DATE DUE

AP 30 '93			

Paradise

Paradise

Elena Castedo

GROVE WEIDENFELD

New York

Published by Grove Weidenfeld
A Division of Wheatland Corporation
841 Broadway
New York, NY 10003-4793

Published in Canada by General Publishing Company, Ltd.

Library of Congress Cataloging-in-Publication Data

Castedo, Elena.
Paradise/Elena Castedo.—1st ed.
p. cm.
I. Title.
PR9155.9.C35P3 1990
823—dc20 89-25640
CIP

ISBN 1-55584-279-8

Manufactured in the United States of America

Printed on acid-free paper

Designed by Irving Perkins Associates

First Edition 1990

3 5 7 9 10 8 6 4 2

To Denny

Paradise

WHEN MY MOTHER TOLD ME I WAS GOING TO Paradise that afternoon, I had no idea what she meant. My father always said Paradise was a hoax invented by priests to seduce nitwits. In Paradise, my mother said, children were always happy, playing in unbounded spaces under clear blue skies, surrounded by fruits and flowers and the utmost good taste.

While my mother passed review of my dress, sandals and front cowlick, I looked through the open window of our pensione room to the small square across the hot street. I wanted to go climb its two squat palm trees, but my mother was attacking my cowlick, a vexing advertisement, she said, of a matching unruly spirit within. She wet it, wrestled with it, pinned it down, although we both knew it would soon dry with the heat of the summer day and spring back up again. My mother couldn't do much about my knobby thinness either. It was going to be the usual "What a pity, the girl looks just like her father" every time we met someone.

"Mami, is Paradise another country, another pensione, or what?"

"Not another country, silly. Paradise is a country estate, a magnificent country estate called El Topaz; the owners are rich—enormously rich."

"Why are we going there?"

"We've been invited. We are their guests. It's a vacation. Our first vacation in the New World." She took a can of condensed milk, a can opener, a tin of crackers and three bananas from the armoire—all our clothes always smelled of bananas—and put them in her bag. "They invited us. It means they like us a lot, because . . . we are interesting, we are educated. We can provide amusement." She locked our pensione room and we went downstairs.

The reason we lived in a pensione and not in a house like other families was because our own country had been taken over by the Assassin. The little potbellied Assassin, whose real name was Franco, wore short little boots over his short little legs and was a monster, so my parents had to flee to France. But France came to be owned by the Nazis, and as luck would have it, the tall Nazis with their sinister big boots were monsters too. We had to flee again. My parents studied a map looking for a place that wouldn't get into world wars all the time. That's how we ended up in pensiones down here in Galmeda, a big city in the South American continent. We were very lucky, my parents said, very lucky to be here.

In Galmeda you mostly looked for jobs, for inexpensive food and for pensiones where the proprietress wasn't so cheap she would do things like providing newspapers for the toilet—instead of brown wrapping paper—which left your behind full of ink. Cheapness like that made my father very mad.

"Mami, there's no war or concentration camps here. Why are we going away?"

"A country estate's a great place, Solita. A country estate is beautiful; it's excellent for your health." My mother handed me a small basket and struggled with my little brother, Niceto, the suitcase and her handbag, but she didn't look disheveled. She looked commanding and determined in her blue suit and blue hat.

"Why isn't Papi here yet?"

"In a country estate, there're horses, lakes . . ." We crossed the front yard.

One problem with this pensione was that San Bernardo Street wasn't paved like bigger streets. It had cobblestones, and if it ever came to pass that roller skates were loaned or given to me, how would I roller-skate over the stones? "Mami, a war isn't coming here, is it?"

"Stop it, Solita. You know very well only morbid people talk about those things. We don't want to be morbid, do we? This is our big chance. You must help in every way you can. Having an opportunity to spend whole days with people is the way to . . . get close to them. If things go well, this will solve everything. It's very important. Very. For you and your brother." We crossed the street. "Now, Solita, remember, 'When in Rome, do as the Romans do.' You are a big girl now, you understand these things."

Should I or should I not say that I didn't understand anything?

Just when I was going to ask about Papi again, he arrived with his small suitcase. For the first time, we didn't have to wait for him forever. His lanky face was surprised, and his red, windblown hair made him look bewildered. I dropped the basket and ran to be hugged, forgetting a girl my age should have dignified manners, like Mami. He had his new smell of sea and sweat. He was very proud to have found a job in the port of San Ildefonso, where they packed sea kelp. "My, don't you girls look gorgeous!" Mami did look beautiful, like the ladies in magazines, except they smiled. She seemed annoyed at his flattery, so I happily took credit for it and went to see how it felt to lift his suitcase. "Where are you going?"

Papi didn't know? How strange. Mami explained. Papi got agitated. I got agitated. I pressed the cowlick; it sprung up, mockingly. Niceto followed me to inspect the suitcase. "Long bird," he said, pointing to the latch. True, the latch looked just like a crane. Papi's green eyes grew very large. "I can't believe what you're doing, Pilar!" he said.

"I warned you, Julian. You're not going to drag me into any more politics, any more danger again. You could have dropped that union stuff. As well as . . ." In her high heels, Mami was taller, so she leaned down to whisper to him.

"Pilar, I explained to you one thousand times, I'm just an advisor; I'm not involved actively; it's a necessary step to establish my credentials. As for the other . . . it won't happen again, I told you. And, wasn't it clear? Wasn't it understood we weren't going to accept any more invitations from those people?"

"The ball was in your court, Julian." Mami's voice was calm. "I don't want to be here while you're doing your . . . advising. The children can use some country air, they can use a vacation."

"The strikes won't be violent, Pilar; this is not Spain! You don't know what you're doing; think about the children. . . ." Papi's whispers about the people we were going to visit were hard to understand. With the blank voice she used when Papi got excited, Mami said if he didn't wish to help her to the trolley and the bus depot, she would go alone.

All the way to the bus depot, Papi kept trying to talk Mami into turning back. I wanted all of us to stay in the trolley and go for a ride downtown. At the cavernous depot, Papi went to buy tickets. The buses were violet on top, dark blue at the bottom and had a red band in the middle. Mami said, "What awful colors; what poor taste." Papi came back. "What superb New World colors! What a rich expression of the popular imagination!" Papi always found something good to say, even when things were bad.

The driver started the bus. Papi waved among the steam and bus colors, his face so upset it made my nose and eyes tingle. I got up. "I don't want to go anywhere without Papi," I said firmly.

"Sit down!" Mami said. "There'll be no nonsense from you."

"I want to stay here."

"You want to stay here, do you? What if Columbus had said that? We wouldn't have had a New World to escape to. You'll love the country. Your father, well, he will come later, no doubt."

Soon Papi's upset face was replaced by the flight of sunny streets. Flocks of houses left together in blocks, not a house out of step. The city market left in one chunk. We went under a railway pass out into the countryside: soft hills sprinkled with fleeced sheep, covered by a blond fuzz that near the road turned into delicate wheat stalks; dashing trees fluttering their leaves upside down in the rivers; rows of vineyards running madly to huddle together in the distance; small adobe dwellings; tortuous trees with black pods.

I saw everything through a wisp of my mother's black hair that had escaped from her hat. Niceto slept on her lap. Niceto always missed the best of everything. The basket with the gift for the owner of Paradise rested at my mother's feet. You always had to bring a gift when you were invited to a country house. Inside the basket slept Pelléas and Mélisande, two tiny puppies. Their last name was Chihuahua. They were foreigners too. They slept in the heat and rumble of the bus with their eyes closed, like dead chickens. "They look like aborted fetuses," Papi had said, and Mami had smiled nervously. The thought of Papi's face made me sad; I couldn't swallow the crackers. How could we go somewhere without him?

There were many things to learn about presents. It wasn't easy for a refugee to buy one for a wealthy host in this New World. From the little money you had left after buying food, you bought something you were reasonably sure they wouldn't have, something that would amuse and excite them, that showed good taste and a certain flair, that made them forget the bearer was poor, that made them think the bearer could be a source of fun, someone they would enjoy having around and introduce to their friends. Giving a rare animal showed good taste. "You be very pleasant, Solita, cheerful and pleasant."

I got thirsty. I got sleepy. After a long time, the bus stopped next to a dirt road spanned by an iron arch. We got off.

"REMEMBER, my little daughter, first impressions are very important."

"I have to go to the bathroom." My mother didn't hear me, walking under the arch that read EL TOPAZ in iron letters. She went to meet a man who stepped down from a red, two-wheeled buggy. I looked around; there was no suitable place to pee.

It was hot, but the man wore a poncho down to his boots. He kept putting his hat on and off between greeting us, loading the suitcase and helping us into the buggy. I sat in front, next to him. He shook the reins, clucked his tongue and the horse took off at a trot. Up and down the horse's hilly buttocks went, an exhilarating view, playing rhythmically with the passing of the eucalyptus trees bordering the road. The man pushed his poncho off his shoulders, revealing a red waistband with a knife. I tried to be polite, not staring at his pockmarked skin, whiskery cheeks or colorless eyes, only at his hands holding the reins, each finger a tree root, each nail a miniature yellow roof tile. He seemed amused when my mother inhaled the eucalyptus smell. "In the houses they have more pretty trees," he said.

"What houses?" Maybe we would end up in another city.

"Where the *patrón* lives; it's called the houses," the man said.

Through another arch the buggy entered a never-ending

garden. We stopped in front of a long, low, columned house, lit and shadowed by the afternoon sun. Dogs of many colors and sizes ran around in great excitement. Women in sky blue aprons came hurriedly from the interminably long veranda. My mother whispered, "Remember, be nice, be nice at all times."

Blue-aproned women and men in blue jackets helped us down and got our suitcase. Three girls, dressed alike in pale green pinafores with rows of tiny buttons, ribbons in their curls and tiny earrings, watched me with curious amusement. Dressing children alike in a family was very bourgeois, a refugee had told me once. The exact meaning of "bourgeois" escaped me, but it had something to do with being dull, not knowing important things. It didn't seem to apply to these girls. I held on tightly to my underwear through my dress. You could never trust panty elastics; they had a way of giving out when you least expected it.

Suddenly, loud music poured from the house and a lady wearing men's overalls came out. Everybody stopped and looked at her. Her hair was cut short like a statue's. She rushed to hug and kiss my mother as if she were her child and hadn't seen her in years. After a while I was introduced.

"I've seen you sleeping, my pretty," the lady said, "the day we took your mumsy and popsy back to your pensione." I hoped my thumb hadn't been in my mouth. Parents' habits of bringing guests to see the children sleeping was irritating. "Call me Tía Merce," she said. She bent down for me to kiss her. Her cheek smelled like herbs. In a babyish tone, she introduced me to the oldest girl, a gorgeous creature, maybe eleven or so, with a noble head of black curls. "Her name is Patricia, not Patti," Tía Merce said with a stern flash of her eyes. Patricia welcomed me with a dimple. Some people had everything. I was then introduced to her slightly younger sisters, Graciela and Gloria, twins who looked like shiny, well-fed cats. They were my age, I was told, and it was all right to call Graciela Grace.

"Ema and Eda, I said do not put so much pomade on the twins' hair," Tía Merce scolded the two look-alike women in green aprons standing behind the twins.

Instead of welcoming me, the twins giggled and ran down the veranda, their curls and ribbons bouncing behind them. The twin nannies ran after them, calling, "Behave yourselves, little ones, come back, little ones, come back!" After careful consideration, I decided that "do as the Romans" didn't apply in this case, even though the twins were my age. First, I didn't have a woman in green to catch me and bring me back, so there was no way to know when to stop running. Second, it was impossible to run as fast as the twins while holding onto my panties, and it wouldn't have looked very refined. Third, I had to go to the bathroom badly—this was no time to engage in bouncing or undue excitement.

The twins came back, apparently very satisfied, and stood observing me. Nobody said "You children go play" or anything to us. After ages we were finally taken to a bathroom as big as a living room with tiled blue arches.

Throughout the warm afternoon, more guests arrived. Some came in the buggy, some in automobiles, masking the smell of lime leaves with a hint of burnt gasoline. In the open back seat of one car sat calmly a tall, llamalike creature with a long neck. "The guanaco!" the girls yelled. After the crunchy sound of hoofs, wheels and tires over the graveled driveway, new arrivals were greeted by the same cheek-pecking and noisy excitement. Tía Merce kept introducing my mother with great pride. The girls observed this intently. My mother smiled happily at every new guest, showing her beautiful teeth in ways she never did around Papi's friends. Everyone brought candy and toys for the girls. Some people had more than everything.

Following every introduction, the twins put on their little performance. Since no one told me anything and my mother had said to keep an eye on my brother, I kept as quiet as possible and looked from time to time at Niceto, who was busy counting the teats of a shaggy dog the girls called Coca-Cola.

AFTER THE BLAZING LIGHT FADED, dinner was announced by a brass bell. The guests walked down the veranda toward one end of the house—or rather houses—where the dining room was, chatting above the rising clamor of strange garden creatures.

Children sat at a round table, next to a huge bay window over the side garden. "This's called the 'old skin table,'" Patricia said. "Because there's always milk or juice or soup spilled on it, and when you pull the tablecloth up, like this, it looks like old skin, see?" Crystal salt containers and butter dishes toppled over. The twins giggled. "Just like the skin in Tía Loli's cheeks," one said, and both laughed.

Niceto kept to himself, observing the raised, contorted leaves and nymphs on an iron wood stove. The girls ignored him; there wasn't really that much of interest in a four-year-old.

Through an opening in the wall, trays were passed from the pantry to maidservants in navy blue dresses with white aprons. The maid serving the old skin table seemed to be in a bad mood. The girls ignored whatever she said.

"You may get creamed spinach tonight," Grace warned me. "It's like green glue."

"Don't worry, just use the usual ways to take care of the puky mess," Gloria said. "I'm using the simplest; spread it around the plate, then claim it's been eaten."

"I'll put it in other places," Grace announced.

"With this maid you have to be firm for the tricks to work," Patricia advised.

I didn't, of course, say it would please me no end to eat creamed spinach, or spinach in any shape or form, or any food they cared to serve me. I was very hungry, but it was obvious that being hungry wasn't the thing to be around here.

"Do you like Christmas better in the country or the city?" one of the twins asked.

I shrugged. The only reason I had known it was Christmastime was because my parents kept saying they couldn't get used to Christmas in the summer.

"What school do you go to? We go to the Villa Sainte Marie. It's the best, of course. We're here for summer vacation; in the winter we go way up to the ski chalet in Llotera."

It was probably not a good idea to tell them I had never been in school. At my age I should have been in fourth grade or so, but we had never stayed in a neighborhood long enough. My fondest wish was to find out what school was like. My mother and the other refugees had given me books and taught me things, like the history of Spain. A tall, lazy dog that moved under the table saved me from having to answer the girls.

"Don't look under the tablecloth or they'll take Vodka away," Grace said. "She's a Russian wolfhound," Patricia informed me. "What's your mother's name?" the twins asked.

"Pilar."

"There's something funny about her. She's beautiful, but she dresses funny. She speaks and acts funny. She's so tall and her skin is so white and her eyebrows are too black."

My mother, sitting very erect at the big table, on the right side of Tía Merce—who wouldn't take her eyes off her—listened to a lean, tanned man with colorful patches on his jacket. It was customary for my mother to get attention from men. I tried to figure out how she was acting funny, but I couldn't see it.

"Mumsy now sits at the head of the big table, where Popsy used to. Maybe Popsy . . . will come one of these days. We know everybody from the big table," Gloria said.

"Not true," Patricia corrected with authority. "The quiet man with the plump cheeks is the world-famous pianist Claudio Arrau, and he came here yesterday for the first time, so you don't know him."

"Patricia knows all about pianists," Grace said. "She takes lessons from Tatoff."

"Tatoff's the best piano teacher in Galmeda," Patricia explained matter-of-factly.

"She gets presents from him; she's so lucky. We never get a thing from Señora Ruimalló, our piano teacher," Gloria complained, dropping a blob of spinach in her milk. "You have to drop it forcefully so it goes to the bottom," she explained.

Since no one was looking at him, Niceto emptied a salt cellar into his mouth. He couldn't have done that in the pensione; salt cost money. Niceto's claim to fame was his absolute tolerance of unlimited amounts of salt.

The serving maid kept bringing more dishes. The girls moaned about all of them and competed to see who could tell more about the people at the big table, which made me feel important.

"The man with the bright patches on his silk overcoat and on his pants is Tío Juan Vicente," Gloria said.

"He's your uncle?" I asked admiringly. All my relatives were in Spain. People who had them made me envious.

"He's not a real *tío,* we just call him that. He owns the lands beyond the train station, many kilometers away."

"Why does he have patches?"

"Because he's an eccentric. You know what that is, don't you?" Patricia asked.

I shook my head.

"It's when somebody does things that everybody says are terrible and everybody loves," Patricia explained.

"We know other eccentrics," Gloria bragged.

"Tío Juan Vicente comes here a lot; he gets awfully bored with his vineyards. They turn mountains of the most delicious grapes into wine. Ugh, I hate wine," Grace said.

I observed the patched man gesturing with his long fingers to explain something to my mother.

"Tío Juan Vicente's an Echaurren." I made the mistake of asking what an Echaurren was. The girls looked at me with suspicion. My mother wouldn't have liked it. "Don't you know? An Echaurren's a person from the Echaurren family, a very old, very important family with lots of eccentrics; they do all sorts of original things. You do know what an aristocrat is, don't you?"

"Of course."

"Tío Juan Vicente says it's not fair for the peasants to be so poor, and he ought to dress like them. So he has Santos, the best designer in Galmeda, put patches on his clothes so he looks like a peasant," Patricia said.

"I've never seen a peasant with patches," Gloria said. "They just wear the tears. Have you?" She asked me.

I hadn't either. We did have things in common. Actually, I don't think I had ever seen a peasant. "Which one's his wife?" I asked.

The twins giggled and spouted droplets of milk, which fascinated Niceto. Patricia hushed them. "He doesn't have one."

"He likes to put on little performances dressed like Mozart or Pontius Pilate."

"Children aren't invited, but we know all the secret ways to see everything and hear everything we want in the houses."

"Mumsy adores him," Patricia said.

Niceto knocked over his glass of milk. The maid came running to clean it up, complaining that the housekeeper hated her, assigning her to the old skin table. The girls ignored her.

"The man in the chocolate suit with the pinkish glasses, he's a psychiatrist. He visits on a schedule. He spends hours on the toilet. He's got a thing about toilets. You know what a psychiatrist is, don't you?"

I had heard of it, but I wasn't sure. I nodded anyway. It was obvious the girls wanted you to know what they did. "Why does he visit on a schedule?" Maybe they would give me a hint.

The twins looked at Patricia. "All psychiatrists visit on a schedule." There was something strange about this, but I had no time to think while the girls talked about the other people. The psychiatrist's wife, with graying hair and the big up-fronts, believed in communicating with the dead. The children called her Melons, but never in front of grown-ups. The dancer with raccoon eyes was called Mlle. Vicky; she had come with Gunther, the German photographer sitting across from Tío Juan Vicente; she was out to catch him. Gunther's feet stank when he took his shoes off to take a nap in the garden; Germans had bad foot smells, they couldn't help it. If I wanted to verify this personally, they'd tell me when to catch him at his nap. Gunther's eyes were beautifully blue, but he pestered the girls, asking them to hold a flower, or a kitten, so he could take their picture. It was embarrassing. The owner of the guanaco, the hairy man with the overflowing neck next to Mlle. Vicky, was bored with his huge factory, which turned beets into sugar, and now painted pictures like chicken droppings. They called him the Walrus, but never in front of grown-ups. . . .

After a while, I realized I wasn't catching half of what the girls were saying, and I worried about not making the good impression my mother had ordered. My stuffed stomach was making me drowsy. On top of that, the girls' New World Spanish was different from the language in the streets where we had lived; it went up and down, and sometimes was sucked into the lungs, almost cutting their breath. They also giggled or whispered. They spoke, spouted, spilled and sucked, and by dessert—a heavenly structure of semolina topped with dark red honey—I couldn't hear anything anymore. I just concentrated on picking the right proportion of semolina and red honey in each spoonful, so that at the end I wouldn't be left with one without the other.

These girls were very knowledgeable, and most of the people they kept mentioning were very important. And they seemed to like me. They hadn't called me a Goda (Goth), the worst insult for Spaniards in Galmeda. Sometimes children in the pensiones where we had lived had called me that, forcing me to chase them, which made the owners of the pensiones say we were going to be thrown out. When someone called one of my parents' friends a Godo, it always started a fight. My mother said their nerves were raw.

My parents' friends weren't important—just refugees like us who lived in rented rooms. Some rented a dilapidated house together. They visited each other a lot. They never brought me candy or toys, but sometimes an avocado, a pear or a bunch of dates if they were available in the yard or in a park nearby. They talked to me in the same way they talked to each other. There were few children left after the war, the exodus, the concentration camp in France and the exile to faraway countries. I was a survivor, they said.

The refugees didn't act at all like the guests at the big table. They didn't move slowly, leaning smoothly toward their dinner partners on one side or the other with a soft smile. The refugees were bony, noisy, and plopped themselves anywhere, even on the floor, with their legs and arms sprawled. They argued, got mad, laughed, patted each other, became sour or excited, but never had soft smiles. They sang songs often, some from the very old days, some from the war. One owned a radio and another a guitar, which they took when visiting. They exchanged newspapers, magazines, books and information about butchers. In Galmeda people didn't eat animals' insides, so the butchers threw hearts, kidneys, brains and livers to the floor for the dogs. It was the refugees' joy. The bad part was that when the butchers saw the refugees beating the dogs at grabbing the innards, they started charging money for them. If a refugee made a great food discovery—maybe a big sack of rice at a bargain—they shared that too. Sometimes Papi clowned around and made everyone laugh, except Mami. I laughed when he tickled me.

WHEN THE AIR on the verandas was black and cool, a young woman in green came to tell Niceto and me to follow her. She said she was our nanny. She smelled like an overly ripe potato, and the odor followed us as she led the way to a white room with bare walls. The candle she carried made ominous shadows. She tucked in Niceto, who was pleased to have a grown-up bed with a carved back, took a china chamber pot with purple irises printed on it and handed it to me. "You pass water now, before you get in bed."

"No, thank you. I don't need to," I lied, expecting her to leave soon.

"Well, then, make the sign of the cross," she said, pulling up the covers.

"Why?" I asked politely. Papi always said the cross was a morbid symbol, used by priests to scare ignorant people into doing what the priests wanted. The nanny seemed angry. "Don't you start getting funny with me, little girl. It won't do you one bit of good. Now, make the sign of the cross."

"I want to know why," I said as politely as possible.

She studied me, looking puzzled and exasperated. "To keep out those evil spirits of the night, who're trying to get in, what else," she said. "Now, no more silly questions."

Well, here it didn't have anything to do with priests. "Where is my mother?" The nanny was taking off her clothes next to a cot at the other end of the room. Apparently, she was going to sleep here; bad news for my plan.

"Your Señora Mamá's room is right there, through those doors, but she won't be in bed for a long time—there's always a lot going on with the *patrones*—so just go to sleep." The nanny got in her cot and put out the candle.

The candle smell lingered. There was no grown-up laughter and chitchat, no distant bus or trolley, no yell to open the door, as there was at home. The night outside was full of the *rick-ricks* and *gorroac-gorroacs* of strange creatures moving in the dark. How could they be evil spirits as the nanny had said? Sometimes a dog barked, then another joined in, and another, until they were all at it.

I had to do something to avoid waking up in a pool of pee. I still had accidents sometimes. These people weren't as terrible as Papi thought. When he came in the morning, how would he act in front of them? Perhaps Mami wouldn't put on her vexed face if he clowned around, and perhaps he wouldn't wave his hands so much to show his two missing fingers. Children in Galmeda made fun of his hand sometimes, but I never told him. When the nanny's breathing sounded like a distant train, I sat on the chamber pot and peed quietly over the purple irises I couldn't see.

Light slivers, like knives trying to get in around the door's shutters, woke me up. What a relief, my bed was dry.

I got up to go exploring. You could get a fix on a place when you saw it before it was filled with humans. Sometimes at the pensione I would get up at dawn, slip out quietly and walk around the empty streets. I ran into stray dogs covered with dew, looked at the houses all freshened up with the night's mist. When the lights of early risers were turned off because the sun had reached their windows, I would go home. It was a muffled world that didn't get in anybody's way.

Now I tiptoed to the door, holding my nose as I passed the nanny's potato odor, mixed now with face cream, and unlatched the shutter to peer out. The milky light had begun to shape weak shadows of the columns. In front of my room, past the edge of the veranda, stood a hill half as tall as the house. Tiny paths, bordered by fleshy flowers, fleshy artichokes and other succulent plants in bloom, curved up to the top. At the crest stood a small tree with glossy leaves and some young lemons. The hill seemed to have an independence all of its own. I wanted to tiptoe through it. I unlatched the door.

The nanny woke up. "You naughty little girl," she hissed, as if I had committed such a horrible crime that the world should be spared hearing about it, "what are you doing up at this hour? You go back to bed this instant."

What could I do? I had to lie there quietly. The early light slid into the room up to the ceiling beams, followed by a racket of birds and now and then a rooster call. It was ages before I was allowed to get up.

"DO YOU LIKE blancmange?"

"Do you like raspberry marmalade?"

"Do you like goat cheese?"

"Do you like palm honey?"

"Do you like poached eggs?"

"Do you like thick cream?"

"Do you like alcayota preserves?"

"Do you like chestnut cream?"

"Do you like yam sweets?"

That's what was in all those little crystal dishes. I loved them all. I had learned to stuff myself in a jiffy, taking spoonfuls from every dish and tossing them onto pieces of French bread, so I could follow girls, dogs and the guanaco, going in and out of heat and shade, to a park, gazebo, playhouse, aviary, and a bounty of fruits, berries, flowers, bushes and trees. I followed them to a children's library, game room, toy room. They cut through large halls, dark dens, empty bedrooms, even the living-room-size bathroom, where the psychiatrist with the pink glasses was reading the paper naked on the toilet. The girls ignored him and continued to run, leaving through another door onto the back veranda. It wasn't the custom in pensiones to run through bathrooms when someone was inside. Gloria, the last of us, left the outside door open. I glanced back and saw the psychiatrist look up from his pink glasses as the sun from the open door hit him like a spotlight.

"We were lucky it was just the psychiatrist," Patricia said. "He doesn't do anything on the toilet but read and try. Others smell awful, or get hysterical. But it's such a short cut it's worth taking risks."

The girls didn't even linger in their toy room, which was the size of the toy store in our neighborhood in Galmeda. I tried to act nonchalant, as though I were accustomed to such toy grandeur, but I was frantic to get to the plate of wooden chickens who ate automatically when a string was pulled, and to some of the building kits, and to the set of miniature pots and pans, and to . . . The girls ran out again.

Whenever we went outside, two small dogs arrived to leap around the girls. "These are Gin and Tonic, and they are not twins," Patricia introduced them. "Believe it or not, Gin is Tonic's mother, but"—she lowered her voice—"they do you-know-what. They're very fine fox terriers." She looked at me. "Are any of your other brothers or half siblings coming to visit?"

"I don't have any more brothers, half or whole."

The girls stopped at an arched doorway, shocked. "You mean that little squirt's the only sibling you have?" They looked at me with pity. Their brother Enrique was in a French boarding school, he was so lucky, where it was winter now and he skied, and they had grown-up half brothers and a half sister who was married and had a baby, so they didn't have to put up with anything their siblings told them, and they were aunts, and it was such fun to go to baptisms and family parties once in a while.

From time to time, the girls stopped to listen with concentrated faces to the grown-ups; apparently, they were trying to get some important scoop, but got bristly if I asked questions. The grown-ups started their days when the sun was at the tip of the sky, coming straight down. At that hour in Galmeda, a cheerful cannon blast from an old fort downtown told you it was noon. By the time the grown-ups went to the back veranda to hold small cups of coffee in the sun, arranged on wicker chairs as in a photograph, everything had settled down. The birds had gone to the treetops; the servants had finished cleaning, polishing, sweeping, beating rugs and smiling at the girls, who ignored them. The patched man sat next to my mother, wearing red jackets with pink or lavender brocade patches in the morning, and patched silk jackets in the evenings. He usually held one of our good-taste gift puppies, and told my mother she had to see his wine cellar and a mare called Ninon who was fabulous. Tía Merce would sing a song with the guitar or cradle the other puppy. Once she said her husband could light his cigars with their stocks and bonds and his paintings if he wished, but she was going to get El Topaz. The girls had no reaction or comments, so I didn't get a clue what it meant. My father was apt to come anytime; I couldn't wait. Would he come by buggy? By car? By horse?

During one of our front-veranda runs, the psychiatrist and Melons were preparing to leave. Getting into his French car, he told Tía Merce he would be back in two weeks, unless she wanted him sooner. He thanked my mother, whispered to her what great help she could be, and asked if she wanted to send a message to her husband. Tell him it's up to him to drop his union involvement, my mother said. I wanted to find out how my mother was such a help, and what union involvement was, but the girls were fast disappearing through the passageway uniting the front and back verandas, and when the Romans ran to the back gardens, that's what you did too.

Anytime I managed to get near my mother, I whispered, "When are we going home?" Days had passed and Papi hadn't come. "I have something very important to do," my mother repeated. "Go along with the girls." Then she was either asleep all morning, up until late when I was in bed, at the big table, or with Tía Merce.

Tía Merce constantly lavished on my mother confident chuckles, fond looks, deep-eyed questions and enthusiastic proposals of things to do. Her hands, ending in brick-colored nails, glided through the air following imaginary paintings, statues, drapery flounces or contours of chairs, illustrating how she planned to redecorate this or that part of the houses. At every air stroke, she asked my mother what she thought. Her nails made me nervous. "Of the light colors, peach is the loveliest," she said. "Everything in a house having to do with light should be peach; lamps, candles, shades, drapes. Then you live always at sunrise, though you get up at noon."

When Tía Merce leaned over my mother, my mother

stiffened; perhaps Tía Merce had bad breath. Sometimes, when there were no other guests around, my mother acted motherly and proposed they study books. "Now, there's an interesting god for you; the bathtub god," my mother would say, pointing at a page. "The Greeks had gods for everything, you see, even for doorknobs." Tía Merce would chuckle, shaking her big bosom. "I only like the gods who float around getting aroused every time they see something moving. This one's Venus, right? I adore those Greeks. *Je les aime,* ay, they really understood *l'amour!*"

Sometimes Tía Merce said things against my father. She had no right.

My mother would even tell Tía Merce things taught me by her or the other refugees, tales about the Egyptians or other ancient peoples and about famous persons. Tía Merce kept saying, as she put imaginary tiaras on her head or togas on her body, "Ay! I should have been Cleopatra and the Greek poetess rolled into one!"

Maybe very soon they would get used to each other and my mother could tell me when we were leaving.

Niceto went around quietly eating rose petals.

CHRISTMAS NIGHT I decided to find out, no matter what, when we were going home. It was my good luck that supper was served in the back gardens, making it easier to talk to my mother without attracting attention. Everyone sat around a live pine tree decorated with strings of *marrons glacés,* bonbons, little angels, stars, shepherds and tiny candles. If the guanaco reached for a candle with his long neck, a servant slapped him away. Several people played guitars. Most sang songs and drank champagne. Every time I started to be happy, I remembered Papi would disapprove of such a to-do about Christmas. Papi had strong opinions and voiced them loudly, which upset Mami. "Why don't you let things be?" she would say under her breath. But Papi would carry on with unquenchable indignation about churches exploiting the poor. I reached a compromise and enjoyed the celebration without getting carried away, which wasn't easy.

The servants stayed in the darkened fringes, under the grape and rose arbors, smiling and whispering to each other. The girls and I ate chocolates shaped like tiny bottles with a liquid inside that burned the throat. I gorged myself on powdered pastries filled with caramel; hot, chewy, small squash and burnt sugar pancakes; cake squares decorated with a glaze silky to the tongue; and long, paper-thin crisp cookies, called little boats. We threw our dinners inconspicuously into the zinnias.

"What did you get for Christmas last year?" Grace asked me. Better let pass the subject of Christmas and presents. The girls stopped undoing gift ribbons when they saw the patched man whispering to my mother. With her long fingers, she opened a round box he had handed her.

"Patricia, when we heard Mumsy say all those things on the phone, back in Galmeda, about Solita's mother, when she said—" Patricia snapped at her and Gloria looked down peevishly at a porcelain kitty she had just unwrapped.

I waited for something else to be said, but nothing was.

My mother took out and admired a hat like a collapsed eggplant with three pompons on one side. The patched man helped her put it on and rearrange the pompons. "It's a genuine Correa."

Tía Merce observed them and seemed angry. She took the patched man's hand. "Come here, *mon chéri,* I must tell you about my special present for you; you'll just die." She drew him away.

All of this was very confusing. I went to ask my mother if there was a present for me, just in case. Her look made me realize my mouth was overflowing with chocolaty liqueur.

"What manners, my daughter. Is this what you call making a good impression?"

"Mami, when is Papi coming to get us? We're in excellent health now, and we've seen a country estate."

"You'll be very happy, Solita; I have wonderful news for you." I got closer to her because of the guitar and the noise. "Merce has decided to . . . well, to start fresh, and to leave the city and move here to the country. Of course, she doesn't want to be here alone and the girls need some suitable playmates, so she has invited me to live here! Isn't it wonderful? Just as I hoped. Dreams are coming true." I made an ugly face. "This will be Paradise for you and your brother; you'll have everything in the world: the best food, fresh air and . . ." The patched man was walking back, laughing aloud, followed by a smiling Tía Merce.

"Live here! But I like Galmeda, Mami. Anyway, when is Papi joining us?" She hadn't mentioned the most important part.

"If he wants to, he can come and visit. If he's not too busy with . . . never mind." Her voice was annoyed.

I ignored her annoyance; this was an emergency! " 'Visit'! What do you mean, 'visit'? I want Papi here all the time, at least!" A tear blurred together the tree's ornaments. "And how about school? There's no school here. I'm never going to go to school."

"Now, no melodramas, Solita. Let's not make things difficult." Mami sternly pushed the pompons back. "I'll see about your schooling. And I don't want any scenes. You get along with the girls; see that they like you. I have enough cut out for me right now. You'll be healthy here, and away from anything happening in Galmeda. This is Paradise; you'll have horses, everything any child would dream of. You're a very lucky girl." When Mami said things, that was the way it was going to be.

The choking that always started to close my throat when things were wrong made the tiny chocolate bottle sit in my mouth as if made of glass. A warm breeze roused the tree's small candles. "Little children, little children, time for beddy-bye," one of the twin nannies said. Our potato-smelling nanny made a motion to me. I followed her while everybody sang a song about this beautiful country.

2

I WAITED IMPATIENTLY FOR THE DAY OF KINGS SO I could dazzle everyone in El Topaz with my knowledge of it. I needed this very badly. We had to stay in El Topaz, Mami kept saying, for some important reason; it was hard to understand what. Also to keep away from Galmeda in case something bad happened; Papi was involved in things a foreigner wasn't supposed to be, that could get him thrown out of the country. But Papi wouldn't do anything like that. In country estates the owners and the guests they welcomed noisily had an elevated way of being that you could have too, if you were smart enough to get yourself invited. So you mostly followed the owners around doing what they did, strictly observing the "When in Rome . . ." rule.

But although I had been doing exactly that, neither Tía Merce nor la Mamota—the servants' boss—nor any of the guests, not even my own nanny, treated me as they did

Patricia, Grace and Gloria. Following them as if I were their shadow hadn't elevated me. Of course, the three had things I couldn't aspire to: dimpled elbows, bouncing curls, plump feet, lavish lashes, commanding blue gazes and a steady self-satisfaction. On top of that, Patricia knew almost everything. However, she hadn't even heard of the Day of Kings. In Galmeda, refugees who came that day always brought me something: a fruit, a pastry or maybe a pencil. They taught me about the thrill of that day in Spain; how before January 6, parents secretly took presents for their children to the three men in town assigned to be the Three Kings. On the sixth, bright and early, in their shimmery regalia, Kings Gaspar, Melchior and Balthazar majestically delivered the presents door to door. It took children forever to stop believing in the Three Kings. One morning when I was my brother's age (could I have ever been so young), I saw my mother hiding a fist-size, tortoiseshell elephant under an iris plant. She then told me that the Three Kings had passed by the yard and perhaps had left a gift for me. I ran directly to the iris plant. She realized I'd seen her hiding the elephant. She never told me about the Three Kings again. I learned about it, though, from hearing the refugees, in spite of Papi's protesting that those were ridiculous, troglodyte customs. So, from the noisy celebrations of New Year's, I carefully counted six days and got ready to dazzle them.

All morning my ears opened up wide for any mention of presents or the coming of kings. Morning went. My stomach and the sun insisted it was almost lunchtime, but no one in El Topaz had said anything yet. Or about Papi coming. Tía Merce, the patched man and the other guests constantly mentioned people they knew who were coming, but never my father. They constantly stirred their tiny silver spoons with the pearly edges into their demitasses. They constantly played games—Ping-Pong, croquet, cards—with their straw hats shadowing and dotting their faces with shifting sunlight speckles, while they listened to records brought by the patched man. Tía Merce constantly got angry with him about the composers he discussed with my mother, or the compliments he paid my mother in that idiotic way that men did. Melons constantly mumbled that the cat was coming out of the bag.

At lunch the *crème au caramel* dessert was gone and not a word had been said about any kings. At tea, after the last macaroon, all my hope for presents, celebrations or dazzlings collapsed. Whoever heard of kings so mean that they would come after tea time, making you wait practically the whole day long?

My hopes didn't stay deflated very long though. No wonder my mother always said, "When one door closes, another one opens." By evening we were told to go to the big bathroom because la Mamota was going to give us all a bath in the huge tub. This was good news in two ways, even though it was a little scary.

First, getting a bath was an excellent way to get to know someone. In El Topaz the person who could make you feel as if you had been noisily welcomed even if you hadn't; who could establish that you didn't have to hide anything and could say whatever came to your mouth, the way the girls did; who could see that you were treated as one of the girls—that person was la Mamota. La Mamota not only bossed all the servants, she even bossed the girls, and they never played tricks on her or disobeyed her as they did their nannies. La Mamota not only knew who was arriving and who was leaving; according to her, she knew absolutely everything that was going on.

So far, la Mamota had frequented the places I didn't: Tía Merce's quarters, the girls' sunny rooms, the storeroom, the laundry, the servants' quarters, the pantry and the sewing workshop, where one or more seamstresses made, mended or embroidered linen or clothes all day. La Mamota passed through corridors, always busy, giving orders and checking lavender-scented armoires, and never even saw me.

Another reason this was good news was that la Mamota did baths only for very important occasions. Baths were normally given by the nannies. Though no one said it, the important occasion was probably that my father was coming the next morning. So, the Three Kings were bringing good things after all!

La Mamota ordered two chambermaids to iron towels to warm them. The balmy evening made this unnecessary; it seemed la Mamota enjoyed bossing chambermaids. At the open door of the bathroom, the guanaco waited patiently for us to finish our bath. Although his name was Boris Godunov, everybody called him "the guanaco." Coming in with the low purplish sun, his long shadow crept through the floor tiles all the way to the huge tub. Guanacos weren't as strong as llamas, but were taller, more graceful and funnier. They were hard to find these days and impossible to catch in the high Andean peaks where they lived. The only way to get one was from a poacher who killed a mother to steal her baby. Guanacos defended themselves by spitting a hideous mess.

Soon the guanaco's calm shadow was joined by the impatient shadows of Coca-Cola, the sheep dog; Gin and Tonic, the fox terriers; Cocktail, a mongrel who looked somewhat and behaved like a fox terrier; and Vodka, the Russian wolfhound. It was their last chance to play with us before dark. The other dogs were standoffish and hung around in their own favorite places.

La Mamota rolled the sleeves up over her powerful arms and soaped the girls, who splashed the bubbles happily. I waited to see how she would get to know me. The twins got impatient. "Hurry up, Mamota, we want to go to the *almacén* and buy candy."

"Pretty soon, Mamota," Patricia said, "you'll call me Señorita, like the other servants. My cousin Beba's only a year older than I, and she has these little titties, so she has to be called Señorita, and I will get some pretty soon, I can tell."

"You have no more breasts than Moses, young lady, and your cousin Beba's a brat, the Good Virgin forgive me. I'll have you know I raised her father and yours, the twins, and your uncle Amito, from the instant they came out of your grandma's birth canal. I was just a girl then, sixteen I was when your uncle and your father were born, but I've always had the talent. And the same I raised your big brothers and sister, and your brother Enrique, the Virgin knows why mi Señora Doña Mercedes sees fit to send him to boarding school so far away. And I still call your Tío Toto and your father 'my boy,' and I've no intention of calling you anything but 'my girl.' Señorita, indeed . . ."

"I've seen an ostrich," Grace told me, always bragging. "Have you? A real one, running through the steppe, not in the zoo." I hadn't, but I noticed Grace had ostrichlike eyes.

La Mamota finished rinsing the girls, being careful not to wet their curls, and looked at me. I gave her a faint smile, friendly, but not fresh. "I don't see why I must have this one in the tub too," la Mamota said, "as if I don't have enough to do. As if I don't have my hands full with my three babies."

While the twins fought for the soap, I grabbed it and tried to soap myself to make her job easier, but this made her mad. "Mi Señora Doña Mercedes has no consideration for me at times, the Saints are my witnesses. I'm still at it, thanks to the Saintly Virgin, who takes pity on this old woman, except for my legs—the Good Virgin could give me a little more help; they hurt an awful lot at night. Ya, the years're catching up with me, and why should I have to be aggravated with a stray child like this one? A foreigner? A Spaniard at that, not even European. Wait till Miguelito, your father, comes and puts some order in this place." La Mamota's gray chignon collapsed. "Such a ribby mouse, this one is. And her mother! Well, I know why old butler Terencio, may he rest in peace, always said, 'Never trust a Godo.' "

I tried to get out of the tub, but she pushed me down. It was best to lie low. "The woman has the nerve to linger here, as if she were another owner, and obviously she hasn't a thing in this world; poorer than beggars, they are." Gray pins fell in the water. "She's not of the same class as my *patrones,* that's plain; she knows nothing of how to behave like a *patrona*, treats the service like they're on her same level. As if they're strangers! Never a little joking, never a little scolding. None at all."

La Mamota was wrong about us being poorer than beggars. Dead wrong. True, we didn't own housefuls of things like other people. But our clothes never had holes; my mother mended everything, except what didn't show. And we owned my brother's crib; I helped my mother carry it for blocks from the flea market to our pensione. Also a suitcase, and my mother's paint set, and other things, and marbles I'd earned playing, and an earthenware pitcher and bowl that my father said were beautiful, given to him by a sea-kelp packer whose mother was a native and had made it. We even gave pieces of bread to beggars sometimes. Even one of my fathers' two pairs of socks, so my father was left with one only. The beggar had come to our door and showed my mother his bare ankles, complaining he couldn't look for work without socks. His ankles had veins which disappeared into his worn shoes.

My mother said we weren't poor because wealth is what you have that can't be taken away from you when you are thrown out of your country: education and will. So she and my father had fled carrying their wealth in their heads. But my mother was serious, and sad a lot. We were going back to Spain the minute the Assassin died. He was going to die very soon, the refugees said. Maybe in a couple of months, killed either by the poison of his own evil or by another general; they liked to kill each other, those generals. Every couple of months they said that. Meantime, you had to help in everything you could so things wouldn't get any worse. It was a good thing la Mamota hadn't seen my father's hand with the two missing fingers.

"Mamota, are you talking about Solita? You mean she's poor?" Grace asked, moving away from me. The three looked at me. La Mamota ignored her: "Me, no one fools me; I know exactly what the Spaniard's up to. I know why she's here; she's hunting, that's what. My Amito already went through that; a foreigner for a wife, but thanks to the Saintly Virgin his marriage was annulled. . . ."

The girls giggled. "Mamota, why do you still call our Tío Armando 'Amito'? His seat cheeks are fat and his hair's falling out, and you still call him 'my little Amito'. . . ." They imitated her voice, giggling.

"You naughty girls, your Tío Amito's not getting fat in the . . . not at all; you ought to have more respect. See, this's what happens when people that just don't belong here overstay their welcome and think they'll be taking over. Leeches, that's what those people are, leeches. Those foreigners . . . When your father comes, he'll straighten up this place, as he ought to. . . ."

My legs sprang, pushed me up through the ceiling to the sky; it bubbled around me, like Sinbad the Sailor when the whale's spout propelled him up, up. Way down, in the tub, was the stinging pain. But I was naked up in the sky; the bubbles had to bring me down; down to the tub again, where I stayed quiet.

"Mamota, hurry up, we want to buy at the *almacén.*"

La Mamota rinsed me. "You're going nowhere; it's near dark already."

"Ay! Mamota, see? You've taken so long," the twins whined.

"You can go tomorrow," la Mamota said, unplugging the tub and calling for warm towels.

"We can't ask our mothers for money until they get up tomorrow morning," Patricia said, grabbing the side of the tub to get out. "Then we'll buy mountains of things at the *almacén.*"

"Yes, yes!" the twins agreed. "Did you hear, Solita?"

I observed the two islands of my knees with the little waves lapping the shores. With the girls' attitude about money, it would be the last thing in the world I would ask my mother. She wouldn't have any. Having an embarrassed mother was unthinkable! Ten times worse than being an embarrassed girl. What could I do? Mami said Papi was never there when she needed him, but now he was going to come.

The sun left the back garden without a sunset, and a low haze cast a steely glow in every room. So far, la Mamota wasn't like the Becasine in books, the person who made you feel you were home, with a group of people of your own. The girls had their Christmas. I was now a girl of the New World and wouldn't be getting presents or the royal treatment on the Day of Kings.

PATRICIA, GRACE AND GLORIA PEERED into the big library and waited for a lull in the grown-ups' conversation about the Genius to ask for money, expecting me to ask too. It turned out la Mamota's big bath hadn't been because my father was coming, but because it was hoped a very, very smart man, called the Genius, would show up. Maybe Papi would come anyway.

Occasionally the grown-ups went to the big library while having their herb teas or coffees with liqueur. The big library was next to the salon, midway in the houses, which was a long row of rooms that started at the dining room and ended in the glass-enclosed gallery. Each room had three doors; one out to either the front or back verandas, which ran the length of the houses, and one to each adjacent room, or sometimes to one of the several passageways that united the two verandas. If all doors had been unlocked, you could have walked all night and crossed the house from one end to another in a straight line, except for a wing that took off at an L and was always closed. There were no indoor stairs in El Topaz. It was fun in the pensione to run up and down the stairs to the safety of the landing, a port to anchor in, then sail again until the landlady ordered you out.

The grown-ups looked at the books' backs without disturbing any from their orderly rows. Only my mother took some of those forbidding-looking books out. When someone sat down, the big library's leather sofas made a hiss under the sudden weight, like someone passing gas sadly. I wouldn't have ever sat on those sofas for fear someone would think I was the culprit.

I couldn't go by myself to wait near the gate in case my father arrived; in a country estate everything was done in packs. In the city you played with others only when you wanted. You could stop and take off to touch either of the silky tips of a snail's antennae and watch each retract independently, or to stare at the lame onion vendor moving like a dancer down the street. You could do nothing, or stand on a park bench to hear the cannon fired every day at noon. You could do things alone and nobody thought you were abnormal. In the city you had independence.

Tía Merce stopped talking. The girls, without any preamble or hesitation, stuck three arms inside the big library, saying, "Money, Mumsy, please." It was more than shocking. Money was related to what the whole family needed; you treated it delicately. Tía Merce went to the sunlit door, handed each girl coins and bills, no questions asked, and went back to pace over the faded rug in front of the dark books.

Until now I hadn't realized how colossally rich the girls were. It was one thing to own toys, pets, houses, horses, cattle, sheep, mountains, cars, trucks, buggies, surreys and huge wheels of cheese, things of vague ownership that other people could use just as much as you. It was another to have money in your hand anytime you asked; that was having total control; that was having no doubts you were colossally rich. The girls even received money when they didn't ask for it! Some guests asked apologetically if *they would mind* taking money because they hadn't had the time to buy a present! It was amazing to see the girls' breezy reaction. They turned to me, "Solita, now ask your mother for money."

We had been invited to this paradise not only because of her, my mother had said, but so that the owner's daughters would have a suitable playmate. That was me. Being something suitable wasn't easy, when formerly you had just roamed sidewalks and a square with two squat palm trees, doing as you pleased. That was my idea of sensible rules. We had to stay in El Topaz long enough for my mother's plan to work. What plan? It was complicated, she said, but I was going to be very pleased. You just had to trust your mother; she was the only thing you had in the entire world, aside from your father, who had to go look for work.

Up to now, all the tight spots we had been in were my parents' or refugee problems; now I had one all of my own. But the sun hitting the veranda plastered the back of my legs, then traveled upward, warming and slowing down my thinking. Luckily, Tía Merce talked again. The girls agreed we couldn't interrupt. "Dull people. Dull, dull." Tía Merce stared at the back of an iridescent book with gold letters. Her voice was watery; it seemed to collect in her underchin before going out. "*Les gents sont* so dull, with a mania to create dullness."

"I entirely agree," the patched man said.

"And you know, my *belle* Pilar"—Tía Merce stared at a brown book—"people only see themselves in comparison to others. So, you know what they do? You know what they do to make themselves happier? They make everybody else miserable. That way, by comparison, they seem less miserable, you see? Can't you see?"

"I entirely agree," the patched man said. "Between misery and boredom, boredom seems better."

"So, my *belle* Pilar, my exquisite Pilar, we have to create our own *monde*." Tía Merce leaned over and took my mother's hand. "Forget the dullards. I refuse to spend my life making others feel better about their ennui, because they irritate me with their nonsensical restrictions." She ignored the patched man's annoyed call. "And that dreadful talk of wages, virtue, balances, ugh, all that tediousness, don't you agree, *ma belle,* my dearest Pilar?"

The patched man seemed very angry at her. My mother

removed her hand to stir her pearly-edged little spoon. "Well, Merce, one must keep certain rules, at least for the sake of children."

"Really," Tía Merce said, "I don't want my daughters to suffer the same mortified childhoods we all had to. . . ." That was decent of her. The girls smiled in approval. "My girls will have enchanted childhoods; three little princesses in *Paradis.* And *ma belle*"—Tía Merce slid her hand on my mother's black chignon—"we can only create *Paradis* with you. You won't ever leave, will you? You won't ruin my paradise; you *are* my paradise. . . ."

The patched man got up abruptly from a sofa's arm without disturbing his demitasse from its saucer. "Merce, enough! Need I remind you of Dr. Kaplan's admonishing? Pilar, it's been long enough; tomorrow you come to my lands, Viñas Echaurren."

Tía Merce's lips almost smiled, but her eyes sent him a furious charge. Or it just seemed so in the dimness? The girls said their Mumsy adored him. "Go drown in the lake," she mumbled.

"Merce, it serves no purpose to get angry," my mother said. "Why don't you use your creativity to turn El Topaz into the most wondrous meeting place, for friends and relatives? It will make you blossom; the girls too." Tía Merce's eyes shone.

Patricia grabbed my arm and gave me a push. "Now Mumsy's not talking, Solita, are you deaf? All right, I will ask your mother."

The girls were still not telling me anything about the conversation that Gloria had mentioned hearing in Galmeda, and that had to do with my mother, so why couldn't I hide something too? "I don't need to," I said.

They hesitated. "You already have the money? So why didn't you say that before?"

I plunged into the sun at the veranda's edge and sharply snapped a blossom off the wisteria. I pressed the blossom's stem end in front of Coca-Cola's face, on and off, making a tiny gaping mouth yelling for help.

"Well, now we all have money; let's go," Patricia ordered.

CRUNCH-CRUNCH-CRUNCH, the garden's gravel growled under the pounding of eight white sandals. *Crshsh-crshsh,* it creaked behind us under the guanaco's dainty hoofs. He came with the Walrus; the two of them traveled together. The Walrus had learned the hard way that guanacos died of loneliness when left alone. The Walrus had promised to take the girls for a ride in the open back of his car with the guanaco, where his erect swan neck permitted him to enjoy the breeze. I kept waiting for ideas on how to get out of going to the *almacén,* but none came.

The girls crossed themselves as we passed by the chapel, a baby church. Something very important about this helped you, but it wasn't talked about, so it was of no help to me. I said, "When a peasant offers you maté, you aren't allowed to drink it, are you?" Since they wanted to smoke because they weren't allowed, maybe they would want to go to a peasant house to have maté.

"We aren't supposed to, but who'd know?" Gloria said. "Oh, Patricia, did you hear Tío Juan Vicente? Do you think . . ."

"Of course I heard, dumbo, do you think I'm deaf?"

The conversation wasn't going the right way, and there were no signs of Papi approaching from up the road. We passed Niceto and the nanny assigned to us, called Fresia, strolling hand in hand. Nannies were supposed to help you.

"Solita's nanny's feeling sorry for herself because she wants to go to the *almacén* to hear the *peones' piropos,* those ridiculous long compliments, and she's not allowed to go."

My mother said the *almacén* owners exploited the peasants with tobacco, drinks and junk, but I couldn't use that argument because the girls would call me a chicken and my mother a wet blanket. Gloria stopped to imitate a *peón* complimenting a maid: "The sun's going down early today, 'cause it's ashamed to be compared to your beauty, Fresia." Gloria was funny. My laughter was half for her performance, half for the glimmer of hope that after this they'd go back. Maybe Nanny Fresia would save me without even knowing it. Gloria warmed up. She was excellent. The girls regarded the grown-ups in strange ways. They didn't take what a person did as a matter of grown-up rights; they observed them with an eye to making fun of them. It was shocking. If grown-ups didn't stick with you, carry you to bomb shelters, pull you away from crumbling buildings, ask for food from foreign sailors, take you to safe countries, find cheap things, use leftovers, where would you be? Why should you make fun of them?

Suddenly, I had a brainstorm. "My mother ordered our nanny not to let me or my brother go to the *almacén*!"

Patricia lifted her powerful curly head. "She said with Nanny Fresia, not with us, did she, and why do you speak funny? Sometimes you speak like your mother."

Maybe my mother would let me not do as the Romans do this once. "I have to go to the bathroom," I said.

"Go after we come back from the *almacén,*" Patricia ordered.

"Can't wait." I ran. If people didn't have to go to the bathroom, what would they do to get away at critical times?

"You better not take long!" Patricia yelled.

I FOUND MY MOTHER painting at her window seat. She was able to go to her room when Tía Merce went to her quarters to have her leg hairs plucked, her awesome nails filed and her hair combed like the statues. Their sunny quarters were near the glass-enclosed gallery, at one end of the houses. Our rooms were at the shaded other end. My mother hummed while putting blue on a black and white eye. The hum created a serene aura around her. How could I penetrate it? My mother would understand if she wasn't too absorbed in her work, because refugees helped each other; that's how you got into better situations all the time, how exile was less terrible, how you could feel not a stranger, even though you were. "Mami," I panted.

Her tall figure in overalls merged with the curled iron bars outside the window. The folded shutters reflected their whiteness on the part at the top of my mother's head, which divided it into two neat black sections joined in a chignon. Everything about my mother was orderly, careful, calm.

"Mami, the girls are going to the *almacén,* and la Mamota, and isn't Papi? I don't want to go, but if I *have* to . . ."

"Calm down, Solita, don't stutter and twitch so. Relax. Now, I want no more nonsense about not wanting to do something with the girls. I told you, we are guests in this house, and you behave accordingly. You should be extremely grateful."

"Yes, but if Papi came, I wouldn't have to go . . ." When we had arrived at El Topaz and I had asked if it was possible to have one peso, she had looked at me as if I had lost my mind. With all the bounty in this paradise, I wanted a peso? She had a point, but she wasn't considering the rule of having what the people you were living with expected you to have, so that everything stayed like Paradise, which, in her view was to go around getting along with the owners of country estates. I had to explain this to her.

"You came to ask me again when your father's coming, didn't you, Solita? You see, my daughter? A mother can read her child like a book. I don't know. Typically, I don't know." She said it tiredly, as if he really didn't want to come see us. She always acted tired about Papi, but here she acted exhausted.

"Mami, why do I have to do everything like them; they are freakish . . . and why Tía Merce? Why should you . . . What did Papi say about these people?"

"Where's that small ship going?" Her hum restored the serenity around her I had broken. She sang about a prisoner watching the sea from his cell window; ships sailing through the freedom of air, water and sun. It always gave me a lump in the throat. Some of her songs were comforting, sad or happy companions, some were strangers, too complicated to get to know, but all were pieces of Spain, hundreds of pieces: a river in the moonlight, hilly villages, old landmarks beloved by a city, the hot-chocolate vendor, the coal man, the miller's wife, the iron forger, people doing things, taking mules to the river, dancing, washing handkerchiefs in the fountain, walking back from fields, going on a journey. If you were Spanish, you sang songs.

"Well, Solita, are you relaxed?" To be relaxed you had to twitch inside, not letting it show. I tried.

"I'm so tired, can't keep my eyes open," my mother mumbled from time to time. "Solita, we are the recipients of great hospitality here, and we should be very grateful."

"You mean we are 'recipients'? I thought we were refugees."

"We *were* refugees, Solita. We *were* exiles. We've been in America for a long time now."

"Yes, Mami, but if we aren't refugees, or exiles, what are we? Nobody thinks I'm from this country. I'm not from El Topaz."

"We mustn't look back forever, Solita, we must look forward. We are in the bosom of highly placed people. I'm walking a tightrope; things are increasingly more difficult; you must cooperate, not make things worse." My mother rested her weight on her good hip. The other had been damaged by a bomb dropped by Germans from their plane on the skylight as my parents were going downstairs. But Mami was clever and could walk so it didn't show. While her brush went from the little paint pots to the photograph, she talked in absentminded spurts.

She didn't agree that the girls were freakish. Everybody had an explanation. The rich had privileges we had to accept. One learned to navigate around them. I was a lucky girl to have playmates and toys and such great food and lovely gardens and everything a child could dream of.

Why was my mother teaching Tía Merce things as if she were a child? Because Merce was convinced that her husband's brothers and friends looked down on her. Why? Because when young she hadn't attended the Villa Sainte Marie or the other expensive schools, nor had she been hobnobbing in Paris with the fascinating people at Maxim's. Although Merce was known as an accomplished guitarist—and what a booming voice she had—it went unnoticed that she had mastered only three rather suggestive folk songs, after which she pretended to stop in order to avoid monopolizing the attention. Under my mother's advice, she was taking classical guitar lessons. Merce wanted to become more cultured than all of them, and show them. We had been lucky; it had worked perfectly for us.

I couldn't see what we had to do with it.

Merce hadn't attended the same schools as the other rich people because Merce's mother was a widow with thin hair who raised her only child by keeping records in a small city hall. The poor, modest woman was very middle-class and had peasant breasts; that's where Merce had gotten hers; that's why she wore camouflaging boleros so much, quite elegantly too. Otherwise, Merce's figure was rather all right. And the reason why Tía Merce hadn't learned things before was because Merce never finished school; she had suffered from melancholia, had no friends, and had found everyone dreary.

And why weren't there any fathers here? Well, when Miguel had met Merce, flocks of women were running after him, as well as after his brothers—because Miguel's first wife was very ill. This was an immense secret, told to me to teach me about life, not to tell anyone, not even Niceto, who was too little; most mothers would never tell their children such things—I was such a lucky girl. It happened that Merce found herself with child, which happens to girls who think with parts below the waist instead of with their brains. Obviously, Merce wasn't of the same class as Miguel, whose family was immensely rich from whale-processing factories. When

Merce realized she was with child, she announced that right after Independence Day she was going to jump in the San Jorge Canal.

In the San Jorge Canal! It was incredible! No dog, horse, or cow that fell into the San Jorge Canal ever made it out alive.

Merce's plan turned Miguel honorable. As soon as his wife died, in the midst of preparations for the fiestas of Independence Day, he married Merce. The next day, with so much excitement, she had a miscarriage.

And when were fathers coming here? Miguel, he, well, Merce had . . . friends he couldn't accept. This was another big secret, not to tell the girls ever, ever, as the girls didn't know: Merce and Miguel were separated.

Separated! A notion so horrible was hard even to imagine! How could something that went together be separated! How could your two legs, for instance, separate? You needed both to get places and a mother and father to have parents. You could lift one leg, put one behind, spread them out, but how could you have each go its own way? This terrible knowledge pleased me. The girls had everything in the world, but also something horrible they didn't know: *separated parents.* But I couldn't say anything when they bragged about all the things they had and how their mother was very everything; very elegant, and very original, and very good in French and very clever about inviting important people. I couldn't say, "Yeah, your mother is very *separated.*" I had to savor it in silence. It wasn't fair. Most times, instead of what you asked for, you were told about what you didn't.

The girls knocked on the window. My mother smiled at them. I went out and followed them through the front gardens. Niceto stood at the gate, content to hold the nanny's hand and blow on a reed. Four-year-olds had simpler lives.

THE *ALMACÉN* was a fancy peasant house of whitewashed adobe with a red tile roof. It was the peasants' supply store, trading post and gathering spot, where they hung around, exchanged a phrase here and there, and listened to a record of whiny mariachi songs, which my mother said were ridiculous but which made me very happy. *Peones* sipped hot maté or bubbly orange crush. Some drank red wine on the sly, allowed only on Sundays, when they had nothing else to do. Some leaned their dark, drooping figures against the walls under the shade of the big eves, or on the long post for tying horses in front. They seemed forbidding to me, but the girls didn't seem to notice them as they went by. The *peones* straightened up when they saw us and took their hats off for a second. I thought their expressions were mocking.

Inside the *almacén* you stepped into another world, dimly lit and cool, with the smell of the fairs of Persia or Alexandria described in the *Tales of Old Arabia:* a mixture of dried fruits, tobacco, maté, soap, violet perfume in tiny magenta bottles, raw cotton fabric, dried herbs, dried meats hanging from the ceiling, bread, beans, mentholated medicines, leather and candy—a totally different smell than the food stores owned by Italians in Galmeda. However, everything was also arranged neatly up the wall in dark cubicles and down alongside the thick wooden counter in bins, barrels and huge glass jars. The *almacén* gave me a cozy feeling of filled spaces and orderly rows. In El Topaz everything else was spacious and erratic. If only we didn't have to buy.

Doña Gertrudis, the fat owner, gushed her greetings. "How very glad I am to see you, Missy Patricia and the Missy Twins!"

The girls went straight to the candy. There were five kinds, some wrapped in wax paper: caramel squares; long cones with yellowish and coral streaks swirling from the base to the tip, which was the first thing to go gooey; rosy hearts with violet words on them, like "For My Sweetheart," or "My Heart Is Forever Yours," which drove the maids to swoon; walnut shapes with a peanutty cream inside; and white mint marbles. Not as many kinds as the girls received from guests, but so tantalizing inside their big-mouthed glass jars. They tried to make up their minds. An ant struggled over the sugar terrain in the burlap sack next to me. If I were that small, I could hide inside the sugar.

In Galmeda we were very careful with our sugar. Once we didn't have to buy any, thanks to a Spaniard my father met, who had come to America many years before. He was very proud to own a swimming pool for weekends and a jewelry store for weekdays. We never used the word "refugee" or "exile" in front of him, only among those who were. To others, we were Republicans. This was very respectable. The word for a nonrefugee Spaniard was "immigrant," but it wasn't used in front of them. The word for the ones still living in Spain was "fascist," and you could say it to them, except there weren't any around.

My father had met this Spaniard while selling the last of the jewels my mother's father, crying, had put all over her when we left Spain. My father told the jeweler lots of stories and made him laugh, and he invited us to eat at his house. As a present, he gave us a large tin of honey from his bees. Although we used it every day instead of sugar, it lasted for a long time in the armoire, and on hot days it perfumed our clothes. The Spaniard paid very little for my mother's last jewels, which were very valuable, because she was her father's favorite daughter. My father said we had no choice, but my mother said he should have taken them somewhere else. She said it was just like him to make honey taste bitter, which wasn't so, it was even sweeter than sugar, and that one of these days she was going to do what she should have done, but never said what.

A boy with callused feet entered the *almacén,* put a cent on the counter and asked shyly, "One caramel." One cent bought the dark kind that turned chewy after being tossed forever from one cheek to another. It was the cheapest, and delicious. Peasant children didn't buy things for themselves, only lard or beans or matches for their mothers, so this boy was lucky. Luckier than I.

Doña Gertrudis' tiny hairs above her upper lip wiggled as

she asked him, "You sure you got permission to buy candy?" She looked suspicious even after he swore on the Virgin that he did.

My father, while buying something for himself, would have railed about a child without shoes, a crime, labor organizing, safety insurance, supporting strikes. My mother wouldn't have said anything while buying him something to eat, like a fruit. She got upset when he talked like that. "Your children need more than words, Julian. It's always the same—all speeches, all words and no do. You need the right people to get a good job."

The girls saw the caramel and wanted some too. Each placed one peso on the counter for an apronful, the way they bought candy. While they held up their pinafores, Doña Gertrudis plunged a wooden scoop into the bin and, one by one, emptied it into the girls' receptacles. "What're you getting, little girl?" She turned to me.

I had to ignore the heaviness in my chest. Whatever I did or said had to fit in smoothly with the girls' mood, so it wouldn't be glaring that I wasn't, and my parents weren't, anything they were. The turbulence that would bring would make "things" difficult for my mother, whatever "things" were. But overdoing it would turn me into a ninny; they wouldn't have any respect for me, and this would bring other problems. "I don't want anything."

Six blue eyes fastened on me. "You don't want caramels?"

"I don't like caramels particularly."

Doña Gertrudis' little lip hairs lifted. "Little girl, I can give you some and open an account for your mother; be glad to."

Even the peasant boy stood at the door awaiting my answer. Grave matters were involved here. Having said no, how could I go back on my word? My mother had said nothing good about the owner, and always said never buy anything unless you had the money right there, no matter what. And was it nice to spend the family's money to get out of a tight squeeze? "No, thank you."

Doña Gertrudis put the wooden scoop back brusquely, or

maybe it only seemed so. "Mmmm, I've been hearing from la Mamota about . . . some of the guests at the houses," she said haughtily.

Patricia made a face. "Maybe Solita doesn't have any money!"

"Solita, guests always have money. Children who don't stay in the servants' quarters; they don't play with us," Grace said.

Doña Gertrudis looked at me as a judge behind the counter. In Galmeda mostly everybody didn't have money for candy; it was something you didn't think about. I said I had money but didn't want any candy. They wanted to know where. I said in my room.

"Mmmm," Doña Gertrudis' mustache wiggled.

"Remember what la Mamota's been saying? Let's go to Solita's room and check on her money," Grace said.

My chest thumped. What if nothing distracted them or Papi didn't show up before they got there? Didn't they know breaking into your house was breaking into you? Papi said Franco barged into your house and forced you to go to church or to jail. But it didn't happen in this country. I never saw anybody in Galmeda break into someone else's house or room. It couldn't be that in country estates it was like the tall-booted Nazis and little-booted fascists, not like Galmeda. Papi didn't like these people. "You can't go in my room because . . . it's my room!"

"It's not. It's our house. Let's hurry in case her mother leaves for Viñas Echaurren; Mumsy got beastly mad at them, so maybe she will, maybe she won't," Grace suggested.

"Why is it that Solita's mother gets invited and the other thing, and maybe Solita will get to . . ." Patricia's elbow cut Gloria's breath. Both she and Grace looked at her with fury.

Gloria was flustered. "We tell Solita other things, so why can't we tell her what we know about her and about her m——"

"Gloria, shut your trap!" Patricia hissed. "This is too important, you turkey. Let's go to Solita's room."

I willed Gloria to tell, tell, but she obeyed Patricia. I had to find out; maybe their secret was what made Mami care so much about whatever Tía Merce wanted. What if every country estate led to another one, and who knows how many more before we got back to Galmeda with Papi? When you meet these important people, my mother had said, one thing leads to another. What if we were somewhere else when Papi came, and he couldn't find us?

The girls left slowly, absorbed in chewing their caramels, and I followed them, trying to figure out a foolproof way to get some of them.

3

ON THE WAY TO MY ROOM, THE GIRLS FOUND TÍA Merce, my mother and Tío Juan Vicente. While Jali, the pet goat, pestered the girls for caramels with her usual brazenness, we followed them. They paid no attention to us: Tío Juan Vicente insisted to my mother how much she'd love his fabulous mare Ninon and his records. Tía Merce got angry at him. My mother tried to make peace. The girls wanted to know if I was going to his Viñas Echaurren; otherwise, they'd check on my money. I wanted to know if we were staying, and ask Tía Merce to stop the girls.

"All right," my mother said, "if it's going to cause such a fight, I won't go to your ranch, Juan Vicente." Tía Merce gave her a hug. Tío Juan Vicente warned, "Merce, you better stop this nonsense, my peach, before you-know-who comes. What a sensational explosion I see ahead."

Gloria whispered, "Who's you-know-who?" Exactly what I was wondering.

"Whoever it is, we'll find out," Grace said. "Meantime, Solita's staying, so let's check on her money."

I tried to explain to Tía Merce that the girls wanted to invade my room without my permission. She didn't understand. "You're not saying unpleasant things, are you, my pretty? We don't say *choses désagréables* in Paradise, my pet." Then why was she telling off Tío Juan Vicente? Mami seemed displeased with me. I had probably said it wrong. Every time I spoke, all three girls talked as one with their sticky, caramely mouths. Mami praised the girls' beautiful hair; she had never seen three more stunning curly heads. This made Tía Merce even happier. But not me.

The girls headed for my room. One thing I couldn't do was cry. Papi was coming, he had promised. Then we were going to rent a house. And I had to start a foil ball. A refugee said once that you could make a ball with silver foil wrappers from confections and sell it. With luck, you could sell it in the United States for lots of money. I was starting a foil ball that was going to be the biggest foil ball ever sold to the United States, and we'd be rich and rent a house all to ourselves.

A young maid cleaning my room shook a rug in the guanaco's and the dogs' faces. "Out of my way, you stinky animals, you think I got nothing to do! Out, out, dumb, smelly creatures!"

The owners of country estates did nothing to help you in unpleasant matters, so you had to grab any opportunity you could. "Let's watch what the guanaco's going to do," I cried.

The girls agreed. "She's a new maid; she'll be sorry she shook a rug in the guanaco's face," Patricia warned. You would have thought maids would be a little nicer to an orphan. They said he didn't belong here with Christian folks, he belonged up in the Andean peaks with the fierce winds and the perpetual snows, that he was a foreigner, a no-man's-lander always crossing the cloud-topped mountain borders. The real reason maids hated him was because he was so different, and because they couldn't kick him and insult him when they were in a bad mood, as they did cats and dogs. Dr. Kaplan, the constipated psychiatrist, said beings kicked those below them on the totem pole. The guanaco was an outsider; he wasn't even on the pole, so he had his own way to deal with kickers and insulters.

We watched him move his jaw, gathering his weapon patiently. We watched the young maid come out again and empty a vase's used water into his face. He lowered his long neck and aimed. Through the air flew a stinky viscous mass which splattered on the maid's face. He had impeccable aim. She let the vase drop and ran toward the kitchen screaming, "Help! Satanás the Devil! He's after me! Help! Help!" The guanaco came back to the spot from which he had been so rudely removed and waited for us, dignified.

We applauded, we jumped. I laughed so hard I had to hold on to my panties in case the elastic burst. I kissed the guanaco on his furry face, whispering happily, "Good show, pal. If they forget about my money, you can have the next caramel they drop." He didn't respond, but then guanacos—unlike dogs or goats—weren't given to great displays of emotion.

The girls observed me as if I were more than a little crazy.

Tía Merce met my mother at the door of the big library. "That man seems to have remembered you exist; he sent word he's coming. I hope you know how to handle it. Don't forget, *ma belle,* it's illegal for a foreigner to foment political unrest."

"Oh, so Julian's coming? Did he say when?" my mother asked.

Papi coming! I knew he would, right now! I sped from the veranda to the front-gardens' entrance, a better spot than the vehicles' entrance to listen for happy motor rumbles. I hid under the giant, blue-bloomed, frog-smelling hydrangea. Late morning spread throughout the sky.

FAINT NOTES FROM the girls' practice on two pianos drifted through the gardens. For a long, long time, maybe three days, I'd waited under the hydrangea, ignoring their pleas to play or watch the grown-ups' performances. I didn't even go to the little library, although I itched to finish *Doña Pepa Goes to Town* and start *Doña Pepa Goes on a Trip.* Doña Pepa, a bragging parrot, impressed her forest friends with invented, fabulous adventures. In spite of my ignoring them, the girls hadn't acted nasty.

"Solita, come!" the girls called. Had my father appeared without my hearing him? On the path toward them, there was a spot covered with leaves. Before I knew it, my foot was thick in cow dung, found in abundance in nearby pastures. The girls exploded in laughter. I limped back and scrubbed my foot with violet petals to cover the stench. My mother was right about having to do what the Romans did every minute. They came to me and Patricia said, "We're playing psychiatric clinic, Solita, to see why you go around whispering to guanacos and kissing them, and going to an *almacén* without money, and hiding under that stinky hydrangea. Let's go." On the way to the playhouse, Gloria pouted, "But, Patricia, don't use awful tonics, or the prods."

"You'll do what the psychiatrist tells you. You want to be cured, don't you?"

I didn't. But if their own mother allowed them to be tramplers and wouldn't help me, who was going to keep me out of their psychiatric clinic? Papi was just about to arrive.

The girls put away anything unsuitable for a psychiatric clinic in their bungalow, which sat at the far corner of the front gardens where a slope of calla lilies went down to a creek. It was furnished like a real house, only everything was smaller. "We know all about psychiatric clinics," the twins boasted. They had visited Tío Jorge, Tío Juan Vicente's brother and the only nonboring grown-up, who washed his hair all day in a clinic, saying his brains were oozing out. And he got electric shocks and tonics that cheered him. He played "train" with them, sliding down a hill on their rear ends. He'd flipped before his wedding to María Pía Ycheñirre, because during a ride, he told Rosita, his lady friend, that he couldn't take her to Rio de Janeiro by airplane, as he'd promised, but was taking her to the town of Tampuco by car, since with his wedding and honeymoon and all, he didn't have the time. This made Rosita so mad she took a pot shot at him with her little hunting rifle, but only blew off a few hairs above his ear and scared the poor horses. Because the horses stampeded, everyone found out about it, and when it got to María Pía, she left him for a baron from Luxembourg, whom Tío Jorge insisted was no baron but a Luxembourg baboon. Tío Jorge didn't supervise Viñas Echaurren anymore and didn't visit; just washed his hair. If they let him out for a weekend, I'd be lucky to meet him, they assured me.

They finished putting things away. Patricia commanded, "Go upstairs, you are patients now." The twins and I settled in the beds. The room had a live smell of fresh wood. Patricia said, "Let's cure Solita first, she needs it most." I didn't agree, but I was just a patient and didn't know what they did. Anyway, this was no time to ruffle the girls but rather to distract them from money or room matters. "Now, tell me why you do these things," Patricia asked me professorially. She whispered, "You have to tell me something secret that's been bothering you."

I looked at the shutters with cloverleaf cutouts.

"What's been bothering Solita is, she's not like other guest children," Grace said. "She's not . . . I don't know what she's not. . . ." Grace was one of the things that had been bothering me.

"Shut up, Grace, you are not the patient; I'm curing Solita now. Do you think Dr. Kaplan or the clinic doctor have a crowd when they are with Mumsy or with Tío Jorge? So put a lock on your mouth. You get unruly and I'll have to use the prods. Now, Solita, what secret's been bothering you? If you don't tell me, it spoils the game."

The prods? It didn't sound good. Normally, I tried to forget what bothered me; now I tried to remember. "Why don't you tell me what secret you know about me and, well, whatever it is?"

Patricia stiffened. "Listen, Solita, *you* are the patient, not us. *You* tell us things. Now, out with it."

I looked at the row of buttons on my chest. To start with, I hated wearing their cast-off clothes. I didn't like cow dung in my toes. I looked at the foil ball in my hand. I worried about getting enough foils. "What's been bothering me is, the candy from the *almacén* doesn't have foil wrappers," I confided.

Patricia's eyes slit. "Listen, Solita, if you want to be a bowl of piss and spoil our game, you'll get your due. We know what to do with guest children who are smart-alecky and game spoilers. I'll use the prods."

Gloria sat up on her bed. "They aren't *really* electric like Tío Jorge's; they're *ortiga* twigs."

"Ya, but they do give you hideous stings that last for hours but leave no marks, so no one can find out," Grace said.

It was time to grab the bull by the horns. My mother didn't understand, and I couldn't cause problems for her. Until Papi came, nobody was doing anything, so I had to; although bragging wasn't polite, this called for scaring them to death so they'd never bother me again. I said with a grave voice, "You know, there was a girl where I lived, called Tonia Ferrolentino. And she bothered me. So you know what I did?" My pause lasted a split second, so they wouldn't have a chance to say, No, and we don't care. "Well, this Tonia Ferrolentino girl, who was Italian . . ."

"So what?" Patricia said. "Mumsy was friends with Javier Cruzat Filippi's mother, and Popsy hates her, but not because she's Italian. Your mother's the only Spaniard Mumsy's friends with. And three-flavors cassata napolitana, and zucchini and the Tower of Pisa are Italian. What has that to do with anything?"

Nothing. But Tonia Ferrolentino was just as much a foreigner as I, therefore had no right to call me names, although as an immigrant she was more at home than we. Immigrants left their country voluntarily and forever. Refugees left theirs against their will and were going back. These girls wouldn't understand any of these things. "So what did this girl do?" Grace asked.

There was no need to tell them Tonia Ferrolentino had called me a *coña,* an insult so awful no Spaniard could take it, even if it meant being thrown back in the ocean with no place to go. "Her family owned a button factory." This established I was harassed by people with credentials of some importance. There was no need to tell them the factory was the whole family making buttons at home. "It's not what she did that counts, it's what I did to her." I paused. They were dying to know. I said proudly, "I threw a big squid head at her. A ripe one."

"A squid head! A ripe one! Did it hit her?"

"Oof! Did it! Right exactly between her blond pigtails; exactly on target." What a beautiful aim it had been! It surprised me far more than it did her. "She had these pigtails midway on her head, like here and here." They gave her the look of an embarrassed dog with the ears pushed back. It was only a look; Tonia Ferrolentino was never embarrassed. Her hair was always perfect; every last one in place, which showed her family fussed with dumb things, something that immigrants tended to do.

"Between her pigtails! Where did you get a squid head!"

"In a garbage pail." Where else would you find one?

The twins were impressed, as they should have been. I didn't tell them what happened afterward. In my rush to defend my honor, I didn't consider that Tonia Ferrolentino—who lived in the green-fence house, kitty-corner from our pensione—was the youngest of seven brothers and sisters, plus uncountable cousins, aunts, in-laws, and undefined "relatives." Since they never sat in the front yard, or strolled on warm evenings on the little square with the two squat palms, I hadn't calculated how many Ferrolentinos were needed to keep flowing such an astonishing production of buttons, and thought they never came out at all. Was I wrong. Shortly after Tonia entered her house howling and grabbing the fishy back of her head, masses poured out of her house and headed for our pensione to scream and wave their arms like palms in a storm at my mother. They called me names, some in Italian. Tonia, in the arms of one of her big brothers, her head wrapped in a towel, milked the situation endlessly, howling every time her family's racket died down.

"So what happened after the girl ran dripping squid brains?" Patricia asked. All three were impressed.

"Nothing. When one of her big brothers started toward me, I went inside, and that was the end of it." I hadn't *gone* inside; I had leapt, flown up the stairs, dived into our room and burrowed through the cloud of dust under the bed. "I swear, that prissy Tonia Ferrolentino never bothered me again." This was true, and later one of her brothers even gave me a bag of rejected buttons, which my mother used on our clothes.

There was silence. They had taken the lesson well. "Did the squid head have eyes and everything?" Grace asked respectfully.

"Yes; sad, gummy eyes." Silence. I smiled happily. From now on, there'd be no insults, no prods, no trampling. Only respect.

A commanding voice called from outside, "Patricia! Grace! Glorita! Come here this instant!" We flocked to the window. Down there, in her gray splendor—bulky gray chignon, bulging gray uniform—was la Mamota. The girls scrambled down the spiral staircase. "What's wrong, Mamota?"

"Plenty's wrong these days, child, plenty; the Holy Virgin

be my witness. Now, I want you to wipe your ears clean of all you just heard up there, you hear me? That child, that . . . I overheard everything. Nothing escapes me, don't you forget it. Never have these houses heard such . . . hooliganism: ransacking garbage pails, throwing rotten squid heads at children, calling names. . . . Imagine the Sacred Ears of Our Lady hearing such things in these houses! Mi Señora Doña Mercedes ought to open her eyes, see what she's brought to destroy our ways, in every front. Now look at you; go and tell Ema and Eda to change you."

"We were just trying to find out why Solita's so daffy," Patricia pouted, "about money, and hiding, and all that."

As they walked away on a garden path, la Mamota's voice complained about leeches and hooliganism until it faded away. The retinue of pinafores after her turned dark pink under the trees; light pink under the sun; dark; light; dark; light; then disappeared behind some bronze viburnums.

The Francoists had shot my grandfather against a wall because he was against the army that was taking over. Could you or couldn't you grab the bull by the horns when the bull owned it all? I had to ask Mami, right now, why wasn't Papi here, why was Tía Merce so important? The play bungalow's window commanded an endless view of masses of leaves casting shadows over clumps of bushes and blooming flower beds. Everything was paralyzed by an idle spell of warmth and the locusts' *whirr-whirrs.*

DURING A GAME of art cards, Tía Merce and the patched man had a fight and he asked to be served *boldo* tea at the park's gazebo, all by himself. The girls scurried after him to try to get some information. I went back to my waiting spot.

The hydrangea had a very irritating droop; it was hard to fit comfortably under it. Surely Papi wouldn't come by bicycle so the girls would make fun of him. He could drive a car, in spite of the two fingers blown off by a German bomb falling through the skylight. He and Mami had waited wounded a long time on the second floor because there were no stairs to go down.

We didn't have to worry about bombs in this country, only about rich people. How could Papi find a car? Maybe he'd found that great job and could borrow one there. Jobs were hard to find though. Papi said the refugee relief organization said they couldn't do anything with a foreign lawyer. This country didn't recognize his degree. Papi found translations to do from French; he even knew some English, but they paid very little, so every day he searched the newspaper eagerly, because that day he was going to find a fabulous job. He found one where they bundled sea kelp at a beach, but he was gone for days, and it upset Mami that he talked to the other workers about organizing against the boss. When I asked about it, she said these were things children wouldn't understand and not to worry. But she wanted him to get another job. When Papi searched the Sunday paper, he gave me the comics, which came in color, with the Phantom in a blue suit. It was great—both of us reading under the ilang-ilang tree. If Papi didn't wave his arms in the air so much as he spoke, the girls wouldn't notice his hand.

Through a gap in the leaves, I saw my mother and Tía Merce strolling. My mother was much taller, so why did Tía Merce seem bigger? Maybe because she acted like a big shot the way Franco did. Tía Merce tried to lock arms, but my mother wouldn't. Their voices became clearer as they approached my hiding place. Passing in front without seeing me, Tía Merce said, "Believe me, it's better to switch from men to women; men's approaches are so much the same, it gets boring. Women have interesting differences."

My mother didn't answer. Later she said, "Of course, Merce, you're enchanting, elegant, wonderful. But I've told you, Sappho is not my cup of tea, and being immersed here in nature, as you say, won't make any difference. I'm tired of saying it: forgo the Greek poetess; collect other poets . . ."

Tía Merce said, "Oh, Pilar, *ma belle,* how regretful. You and Juan Vicente are ganging up on me, and now, even after we found out about Julian, he thinks he can . . ."

"Juan Vicente and I have your welfare in mind, Merce. You must take Dr. Kaplan seriously. He has the . . ." My mother's voice trailed off as they went behind the old oak's massive trunk. My mother and the patched man were very nice to Tía Merce. How could they be ganging up on her? So, when was Papi coming?

Hunger tugged at my stomach, but I wouldn't stop listening for happy motor rumbles. Soon things would be set right again. In Galmeda I did what pleased my parents quickly and well, such as eating an egg in my soup, even if it was still slimy, finding something Papi had lost, or looking after my brother. My mother and I were together when she dressed Niceto, or we ate raw clams in the fish market, or carried vegetables back home. Here in El Topaz, my mother had things to do, but I didn't know what. I had things to do, but she didn't understand about them. My brother was under Nanny Fresia's care, and neither of us had a part in it. Trying to help take care of my brother would have made the girls say I was putting on airs.

In Galmeda people didn't expect you to do what you couldn't. Refugees weren't as good as other people, but they weren't *under* anybody. Being under others was hateful. A motor's rumble came from the distance—then the tumble of tires over the small bridge at the bend of the road.

He was here! Papi was here!

4

A CAR WITH A COVERED WHEEL ON ITS BACK circled the driveway. Would Papi be coming with refugees? No, I had to remember we weren't refugees anymore. Besides, where would refugees find such a fancy car? Someone else had invited him. "My father is here," I boasted to the girls while jumping happily, "my father is here."

A jumble of people and animals rushed out to the front veranda. Manuel, the head butler, ran to turn on the huge battery radio; Tía Merce liked loud music when guests arrived. My mother suggested instead a record called Dvořák. Tía Merce agreed and grabbed the patched man's arm, whispering, "Now, Juan Vicente, my pet, do I keep my promises, uh?" He kissed her hand while they went down the steps to do greetings.

I braced myself for all the kissing to be done. Grown-ups approached each other's cheeks within a hair of touching, but we had to press our lips into all sorts of smelly textures that ranged from scrappy to spiky, from powdery to droopy, from clammy to gummy. And after the deed was done, it was impolite to wipe your mouth to keep something slimy or dusty from entering it. You had to stand there smiling with lips smeared with odd things.

With the refugees you didn't have to do prearranged things; your body just did normal things. Some hugged you; some pulled your ear, which wasn't so cute; some grabbed your nose with their knuckles, which was funny; some patted you or pressed your shoulder; but it was all cheerful and comfortable.

The first one out of the car was the photographer with the smelly German feet, acting as if he were delivering royalty. Mlle. Vicky, the dancer with raccoon eyes, jumped to help him with a suitcase, which I knew a lady wasn't supposed to do. Then came a tall, stiff woman, older than my mother. Her long blond hair, hanging down like a girl's, was stiff as straw. The girls moaned at the sight of her. "Ugh! María Teresa, the contessa!"

Since the girls' eyes looked sourly at her, it was safe to ask questions. "Why is she so stiff?"

"She fancies she's the Eiffel Tower, or something, because ages ago she was a model in Paris. She's icky. She loves Mumsy to death. She hates us. We hate her."

The straw woman gave Tía Merce a stiff peck and a killing glance. Tía Merce chuckled without her usual confidence. "Mari Tere, what an enchanting surprise! Ay! A Dior cape, isn't it?" Tío Juan Vicente, amused, whispered to Tía Merce, "My, do you have your hands full. At least you should be happy *he* didn't come."

The straw woman turned to give my mother a cold stare that made my stomach knot. Grace complained, "Patricia, you always say we'll do something terrible to the contessa so she'll never come back to make Mumsy do whatever she wants, but we never do it."

"This time we will; I have a plan. We can get rid of

anybody we don't like." The twins looked at their older sister with admiring expectation.

After the straw woman glanced at the girls, she turned to me. I stretched my lips to fashion a friendly smile. Looking at me as if I were a rare beetle, she asked, "And who may this be?"

"I'm Solita."

She didn't say anything like, My, what an interesting name, just stared. "Well, my name is Soledad, Solita's for short." If the occasion required more, I would add that I was named after the famous book of poems. My parents always liked for me to say it; then maybe the straw woman would like my mother.

The girls looked at me aghast for talking. But Mlle. Vicky said, "How lovely," and she, the German photographer and the patched man, even Nanny Fresia from the distance, smiled at me. Maybe now I could talk with the grown-ups, in spite of the girls' sour look. Tía Merce said in what sounded like an apology. "This is my friend Pilar's child." Fortunately, the straw woman turned her cold stare on Tía Merce, so I didn't have to say anything else. Tía Merce's underchin trembled. She glanced at me and whispered sternly, "By the way, my pretty, la Mamota's been telling me you're not behaving quite properly. I grant this won't happen again, will it, my pretty."

Was this a question? I pressed my cowlick. Luckily, Tía Merce went down to greet a small man coming out of the car. At times it was an advantage that in country estates grown-ups didn't focus their attention on children for very long.

The girls still stared at me aghast. They whispered. Gloria said, "So, for now she won't be going to . . . you know . . ."

Patricia told her not to talk so loud, so I couldn't hear any more. But soon Patricia couldn't resist showing off how much she knew about people, which was fine with me; it was the easiest way to find out things. "The pretty man's Claudio Correa, a famous hat man. Everybody famous or important comes to El Topaz."

The famous hat man filled his suede clothes very well. A few neat wisps of hair fringed his suede beret. Tío Juan Vicente seemed happy and got busy shooing the excited dogs and Jali away from the hat man's neatly pressed trousers. The guanaco arrived on the lookout for cigarettes, abundantly lit and carelessly handled on these noisy occasions. I hoped the hat man wouldn't ruffle Tía Merce and make her upset at me too. "What's a hat man?" I asked, my eyes still locked to the car's dark insides.

The girls weren't horrified; by now they were used to my abysmal ignorance. "He draws hats and owns a shop that makes them." "And the elegant stores sell them for oodles of money to distinguished women." "Mumsy's very clever to get him to come."

The hat man kissed my mother's hand. Instead of acting dignified as she did when men got idiotic around her, she smiled. He said, "My shop's on strike. Those unions have Galmeda up in arms. What trouble, what troublemakers."

My mother stopped smiling. I kept looking at the car, but a big man took forever to get out. He went to shake the ladies' hands slowly and gave my mother a penetrating look.

"That's Marco Polo," Patricia said. "That's what Mumsy's friends call him. He's traveled so much he has an accent."

"He has sons scattered all over the world." "A Chinese son, an Indian, and . . . Burmese and Mexican and . . . others."

No one else was in the car. Papi hadn't come. Could I run and hide in my room? No. Could I dissolve the lump in my throat? I had to. Had he gone on sleeping when they picked him up? It always took Mami forever to wake him. Julian, Julian, she called, get up, Julian. She sprinkled water, she threw his bed covers off. He often caught a cold but didn't wake up. Once Mami yanked his bedclothes so hard he went with them; his head hit the floor, his legs stayed on the bed. We went to market. When we got back, Papi was still in the same position, asleep!

Or had they decided there was no place in the car for Papi because Marco Polo's behind took so much room? What was happening in Galmeda? Had Papi given the guests a message for us? More than anything in the world, I needed a magic carpet; not even an elegant one with silky fringes that flew like the wind, just an old, used one from the flea market.

My mother didn't seem upset that Papi wasn't here. She laughed at what Tío Juan Vicente told the hat man. Tía Merce fidgeted around the straw woman. While the twins stampeded down the veranda, doing their usual running away, I went to ask my mother about Papi. But she was talking with the others. It was now widely considered that I lived here, so I had to follow the twins. On top of my distress, it made me feel perfectly idiotic and a touch disgraced. And it was hard to run as fast holding on to your tears and your panties. For some reason panties were the only things you didn't inherit from others, so I didn't have any of the twins' cast-off fancy ones with infallible elastics.

The sight of the guests' candy, especially the bags of meringues, eased the lump in my throat considerably; delicious eating, gigantic foil wrappers for my foil ball, and a reprieve from buying sprees at the *almacén*. One thing you learned at country estates was to get what you could when guests arrived. As the music blared out, in the midst of cheerful confusion, picking up puppies, kissing and "My, haven't you grown," and "My heavens, you're making me old," the girls acted quite civilized. They had to offer candy all around, but lately they complained that I never refused, as polite people had to. I didn't want to be that polite. You couldn't stuff your mouth and your pockets blatantly, but I helped myself in a decorous manner and even handed some to my brother, and the girls couldn't make a fuss. It was another story later when the guests were out of sight.

La Mamota and Manuel instructed the men servants on what to do with suitcases. The guests chatted away. For some reason the girls followed them with interest; they had something important to work out. Maybe it was related to what they knew about me. In any case, the guests had to tell why

Papi hadn't come. Maybe some guests turned out to be the next best thing to refugees. Maybe they'd tell the girls to be fair. What if a batch of guanacos descended from the high Andean peaks? It would please the guanaco tremendously. He'd been lonely. They would be his friends.

LEANING AT THE END of the gallery's wall made of glass panes, the girls observed the grown-ups settled comfortably on fat, flowered couches. They wouldn't go any closer. I could hear meringues crumble between the girls' teeth and imagine the sweet invasion of white powder. Meringues were good for sad throats, but I hadn't managed to snatch one from them. Niceto went from lap to lap, flirting and extorting bonbons; it was disgusting.

The guests' skins glowed in the dying orange light entering through the glass. They hadn't mentioned Papi yet, nor anything that seemed related to whatever it was the girls didn't want me to know. The guests kept mentioning Galmeda. My mother could ask them about my father. I could talk to them.

The refugees always told each other about meeting clever people in this country who were antifascists, and news about refugees in other countries, and how thrilled they were to be in this quiet one, going to the fish market, opened by two Spanish refugee brothers, to eat raw clams; going to the university theater, started by two refugees who'd worked with the poet García Lorca; sitting during balmy nights under a squat palm tree in the little neighborhood squares. They talked less and less about how they'd managed to get rescued or to escape, or to take a cargo boat to the New World, or which countries had not let them in, such as the United States, even though they had jobs waiting there teaching, or linotyping, or making furniture, because its president, called Roosevelt, was the Assassin's friend; and they never said they were homesick or missed their families, although my mother said they all did.

The long-legged group related tales about their trip to El Topaz as if they were fascinating and astonishing, with oohs, ahas and laughter. Would they take us back to Galmeda in their car? This cheered me up.

While Tía Merce sang with the guitar, I surveyed the gallery, wondering who might treat me as if I was someone to be taken into account. They were all in a titter about the espresso brought by Manuel, made with a new contraption the hat man had brought from Paris. Other coffee makers had been brought before, and they always said the same thing, "*Delicioso,* absolutely *delicioso!* How did we have coffee before! Coffee will never be the same!" The straw woman demanded cognac in hers, then kept pouring more from the bottle, looking at my mother as if she wanted to harm her.

The girls had something in mind for the straw woman. They said she was an ex-model, an ex-widow and ex-married, and after their witches' rites and their smear trick she was going to be an ex-guest at El Topaz. She was the widow of an old Belgian count, but money had to be paid to get his title, and he had left none, so she was using the money that a younger, wrinkle-faced *yanqui* who owned copper was giving her after they divorced, to get the old Belgian's title. I wouldn't have been able to tell the girls anything like that about my parents' friends.

Tía Merce was nervous with the straw woman and thrilled with the hat man. The hat man looked at my mother as if she were a hat. He told her her face was made to wear hats. She didn't say anything about Papi or going back in their car. The Walrus sniffed at something his hairy fingers took from a small jeweled box. The patched man put a record on the Victrola and raved about Bach, which my mother liked, but which the girls complained was only good with horror shows. Mlle. Vicky said, "Gunther, Gunther," to the photographer, as if he didn't know his own name. She moved her long legs, revealing under her many-banded sandals a bright, deep purple foil wrapper with squared ridges, a king of wrappers.

Now I absolutely had to go near them. How could I do it without Tía Merce noticing? When I was near her, she made me think of all the places a girl like me should be instead of where she was. A girl like me turned and twisted too much, had a disorderly cowlick, a shrill voice, and should be made over again; nothing was salvageable. "I'm going to talk to the grown-ups," I whispered, so it wouldn't take them by surprise.

"Do what? Solita, has your brain turned to muck?"

"Why?"

"Why? We don't go around talking to grown-ups."

"Why not?"

"What do you have in your brain, Solita? They're boring."

"If you find the grown-ups so boring, why do you listen so much to what they tell each other?"

"How else are you going to find out things or make plans?"

"By asking your Mumsy, or one of them."

They looked exasperated. "Solita, you really think grown-ups are going to tell you the truth? Grown-ups tell you what's polite, dummy. They never tell you the fancy things you can tell your cousins or the girls at the nuns' school."

"What's tickling about grown-ups are the fancy things you find out on your own by watching them," Grace said.

"You already made a complete fool of yourself, yakking to María Teresa when she arrived. Didn't we tell you we hate her?"

The girls had cast a paralyzing net around us. In country estates you had to do a lot of waiting because people planned things and wouldn't tell you about it. So you had to learn to keep quiet. In Galmeda the only thing I couldn't say was something against this country. My mother told the hat man, "I have a hat of yours, a gift from Juan Vicente; it's a work of art." This made the patched man smile. The collapsed eggplant a work of art? Would this be fancy? It then occurred to me I didn't have any cousins or school friends to tell fancy things to.

"Very interesting magazines," the straw woman said, browsing at some my mother had asked Tía Merce to order.

"They were Pilar's idea," Melons said.

The straw woman looked furious. She put a cigarette in a holder and with a sour smile asked my mother, "And how is it that you met our little Merce?" Tía Merce didn't move.

Melons said, "You know, the day Mercedes met Pilar, she called Dr. Kaplan, my dear husband, at midnight, to tell him she'd met this divine Spaniard. Mercedes was in a highly agitated state, and my poor dear had a terrible cold."

"Leticia," Dr. Kaplan said.

The Walrus chuckled. "Leticia, you don't have to call her a Spaniard. Why, Pilar is practically one of us. . . . What I mean is, she's not an inferior race, I mean, we all have Spanish blood. . . ."

Mlle. Vicky's sandal covered the bright purple wrapper.

Melons' words roused Tía Merce. "True! That night"—her chin sagged happily—"I had a *petit* dinner to introduce Armando, my available brother-in-law, to a friend's daughter. The butler said the photo retoucher had come, so I went to pay her, and the minute my eyes saw Pilar, I recognized the presence of an *esprit extraordinaire*. I invited her to stay for dinner. Armando, my brother-in-law, insisted on taking Pilar home. Was my little friend miffed! Then I saw Pilar at a party at Armando's house . . ."

"He invited both Julian and me," my mother interrupted. The twins said their youngest uncle had a hothouse with trees inside, a Land-Rover with a battery phone line, a stuffed-parrot collection, a full-size bronze of Napoleon, and had entertained French Olympic champion Henri Oreiller in his ski chalet. They said they had seen my mother at their house once when their uncle was there, but Patricia wouldn't let them say anything more. I never knew my parents had visited someone with all those things. Parents led mysterious lives. Sometimes you wanted to know where they went and be part of all the excitement, sometimes you didn't care, but now I did.

Mlle. Vicky's sandal made a rip on a corner of the bright purple foil. But it was still usable.

"Yes, and the minute I saw him, *son mari*"—Tía Merce bent up her wrist—"I could tell he's a *petit macho espagnol* type, the possessive, unreasonable type, not at all up to Pilar's level . . ."

The straw woman muttered, "That does it!" dropped her cup and left with her cigarette holder up, leaving a trail of smoke. Tía Merce ran after her. Everyone was startled. In spite of this being obviously fancy, the girls said there was nothing fancy going on and left in a hurry to follow them.

This was my chance. With great daring, I crawled to Mlle. Vicky and picked up the purple foil. I waited for someone to talk to me. Melons said, "María Teresa's never been able to control her jealousy." Not one grown-up asked me a thing, such as what I wanted to be when I grew up. These El Topaz grown-ups weren't well disposed, rather the opposite of refugees. The only one they noticed was my brother, due to his large eyes, his reddish hair and his unworldly answers, which they found enchanting.

I headed for the little bathroom, admiring my purple foil with ridges. As big as El Topaz was, there were only two places where you could be left alone. One was the little library—a small room with children's books going up every wall. The other one was the little bathroom at the end of the houses, which looked out over the sloping calla-lily field stretching below the front gardens. The door scratches, done by dogs who had occasionally been locked there, made interesting or funny pictures that made me laugh. No one else used the little bathroom because it was so popular with bugs.

As I approached a corridor joining the two verandas, I heard a very angry voice: "Just as I suspected, and if you want to see me again, my little Merce, you better throw that barbarian woman out! I can't understand you! You told me what happened in Galmeda, and you let her use you for her designs? She won't get away with making a fool of you! I promise you! She'll be sorry!"

Tía Merce's voice said, "Mari Tere, she's just staying away from Galmeda, darling; stop threatening, you're acting silly."

That was true. Under the corridor's massive door, I saw six small feet. The girls were listening too. I continued on to the little bathroom. I sat comfortably and admired the purple wrapper on my foil ball. It was getting dark. A lonely froghopper bug persisted in its delusion that it could climb up the slippery bathtub, probably looking for its mother and father. If it was my father Tía Merce had mentioned, it was silly to call him *petit*. Thin yes, but *petit* no. He was practically as tall as Mami. Tía Merce's French was terrible. People here talked about my parents, whom I knew so well, as if they were actors on a stage, figures in a political magazine, strangers. Even la Mamota carried on about my mother. They were trying to fit my parents into some new place in an odd order of things. So where were my brother and I to be fit in? The froghopper bug never made it.

WE RAN AND ROLLED on the slippery green of an alfalfa field, leaving flattened areas. The girls were in a bad mood, apparently from something the straw woman had said, and it had something to do with me, but they wouldn't tell me. "Too bad Solita's never tasted the marvel fruit," Grace said. "It's the most delicious in the world, but there're so few and the grown-ups take them."

"I think there's a marvel fruit available now. Would you like to taste it?" Patricia asked me.

I managed to agree without showing enthusiasm. You could be emphatic here about disliking things, never about liking them.

We didn't go to a fruit orchard, but to the vegetable patch. The chief gardener's white dog was there sniffing a squash plant. Tonic went berserk wiggling his stub tail, running around the dog and sniffing its behind. "Tonic's going to get his bullet out in a minute," Gloria said. Sure enough, a glistening red bullet came out like lipstick between his legs.

Patricia looked around to make sure no one observed us. "Mario's dog's too tall; we can wait all day for something to happen. Let's go get the marvel fruit." Tonic waved his behind frantically. The twins wanted to stay in case Tonic accomplished what he was attempting so strenuously. They complained there was always someone forbidding them to watch the dogs doing . . . they rapidly put one finger in and out of another curled one, which was the way they referred to the no-name thing, so the nuns wouldn't hear, they said. You learned a lot at nun schools.

Though I wanted to eat the marvel fruit, I was glad they decided to stay. Anything related to the no-name thing was very wrong, but extremely interesting. Just as Patricia predicted, Tonic flashed his red bullet in the breeze, then began to cry and whine. "He goes loony; let's help him," Gloria said.

"Gloria! You got mold in your brain, as usual! Imagine if Padre Romualdo hears you!"

"Padre Romualdo's not here," Gloria said, "and he's not going to tell us about bullets; he just scolds Mumsy and her friends. I want to see where the bullet goes and what happens." Gloria had a point, but her sisters cried, "Revolting!"

"Maybe. But cousin Beba says the bullet grows like a hose, explodes in the girl dog, and the pieces turn into puppies. Don't you want to see the hose?"

This sounded sensational. Then suspicious. According to my mother, babies came from an egg inside the mother.

"Cousin Beba never told me that," Patricia said, offended. You couldn't blame them for bragging about cousins, aunts, uncles and grandparents; it was too fantastic. When we got tired of waiting, we went to a patch. Grace picked a gleaming red fruit, almost unreal. She ceremoniously handed it to me. "The marvel fruit. Bite a big piece, and chew it fast, to get the most deliciousness out of it, and get that wonderful feeling."

I was touched by Grace's generosity, especially because Gloria looked resentful. "What if Padre Romualdo insists we go to confession? Don't give it to her."

"Let's split it in four," I offered, "or five, to give my brother some." I was touched by my generosity.

"No. We've had it many times before," Patricia said. "The next one will be for your brother."

Well, all right. I eagerly bit into the marvel fruit, and the instant the juice flooded my mouth it turned into lava. My tongue quickly pushed the fire out of the way, to my throat. The inside of my chest got stabbed by hot spurs going down. I gasped for air. Was Patricia laughing? And Grace? Their faces appeared and disappeared between my tears and, yes! They were laughing!

I ran to the houses, a flaming torch. Patricia and Grace ran after me, singing "*Ají, ají colorado!*" and laughing so much they couldn't keep up with me.

The grown-ups were sitting on canvas chairs around the pool. My mother was telling them that Salvador Dali had been hired as a young man to decorate windows in New York.

I was in such fire, such indignation, that I crashed my mother's Dali story and her "Spaniards don't cry," and the entire history of Spanish valor, and threw myself at the mercy of the canvas-chair group. I blurted, cried, made a disgraceful spectacle of myself, but a plenty justified one.

"Calm down, Solita," my mother said. Calm down? I pointed to the scorched pit of my mouth, to the rest of the marvel fruit, to the two girls giggling behind a pomegranate bush. I glanced at the others to gauge the severity of the punishment coming to the girls. The sooner and harsher the better. Were Tía Merce and some others smirking? It seemed impossible, yet that's how it looked. They weren't indignant? Shocked? They were amused? It was bewildering. Now my mouth had to stay closed to hold a new pack of sobs trying to burst out, this time in confusion, not in righteousness.

Tío Juan Vicente looked at the fruit. "It's *ají colorado,* powerful stuff; children shouldn't touch it." The famous hat man said, "Amazing red." The straw woman said, "Aren't there toy rooms and game rooms to keep children occupied here?" A smiley voice said, "Ay, these girls are impossible, aren't they?"

Tía Merce clapped to the nannies. "If you don't do a proper job of supervising, I'll send you home and bring your cousins."

My mother brushed the fruit to her lips and quickly washed it with cherry juice. "What's this commotion, Solita? What a Sarah Bernhardt production. Go rinse your mouth and change your pinafore; it's all wet. And stop eating junk; you should eat only at mealtimes." She continued her story about Salvador Dali throwing bricks at the store windows, creating a huge brouhaha in the streets of New York, because his decoration of dusty old bathtubs and naked mannequins covered with spider webs had been washed by the store's cleaning crew. The canvas group laughed.

Although none of them, sitting there in the light and shade waves from the pool and the magnolia, knew I had embarrassed my mother, I did. I went down the veranda to my room, looking at the planked ceiling in an attempt to make the tears go back inside. They went into my ears.

I didn't change my pinafore. I took my magic flying carpet from a secret place. I flew far, far up, so high I was a speck from Earth. All the way to Galmeda, I didn't stop until I was over our square with the two squat palm trees. Through the three-paned opened window, I entered our room. I told Papi what had happened and wet him with tears. He was angry, gave me a hug and said, I'll take you away from there, and we'll live here and you can play in the square with whomever you darn please.

The white wall next to my bed always had new figures to discover. Had it been so shameful to have cried in front of everybody? At least my mother hadn't gone on about this or that Spaniard not crying: "Did you see Alphonse the Sixth crying when he was told during a trip that the Moors had rebelled because his French wife and the archbishop had violated the Main Mosque—did you? Did you see Alphonse the Tenth, the Wise, cry when the pope didn't permit him to take legitimate possession of the crown of the Germanic lands—did you? Did you see the Visigothic king crying in Toledo when he learned his son had been converted to Catholicism by his wife and was challenging his power—did you? And you're going to cry for that small stuff?" It never seemed so small to me. And of course I hadn't seen any of those people that my mother made live among us. They were unknown in San Bernardo Street, or here.

A plaster design in the shape of the *ají colorado* made me furious again. I was never, ever going to do anything with the girls again. Not even sit at the table with them, ever. Even if we were thrown out of El Topaz and my mother and my brother and myself had to starve to death, or worse. Starting after teatime, since it was that time already. Why had Salvador Dali, a Spaniard, acted like a crying brat, and the canvas group had found his shameful tantrum funny?

TEA WAS SERVED under a linden tree. The girls' pouring of salt from tiny silver ladles on their avocado canapes revealed no remorse or apology. It made me furious when the salt I put on my canape stung. Gulping chocolate milk, I said, "You lied to me."

"You have a chocolate moustache; you always do, Solita."

They weren't going to intimidate me. But I wiped and did have chocolate. "You did a treacherous thing." This was a good word from *The Junior Three Musketeers.* The twins seemed to be making mental notes to ask Patricia what it was.

"Solita, you're a real crybaby and a spoilsport. Running to the grown-ups like that. . . ."

I bit my glass of milk, not hard enough to break it, just enough to give it a jolt.

"Where have you been, Solita? Guest children always have jokes played on them, if they toady up to the grown-ups."

"What María Teresa said will happen is not Solita's fault," Gloria said. Her sisters silenced her with dirty looks. She said Padre Romualdo was going to scold them about the *ají colorado*.

"It's ungracious to get mad and be a boor," Patricia said.

What to think or say? I was saved by two maids bursting onto the terrace teasing Nanny Fresia about someone called José.

That night I was awake when my mother came to her room. I called to her in whispers: "Mami, what are we waiting for to leave? The girls *are* freaks. They're scary."

"Unwarranted fears, my daughter. They're just prankish, rich girls. Just learn their ways and navigate around them."

There I was, in a sea full of hidden rocks and unexpected vortexes without a pilot. "When's Papi coming?" My voice cracked.

"Whenever he wants." She kissed me and Niceto good night.

You couldn't just postpone bad things, you couldn't lie about what could be discovered, you couldn't scare people; you had to work harder, you had to *plan* for things to happen.

OUT OF THE BLUE, the straw woman announced that she didn't want to watch the Charlie Chaplin movies brought by Marco Polo, she wished to horseback ride to the big lake to play cards on the boats. Tía Merce immediately ordered a general ride. But I didn't know how to ride horseback! The last thing in the world the girls wanted was to go anywhere with the straw woman. They considered some options. They said that the straw woman stuck a hot pepper in her horse's asshole to make it frisk like a show horse, so they considered stuffing several hot peppers, so rather than just itch and get frisky, her horse would be stung to a frenzy and throw her off. "Well, at least riding will be fun," Gloria said philosophically.

Before Nanny Fresia made me put on riding clothes, I ran to my mother's room to tell her I was staying here. She was sewing ribbons on her espadrilles and humming "The Four Mule Drivers."

"Solita, these are the things you will learn while we're here. You won't be a little savage much longer. Soon, you'll learn to dance from Vicky. You're a very lucky girl. You must learn, as quickly as possible."

"But I don't know how to horseback ride!"

"Just do what the girls do, they'll tell you."

Ask the girls! I'd die first. "I don't want to, Mami."

"Solita, you don't want to be rude, you don't want to offend your hosts." Why did mothers *tell* you what you didn't want? You were the only one who knew. "Let's not start pooh-poohing what interesting people do, Solita, like your father. Look, ribbons make these very sporty. In the country you wear sporty clothes."

"But, Mami, horses are huge and scary."

"Horses are huge and scary? What if El Cid had said that? And Saint James of Compostela? What if the brave knights and ladies you see in the paintings of El Prado had said that . . .?"

This went on for as long as it took to tie the ribbons around her ankles. Mercifully, she didn't go on comparing my puny plight with the centuries of invasions endured by our ancestors and the bravery they had displayed. I never knew that horses and my mother's much-touted Spanish valor went together. But the very real ones in El Topaz were frightening, the one pulling the buggy gigantic. In books clever horses were children's friends. My only riding experience went way back to a refugee whose son never made it out of Spain and who gave me rides on his back on all fours. Through the window I saw Nanny Fresia coming. Leaving Spanish valor for some other time, I ran out the opposite door.

I joined a scattering of grown-ups who seemed quite satisfied to be wearing tall boots and pants with flared hips, which looked as if they could flap and take off. Some ladies mentioned the eagerly awaited Tío Armando, which made the girls very uncomfortable. The grown-ups made the sign of the cross as they passed the chapel and lamented that the sky was so pale.

Horses, huge horses, were being brought to the cart yard. I saw Nanny Fresia coming. I hid in a cloud of perfume behind a plump lady who wore a net over the red hair under her hat. She kept rattling bracelets in agitation. "A *criollo* saddle for me. Who's in charge here?" She was joined by a lady similarly jeweled, dressed, coiffed and hatted, with black, curled bangs over fiery blue eyes. The girls had said she wrote poetry and her husband owned pharmacies. Tío Juan Vicente, with leather patches on his riding pants and a rifle on his shoulder, said, "Poor pumas, they've no idea Juan Vicente Echaurren's on the loose."

Nanny Fresia looked around. I suppressed coughs from the fumes of the perfume. "Where's Marco Polo? He's vanished," a voice said. "Soon he'll add to his brood some from El Topaz," another voice said. Someone asked, "Why the name El Topaz?" "Because of the color of my eyes," Tía Merce said, turning her horse toward the road, "and the golden sun, wheat hills and the golden life."

Suddenly, a young woman I'd never seen, with flowing reddish hair, arrived galloping, as if from nowhere. Her reddish horse was as spirited and eager as she. Tía Merce introduced her. "This precious girl's one of the many daughters of my good neighbor Jaime Undurraga; he owns the lands between us and the Echaurrens. Which one are you, my pretty?"

"María Cristina." She was beautiful, with flushed cheeks and a perfectly tailored riding habit. She pushed back her hair as she handled her nervous horse with elegant ease.

"Won't you join us for a short ride, dear?" Tía Merce said.

"I don't mind if I do," the precious girl replied demurely,

as if she hadn't joined them already. Patricia and the twins observed her wistfully; if only they could be that old and independent.

A woman whispered that María Cristina, at eighteen, was too young to be dyeing her hair mahogany. "After you've had a few children, you're entitled to mahogany." Others whispered, "I bet she found out Gunther's here." "The Undurraga girls are getting desperate." "They keep their mansion in Galmeda closed, did you know?" "Of course, they pretend to be here on vacation, and the girls have to prowl around here for slim pickings." "If Jaime Undurraga knew a daughter of his was here blushing at Gunther! The whole slew have strict orders to look for marriageable money only."

The precious girl moved next to Gunther and acted as if she had a secret she was willing to share with him. Mlle. Vicky tried to insert her horse between theirs, but the beast balked, opening his nostrils wide. My mother had said the photographer wasn't a bad German, just an "innocent boy" who'd come here to America for a peaceful life, and since he was so handsome, society girls flocked to his studio to have their pictures taken.

"Vicky shouldn't be so worried," whispered the black-curled-bangs lady, whom the girls said was spiritual. "These Undurraga girls are so dumb, they are apt to applaud in a concert between the movements of a symphony." She smirked disdainfully.

"She talks like a duck," Tía Merce said in a duck's voice.

Amazingly, even when you were as old and pretty as this precious girl, and could gallop as well, you still had to be careful about everything you did.

My mother arrived in her ribboned espadrilles and the black overalls she'd made from pieces salvaged from a burnt-out factory. She had charmed the guard into letting us inside to look through the charred bolts. Our clothes had sprung from those ashes. Everyone stared at her. The straw woman let out a snort. My stomach knotted. Finally Tío Juan

Vicente said, "My dear Spaniard, how charming, how impractical. Claudio, wouldn't this charming, impractical person look *sensational* in something . . . brisk? Yes! Fresh, like reeds in a pond; striped pants, green safari blouse, white riding boots. What say you, Claudio?"

"Mmm," the hat man said, squinting to look at my mother. "She definitely needs drama, none of that charming stuff . . ."

The straw woman whipped her horse and held him back, so he did jumps in place. Tía Merce turned to her and said, "You behave yourself, *mon chou.* Hold that fire of yours; leave her alone. . . ."

My mother barely smiled and climbed on a horse held by Alberto, a strong-armed man with a goatee, and his son.

Nanny Fresia came toward me. Luckily, she was stopped by the Walrus' yells to get out of the way, as his car was backing out of the garage. Evaristo, the chauffeur, got out, picked up the guanaco with difficulty and put him in the open back seat.

Nanny Fresia reached me at last. This was the time to do like heroes in books and think of *something* to get me out.

ONE LOOK AT THE guanaco and I got an idea. (My body was skinny, but my brain could come up with great ideas!) I said to the girls, "Didn't the Walrus promise to take you in his car's open seat with the guanaco? Are you asking him now?" The girls were charmed. They begged and noisily reminded the Walrus of his promise. He agreed. I was saved! The guanaco closed his eyes in the breeze. I waved to Nanny Fresia ecstatically.

Along the road, we approached a palm forest. The girls pointed at two horses tied to a palm and pounded on the car's back window. "Leave us here! We've had enough car riding!"

The Walrus told us he would pick us up on his way back. Evaristo said, "The young ones shouldn't be left alone in these parts; there're big wild animals, Señor." Big wild animals?

The three girls yelled, "What has that to do with us! We've been here a trillion times before!" The Walrus agreed that the little ones knew these parts well. The guanaco fidgeted.

"Don't you go into the brush," Evaristo told us. "Missy Patricia, the pumas there, you know. You don't hear 'em, then swoosh! they're right on top of you. . . . And the cougars also, Missies. Also the *culpeos,* those mean black lobos, Missies."

"We know, we know," the girls said.

It seemed my idea hadn't been such a good one after all.

"Yes, girls," the Walrus admonished, "stay on the road, not in the forest or near the brush; we'll be back shortly."

I'll go with you, I wanted to say, but I didn't, being even more scared of the girls than of pumas, cougars and black lobos.

I WALKED CAUTIOUSLY in case the girls were planning a dirty trick, yet going under the tall palms, feeling their long, fresh shadows pass silently over me was thrilling. "Here we get our palm honey," Gloria said, pointing to the buckets on the palm trunks. "Mumsy sells some too. Big trucks come to get the barrels, then it goes into cans in the town of Topotilla."

Patricia observed the two horses. "Mumsy took Rabelais, so if one of these is María Teresa's, she didn't take Mumsy with her like she always does."

"If one is María Teresa's, we didn't bring hot peppers to stuff up his ass," Grace lamented.

"Let's use *ortigas,*" they said, laughing with delight. I hoped they wouldn't ask me to stuff those stinging weeds! Luckily, they didn't find any. "Listen: first, if María Teresa's around, we'll let the horses loose," Patricia declared. "When we get back, we'll play witches, and third, we'll do the smear trick."

We tippytoed for a while, leaving the shadow-striped palm forest and entering the brush near the foothills. The silence was eerie. Sinister dark mushrooms sprang from a dead log. "I have to pee," Gloria said. I was going to go there too, when one of the horses caught my eye from the forest. A horse is an animal, but this one was suddenly looking at me with a knowing eye. According to Nanny Fresia, the dead came back to get inside animals, who then understood what you did. What if this horse had been a handsome prince or a fierce general? I peed behind the dead log.

I turned around, and leapt in terror. Above me hung a huge black lobo tied open between two trees. His insides showed a horrible geography of wounds and torn bones; his head hung hideously. I froze until I heard Patricia say, "Solita, c'mon, let's go." I turned to the girls, feeling sick.

"Solita, don't tell me you're scared of a dead black lobo," she said, studying my face.

"That's how they scare away other black lobos," Gloria said.

"Gloria, you don't know anything," Grace said. "This one had rabies and had gone crazy biting everything; he's hung up like that to scare the rabies away." Gloria admitted that was true.

As we walked through the brush, we heard a strange singing. The servants talked about many creatures and mountain spirits. It was warm, but I was chilled to the bone. We heard cavernous voices. I wanted to run, fly back to the road. But Patricia put a finger to her lips, and the three tiptoed in the voices' direction. I could do nothing but follow.

The voices came from a bamboo-covered gorge, hidden from view by brush. We crouched at the edge and looked down between the thick shoots. There was a cave down there, roofed by the bamboo. A tiny stream meandered in the middle, between patches of moss and spotted stones. We could see Tío Juan Vicente's back. He was talking while removing his patched suede jacket and his shirt. Patricia put a finger to her lips. "Don't you love the music of these grottoes?" he asked someone moving behind a thick plant. "This sweet little babble, the whisper of breezes, the songs of the cicadas . . . Ever since I was a child, I've loved the enchantment of these grottoes. Such a secret, poetic, erotic world!"

We were hardly breathing. He unhooked his suspenders. "I was deflowered in a most poetic way in a grotto like this one, at age twelve, by my parents' favorite servant." He took off his socks. "Ah! The moss tickles my feet!" He struggled with his riding pants. "What's your favorite love music? Mine is definitely Wagner's love duet, when Tristan loves Isolde before his death." He sang a few notes. "It gives me goose pimples. And that crescendo!" he lifted his arms higher and higher. "Really, you must come to my *viñas,* hear my recording of the Berlin Orchestra under Gerd Rubahn. It's superb!" As he bent down to step out of his underwear, we got a good view of his white behind. Each cheek had a clover leaf painted on it.

An exploding giggle escaped Gloria, in spite of her covering her mouth with both hands. Patricia's "Shut up, you idiot!" made Gloria lose her balance and fall on the bamboo roof.

Tío Juan Vicente straightened up in a hurry and looked up. He must have seen some color receding up there. Whoever had been moving behind the lush plant stumbled. We ran while Tío Juan Vicente said, "Not a puma, silly darling, just some peasants. . . ."

We raced and leapt to the road. Patricia scolded Gloria over and over. What a relief it hadn't been me.

"Why does Tío Juan Vicente paint his rear end?" Grace asked.

"You know why, because he's an eccentric. He's got a thing about decorating. Some people paint their faces, he paints his behind." Patricia really did know a lot.

I wanted to change the subject, but suggesting it wouldn't work. You had to make them want to. I said, "It's just like an eccentric to take all his clothes off for such a tiny stream. Not what you call a swimming hole. More like a toe bath."

The twins laughed, which was gratifying, but Patricia said, "Don't be stupid. Tío Juan Vicente was up to something naughty."

"You mean like using his carrot thing?" Gloria asked.

"Patricia, who do you suppose was there?" Grace asked.

"Probably the str—— the blond woman," I said.

"I don't know," Patricia said. "If it was her, we could have let the horses loose, if it weren't for your idiot twin."

At the road, out of danger from wild beasts, my stomach was feeling even worse. It couldn't have been. . . No, it couldn't be. My mother had left riding next to the hat man.

In a while the Walrus car approached us. "Hello, girls; hope you weren't too bored just waiting here on the road."

5

UNDER THE MORNING SUN, MY MOUTH WATERED observing the last of the bright bags, bars and canisters in the girls' arms. "María Teresa thinks she's Rita Hayworth or something, just because she'll be a countess," Gloria grumbled. "She took Mumsy away for long times. Popsy hates her. She locks doors to keep us out."

The girls were odd about sharing; they wanted no one to share time with their Mumsy, and they wouldn't share their sweets with me. But I made a solemn vow to get some. It was a matter of principle. Of course, my expectations didn't extend to the chocolate bars; you had to be realistic. The brightest prospects were the noisy and ribboned cellophane bags. I watched those closely because sooner or later they fell apart from the thrusts of sweaty and sticky hands. You had to be fast as lightning to retrieve what fell from them before the guanaco and Jali, the goat, did. Both knew about the cellophane loopholes; both had a sweet tooth and swift lips. They consumed anything in a flash, wrappers and all. However, even when rushing for a treat, the guanaco had gentlemanly manners. Jali was pushy, but she got away with it because of her charm. The dogs and the latest orphan lamb, received as a pet, were oblivious to these competitions.

Patricia said, "Let's snoop in María Teresa's room, now that all the grown-ups are out at the soccer field watching El Topaz play Viñas Echaurren." It was a daring idea. While I attempted to snatch some nougat from Gloria's pocket and got only lint, the girls took the straw woman's silk slippers and put them on the famous hat man's bed, and his aftershave in her necessaire. They warmed up and raced from room to room switching things: their Mumsy's big bras with Dr. Kaplan's shorts; the red-bangs lady's high-heeled slippers under Marco Polo's night table; Melons' corset in Tío Juan Vicente's armoire; his skinny silk pajamas under the Walrus' pillow; the Walrus' suspenders in Melons' suitcase; the black-bangs lady's stockings in the photographer's bag; Mlle. Vicky's eyeliner in the famous hat man's shaving kit. We couldn't wait to see what would happen when the guests put on the wrong panties, or the wrong makeup, or thought someone had stolen their belongings. Then we dressed, made up, moved and talked like Mlle. Vicky, Tío Juan Vicente, Melons and others. Gloria put on, then took down, the culottes of the pharmacy man's wife who wrote poems, the way the girls had seen in a bamboo grotto, while Grace, pretending to be the Walrus, whimpered, then the twins bumped against each other and Gloria whined like a field mouse; they were funny. You saw amazing things in country estates.

Then they headed for my mother's room to try on her clothes. This terrified me; my mother had such old underwear, and what if her only good blouse got damaged? Why didn't we open the aviary and let all the birds fly free, I proposed. The girls gave me their "you have a brain made of cow dung" look. "You have a cow-dung brain," Patricia said.

"Those birds are very rare and extremely valuable." The twins nodded. Who could understand these girls? They did naughty tricks to everybody, but some things, such as freeing poor birds, were off limits. Luckily, they decided to look around for something else to do to the straw woman. While munching gum drops, they discussed the party they had witnessed the night before in the gallery. "I heard la Mamota whisper that María Teresa's going to 'expose' Solita's mother, and her husband will find out," Grace said. What could the straw woman "expose"? She probably had learned about my mother's bad hip and contrived walk, which Papi knew all about. The straw woman was a witch.

After we passed Beethoven, the German shepherd and top patrol dog, I hit Grace's elbow, trying to make her drop her mints. "Have you ever seen an ostrich?" she asked me, biting a nougat. "I have. Running down the grassland with its ugly eyes."

"Listen, Grace," Patricia said, "just because we were carsick and didn't see the ostrich, you think you're Napoleon." They fought about the ostrich until I burst. Swallowing a lot of unused saliva, I yelled, "You should share your nougats with me!"

They were shocked. They had the bad taste to bring up their Mumsy's remark about my not behaving quite properly.

"Solita, if your parents' friends gave us gifts, we would share candy with you, but your mother doesn't know anybody."

"She knows the Ferrolentinos," Gloria said.

"Ugh, Gloria, that sounds totally low-class. Is it?" Grace asked Patricia.

"Of course. I bet Solita doesn't even have ancestors."

This was troublesome. I should ask my mother. Patricia was wrong. My parents did know people. Sometimes Mami invited a friend or two and served tea and cookies with little blue napkins. Papi brought lots of refugees all the time, which upset Mami. Then Papi started bringing locals, who talked about politics and strikes, and Mami liked it even less.

We passed my mother, Tía Merce, and the straw woman. My mother said the girls looked lovely. This pleased Tía Merce very much, but angered me and the straw woman. The girls got away. "María Teresa's vicious; in Galmeda she killed Louis XIV, our pet mouse, with her umbrella, just because he wanted to go up her leg. Ugh, her feet are ugly, with those yucky veins popping out."

It was strange to hear the girls talk about Galmeda; Galmeda belonged to me, not to them. They said their neighborhood had huge gardens and walls, but I never saw such a thing, although I did go around in Galmeda with Papi. I had to run to keep up with him. He rushed, rushed, rushed. The minute he arrived at the pensione, he was out again. It was hard to pant and talk at once; you couldn't tell complicated things, a few words at most. Still, going to deliver translations with him was the best thing ever. He got into big discussions with everybody, was always late and had forty thousand things to do. No matter how many he got done, he had forty thousand left.

Next to the garden pond, I retrieved a green mint! I was a lucky girl, as my mother said! In spite of this, a *tocuar* sang "*Tacuarí! Tacuarí!*" which according to Nanny Fresia meant you were doing things wrong. We passed Nanny Fresia with Niceto in tow. She whispered to me, "Did you hear the *tocuar* laughing at you, little girl? Are you going to tell me you can think of no better way to get a share of candy than to fight with a goat and a guanaco?" They had a nerve, she and the *tocuar.*

"This isn't a fight, it's just a game," I whispered, and moved on. But my thoughts whirled. First, it seemed she knew my secret that my parents had no friends who could bring me sweets. Second, she didn't hold it against me; on the contrary, she appeared to be on my side. Third, she was right. Following the girls through the diamond-patterned boxwood maze, I said, "I bet I can throw candy farther than you can." There was mild interest. Everybody knew they were far better shots. "I bet I can throw candy all the way to the other side of the aviary." They answered with self-confidence that even with a slingshot I couldn't, which was true. "All right, let's all throw. Give me one."

Even Patricia fell for it without a hitch. There was candy strewn all over the boxwood maze. We picked it up, dusted it on our puffy sleeves—as the folds didn't show the dirt much—and ate without anybody saying anything. Of course, the girls had won every time, and so had I.

I told Niceto to share what I gave him with Nanny Fresia. He refused. "You're a selfish baby," Nanny Fresia told him, "but your sister's a big girl, so she's not selfish." I had to live up to this new, flattering image, so I gave Nanny Fresia lots of candy. Only later I realized I'd been had just like the girls.

The Walrus went by telling the black-bangs lady, "I'm thrilled you think I'm so thin I could fit the lovely silk pajamas you left me as a surprise!"

GRACE BURST into the pool house as we were undressing. "Patricia! Hurry! Hurry! María Teresa's telling Tía Pilar some things, and I just know it's fancy!" Patricia and Gloria ran and jumped into the pool as if they had to save somebody. I followed them. Tía Merce stopped singing; the others, stretched on chaise longues, looked at the straw woman. Marco Polo arrived in a bathrobe, teetering in high-heeled slippers with red pompons at the end of his hairy legs, complaining his slippers had disappeared. My mother got up and walked away. The straw woman followed her, talking angrily. My mother ignored her. The straw woman said strange things louder and louder: "You're just using Merce. It so happens María Paula Oyarzún told me every word Merce had told her before you came, but forget it, it won't happen. You're just a glorified maid, that's why you're here. . . ."

My mother went into the pool house and locked the door.

The grown-ups dispersed. Tía Merce put her guitar down and walked off with the straw woman, who swung her arms furiously, screeching, "How can you fools stand that social climber!"

The twins bombarded Patricia with questions. Patricia, whirlpooling the water in a corner of the pool, said, "You know very well what she was talking about."

I said I didn't. The twins turned to me, then to Patricia.

"Well . . . it's because your mother's . . . odd," Patricia said.

"My mother's not odd," I said.

"Maybe María Teresa can't stand Solita's mother because, you know. Also because her name is not distinguished," Grace said.

"Not all the guests have distinguished names," Gloria corrected, paddling.

"Yes, dummy, but Mumsy and her friends say they're *marvelous characters.* I doubt whether Solita's mother is a *marvelous character.* Has she done one thing on the spur of the moment that's tickled anybody?" Patricia challenged. "And María Teresa can't stand immigrants; that's why she doesn't like Solita's mother."

"We're not immigrants," I said hotly. "We are Republicans."

"Maybe, but we come from Spanish dukes and counts who came here a long time ago," Patricia said. "And why is it that your mother never mentions anybody with distinguished names? Or important? She talks about statues, Egyptians and dead people."

In the New World, people were more distinguished than in the old one? Weren't those who had done amazing things distinguished?

"But Solita doesn't have thick skin, hairy chops or a crown cowlick like low-class people," Gloria said, paddling.

"Solita's not totally low-class, dummy," Patricia explained, "just not distinguished."

I didn't say a word about their father being *separated* from their very this-and-that mother. "My mother knows a lot, and that's important." We looked at the straw woman walk to the pool house. A cowlick in front wasn't as low-class as a crown one? I looked at my face on the water's surface, but the twins' swimming broke it into puzzle pieces. At least I didn't have to worry about hairy chops. So the girls went around calculating how much hair people had, where and in which direction it grew? My parents and the refugees said people in the New World graded each other according to how they looked. In Spain everybody looked the same. It was true that the servants in El Topaz had dark skin, and the guests light skin. Evidently they were different in other ways too. Hair and last names had important meanings.

The straw woman stopped in front of the pool house door. "And who put shaving cream in my necessaire to hint I have excess facial hair? Tell me that!" The girls ducked under to laugh.

I DIDN'T THINK games could get rid of anybody, but the girls insisted that "Witches" would spook María Teresa. I favored plans such as their last one, to scare her horse to make her fall on the wild artichoke plants, although that hadn't worked. For the game of "Witches" I claimed a white and black rug that was thin, therefore fast. We had to follow paths under our rugs, repeating their geometrical designs. That way we entered an invisible domain, totally out of reach of the grown-ups, and turned into powerful witches, capable of throwing spells that would spook people we didn't like and make them leave. But if we collided and didn't follow the paths correctly, we put ourselves in grave danger of being invaded by other spells. After covering the rugs' patterns, we won that territory, and immunity from invading spells. The rugs were called Tampuco because they came from Indians in the southern town of that name. I didn't know what Tampuco had that was connected with witches. In Spain there weren't any spirits or other inexplicable beings. The bad ones there were fascists, exploiters of labor (labor was men in factories with smokestacks that whistled, and who had families to feed), bad kings, invaders, religious fanatics, treacherous courtiers, and so on; strange people, but explainable. When we were sweaty and exhausted and had won complete immunity, we sat on the conquered territory. Dr. Kaplan entered the salon, telling Melons, "It's all right, my dear: taking and hiding his suspenders was motivated by an unconscious desire to make me jealous."

We left and the girls headed for the cow barn to implement their plan number two against the straw woman.

"I'll wait here for my father," I said. "He's coming."

"Solita, why do you brag and lie about your father coming?" Patricia didn't call me a liar, just said I'd lied, which was an improvement.

"I didn't lie. He wrote and said he's coming. He just didn't come with these guests."

We climbed the fence to the yard where the calves turning into heifers loafed or shoved each other in good humor. As soon as they saw us, they came to get the grape leaves the girls fed them, which they adored. Justino, a stableboy, saw us. "Missies, don't. You know grape leaves give calves the stomach cramps." We ignored him. He attempted to run the calves away from us, but they got feisty and tried to horn him with their little stubs. Justino gave up. The calves and the girls knew exactly whom to ignore, so that you could get to do what you wanted.

The girls didn't find whatever it was they were looking for in the cow barn for their plan, and went looking for Tonic, the young fox terrier. I was about to break down and ask questions but refrained myself. "C'mon Tonic," they urged him. "Help us." Tonic wiggled his stub tail and performed some stunningly graceful leaps. I followed the four conspirators toward the fishbone pines. Mlle. Vicky stormed down a garden path steaming mad, followed by the photographer carrying ladies stockings and insisting he had nothing to do with them. Then, in the shadow of the araucaria pine, Tonic relieved himself—nothing new or interesting—and cries of triumph pierced the afternoon sunshine: "One coming for María Teresa!" As soon as Tonic finished, Gloria took two foils from her pocket. I thought she was going to make a foil ball too, but instead she carefully wrapped Tonic's stool and said, "It's warm, but we've got to get it before the gardeners do." At that point I couldn't resist any longer and asked what was up.

"We scatter these poops around the grown-ups we don't like."

"When they step on one, it's a riot! Some do little one-leg dances. Some pretend nothing's happened; they go aside casually to rub the gooey sole of their shoe fast, fast, fast, pretending to agree with what's being said, as if they're only listening."

"This's one for María Teresa. Tonic eats rotten leftovers from the other dogs' dishes, so he puts out specially stinky ones," Grace gloated. How was this going to get rid of her?

"When María Teresa's mad, she explodes like pond-scooping dynamite and leaves in a fury."

"Just imagine those silk slippers she gets from Paris that she brags about, soaked in our surprise." "Let's keep the guanaco around here until she steps on it; nothing bothers him more than women's screams; it pierces his ears." "What a lovely sight; her silk slippers soaked, her face splattered," they said wistfully.

"Actually, she's lucky; this one's firm, not messy." Grace got serious. "Patricia, what if someone else steps on it?"

"It'll be on her doormat, silly. She'll step smack onto it." I hoped they wouldn't ask me to place it.

"I don't have any more wrappers to pick up the other poops," Gloria fretted. The two looked at her, then at my foil ball. I put my heart in suspension.

"Solita has plenty. Give us some foils." Grace made a move to get my foil ball, but I jerked out of her reach.

"Solita, you give us some foils."

"No!" There had to be a limit to what you had to do; they wanted to jeopardize my family's entire future for a dog poop.

"I can't believe this," Patricia said. "Those are *our* foils, Solita. I can't believe you think you can hog them all."

"They're not yours." I tried not to panic. "You threw them away, and I picked them up, so they're mine."

"Everything here is ours. I can't believe how selfish you are! We give you everything, everything, and you can't even share a couple of lousy wrappers that we need badly," Patricia said, getting closer. When I told her to use leaves, she raised her voice. "Not when we have foils. Solita, give me the ball."

I refused, and they grabbed me. There was pulling and tugging, and the ball left my hand. Patricia tried to remove a foil, but it was a well-made ball. She tore a lot of slivers. After she made a mess of it, she gave up. "Here's your stupid ball. You can't even get a decent wrapper out of it."

"That stiff ball doesn't even bounce," Grace snickered.

While rubbing my scratched arms, I silently summoned a dozen hunchbacked, warty fiends to come beat up the girls. Instead, Ramón, a front-gardens gardener arrived. He picked up Tonic's stools with a spade and carried them away to whatever secret places he hid them. The girls glared at him, then at me. I didn't move, which was the brave thing to do.

"See what you've done, Solita. Half our supplies lost, after we waited forever. You've ruined a masterful plan."

I turned the ball in my hands. Now it was rough-surfaced and smaller. How much was this going to set me back? There was no bed of my own here to hide in and let the tears out; everything belonged to the enemy. I couldn't spit. And it was cowardly to leave at a time like this; being cowardly was the end. You had to wait for your burning face and scratches to cool. You had to stand and act as if you didn't care. You had to look at a bush, not at them or the foil ball, while they glared.

Then, as I feared, they gave me Tonic's one contribution to deposit on the straw woman's doormat, which was conveniently brown. They were still furious.

"Are you a telltale?" Patricia asked.

In Galmeda the idea of being a telltale never crossed your mind. What could you telltale to your parents or the refugees?

"Of course not. Did I say a thing when you put garlic paste under the guests' pillowcases at nap time? Or later when you went around laughing at the guests with red ears, saying they'd spent hours rubbing with liters of cologne to get rid of the smell? Did I say anything when . . ."

"All right, all right. If only one turd isn't enough and María Teresa doesn't leave, you're going to be mighty sorry."

DURING SIESTA, while the girls waited for the straw woman to come out of Tía Merce's room and go to her own, I went to the giant hydrangea and waited for my father. They were still angry at me about the foils. Tío Juan Vicente came out of his room demanding to know who'd left a corset in his armoire as a hint that his middle was spreading, a patent lie. When I got tired, I went to my mother's room and stood next to her bed, hoping she'd ask about the girls and tell me about Papi and the straw woman. Except for her black eyebrows and lashes, with her eyes closed she was a marble statue. "I'm so tired," she said. After a while I asked when was Papi coming. She turned to the other side. "Your father, he has this idea he's going to be this country's number one in labor negotiations. He's just trying to live through his father, that's all. Never mind. Go have tea with the girls, my daughter. We'll solve this."

We'll solve what? What was labor negotiations? Wasn't Papi's father dead?

At the table the next afternoon, the girls whispered to each other. Niceto dipped buttered bread into his hot chocolate and counted the tiny yellow dots clinging to its surface.

Patricia held up her *allulla* bread importantly. "You won't believe what happened last night. The bad part first: Claudio Correa got mad. He said someone was 'casting aspersions,' leaving makeup on his night table. It took Mumsy a while to calm him down. But . . ." She whispered something.

The twins sputtered chocolate milk happily. "She must've squashed Tonic's turd!" Niceto put a spoonful of salt in his mouth, profiting from the confusion. The girls whispered again. "You also heard María Teresa screaming last night?"

"Yes."

"Did you hear her screaming Mumsy was being 'betrayed'?"

"I didn't hear a thing," Gloria pouted.

"Gloria, you're always a comet out of orbit," Grace said. "Patricia, what was María Teresa screaming about?"

"Topsy-turvy." Patricia never said, "I don't know"; it was always "Topsy-turvy." "No doubt she's furious because she says Mumsy's too easy on us. Mumsy kept telling her there was absolutely nothing to her suspicion, but María Teresa insisted. Then she woke up la Mamota in the middle of the night—"

Gloria interrupted: "I bet it has to do with what we heard Mumsy tell her friend Mónica on the phone in Galmeda—"

Patricia and Grace hit the hand Gloria was holding up and it smashed buttered bread on Gloria's mouth. So the straw woman was involved in the big secret too?

"María Teresa treats la Mamota like an ordinary servant," Grace said.

"Well, la Mamota used to be just a nanny," Gloria said, flustered, wiping butter off her face.

Patricia shot, "All right, I won't tell you what happened."

"Please, please!" we begged.

"Well, last night it was like a live chicken coop at the servants' quarters. La Mamota woke up Nanny Ema. Ema woke up Manuel. Manuel woke up Evaristo, and told him to drive the contessa to the bus."

"Drive her to the bus? In the middle of the night?"

"That's nothing. La Mamota said this morning that Evaristo thought he was driving the contessa to the public road, but María Teresa said no, she wasn't going to spend 'one more minute' in El Topaz waiting for a stupid bus."

She wasn't like Papi, who loved the colors of the buses. "So what did she expect, Superman to come, zooom! and get her?" My funny remark was to let them know I was with them about the straw woman, but it made Patricia madder.

"Listen! I'm doing you a favor telling you this, so shut up. Well, María Teresa told him to drive her to Navidad, and they had to wait hours for the five-thirty morning train. She's so unreasonable."

"I know Mumsy got really sick," Grace said. "La Mamota asked for manzanilla brew, and had to give it to Mumsy in spoonfuls."

"All that just for a little fox terrier turd? María Teresa's got mold in her brain," Gloria said. "She thinks she's this year's Cadillac model. All the grown-ups have moldy brains."

Patricia turned to me. "Solita, you don't deserve to hear this; in spite of you, things turned out fine; María Teresa left forever." I leapt, having more than one reason to rejoice.

"I hope she put her dirty slippers on her chic clothes in her suitcase before she realized it," Grace said.

"I'm not sure, but we can get rid of selfish people who hog things that don't belong to them," Patricia said, looking at me.

I should have given them foils. Long-range plans didn't work; each minute you had to save your skin right then and there, by yourself, and in ways that wouldn't come back to haunt you.

"It's no fun playing with the same child all the time," Grace said. "Solita, why have you been here so long?"

How did I know why? We went from country to country, from place to place, because things happened to us. We were leaving the minute my father came. Meantime, you had to learn to navigate around perilous rocks, as my mother said.

"We have been here this long because my mother wants to," I said, but not too defiantly.

"And Solita, you don't know anything. You can't swim, don't even play Monopoly. Children who come visiting know these things. I bet you don't even ski or horseback ride, do you?"

I stopped chewing. This required concentration. "Yes."

They looked suspicious. "Are you a good rider? I bet not."

Sun flooded the yellow tablecloth. "Yes, I am."

"Do you ride *criollo* or English?"

"English." Who knew what the other thing was, and even if the English had stolen Spain's gold from the New World, at least they were people more or less like us, and had a famous writer.

"You really ride English?" Grace and Gloria were impressed.

"Yes. Hear the *yohes*? I think my father will come today."

"Mumsy says Tía Pilar's husband's always looking for work," Grace said. "When men looking for work come to El Topaz, they stay in the servants' quarters. And how come you eat so much? That quince you're eating's ours, you know."

"It's just that you set a bad example, Solita. Then the maids say we have to eat too," Gloria explained apologetically.

Niceto quietly observed a transparent quince slice.

"You're selfish and won't share anything with us, so from now on we won't share either. You have to ask us," Patricia said.

I reached for the brick-colored bar made of quince preserve, not to lose a minute before things got worse. Patricia grabbed my wrist. "Are you deaf?"

The valiant little tailor in the stories won over the mean giants because he was smart and thought of good wiles. What would work here? "My father knows magic tricks. He can cut anything in half and make it whole again, before your very own eyes. And he can teach you."

They were silent. Then Gloria burst out, "I want to learn to make coins disappear and to make cut things whole again, Solita. Will you ask your father when he comes? Please?"

I reached for the quince bar. But Patricia said, "Wait a minute. Your father won't come. And even if he did, all we have to do is ask Mumsy to tell him to teach us. And you can't have that." She took my slice. I got up and headed for the little library. If I opened a book and pretended to read, they would get bored and leave. I reached for the beautiful story of the girl-queen of Maori, who was fair and was respected by all her subjects, but they said, "That book's ours, you can't touch it." Each time I reached for a book they repeated the same thing. I looked for the story of the dog in the manger, because they didn't want their books anyway, but I couldn't remember where it was. I gave up and went outside. They followed me. "Solita, you can't stand in the veranda; it's ours." "Solita, you can't sit on the bench; it's ours." "Solita, you can't go down the steps; they're ours; you have to jump. Jump!" "Solita, you can't walk in the driveway; it's ours. Don't touch Coca-Cola; she's ours."

My father could show up suddenly. The girls followed me to the road. I couldn't stand there, it was theirs. I got off the road, went through a barbed wire fence and into the field. The girls stopped. "You're not allowed to go in that field," Patricia ordered. "Those are bulls beyond the ombu tree, even Thunder is there." Coca-Cola and Cocktail wanted to come with me, but Patricia didn't let them. They frisked and waggled, confused. I continued down the field. "Those are the father bulls! As soon as they see you, they'll chase you! They'll trample all over you!"

I continued down the field. Four bulls rested under the fat trees. My walk wasn't fast, to show the girls didn't scare me, or too slow, to show the bulls didn't scare me. My face was set in a plaster of fear. A bull looked at me. Calculating how long it'd take to run to the side fence, I cut diagonally. If a bull made the slightest move, I'd have time. When I was near the side fence, a bull got up. He moved toward me, his tail restless, his head arrogant. Even though I could practically touch the fence, I lost my nerve and went through the barbed wire so fast it made two gashes near my knees. The bull stood for a minute, then bent down to eat grass. The breeze made the sweat on my forehead cold.

The thing to do was cut through to the public road and hitch a bus with the beautiful colors that my father loved to Galmeda. But I would get lost. It was better to walk to the road at the bottom of the hill. I remembered the story of the lovely orphan princess sent with her nasty stepsister to another kingdom to be married. On the way, the nasty stepsister roughed up the lovely princess, put on her clothes, and when they arrived said she was the princess and the princess her maid. The real princess looked so sad that the king ordered her to tell her sorrows to the fireplace. She did, and the king, who was listening on the other side, unmasked the nasty stepsister and all turned out well.

"We'll see how good you are at riding English!" Patricia yelled. "Tomorrow we're all going for a long riding trip! This time you won't get off!"

Farther along the road I went down a culvert and sat under the bridge. The spot had been used as a bathroom, but better to be hidden than squeamish. A breeze traveling from the distant hills to the fields took away some of the stench. On the hills, sheep milled around the water trough, and lambs' calls came faintly. Next to me a few weeds bent down and shivered. I put my hands on my forehead and my elbows on my knees, and I cried for a long, long time. By order of the king.

6

NANNY FRESIA TOOK ME TO THE HORSE YARD, holding my hand as if the graveled course were a street with heavy traffic. Two black-and-blue butterflies were chasing each other. She crossed herself. "It's bad luck, those ones." My britches—formerly Gloria's—were too big at the waist, but that was the least of my worries.

I ran and jumped on a huge white horse; he raised his front legs up in the air; we leapt over fences, fields and earthquake craters; I saluted the girls and la Mamota with a wave of the hand; their mouths dropped open in amazement; they looked up at me; they said, Because you are so brave, we consider you one of us; from now on you are just as good as we are.

My hand clutched Nanny Fresia's tightly.

The saddled horses formed a long line, each tied to a post. Coca-Cola and the other dogs ran about in a frenzy, teasing the horses by racing around their legs. The horses looked straight ahead nonchalantly while trying, unsuccessfully, to kick the dogs. The guanaco watched the scene calmly. Jali returned to the empty gardens to eat forbidden flowers. The girls, in their matching jackets and britches, sliced the air with child-size whips. The grown-ups milled around in their riding outfits.

"Merce, where are we riding to?" someone asked.

"We'll ride to the Caída de Satán—Satan's Fall. It's a very impressive sight," Tía Merce told my mother, "the deepest hollow left by an ancient earthquake."

"Oh, no! Not the Caída de Satán!" Mlle. Vicky contorted her arms. "Let's go to the bigger lake, Mercedes. The bigger lake's so incredibly marvelous, don't you think, Gunther? It'd be so marvelous to camp on one of the islets among the reeds . . . sooo romantic, the Garden of Eden. . . . One can skinny dip. . . ." She giggled. "Gunther, do you like camping? Well, how about picnics?"

"It's not a good day for swimming," Tía Merce said. "We'll go to the Caída de Satán."

Nanny Fresia squeezed my hand, whispering, "You shouldn't go there, little girl." Easy for her to say; I agreed totally; there or anywhere, but she wasn't doing a thing to get me out of it.

"Not the Caída de Satán," Tío Juan Vicente complained while getting on his horse. "What a dreadful precipice. Vicky's right; let's go to the bigger lake and row to some of the islets."

Above the voices Gloria said to us, "Tío Juan Vicente won't go to the Caída de Satán because he's afraid the Devil'll throw him down the precipice." She said it too loud; everyone heard it and laughed. Gloria was mortified.

"Peasants won't go anywhere near the Caída de Satán," Tía Merce explained. "They believe that's where the Devil dwells."

Nanny Fresia bent down to my ear. "It happens to be one of the Devil's favorite places." She made tiny signs of the cross. "He throws unconfessed souls there, down to the Basilisco, who loves to abuse them, and they have to stay down there until someone prays and commissions masses for them. If you go near the Caída de Satán, you'll hear voices, 'Jump, jump,' and you will jump, because that's what the deputy devils will make you do. You'll fall down right into the slimy arms of the Basilisco." She made more tiny signs of the cross. "Satán will drive you to jump."

Nanny Fresia had a way of worrying you about distant dangers when the problem at hand urgently needed a solution. When you had to avoid getting on a horse, she'd tell you about falling into slimy arms in the void. So far, I was solving the problem with politeness; every time it was my turn to get on a horse, I politely deferred to someone else.

"I say the Caída de Satán's not the place to go today," Melons cautioned, crossing her hands in front of her ballooned blouse. "When you get to my age, if you're sensitive, you learn to let yourself flow with the forces that hum around you. Every force this morning says not to go to the Caída de Satán." That last part was the only sensible thing I'd ever heard Melons say.

Mlle. Vicky asked her teasingly, "Well, is Dr. Kaplan coming or is he afraid?"

"Dr. Kaplan has work to do." Did she mean he had to read on the toilet? Now he could spend hours there undisturbed. Melons smiled like a person who knew everything. "As for you, Juan Vicente, my boy, watch that rifle. Don't put on a show." She was helped into the surrey by the driver and looked at the sky. "I think there's a storm brewing."

Tía Merce looked impatient. "What nonsense, Leticia, there're no summer storms in my lands. Of course Juan Vicente'll be careful. He'll show Claudio how to trail a puma, that's all."

One of the friends of the girls' uncle proposed, "Let's go to your Virgin Mary shrine, Merce, that glassed-in, bigger-than-life statue. They tell me it's full of flowers made from bread, and it's perfectly dreadful," she laughed.

"No, no, if we're going for statues, let's go see the Christ at Cross Hill," another one proposed. Everybody talked at once. Everybody disagreed. Maybe the trip would be canceled. "Later," Tía Merce said. "Now, let's go! To the Caída de Satán!" They disappeared down the road in groups. Tío Juan Vicente and the famous hat man flanked my mother.

"Now we take care of the young ones," Alberto, the groom, told his son. With the racket of hoofs, birds and talk it was hard to hear motor rumbles from the road. My father could arrive soon. He said people who loved horses had horses' brains, so we would stay, and I'd show him the gardens. He was supposed to arrive with some other guest; this time it was true.

But there were no motor rumbles.

ALBERTO YELLED, "Your animals are ready, Missies!" The horses Patrician and the twins Graceful and Glorious, a present from Tío Juan Vicente when they were colts, had the eyes of sleepy lizards and seemed incapable of making any decisions.

Decisions. "Listen," I said to the girls. "Wouldn't it be great to stay here and tie the three pedal cars like a train?" No interest. The twins were engaged in a sword fight with their riding whips. "I'll pull you; you sit in the cars and I'll be a human engine going '*Chuga-chooga-chuga, too tooooo!*' " Still no interest. Then I had the greatest idea yet. The girls complained constantly about what was played on the battery radio, such as music called Impressionist, which sounded like noises from a full bathtub. They never tuned in the good shows—"Dracula," "The Mad Dwarf" or "The Body Snatchers." "Listen, let's stay and hear 'Dracula,' I said forcefully, which was more persuasive and masked any signs of fright. Still no interest. "We'll turn it on really loud, especially that scary laughter and organ music, when it goes 'Ha! Ha! Ha!' "

"Don't be stupid. 'Dracula' is on only after dusk. Besides,

we want to go and find out who goes to the bamboo grottoes with Tío Juan Vicente." They mounted their horses and, buried inside deep saddles full of stuffing—this was *criollo*—waited for me.

Finally, there was only a black horse and me, standing under the canopied pine, holding on to my pants' waist, standing tall, not to show how scared I was. Tía Merce was the last grown-up to mount, and Alberto called to her, "Mi Señora Doña Mercedes, we need an animal for the little girl there, under the old pine."

Tía Merce was leaving. "There's a horse left, Alberto. What's the matter with you?"

"That's Lucero, mi Señora Doña Mercedes; nobody wanted him. Don't know why Señor Don Armando made his brother, mi Señor Don Miguel, buy that brute." Tía Merce seemed irritated and eager to join the others. "Well, give her whatever's left."

Alberto shook his head. "Lucero's good for polo, mi Señora Doña Mercedes, not for children. He's also got an English saddle. There's no animal for the little girl. If my son gets another one from the pasture, you'll all be by the poplar creek by the time it's saddled. Sorry, the little girl's out of luck today."

It was hard not to leap and laugh. Nanny Fresia whispered, "See? My prayers have been answered; it's going to cost me a whole candle; you're costing me plenty. . . ."

The girls were taken aback, then yelled, "Solita rides English, she rides English, and she's a very good rider!"

"Give her whatever's left." Tía Merce whipped her horse and trotted away, lifting dust that made Gin and Tonic sneeze while they ran behind her. She disappeared past the bridge.

Nanny Fresia returned to the house with Cocktail, the presumed fox terrier, telling Niceto that being rich wasn't a bit of help to people's good sense, not a bit, and reneging on her candle deal. Jali greeted them with acrobatics. I wanted to be a goat.

Alberto put his hands grudgingly together for me to

climb onto the black beast. His huge belly was crossed by protruding veins, and his black private parts shook when he moved. Sure of having little control over my legs, I stiffened them, so my knees wouldn't collapse in Alberto's hands. Spaniards are courageous. The girls watched me. My legs didn't collapse; my left one went over. I was really sitting way up above the world!

The famous English saddle was just a leather piece with a small mound in front, the saddle equivalent of being naked. Alberto put my feet, now distant pieces of ice, in the stirrups. He shook his head and mumbled while adjusting straps: "Don't like children riding this kangaroo. Even if they ride good. Told my *patrona.* Of course, a man tries to do his job, and who listens? Now, little girl, no kicking Lucero's ribs; he's more ticklish than a hare. And no whip; this brute's no shy mouse. If something ahead's white or bright, specially on the way back, stop dead. Then go slow. Even a scrap of paper or an old pan, he thinks it's a gigantic puma about to eat him up; that's how bright he is. And no running, or the fool's likely to take off like a herd of bulls is after his ass. If another horse starts to gallop, hold the reins short, to your chest; this berry head's got to be in front of everybody. Specially coming back, hold on tight; he comes home like his house's on fire." He slapped Lucero's neck to indicate he was through. This made the neck jerk back, which jerked my stomach up to my mouth. "Just hold the reins short, little girl, and no whipping and trying to show off." He needn't have worried about that. However, it would be nice if the girls thought the only reason I wouldn't show off was because Alberto had said so. He turned to an old man on a bored horse. "Tomás, stay close to Lucero, right close, and don't let him get out of hand, specially on the way back." The old man nodded, seemingly too tired to say anything. Alberto turned to the girls. "Señorita Patricia, see that your animals stay down to trotting, specially on the way back; you know that devil Lucero, how he takes off when he hears galloping, specially coming home. . . ."

Coming home—a possibility in the distant future. Meantime, with my upper body rising stiff and expectant from the saddle, I listened intently for motor rumbles. Nothing. Nothing.

The girls' horses headed toward the bridge. Lucero followed them, and I was inescapably going wherever he was. I was empty; my inner parts had gone elsewhere. My left hand clutched the reins, my right one latched firmly onto the saddle's puny mound. I switched hands. Which hand should do which job? The horses made a hollow *clickety-clat* over the bridge's logs. Lucero too. So far, I was still alive. Patricia looked back. "Solita, you said you were a good rider and you're holding on to the saddle!"

"Revolting!" Grace said.

So you weren't supposed to hold on to the saddle. How did you stay on the horse if it wiggled or jerked? What a reckless waste to have one hand just dangling instead of clutching something.

Next to us rode the old man on his bored horse. "Ignore Tomás," Gloria whispered unnecessarily; the only thing I wasn't ignoring was the big horse's head in front of me. "Tomás is the horse nanny." Gloria's explanations were usually practical.

"We know how to get rid of Tomás when we want to," Grace whispered. "He's even dumber than the house nannies."

We rode down a lane bordered by poplar trees. My eyes had no use for the fields on one side or the soft, fuzzy hills on the other. They fastened on Lucero's ears in front, trying to read into their wiggling what he could be planning to do. My stomach returned, and went up and down every time Lucero jerked his head.

Buried inside their *criollo* saddles, the girls looked at me with undisguised admiration. But they seemed to be waiting for something to happen.

At a bend in the road, Lucero saw two riders ahead. Right away, he walked faster, without any consultation, much less permission, from me. Surprisingly, I didn't slide off the rocking saddle. My stomach fled again, leaving a cold, empty spot, so I wasn't nauseous anymore. Lucero caught up with Ruperto, the *peón* who sang with a guitar and the one with the refreshment baskets. The girls and the old man kicked their horses to keep up with me. As soon as Lucero saw grown-ups ahead, he quickened his step and reached them. Tía Merce was saying, "*Mon empire,* my *chers* friends; it goes on and on, as far as your eyes can see and farther yet, and it's all *à votre disposition.* Were I Cleopatra, I would be taking you on my barge. . . ." This was not very interesting.

Lucero moved near Tío Juan Vicente. He was instructing the famous hat man: "Press the knees to the horse's ribs. The faster you go, the tighter the knees. No, no; your feet toward his belly, not out. Right. Now, stretch your torso almost parallel to his neck. No, no, your knees in place; you must show him who's boss, Claudio." The famous hat man giggled nervously. This answered one of the things that was on my mind.

I wanted to hear more, but Lucero moved ahead near Mlle. Vicky. She was lecturing the photographer on how to hold the reins gracefully: ". . . dancing makes your body limber for *every* activity. . . ." Not much to learn here. I didn't care whether I stayed on a horse gracefully or not; the thing was to stay. Mlle. Vicky got so close to him their boots almost collided. Both their horses looked back with worried eyes. She purred, "Ever been in a bamboo grotto? It's secret, sensual." Suddenly, it occurred to me a saddle could slide and put me upside down under the horse. One more worry.

Again Lucero positioned himself ahead of everybody, and the girls and Tomás followed us. We passed some peasant dwellings.

"We can go for kilometers and kilometers that are ours and never see anyone," Patricia boasted. "Very few people in the world can do that; Mumsy says in Europe nobody can."

Women with children hiding behind them waved or came to offer Missy Patricia and the Missy Twins "a little bit" of maté, with either "a little bit" of home bread or papaya or whatever they had. They bent down while offering, as if everything about them was a little bit, including themselves. They didn't seem to notice how jittery I was, nor appreciate my being on Lucero and riding English. The girls barely acknowledged their greetings. "You see people around here," I pointed to the women.

"Oh, but those are peasants," Patricia explained.

I ignored fields, corrals, cattle, sheep, weedy slopes; riding required devoted concentration. When we reached the palm forest, Patricia gave a nod, and the three yelled, "We're going to the bathroom!" and left the road. Looking up into the roof of lacy umbrellas, so gracefully moved by the warm breeze, I pondered the logistics of peeing without getting off a horse. "Tomás, you heard us, go the other way, we're going to the bathroom," Patricia ordered. "There is a bathroom around here?" I asked.

The twins giggled. Tomás mumbled, "Do me the favor, you stay here, Missies. Don't you go into the brush, the pumas . . ."

"Yes, yes, and the cougars and the black lobos too," Patricia mocked him, and he went to the road.

"That's how we get rid of Tomás, so we can do what we want," Gloria explained. "When he comes back, we're gone, so he takes a nap on his horse." The three started toward the brush.

"Don't you think we should do what Tomás says? It may be dangerous," I suggested. Tomás wasn't the Phantom, for sure, but he looked better than nothing, in case Lucero started acting up.

"Are you afraid?" Patricia asked. "That black lobo's dead, and the puma we found here turned out to be Tío Juan Vicente."

"We'll see who he takes to bamboo grottoes," Grace babbled.

"Wouldn't that be fancy," Gloria said.

"I think we should pee and get out," I said. "It wouldn't

be fair to the horses if a cougar leaps on them." They ignored me.

We slid off the horses and tiptoed, peering down bamboo grottoes. All were uninhabited. They climbed on their horses and waited for me. Every time I tried to put my foot on the stirrup, Lucero moved away. A rude animal.

"You said you are a good rider, and you don't know you push the horse against a tree so he can't pull away from you?" I wasn't about to push that black mass of nerves and hoofs anywhere. They had to fetch Tomás to help me. It was humiliating, but better humiliated than crushed to a pulp.

Ahead, the girls went to pick blackberries from a thicket hanging over a dead tree. I stayed put, holding the reins to my chest. So far so good. Behind my side of the thicket, Tía Merce's voice said, "Don't worry, I don't grieve over María Teresa. Have you seen Ruperto? Ooooh, he has the most virile . . . voice. I'll have him . . . play me some chords. . . ." Tía Merce chuckled.

Tío Juan Vicente laughed. "*Bien,* my pet, and listen to me: stick to one side of the fence, my dear, and be more discreet—"

Tía Merce interrupted. "You! You talk about discreet! We weren't five minutes out the other day that you and Claudio disappeared. I bet you took him to a bamboo grotto, hmm?"

"Marvelous, it was marvelous. Except we were disturbed by peasants. It's beyond me why you permit them to go up the mountains when we're there. Mine wouldn't think of it!" I had to tell the girls right now! This instant! It had been the famous hat man in the bamboo grotto. They weren't going to believe me.

Tía Merce answered that he had no lands, but a cuckoo clock, because his Teutonic foreman ran it as he had run concentration camps. Tío Juan Vicente got mad and said his brother Jorge, not he, had hired the foreman before losing his mind over María Pía running away with the baron, and in any case, his lands produced and hers didn't. He told her to listen to Dr. Kaplan and stop seducing her father *and* mother, that you did either one or the other. Now Tía Merce got angry. "Oh, that sap with his pink glasses and his seduction talk. . . ."

The girls came back. I told them. They said I had wool ears and a cotton brain. They didn't believe a word of it.

Near a peasant house, the girls spotted some green fruits on a tree. "*Lúcumas*!" they shouted. "Let's gallop to get some." My mouth cried "No!" without my permission, and they looked at me. I glanced beyond Lucero's ears, trying to look as unconcerned as possible under the circumstances. Then I glanced quickly at Patricia to guess what she was thinking. She still seemed to be waiting for something to happen. Warily, I followed them.

A woman from the house picked some *lúcumas* and brought them to us. "That's José's mother," the girls said, expecting some reaction from me. But I was reacting to other things. Lucero kept moving his head impatiently; he wanted to keep going. Don't lose your patience, Lucero, don't wiggle like a worm, don't leap like a grasshopper; wait for the girls to finish eating. Tomás, stop Lucero from your bored horse if he suddenly bolts your way.

"You mean you don't know what's going on with José and your own nanny?" Patricia was saying. "How stupid can you be?" I hadn't thought about it. Suddenly the idea of Nanny Fresia going off with some man bothered me. Now I greatly respected her. She was the only one to worry about me on this absurd trip, was even going to spend money for me. I asked lamely what was going on.

"Nothing. Your nanny used to be sweet on José before she was a nanny. But now her head's swollen, and she thinks José's too low for her, because he's just a plain *peón*. But he's really stuck on her. That's what la Mamota told the cook."

The brilliant yellow pulp of the *lúcumas* was truly the most delicious treat in the world. I began to feel better.

When the grown-ups appeared, José's mother started to cry, revealing gaps, like a piano with black and white keys. Her callused brown fingers chased flies off her face and pointed to a dog-size house flanked by tins of flowers and a cross on the roof. She said her "little angel" had gone Up There three days ago. She begged Missy Patricia, please, to ask her Señora Mamá to put a candle in the chapel to the Virgin, since Padre Romualdo hadn't baptized her little angel yet. Patricia agreed. The woman kept thanking her as if Patricia had given her a new house.

The girls' horses listened with bored faces, but not Lucero; he moved restlessly toward the road. I held the reins to my chest as the groom had said, to show Lucero who was boss. Lucero turned his head back, surprised that I could give a command—and he obeyed! My brain was more powerful than Lucero's brute force! Things were going to be all right after all!

Patricia relayed José's mother's request. Tía Merce chuckled and said the peasant's superstitions were so picturesque. My mother stopped and asked if she wasn't going to find out why the infant died. Tía Merce was taken aback. "Pilar, *ma chère,* my *capataz* handles requests in El Topaz. It's up to him to ask me if I want to see them in my *despacho.* Surely you don't think I'm going to be bothered with a couple of candles for the chapel?"

I had peeked into the *despacho,* a forbidding room at the end of a dark corridor, whose oval, nail-studded door was always locked. It had a stained-glass window with a crest that cast a spooky yellow light onto a carved desk and a heavy carved chair. Tía Merce sat there sometimes like an empress, to chastise, warn or reward *peones* for things the *capataz* had told her. Peasants went by there regularly in a long line, to get paid. It had some obscure, bloody history, the girls said, but they didn't know exactly what. I remembered Bluebeard had put his wives to death in a similar room, and was always afraid of getting locked in there.

"Merce," my mother persisted, "how's this woman with those children going to walk kilometers to see the *capataz*? Or you?"

The girls thought my mother was odd and said dumb things. Did she, or didn't she?

"*Ma chère* Pilar," Tío Juan Vicente said kindly, "half their children die. It's natural to them, they neglect them. When my socialist friend Ramiro Valdés's elected senator, this will end." He turned to Merce. "My pretty, I tell you and tell you; get a good administrator, let him deal with these things."

"All the former SS officers have been taken, Juan Vicente," the Walrus said. "They're the only ones who do a good job running haciendas."

Tío Juan Vicente agreed. "Armando's always trying to lure mine to his horse farm."

My mother was calm. "Only dying of old age is 'natural,' Merce. If the infant died of an infection, the other children might catch it. If it was neglect, the woman should be told."

Tía Merce smiled as if my mother were my brother's age. "Pilar, *ma chère,* you don't know how ignorant these people are, and how stubborn. They get children like colds, all their lives, from eighteen to fifty, often from many fathers. They have their fun, then half the infants don't survive. They say yes, yes to anything you tell them, then bury your medicine and give a sick child goat urine because Tomasa, the *curandera,* said so."

"Half of them get killed by Tomasa," Tío Juan Vicente said.

The Walrus asked, "Why do you want more of these primitive people around, anyway?"

"Tsk-tsk, Arturo," Tío Juan Vicente scolded him, "it isn't nice to say such things. You must be more progressive."

"I know how Pilar feels," the spiritual lady with black bangs and blue eyes said sympathetically. "It tears the linings of my heart. That's why I have so many extreme-left friends. But let's go; there are too many flies around here. Merce and Juan Vicente are right; there isn't much you can do, unfortunately."

My mother dismounted. "I'll find out what symptoms the child had, then we'll ask Dr. Kaplan." She walked, very tall, toward the woman. Now the girls were positive my mother was crazy. Were they right? What would a man who spent so much time on the toilet know about this woman?

"Pilar's a character," Tía Merce chuckled indulgently. Did this mean she was considered a marvelous character? Probably not.

Tío Juan Vicente whispered, "Well, as long as Pilar's here, my pet, you won't try to steal my administrator. Did you see her face when she heard he was a former SS man? In truth, Spaniards are very rigid people, no flexibility at all. I can see why she went for Julian's rebellious commitment to extremes, but, of course, after the war she hates it."

These people were against rebels, and it seemed my mother used to be rebellious, but now was that way only about very few things. You had to decide whether to go along with people who did wrong things or fight them, but it was very difficult, because no matter what you decided, you were going to pay for it. You had to watch how it turned out for other people and see what was best.

José's mother advanced shyly, several children clustered behind her, like one big body with many dusty, blemished legs. My mother talked to her. The woman wiped tears with her dirty apron. The grown-ups became impatient. My mother did these things; she suddenly took matters into her own hands. Once she grabbed a Gypsy girl, bigger than I, saying she was filthy with parasites, and threw her in the pensione's tub. The Gypsy girl screamed that water spirits would kill her and kept trying to climb out of the tub, but she was no match for my mother. The other pensioners were furious, saying they were going to get infected, robbed and cursed. The Gypsy girl left outfitted in my mother's oversized clothes, throwing curses at her, and shiny clean. The pensioners were fed up and complained to my father. He apologized, and told the women that ladies in this pensione had the best fashion taste he had ever seen. He told the men war stories. The pensioners blushed and laughed and patted my father on the shoulder.

Strangely, in El Topaz they liked my mother but said odd things about my father. Melons said once that Mercedes hated him because she hadn't seduced him, and someone agreed that he had to be the seducer, and Melons said he had a roving eye for every skirt except Mercedes', maybe because she wore pants, and they all laughed except Tía Merce. I wasn't sure what seducing was.

A refugee said once that my father's father complained that he chased skirts instead of sticking with his law studies. My father liked to know about the world. He liked the justice system of tribes in Africa, who were very pragmatic, which he said meant "realistic," which meant "down-to-earth," which meant "sensible." I didn't remember my grandfather, who'd been killed by the Assassin, but I was told he loved me very much, even though as an infant I was bald, which is even worse than having a cowlick in front.

The precious girl from the neighboring lands arrived galloping, as usual, which made Lucero nervous, and me and Mlle. Vicky upset. My mother finished talking to José's mother and remounted. The trip was resumed. Lucero made some large strides, and I pulled the reins with all my might. *Fabuloso!* as my father would say; Lucero slowed down! If only it worked coming back. I glanced at the girls to see whether they fully appreciated my mastery over the gigantic beast. They were busy wiping *lúcuma* from their hands into the woolly layers of their saddles.

THERE WAS SOMETHING to be said for horseback riding. The horse did all the work, and you tried to enjoy yourself. Mlle. Vicky asked, "Why do peasants, especially the women, have no teeth?" Finally a sensible question; I had wondered the same thing. "The soil here has little calcium, so even milk has little of it," Tía Merce explained. Strangely, all the calcium got into Tía Merce and her friends' food, none into what the peasants ate.

We heard galloping behind us. Lucero tensed and walked

faster. I wanted to look back to give a "Stop" glance to whoever was breaching the safety rules about galloping around Lucero. I couldn't, because he started to trot, ignoring my fierce pulls. Had he decided I was too scrawny to be boss in spite of my superior brains? Had he realized I wasn't a normal, distinguished guest? I grabbed the seat and prepared myself for the worst.

Marco Polo galloped by with his nose up in the air, showing off, as Melons had said. I was so jittery I almost screamed. A low branch hung ahead. It hit him. He screamed and nearly fell off. You had to worry about trees attacking you too! He turned around slowly. A gash on his forehead dripped blood. It made me nauseous. I began to feel dizzy. . . . I opened my eyes wide to steady the world. He said, "I was trying to catch up with you, and didn't see that branch."

One of the culotted ladies went to take a look. "The blood won't cause a flood, but you'll have an egg-size bruise."

"This happens to everybody not familiar with *mesetas* bordering a precipice," Tía Merce chuckled. "It deceives you into thinking trees are taller than they really are."

"It happens to every macho trying to show off to the ladies," Melons mumbled from the surrey. "It serves him right for not sending a cent to his sons, just bragging about them."

"I think I'll go back to the Himalayas or the Amazon," Marco Polo said. "It's safer." I looked at him furiously; now my stomach was queasy and Lucero had shown me *he* was boss.

"I warned you," Melons said with her know-it-all smile. "The forces said not to go to the Caída de Satán today."

Melons was a jinx.

"Of all the fun in the country,
the rodeo's the very best,

there go the men on their horses,
showing valor and skill,
sporting colorful *mantas,*
like cherries in a cherry tree . . ."

Ruperto sang while everybody rested against the big cottonwood trunks before heading back. The song, the pastries and the cold drinks made everyone happy. Resting my behind by lying sideways made me happy. Then the Walrus had the awful idea of asking the spiritual lady to recite a poem. The poem was clear as mud, but everybody applauded. Just when I thought we were free, the lady with curled red bangs cleared her throat to recite. While she droned on, I watched a buzzard plane smoothly in the lighter sky near the mountains, then I heard Melons whisper, "Mercedes, why do you hate him? He isn't a boorish clown; I even found his missing fingers charming."

I bit into my pastry and drank papaya juice. Melons hadn't seen my father's severed fingers to find them charming. It had to be someone else. Of course, Melons always said crazy things.

"But, Leticia, why did she leave with him?"

"Mercedes, use your head; you tell me his father was a union organizer. If he'd stayed, he would have been killed. . . ."

"Imagine, a laborer's son! But why didn't she stay with her own family? They were very well placed. I just can't understand."

The girls said Tía Merce was very everything, but if she was talking about my parents, she was asking very dumb questions. I shook the stalks of a few tulip-shaped mushrooms.

"During wars things happen, Mercedes; social barriers get broken. Naturally she resents so much having left her country and family and painting for him, she's now chasing after comfort, social position. I can see right through her. You too, Mercedes."

"*Ou la-la,* Leticia, you scare me. But *merci* for the tip; I can feed that resentment to keep her here. . . ."

"Listen, Mercedes, just because you're in my husband's care, I don't have to put up with your plots; you have to be it all: the baby in the baptism, the bride in the wedding and the corpse in the funeral. Remember, she isn't staying here because of you, she's waiting—" She was interrupted by Tía Merce's abrupt move.

If they were whispering about my mother, I knew what we were waiting for; we were waiting for my father. The poem was finally over. Luckily there weren't any more ladies with curled bangs who recited poems. Tía Merce asked my mother to recite something.

My mother said, "This is by Antonio Machado: 'Between life and dreams / There's a third thing, / Guess what it is.' " Everybody looked confused. They didn't think it was a poem.

Tía Merce headed for her horse. "We'll take a peek at the Caída de Satán and go back," she decreed.

I pushed away the groom's words about coming back on Lucero. I had stayed in one piece so far; I could return in one. Papi could arrive in the next second. Even if he came by bicycle, I'd sit on the handlebar, the way I used to when we went for rides.

SHOTS SOUNDED on the other side of a hill. A tremor went through Lucero. His ears pricked nervously. Tío Juan Vicente appeared, galloping downhill. The famous hat man followed him at a trot, clutching his saddle. "Look! He's holding on to the saddle!" I cried. "He doesn't know how to ride very well."

"Let's find out if they shot something; maybe a puma," Patricia said. The girls whipped their horses into a canter.

Lucero trotted after them with me bumping like a watermelon. Hands, stay away from the saddle whatever happens; legs, grip hard. . . . Good advice, but the belly was so huge my legs bounced away from it. Concentrating on my legs, I forgot to bring the reins to my chest. Lucero started to gallop. I grabbed anything within reach: the saddle, the mane. Lucero and I tore past the girls. Ahead, the grown-ups looked back when they heard a gallop and hastily got out of the way. A lady screamed. As soon as we passed them, Lucero slowed down to a trot, then to a walk. Saved! I was saved!

I tried to steady my trembling arms before the girls saw me, but Lucero's ears picked up a gallop. Behind us Tío Juan Vicente, leaning over his horse, one hand securing his rifle on his shoulder, yelled, "Don't worry, my child, hang on! Hang on! I'm coming to the rescue!"

What did he mean? Lucero's eyes rolled back, his muzzle stuck forward; he took off, left the road, faster and faster through an open *meseta.* I leaned my body over his neck, as Tío Juan Vicente had told the hat man. This did nothing. I tried to wrap my arms around it—which Tío Juan Vicente hadn't said—but the absurd neck was too thick. My hands kept slipping off the mane, which for some wicked reason had been cut ridiculously short. The area where we were headed suddenly disappeared from my view, as if there was a huge void. A void! The Caída de Satán?

Running horses and yells escalated. "Stop, child!" "Stop, Solita!" "Stop, girl!" "Jump off the horse, child!" "Off the horse!" "Jump! Jump!"

Jump? Nanny Fresia's words bumped up and down in my mind: "The Devil drives you to jump. . . ." There wasn't much time to think; we were getting closer and closer to the edge.

"Jump, child! Jump!"

Lucero was running like a devil, but I was still on. Surely even a lunatic horse had enough sense to stop before he reached the edge of a precipice. On the other hand, why should anybody trust a horse, especially a crazy one? The edge over the void was near. . . . I slid my feet from the stirrups, swung to one side, bumped a few times and fell down into the scraggly ground.

Was I in one piece? Unbroken? This was a time to cry. Spaniard or no Spaniard, I decided I would. But my face wouldn't cooperate; my mouth was a leather hole, my tears dust. Maybe Spaniards never cried because they were as scared as I was now. The *tacata-tacata* of Lucero's hoofs slowed down, but I didn't look. I never wanted to see that berry-brained animal again. I stumbled up and dusted myself clumsily. I tried to walk, but my legs were tiny and didn't advance any. Not being on top of Lucero made me a midget.

Tío Juan Vicente jumped off his horse with a terrified face and took me in his arms. "Brave girl, bravo, bravo." Obviously he couldn't see the huge fear still bumping inside me.

Other grown-ups arrived trotting, galloping, oohing and aahing. "What a close call!" "Good Heavens, the Caída de Satán!" "She did the right thing!" "Could've broken a leg, her neck, how atrocious." Tomás came shaking his head, as if this had been all my fault. Tía Merce scolded him. "You're supposed to watch the girls. What in the world do you think you're supposed to do, Tomás? Give the child your horse; walk to the nearest peasant house, the Piñeiras, I believe, and ask for the horse they use. Bring it back later with something."

Tomás removed his hat. "Sí, mi Señora Doña Mercedes."

Tío Juan Vicente picked me up and put me on top of Tomás' horse like he would a sack of corn. The *criollo* saddle received me, warm and soft. My mother came close. "You did very well, my little daughter, you did the correct thing." She blew me a kiss.

The grown-ups smiled at me. "What are you thinking, Solita?" the black-bangs lady asked with interest.

I didn't say that Tío Juan Vicente was the most blundering idiot in the entire New World, that he had rushed to "save" me and had nearly gotten me thrown down a precipice, that although he'd been nice to me afterward, I hoped never to see him again. I said what I had been thinking before. "I was thinking how silly those children's horse stories are."

"What do you mean, Solita?"

"Because Lucero looks all bright and alert, but he isn't as intelligent as a worm. I won't read those stupid stories again."

"How adorable," the black-bangs lady said. Others laughed.

My mother asked me, "Did you thank Juan Vicente for his concern?"

"Don't be silly, *ma belle,*" Tío Juan Vicente said, "let the child get her bearings. I'm still pretty shaken myself, you see."

We headed home. The girls observed me from a respectful distance. I felt like one of the pictures of their distinguished ancestors hanging in the salon. I waited for them to get closer.

IN COUNTRY ESTATES the thing to do was to be brave. All the grown-ups talked about me. It was glorious. The precious girl got closer to the German photographer. "I'm all shaken up about the child," she said brokenly, giving him the look of a dog seeking protection from his master. He was also upset. "Why didn't I bring my camera! Could have shot the little girl's jump." The precious girl pouted to console him. Mlle. Vicky consoled him too, saying perhaps he could take shots of her dancing, with or without whatever he wanted. He glanced with embarrassment at the precious girl.

Tío Juan Vicente smiled at me and whispered to my mother, "Pilar, you stayed so cool; weren't you worried?"

"Juan Vicente, if I didn't stay cool about things like these, would we have survived the war? The exodus? The concentration camp? The refugee ship?"

She thought I couldn't hear, because she never mentioned

those things. She told the refugees the war had ended years ago, why talk about it? They talked about the war's politicians and factions, but never about us there, except when they remembered something funny. But I knew it wasn't funny; it was terrifying.

The only one who did talk about what happened to us then was Nuria Puig. While fleeing through the snow-covered Pyrenees, she'd made a hole in the one orange they had to eat, and every day she squeezed juice for her and her husband, but he wasn't strong and died anyway. When I asked my mother how we made it, she said Nuria Puig was only happy at funerals, that if you summoned up sad things, instead of fighting for better ones, your brain would breed swamp creatures. I imagined Nuria Puig in a stagnant lagoon, perhaps with a frog on her head, like the picture in a magazine loaned to my parents.

My curiosity stayed the same, but the refugees' only answer to my questions was "That chapter of our lives is over; turn the page," or "That bad act ended; on to the next act." I never found out anything. Patricia and the twins always talked about their baptisms, their birthdays, the beautiful parties they had attended and the important people, like bishops and ambassadors, who'd been there. I couldn't tell them anything. But they hadn't jumped off Lucero. Finally, they rode up to me.

"Were you scared?"

"Not much."

My voice came out a little shakier than I intended, but they didn't seem to notice. Why not milk the situation to the fullest? "This Tomás horse is an ox," I said, pushing aside a slight sense of shame. "And this *criollo* saddle is hopeless; it makes you feel like a baby in a high chair."

All the way back, I talked as if I were the girl-queen of Maori. "It was the famous hat man in the bamboo grotto," I said. They didn't deny it. Even la Mamota was going to treat me as if I was like other people. Papi was going to be so proud of me; maybe he was in the houses already! Basking in the girls' respect, I saw all sorts of beautiful things I'd been too scared to see before. It was hard not to act gleeful.

In truth, El Topaz was a fine place; everybody admired me. Instead of my father taking us back to Galmeda, it made more sense for him to live here with us. Tía Merce was so fond of my mother it couldn't take too much effort for my mother to convince her. My mother could do anything she made up her mind to do. My father could also teach Tía Merce many things. And he could make everybody laugh, like in Galmeda. "Stupendous!" Papi was going to say about my brave jump.

7

LA MAMOTA GAVE US ANOTHER BATH—AGAIN, NOT because my father was coming, but for the arrival of a very, very famous pianist. The girls complained that the party in his honor was going to be a yawning bore. Not so. Because they filled all the dog dishes with champagne, the animals howled and stumbled and chased each other all over the salon. It was the best party ever. The very, very famous pianist left to give concerts all over the world.

The next day a *peón* who wasn't from El Topaz came to bring word from his *patrón* that labor strikes had hit Galmeda.

"Please, don't mention labor strikes," the Walrus said.

"I hope your husband isn't involved," Melons told my mother.

The *peón* also had a message from my father that he was coming! And was taking the girls for a ride to the nearest town! I brought up the ride all through dinner. It amazed me that the girls were glad my father was coming, though they wouldn't say why. It didn't matter; things were really looking up.

The next day I got dressed early to wait for my father. He was coming. It was official. But in spite of my ride and jump from Lucero, Nanny Fresia held me prisoner in my bed as usual. Probably Papi hadn't come before because he couldn't borrow a car. In Galmeda he met a dentist once whose family was well situated—which meant they never ever had to go find money—but weren't just bourgeois, which meant they liked my parents and enjoyed themselves intelligently. The dentist told Papi to borrow his car sometime, but maybe had used it all the time to chase patients; most people didn't want to go to the dentist. Or maybe Papi had found that great job he was looking for, and it was too great to leave it. Papi was very smart and could get a great job if one was available. Maybe he'd arrive in the next few seconds, while I was all dressed to go but a prisoner in the dark.

Light from around the shutters shaped the ceiling beams. I waited for some part of Nanny Fresia to move; if you woke her up when all of her was asleep, she'd be cross. Finally her tongue swished. I said, "I have to go to the bathroom."

Right on cue, her sleepy voice said, "Get the chamber pot."

Bravely I ignored her and went to the door. As expected, she said, "Where do you think you're going, little girl?"

"To the bathroom; this has to be in the bathroom."

Instead of saying "All right" and going back to sleep, she opened her round tin of Nivea cream and yawned, "You can't go out yet, little girl. Maybe some *ánima*'s still in the gardens."

"What do you mean, 'some *ánima*'?"

"Ay, you're going to turn me crazy, little girl; never had a child ask such dumb questions! *Ánimas* come out at night. You mean to tell me you haven't heard them? They come after dusk; they leave when the roosters sing. Haven't heard one rooster yet."

"I'm just going to the bathroom."

"Maybe you are soft in the head, little girl. What if Quirincho gets you? He steals children, that hunchback devil."

"Why would he steal children—is he a Gypsy?"

"A Gypsy! Quirincho a Gypsy!" She turned on her creaky cot, laughing. "Wait till I tell Ema and Eda! Quirincho's an *ánima,* little girl, he steals children." I asked why. "How would I know? To make mischief, like the others." What others, I asked. "Puff! There're lots of *ánimas.* Later you'll be careful about Trauco, when you turn a young lady. He springs up laughing and gets young girls in the, you know, interesting state, big . . . you know. He's a warty midget with a little stone hatchet on his shoulder."

I asked her what did she mean. "Trauco jumps out of the shadows on a girl's back, and he hits her with his little hatchet, in the walnut in the neck, where the back starts."

I felt my neck. True, there was a walnut there. I asked her how did she know all that was true.

"How do I know! It happened to my very own sister, Teresita, when she went to fetch a rabbit from the trap at Boldo Hill and got to lingering, picking cherries from that old wild cherry bush, and started back past dusk, and whammo! Trauco got her."

"So what happened?"

"He must'a been laughing really loud, 'cause Teresita delivered twins, Rosita and Eldebertito."

"But I just have to go to the bathroom through the veranda. Besides, Beethoven and the other dogs will protect me."

"The dogs! Little girl, a dog can't do a thing to an *ánima;* it's like biting air. By the time a dog barks, it's too late; they've done their mischief. You go out now, and this *ánima* who hasn't been keeping track of the sun might grab your leg from the veranda's edge and pull you down, and that's the last we'll ever hear of you. Now use the chamber pot and go back to sleep."

How could I go back to sleep? Slowly the last night noises died out. They were probably just strange animals. Servants were ignorant, but they knew these parts, and we didn't. There was no reason, really, to go out before outside turned sunny. Papi always had trouble waking up early anyway.

WHILE I WAS waiting for Papi, all dressed up on a veranda bench, Nanny Fresia taught me how to knit with two wooden needles. The girls complained mightily about having to practice the piano with hats on; I had told Nanny Fresia so much about the ride with my father, she had convinced the twin nannies to dress up the girls too. Melons went by smelling like crushed roses, holding a puppy, and asked me why I was knitting with gloves on. When I told her my father had announced he was coming, she put the Chihuahua puppy down. "Your father's all talk, talk, little one. Disregard what that charming man tells you; he'll give you loads of grief." I disregarded what Melons told me; it caused me grief. Papi was coming today. I had to tell him about Lucero. He had to fascinate Tía Merce. Then she would ask Papi to stay here.

Knitting was something that girls did, although Patricia and the twins didn't. It demanded concentration, which wasn't easy while kicking a guanaco and a goat to keep them from nibbling the yarn and making it slimy. If you passed the needles and the yarn right, it would make a sweater to be sent to my grandmother, or socks for my father. Better start with socks, the most important thing in civilization. Without a sweater you'd be cold, that's all. Without socks you could do nothing; you couldn't even drink an espresso at a café counter on a hot day with someone who might help you get a job.

In Galmeda I'd been very useful about this. Most mornings my father raised his head from his pillow and asked me to find his socks. Depending on where they had chosen to lie all night, it was either a simple operation or a feat. If they were curled, limp and dejected in puffy clouds of dust under the bed, it took a deep, courageous breath to dive in to get them. No matter how far under the bed, how thick the dust, or how many odd objects appeared in the dark, I didn't retreat. I handed the socks to him, avoiding the spots hardened by the rubbing of toes and heels on his walk to the bus stop to look for work. The soft parts were more pleasant.

Knitting was magic. You maneuvered the needle—under this way, pass, come out, under that way, like doing a dance—and soon you had a fabric with a pattern! Then garments, like the blue sweater I had on, knitted by my mother long ago. It had shoulder pleats—this was very elegant—and purple and violet streaks across—this was very artistic. My mother knew how to be artistic. Nanny Fresia said I looked ridiculous. That the sweater was funny and too small. She didn't know a thing about wearing what you wanted; she insisted I dress in the girls' castoffs. She said what I'd brought from Galmeda was unusable, said it was too warm and ordered me to take off the sweater. I ignored her, because my father was coming, and when you had a father around, a nanny could go hoarse giving orders and you didn't give a hoot.

My mother and Dr. Kaplan walked by without seeing me. "If my therapy to have Merce here and channel her libido into artistic, creative pursuits doesn't work," he said, "heaven help her. She's bent on a self-destructive course." That was very odd language.

After a while, knitting was all the same and it didn't look at all like a sock. I had to take the sweater off. I was about to go check whether a praying mantis changed colors on a yellow flower when I heard a motor's roar, probably one of those long cars. The girls stopped playing and ran out. "Sounds like a huge limousine," Grace said. I had little time to think; it'd be here in no time. If it was Papi, I could stay put so he would see me, so ladylike and grown-up, knitting him a future sock.

A dusty old motor bicycle zoomed by toward the gates. I dropped everything and ran, ignoring Nanny Fresia's yells. "Get that yarn, you bad girl! Look! Look at that cursed beast and goat fighting to chew that beautiful yarn! You dropped your hat! Come back, I tell you!"

It was Papi! I hugged him so hard it made him laugh. Mami was right; the country air was making me strong.

"How are you, treasure? My, I think you've gained a kilo and grown a centimeter!" It was almost worth not seeing him for so long to hear that. My insides burst with energy, ready for what he might say, such a different readiness than the one for the girls, which was always for a defense. "What a dress," Papi smirked. "And gloves? Why are you wearing such *cursi* stuff?"

My body encased in Gloria's dress *cursi*? *Cursi* was the worst thing in the world: gold-trimmed figurines of little shepherds; sugary violin music; lots of big words pronounced slowly (one big word said fast once in a while was good); bouquets in your sofas, drapes, pictures, vases and rugs. After meeting *cursi* people you laughed at them; they were not to be considered. Gloria isn't *cursi,* Papi, I almost said. I defend Gloria?

We walked to the house. Should the sock be a surprise? What if it got so boring only one sock got done? "Papi, I was knitting." I checked his face to see how impressed he was.

"What do you think of my bicycle?" he asked proudly. He should have known I was impressed. He was going to be too when he learned about my horse jump. "Papi, I have a foil ball."

"I have a terrific job; wait till I tell your mother."

"Mami was in the park; they went there for a walk. But now they're by the aviary." I kept up with things and could give useful information. No doubt the grown-ups would tell him about my horse jump. "Papi, wait till you see the guanaco."

Papi walked with that nervous stride he took when he was going somewhere and was about to be late, moving fast, the muscles in his arm where I hung tense, hard and shifty, his face down, the ridges around his mouth restless, his eyes not focused on where he was walking because they had already arrived where he was going. I'd always wished my eyes could see those places in advance too, and now I knew everything about this place and he didn't. It was strange; it made me feel like a mother.

Instead of taking the road, I led him through the winding paths so he could see the many flowers and bushes. I had to warn him about stinky or bitter-smelling ones, show him the sweet or exquisite ones. He went on walking fast, his eyes somewhere else.

A smiling Nanny Fresia walked toward us with Niceto in tow. Papi made a big fuss, kissing him and picking him up. I got my patience ready; it was going to be the usual asking Niceto questions, him answering cute remarks and widening those huge brown eyes like Mami's, and Papi laughing. Niceto was cute, but grown-ups exaggerated his wonderfulness.

Mami and the others were around the aviary, holding demitasses. Maybe with the birds' chirping they hadn't heard the motor, because none ran to stage the usual welcoming routine accorded to guests. Papi went to give Mami a hug. Mami was polite, the way she'd been with the lady friends of the girls' Tío Armando. Tía Merce gave Papi a cheek peck with the same smile she had when a maid or a *peón* mispronounced a word. The others made polite noises and handshakes, then continued to talk about Tío Juan Vicente's plans to ride his fabulous mare in the Bois de Boulogne in Paris. The disquieting oppression about my father that sometimes crept over me started to grow.

Only Melons talked to him. "I was an honest young woman," she told him. "I'm now a no-nonsense middle-aged woman. And I'm working myself into an ornery old woman." My father smiled politely. Someone whispered, "She was a crazy young woman, is a crazy middle-aged woman and will be a crazy old woman."

They all went to play roulette. Papi trailed behind and grabbed Mami's arm. "I found a job at this huge new electric plant." She smiled. "Pilar, what's going on? Some hysterical woman who called herself 'Contessa' María something or another, she called me to threaten me that if you don't leave she'll tell my boss I talk to the unions! She said you and —"

Mami said, "Nonsense, Julian, she's crazy, and insanely possessive of Merce. And you are not one to talk."

The girls, still in hats and gloves, arrived bristling. "We were told we would be taken for a ride to Las Cabras," Patricia hissed. "You think that dirty, noisy bicycle's a limousine?"

The only one who was pleased with my father was Nanny Fresia. I ignored the girls. They were distinguished. But I was a girl who could not only ride English and had jumped off Lucero; I was a girl with a father who was here.

Tía Merce's disquieting chuckle shook the fine, white peach fuzz underneath her chin, toward her throat, which could be seen against the light. She said, "Julian, the girls are still dressed up for the ride you promised them."

"Of course, of course," Papi said, waving his arms. Patricia refused to go. The twins relented. Papi put Niceto and me in front of the seat, on the bar, and the twins squished on the back rack. My mother complained it was unsafe, but Papi played deaf to it. We took off for the road, bumping and holding on tight.

At the public road, every passing car laughed seeing three girls in hats and gloves on a battered motor bicycle. Papi beamed. I didn't know whether to be happy or not. "I got a great job!" Papi yelled to the wind. "In the new hydroelectrical plants!" I held on to Niceto. "It's incredible, heroic really, the workers like ants in a mountain!" A bus went by; everybody laughed. Papi went on about a so-called engineer who probably got hired through family influence, and another one who noticed Papi could read maps and manuals in

French and English, "and lets me use the motor bike whenever I want! Isn't it stupendous!"

Suddenly the motor started to putt-putt and slow down. Then it stopped. Papi got off, cursing. We stood by the roadside while he tinkered with the motor. Cars slowed to look. After a while Papi put Niceto on the front and told us to push while he tried to start it. People in passing cars laughed at us. Grace said hotly she'd never been so humiliated in her whole life. Finally the motor started and we headed back without having seen Las Cabras. We arrived dusty, disheveled, sweaty and with dirty gloves. Gloria had lost her hat.

The twins didn't tell about the bicycle breaking down. Grace was too mad. I think it would have been fun if she hadn't been there. Everybody went to their rooms to get cleaned up for lunch.

In my mother's room, she and Papi were talking. "Of course I would've come sooner. I couldn't, Pilar, but—"

"You haven't even tried to approach a respectable law firm."

"Pilar, you know about the law against hiring aliens! Of course I went to the Ministry of Justice! Three times!" Papi seemed very angry at the people in the Ministry of Justice.

Mami said, "Be patient," which she always told him. Papi got mad. "You going to hear me or lecture me?" They saw me at the door and told me to go to lunch.

I waited, but nobody came, so I went back to their room. I pushed the door. I pushed harder. The latch moved, and the door opened. What I saw in the dim light froze me; it was one more assault, one more piece of evidence of how things were and shouldn't be. My mother was naked, with her legs bent out; my father was naked over her. He saw me. "Close the door!" he snapped. Close the door in front of me or behind me? My father had never yelled at me before. Clearly, what was happening was the no-name thing that was so awful it could never be mentioned, what animals and ignorant maids did, what the girls said was comical, grotesque and shabby.

I went to the gardens. All that was connected with births and here I was, having been birthed. But it seemed too awful to be analyzed. I stretched on a chaise longue and fell asleep.

AFTER DINNER I begged Nanny Fresia to let me go to the salon instead of to bed, to stay near my parents. Nanny Fresia was as easy to sway as the ancient oak in front of the gallery. But I didn't have to stay mad in my bed until I fell asleep; my parents came into Mami's room. A cheerful, warm strip of candlelight leaked under the closed door between our rooms.

Mami asked something. Papi said, "Translate manuals, read maps, codes, carry his equipment . . ." Mami mentioned the bicycle. "The engineer—English parents, born over here and speaks Spanish with an English accent—noticed me, asked me if I could drive!"

I felt sorry for the girls. I felt superior to them. They had all these houses and toys and money to shop, but there were uncountable kilometers and undetermined spaces and unknown places between their mother and father.

Mami asked something. Papi said, "About five hours' drive, then up the cordillera . . . No, no women; cut the sarcasm. No, Pilar, I can't ignore the Trade Unions Congress. Be reasonable! It's large, has wide ties; it's my great chance to be an advisor, be trusted by a major organization. You don't know this country; the incredible class stratification, and racial too, and priests and the rich . . . No, not dangerous, Pilar, not 'the same story all over again'. . . if the unions get ugly, I'm out. Not dangerous; there's no reason for you to be here. . . ."

They lowered their voices. I put my head at the foot of the bed to hear better. "It's a peaceful country, Julian."

"A perilous myth, Pilar, invented by the intelligentsia so they can go on having their comfortable life and do nothing . . . They've always had violence, never organize effectively.

If I get a job at the Ministry of Labor, I'll be an indispensable mediator."

Mami whispered again. I hung my head near the floor. "They're educated, Julian."

"Educated! They glue books on the wall for show!" I could only hear a word here and there. His voice said, "Degenerate Juan Vicente . . . appalling blimp."

Her voice said, "So nice to you . . . a warm person . . . he's socialist, you know." Then came *bsss-bsss-bsss,* like striking a match on a matchbox.

"Yes, you're a great lover, but I'm worn out. Nothing but promises, but every cent's for you, every minute for your self-promotion. And your . . . well, maybe, maybe, if you stay out of the strikes . . ."

"Pilar, be reasonable. You'll be so pleased."

Papi whispered. I slid just a bit more, and suddenly everything went and I crashed onto the floor and hit the door. Nanny Fresia woke up screaming. Niceto started crying. Papi opened the door and saw me struggling inside the bedclothes.

"You little sneak," he said, and ordered me to go to bed.

The door closed. The strip of candlelight went off. Our two rooms were dark and quiet, with my mother, father and brother, all together. Later Mami would tell Papi about my horse jump.

DURING LUNCH Papi sat at the big table. He had been out with the grown-ups, playing croquet with a sarcastic face, drinking espresso in the sunny back veranda with an irritated face, listening to the news about the strikes on the radio with a worried face, or whispering with Mami in a reasoning voice. Or he had disappeared. I still hadn't hung on his arm or told him about the guanaco or pointed out what was most interesting. He hadn't told me anything. But he did ask me once, "Would you like to come to Galmeda and ride the motorized bicycle?" I said, "Let's go!" and he laughed, raising his nostrils. You never knew when grown-ups would laugh. I ran to tell Mami. She didn't make the same stern face as when I begged her to go back to Galmeda. She said, "Maybe." When my mother said maybe, she meant maybe.

The psychiatrist with pink glasses was talking to my father about the people in the magazines we had back in Galmeda. "It's inconsistent for Hitler to commit suicide. "I'm sure he escaped somewhere, maybe to our country. . . . there are so many rumors. . . ."

My father said, "Doctor, Hitler's suicide *is* consistent; it is the quintessential"—he always used that word—"scorpion's act—spreads poison and, when threatened, turns it on itself."

"An acute observation," Tío Juan Vicente said. "However, I think it rather impossible that he could have done such awful things. The German soul—Brahms, Schumann, Wagner, Mahler . . ."

My father looked at Tío Juan Vicente as if he were a slug.

"But Juan Vicente," my mother said, "don't you remember the Germanic tyrant Ataulf?" Nobody seemed to. "In the fifth century, Ataulf led his Visigothic barbarians through Hispania, under the pretext of helping the Romans."

"And as usual," my father said, "they burned, raped, killed and took over, just like their descendants the Nazis did."

"Oh, Julian, you speak so . . . forcefully," Mlle. Vicky gushed.

"The English were as naive about Hitler as the Romans about Ataulf a millennium and a half ago, till it was too late," my mother said.

"That's right—ignorance of history. It's going to take the world generations to recover," Papi said.

I looked at the girls; now they were listening to the big table. They would see how interesting my father was.

"It's the same, the same," the psychiatrist said. "Cultured

people aren't interested in being rulers, only demagogues are."

My father launched forth passionate words I'd heard before: brown shirts, workers' exploitation, invasion, genocide, treaty, deportation, betrayal, tyranny. Only the psychiatrist and Mlle. Vicky listened. Tía Merce and the others looked bored.

Maybe they looked bored because when you were in another country you had to act more like the people who owned it. You tried to bring your voice up or down or suck it in as they did. When doing greetings, you didn't lean back with open arms, you leaned slightly forward and shook hands limply. If you were a girl, you had to know whether to open your eyes wide so they'd find you polite, or say something so they'd find you smart. When laughing and talking, you had to know whether to let the air out through your nose or your mouth. Some refugees soon learned and no one found them odd. Others never seemed to, and continued to expel their middle-of-a-sentence laughs through the nose, as if they were back home. There were so many things Papi needed to learn.

He talked about the United Nations. "Oh, Julian, you talk divinely," Mlle. Vicky gushed. I looked at the girls.

"Don't you adore Paris?" Tío Juan Vicente said. "I agree with Claudio Correa that it's the only place a civilized person can live. You open your shutters in the morning, and there's Notre Dame! And French music—the divine Chopin!"

My father said, "I brought a record of the most outstanding personality in the United States today—Paul Robeson."

"Who's that?" Tía Merce asked, and turned to Tío Juan Vicente to ask about his horses. Papi's face was furious.

"Isn't your father taking you home?" Patricia asked.

"Oh, so we don't have to worry about—" Gloria stopped when Patricia kicked her.

"He's funny. He has a cockscomb of red hair," Grace said.

"He's got missing fingers—how come?" Patricia asked.

"It was a bomb. During the war."

"Oh, c'mon. War only happens in the movies," Patricia said. "Makes him look like a *cornudo.* People let each other know who's cuckolded by pointing their fingers this way, like cattle horns."

I pretended not to hear.

"What does your father do, anyway? La Mamota said he's a construction worker." Reading their faces, I couldn't tell whether this was good or bad. It didn't look good, so I said nothing. I didn't have to follow the rule to stay with them even when they were mean; my father was here. I got up, went to the big table and whispered to Papi, asking if it was all right for me to go out. The girls watched me curiously.

"Well, of course, treasure," he said, smiling.

"We're going for a walk, right, Papi? After lunch?"

"Of course, treasure, right after lunch. Wait for me."

As I went behind Mlle. Vicky's chair, she turned to me. "I'm going to teach you to dance, little one, very soon." She winked.

"That would be stupendous," my father said to her.

I pushed the big dining-room doors and went out into the reception room. I'd been bold! I'd been defiant! I was on my own! I could tell him about Lucero! But I had missed dessert.

TIME CRAWLED in the reception room and Papi didn't come. The girls went by to their siestas. I told them I was going for a walk with my father. Finally he came out and said he was going to the gallery to hear the news for a little while.

Where should I take Papi? He had taken me and Niceto to San Toribio street once, to Charley's, which Papi said meant "Little Carlos' Place," but "Charley's" made it sound exotic, and bought us each a whole Coca-Cola and a whole pastry. After waiting for a long time, I went to the gallery. Papi wasn't by the radio. The twin nannies, Ema and Eda, said el Señor Julian had gone toward the park with la Señorita "Madmosil" Vicky, and giggled.

I went to look for Papi. At the road I shook out the transparent tiny rocks that got inside my sandals. No one was in the dark woods but a white snake. I followed it as it slithered toward a lazy stream at the park's end, but couldn't catch it. Suddenly the most exquisite perfume overwhelmed me. I looked down. There was a tiny white flower near my sandals. I kneeled down to examine the miniscule arms reaching out of the undulating cup. It was astonishing that such a tiny thing could have such power, just growing there, calmly being itself.

Then everything exploded. "You wicked little girl!" a shrill voice said behind me. "Why are you in the middle of nowhere, alone, on your knees, getting your dress dirty!" Nanny Fresia had turned into one of those devils she was always mentioning. She pulled me by the arm as if I were going to get lost. My face burned with humiliation. "I'm going for a walk with my father."

"Very funny. You better not wander out alone, little girl, or I'll tell your Señora Doña Mamá, and la Mamota if I have to! You stay where it's proper and fitting!"

She left me in my room. Niceto slept. Why was wandering alone improper? In Galmeda you could wander all you wanted. Everything was neatly arranged in methodical streets: four houses and you were at the end of your block; another half block, at a friend's house; another block and you could tease an irritable bulldog by standing with an inscrutable smile outside his gate and watch him get hysterical. Streets were either old, with cobblestones; not so old, with squared, flat stones; or highly modern, paved with the smoothest of cements, wonderfully suited for roller skates and bicycles, if you were lucky enough to borrow some. Tiled sidewalks let you walk feeling very proper. However, the tiles' sixteen ridged divisions made them unsuited for roller-skating; they rattled your brain to a frazzle.

In Galmeda you walked two blocks in any direction, any at all, and you knew exactly what to expect: an Italian in a tan apron behind a corner store's counter, surrounded by pickles, olives, tired vegetables, coffee and packages. They all had tiny broken veins on their faces, owned the store and wore their bad moods as a badge of national and occupational superiority. Being just Italian or just a food-store owner wouldn't make you so proud, but a combination of the two did. Everybody was informed of this by the store owner's sons, who played in the square. My father said Italians were all right if they hadn't supported Mussolini. How would you know if they had?

You saw scores of people in front yards and windows in the city: widows with sagging necks; old men with canes; a large family with woolly hair, all of them except one—where did he get his glossy straight hair?; matrons with pigeon breasts looking out to the sky; a thin woman with a birth mark; parrots, canaries, lap dogs, cats doing miracles of equilibrium on window sills. You could wander all you wanted in a city, and who would mind when there was so much going on? It would be best if we went back to Galmeda.

Mami didn't seem thrilled to have Papi here, but they had talked a lot. I couldn't tell anybody about the no-name thing.

After siesta I found the girls at the swings under the linden trees. Now that I could leave them if they started acting up, I wanted to play with them. Luckily they were preoccupied, so they didn't ask about my walk with my father.

Gloria proposed they hide behind the goose house. Grace said it'd be a shame not to see them making fools of themselves. I asked see who? "We just found out Mlle. Vicky's planning a dance class for tomorrow. We've been lucky since Gunther was seen by the river's lower end, romancing María Cristina under the date palms, because it made Mlle. Vicky sulk. But now she's happy again and wants to suck us into a class; it's horrible!"

I asked why.

"Haven't you seen a dance class? Nothing, nothing's more ridiculous. They prance around in bloomers and shorts pretending to be leaves in the wind or twigs in the river. Tío Juan Vicente tippytoes around in a satin bloomer, very serious, saying he's a white snake in the black forest, or a river sprite."

"You should see Melons standing still and twisting her wrists; she's a storm over the Andes."

"And the Walrus, on fours, like a rhinoceros."

I couldn't wait to see this zoo. It sounded like wonderful fun. My father was going to be so pleased to see me learning to dance. Maybe he'd meant for me to take a dance class first, then we'd go for a walk. I was going to try very hard in the dance class. "But why don't you want to join the dancing?"

From their swings the girls stretched their necks like fighting roosters. "Because! We hate making fools of ourselves! We've boycotted the classes forever, and won every time because we stick together. You'll be one more to give us weight, Solita."

We took turns swinging high up in the air, then leaping onto a garden table. It was thrilling. It was dangerous. But some things you couldn't help doing.

8

PEEKING INTO ONE OF THE SALON'S WINDOWS, THE girls huddled together, a mass of flounces, lace and ribbons. They giggled or made derisive noises. After a while I asked, "Can I peek?" I had been looking for my father. "Be my guest." Gloria let me into her spot. Gloria was quite capable of being a decent human being.

Papi sat on a couch, watching Mlle. Vicky command the salon. Wearing a black maillot, as good as naked, she tried different sheet music at the grand piano. Velvet sofas, game tables and rugs had been pushed against the walls. The tall windows, usually shuttered, were open. Ghosts and witches had departed with the shadows. The portrait of Miguel Armando Mate, an ancestor the girls bragged about constantly, glanced ahead, oblivious to the animated grown-ups, in shorts and bloomers as predicted.

Papi had said how stupendous it was for me to learn to

dance. Mlle. Vicky clapped for the class to start. She came from some indefinite country and had indefinite parents. She had trained in Germany in a famous dance company, so she could gush in German to the photographer. She spoke without an accent, and it was hard to tell what she was. She wasn't rich like Tía Merce; she didn't have one of those northern Spanish names considered so elevated here; she didn't know about history or poets like the refugees; she didn't follow the same sugary courtesies as people in San Bernardo Street, whom the refugees called petit-bourgeois or lower-middle-class. So what was Mlle. Vicky? She was someone who played the piano with great force. She smiled at Papi.

We giggled about Tío Juan Vicente's black-and-orange-striped bloomers, velvet bodice and white tights; he looked like a conquistador and gave me a funny feeling of being in a history book. He sat on the window sill to adjust a slipper, murmuring, "Ah, Scarlatti! How bubbly!" He saw us. "Little ones, come in and join the dance!" The girls ducked. "Come in, *dépêchez-vous!*"

I looked at my father on the couch. "I'm going in," I said.

The girls let go of the window's iron bars and stared at me as if I were the madwoman of Paris in the radio show. "You can't go in. Boycotts have to be observed by everybody," Patricia ordered.

I opened the salon door and went in.

Tío Juan Vicente took me by the hand—"Are you ready to take up flight, little sea gull?"—to join the line, arms stretched, making a circling caterpillar. It was exhilarating to run to the beat of the music. At every turn, the girls' faces in the window flashed by. They never boycotted their piano lessons, so why should I boycott dancing?

I looked at Papi to see if he was pleased with the way I was learning, but he was looking at Mlle. Vicky. She ordered the circle to break, and for us to be ocean waves falling over rocks. We all curved our bodies, bouncing and retreating. I knew about waves. The photographer seemed uncomfortable, perhaps expecting the precious girl from the other lands to show up and see him turned into a barefoot wave. I kept my distance.

My mother looked so beautiful with a disheveled chignon and flushed cheeks. She was invited places because she looked so good. I saw a future full of invitations for Niceto. As for me, if a war caught me and turned me into a refugee again when I grew up, I was going to be in a pickle, because my looks wouldn't fetch any invitations. Maybe they'd like my dancing. I wanted my mother to see my wave, but Tía Merce whispered to her, "You are the rock," and crawled all over her. My mother moved away, but Tía Merce's wave was huge and followed her around the room. Tío Juan Vicente snapped at Tía Merce to stop it. Marco Polo was a running wave with loose-hinged hands—two flopping squids.

We had to be a tree's last leaf in the autumn. I didn't like hanging like that, would rather have flown as a hummingbird. But Mlle. Vicky winked at me in approval. Then we were a record player until we were dizzy—that was fun—then turned into floating logs. Rolling was better than floating. Some grown-ups floated up, some down. Melons was a dead log on still water. Papi didn't look at us, the dancers, as much as at Mlle. Vicky.

Tía Merce floated toward Tío Juan Vicente and whispered, "Listen, my peach, can't you mind your own business?"

He whispered, "Just trying to help you, dear Cleopatra; why hang on to a hopeless case and stir up the consort? You'd be better off with him than someone else; think about it. Just because your father abandoned your mother . . . Oh, how was Ruperto the other day?" Tía Merce chuckled. I rolled their way to hear better, but when they saw me, they just floated silently.

The girls weren't inside to hear me speaking to grown-ups, so I asked Tío Juan Vicente, "Why do you wear bloomers to dance?"

"Why, what a curious little log. I'll tell you. Dance is movement and should be ethereal; one shouldn't see buttocks, you see, they're the total opposite, made to sit. Dance is long, slim, buttocks are round, fat; dance is light, buttocks, solid. In dance, buttocks are an absolute no-no." Was that why he painted his? He had a thing about buttocks. He rolled down the river and whispered to the famous hat man, who bumped at every turn as his uppity behind got in the way, "You're a terrific log, darling."

"Shhh," Mlle. Vicky barked. "Concentration. No talk. Now, I want to see lovely lotus flowers opening up on a sunny morning. Lovely, not limp ones." I tried, but it was hard; somehow limp and lovely went together. I glanced at Papi. He still didn't see me.

When the class ended, Tía Merce rang a bell and serving maids brought lemonade. I flopped next to Papi. Maybe next class I'd get better and he would watch how well I could dance. Mlle. Vicky glanced at him. "I'm so very pleased your girl joined the dance. She did very, very well. I wish Merce's girls would show the same interest. They won't even try."

"Vicky, it's up to you to inspire them," Tía Merce said.

"Ay! I have a divine idea! We'll have a performance for Holy Week! Seeing this child has inspired me. We'll have lessons so the girls get enough training." She looked at my father again.

What Mlle. Vicky had said was great, almost as great as being in Galmeda, singing, talking and fooling with the refugees.

EVERY HOUR, all day, Papi listened to the news on the radio about the strikes. This made the other guests, especially Mami, mad. He wasn't even at the table for dinner. Mami had the face she wore when she was upset but didn't want you to know it. Tía Merce kept making funny remarks about my father and Mlle. Vicky's absence. How silly to make such a fuss. Papi was a busy man. In Galmeda many times he wasn't home for dinner.

The girls hadn't forgotten about the dance class, because they didn't talk to me but whispered about some sinister ceremony they were planning at their playhouse. They complained the *quenelles de poisson* were like cat's vomit rolled in flour. "At least we don't have to hide snails like yesterday," Gloria said.

"Ugh! The snails were Tía Pilar's idea. I would rather eat a fly than a snail. At least they're crunchy," Grace said.

I kept mum about picking snails from the garden for my mother. Once I forgot to close the soaking pot and they were on walls, ceiling and beds at the end of their shimmering trails.

After dinner the grown-ups decided to have their coffee in the gazebo. I wanted to go see if Papi was in the park; I still hadn't shown him a thing and no one had told him about my horse jump. When the girls heard guitars in the park, they went too.

Papi wasn't there. Tía Merce, Ruperto and the precious girl—who had arrived galloping as usual—played guitars. She tossed her long mahogany hair next to the photographer. A wreath of flowers braided in her hair had turned her into a wood nymph or the youngest of the twelve dancing princesses. Every time her duck's voice sang alone, the dogs—except Cocktail, who had tolerant ears—drifted away. The Walrus clowned in the middle of the gazebo, and the black-bangs lady did contortions, or maybe it was supposed to be dancing. Papi and Mlle. Vicky arrived. Tía Merce giggled with delight. Mlle. Vicky glanced haughtily at the photographer and joined the dance; she could really dance. Mami left looking angry. Tía Merce and Tío Juan Vicente followed her. Patricia stiffened her arms down, meaning we should keep quiet, this could be fancy. I tried to hang on Papi's arm, but he looked worried and went after Mami.

Mlle. Vicky sat down, and everyone around her stared at her in silence. Melons said, "My dear Vicky, you're turning breezes into gales. Are you desperate enough to fall for

Mercedes' little games and to try to sweep up a man who's not yet available?"

Mlle. Vicky said with agitation, "You're the one who's making an earthquake out of a tremor. I didn't provoke a thing; why's she so angry? Anybody can do anything, but Vicky, Vicky's just . . ." She wiped her tears with a corner of her blouse. This was not good manners, my mother once said; you should use a handkerchief. She hadn't said what to do if you didn't have one. Mlle. Vicky's voice shook. "Leticia, you said that when Armando comes, I won't stand a chance, so what's this, I get nothing?" Again she misused her blouse.

We froze at the edge of the gazebo seat. It was embarrassing to see a grown-up acting like a sissy. The Walrus whispered to the black-bangs lady, "Was Vicky taking advantage of the fact that he was mad at Juan Vicente?"

"No, no," the bangs lady said, "you men never understand a thing about each other. He couldn't resist a damsel's flattery; when the siren sang, he melted. And Merce's provocations and innuendos probably affected him. It's possible he also heard something about Armando."

Melons turned to us. "You nosy girls, go play."

In spite of Melons having ordered it, the girls left to check on their Mumsy and the others. I quickly finished my milk then drank the girls' milk, while thinking what to do to keep them away from my parents; something was very strange.

Patricia grumbled, "Who does Melons think she is? What a witch. She won't even let us see her daughter Lolita up close."

"Lolita?" I had no idea Melons had a daughter.

"She keeps her in a jar."

"Melons was going to have a baby, when she was old. But there was no baby, but something. She keeps the whatever in a jar with a plate that says LOLITA KAPLAN ESTÉVEZ, JULY 5, 1939. But she's never let us see her up close," Patricia grumbled.

"I don't believe you. Show me," I said. This was a good way to keep them from snooping in my parents' direction. They agreed. We peeked through the door glass in Melons' room. The psychiatrist was reading, not in the toilet this time, but in a stuffed chair.

"Over the chest of drawers, see?" Patricia whispered. Something floated inside a domed jar. They hadn't lied.

"When the baby didn't come, she went to the loony bin again," Grace said.

"She met her husband, the doctor, because she was cuckoo in the first place," Gloria explained. "Mumsy says it's disgusting."

I wasn't so sure. Melons seemed to know what others didn't. A tiny thing in a glass jar had her parents always with her; they protected her; she didn't have to fend for herself all the time.

"So, what was going on at the gazebo, Patricia?" Grace said.

"It's clear as water! Mlle. Vicky was misbehaving, and some of the other women got mad," Patricia said. We wanted to know how. "Didn't you see her with your own eyes? She danced wiggling her hips, like this"—Patricia's lack of a waist made it hard to see the misbehaving wiggle—"like bad women do it in those shows for men. Tía Pilar was the maddest—didn't you see her?"

"That's fancy!" Grace cried with satisfaction. "Isn't it?"

"I saw posters in front of one of those bad places," Patricia bragged. "You should've seen the bad women with shells in their crotches and titties instead of clothes."

"Patricia sees everything," the twins said admiringly, taking another peek at Melons' room.

"You naughty girls! Stop that this minute!" Ema ordered. "Go wash your hands." Things were looking up; all four of us were being scolded, not just me. Was it because I'd been brave or because my father was here?

SOMEONE SAID my father had gone to the animal baths to talk to the *peones.* The girls let me borrow their brother's bicycle to pedal there. They followed me. As hundreds of sheep in the corrals lifted their heads nervously, wondering what was up, I lifted mine looking for him. Maybe the veterinarian knew. He barely nodded to us, mopping his bald top worriedly. "This isn't the right time to dip. You didn't put out the salt licks with the roundworm medicine," he scolded the *capataz*. "There's too much creosote for the lindane. Everything's done wrong here, at the wrong time, year after year," he scolded, mopping his head.

"Señor Doctor," the *capataz* said defensively, "I do what I can. La Señora Patrona doesn't give me the money to buy; am I going to invent it? Mostly she wants things done in the houses."

"The vet's a crab, like María Teresa," Grace said.

At the gate a *peón* poked a sheep's behind with a long T pole. She entered the corridor, but when she smelled the pungent odor of disinfectants, she tried to backtrack. Another *peón* pushed her into the canal. She fell and swam desperately to the other end, holding her head up with opened nostrils. Just when she was reaching the end and thought she was safe, another T pole pushed her head under the foul sludge. "If the head stays dry," Gloria told me, seeing my horrified face, "the screwworms, ticks, lice and scab mites go there for safety, and later suck their brains out." Patricia and Grace grimaced. "Ick, Gloria!"

More sheep went through the ordeal and came out looking half dead. Things were like that sometimes; you couldn't go back, you couldn't fly out, they pushed your head under.

When our arms got tired from hanging on the corrals' fences, we bicycled back to the houses. The girls headed to the avocado orchard to have a private meeting. Nobody would come around there while the sun scorched the air over the prickly pears and dried weeds, and the fallen leaves, of a distinguished greenish-brown color, announced even a field mouse. Maybe they were going to talk about the big secret they were keeping from me, so I followed them. They didn't stop me. We dug up pipes. There was no end to what you could learn on a country estate. You massaged a ball of clay, sank your thumb in the middle to make a cup, poked a side hole with a hollow cane, tightened the clay around it and you had a pipe! If there was no store tobacco, crumbling dry grape leaves would do. In the shade of the adobe wall, we crossed our legs elegantly and puffed, totally grown-up.

Patricia and Grace argued that I couldn't be trusted because of the dance and my father. Gloria said I could. I said they should be grateful I had danced for them. They thought about it and agreed! Then I defended my father and they left it hanging. They warned me their plan wasn't for people with weak stomachs. I stood firm, because what mattered was that I had an all-right father. After a lot of negotiation, they finally agreed to let me know about their rustic playhouse plan, providing I let them cut a cross on me with a chagual bush's splinter and swear I would say nothing even if it caused me death, or they would spit at me like guanacos. I agreed. My father wouldn't let anything terrible happen to me; that was something fathers did. They protected you.

When Nanny Fresia saw the bloody cross on my knee, she was very angry; this was toying with Satan, she said, and ordered me to go to my mother's room and ask for a bandage.

As I entered the room, Papi said, "But Pilar, I've told you and told you, there's nothing to it. Won't you listen? And how about you and that Armando Larraín, that parasite!" My mother left. Papi came to give me a hug. His eyebrows drooped and his mouth went lopsided; he looked very upset. "I have to go back to work, my treasure. I'll come back when I can. . . ."

This was the last thing I'd expected! I'd let a cross be cut on my knee, held my ground with the girls about him at tremendous risk, was going to participate in a sinister deed, which could be dangerous—and he was leaving? Questions rushed and tangled in my throat. Why aren't we going with you? Why are we here? The girls know something. Nobody'll tell me. I'll knit you a sock, I'll be useful; maybe the Assasin'll die tomorrow and we'll go back to Spain, but here we won't find out. . . .

"What do you want me to bring you next time, treasure?"

"Why don't you stay here, Papi . . . and live here . . ."

"Solita, be sensible." I couldn't see his face. "Maybe your mother will leave here soon; I'll be waiting for you. I'll come every weekend, it's a promise. So, what present do you want?"

"Every weekend? Like when you went to San Ildefonso? Then bring me a dress. But why can't we go with you, Papi?"

"Ask your mother. I promise to bring a dress. What color?"

"Any." I couldn't have cared less; it just had to be my own.

"I must say good-by to the others. Niceto wants a soldier?"

"Yes, but get one with a firm neck. He takes dolls' and soldiers' heads off. He likes to see a row of heads in mud."

Instead of being outraged at this savagery, Papi smiled. No doubt about it, the rich and four-year-olds got away with anything. "Papi, mothers and fathers . . ." I wanted to say, "should be together," but the path to those words was blocked. I saw Lolita floating in front of her father reading the paper.

"I'll bring you children back, you'll see; your mother will let you know pretty soon. It's a promise." I disregarded what Melons had told me about disregarding what my father told me.

Papi said good-by to everyone at the gallery. Tía Merce turned the huge battery radio on and hugged him with eyes happy and bright. Mlle. Vicky cried again, but this time wore a dress, so she couldn't use her blouse. Papi gave her his handkerchief and asked for it back; he only owned one. Mami was polite.

The way Papi moved and walked, with the front of his jacket closed over his thin chest, with his red hair carefully combed, with the others looking at him—it all hurt. I wanted to cry for the pain of his impending absence and the renewed distance of the half-closed shutters protecting the windowpanes over San Bernardo Street. . . .

Out through the entrance yard, the shadows of Papi, me and Niceto merged into one and slid next to us, inseparable. But our joint shadow disappeared when we entered the shade of the sugar pine. Papi got on the cycle. Even when, like Lolita, you had a father with you, he could have a lot of worries and things to do, and no matter how much you needed to talk to him, you could end up just floating like her. The cycle—with Papi's arm waving good-by—disappeared behind a trail of dust. Anyway, my eyes were too blurred to see. Niceto held my hand and went on waving good-by.

Papi never heard about my horse jump.

9

"*CHIIRRI-PURI-PURI-PUI*," THE *PURI* BIRD SAID, and flew to the pepper tree. I continued to look out our bedroom door at the clean, gloomy morning shining coldly over the lemon leaves. "Hurry, little girl, the girls called you! And mind what you do, the *puri* bird's warning you about something." Not only Nanny Fresia, even the birds bossed me. Papi hadn't come for the weekend; he probably couldn't get the bicycle. How about staying in my room forever? That struck me as brilliant. Except my room was dark, and the only thing to do was watch the wall from the bed, especially when the low sun made the plaster indentation into amazing designs. The girls came to pick me up, and we went to their peasant playhouse.

"Solita, you're the sentinel. Stay at the door; don't look inside. It's your job to keep this a secret." Inside, Patricia gave orders to the twins, who dug the grave on the dirt floor quickly with their small spades. "Dig deeper this time, and don't you get your pinafores dirty, or la Mamota will ask questions, and Gloria, you always give the whole thing away. Solita, if you let anyone sneak up on us without warning, we are done for; then you'll be done for." This was my chance to be one in four, and I was going to do it right. It was hard to scan every path to identify anything moving through the artichoke fields or the chestnut trees, avoid soiling my—Gloria's—dress on the doorframe, and not look inside, all at once.

Grace covered her nose and mouth with her pinafore. "It's a hog's bouquet in here—enough to gag a maggot."

"Don't stop digging! We have to pour more dirt over the other corpses," Patricia ordered.

"If I dig anymore, I'll fill it with my vomit," Gloria said.

"I decide when it's deep enough," Patricia said. She looked and pronounced it deep enough. She dropped the lamb, trying to cross its front legs over its chest, but they were too stiff. They threw dirt until it was covered. "Gloria, you walnut brain! Take that cross out. That's a dead give-away; we'd never get another lamb for a pet." Patricia looked at me at the doorway, holding my nose. "Solita, if I catch you peeking inside again, you'll be sorry." They held candles solemnly, which was silly with such strong sunlight outside.

"Why did it have to die?" Gloria sniffled.

"I don't know," Patricia said pensively. "No matter how much fruit juice I give them, they still die from lack of vitamins. I'll give the next one twice as much. Let's get the ceremony over with; it's teatime." They asked several names to protect the lamb on her way to a place called Limbo, promising four candles if the lamb arrived there without mishap.

I was so absorbed thinking what those names would do with candles that I didn't hear steps until a voice startled me. "Hello, little wood nymphet. Why are you here all alone looking so sad? You look like you're going to a funeral." It was Tío Juan Vicente with the hat man.

We hadn't agreed on an alarm signal! All that occurred to me was to slam the door shut and lean against its dusty planks, forgetting my clothes. Heavy breathing let me know the girls were trying to get fresh air by positioning their noses at the cracks between the planks. "I'm . . . waiting for Patricia and the twins." What a feat to have told the truth without giving secrets away.

"Claudio, this peasant playhouse was my idea, you know. I convinced Merce it was a truly gracious and democratic thing to do—after all, the peasants should not be ignored." While he talked, the heavy breathing got worse. Finally they departed for the river, saying, "We'll let you little ones play your lovely childhood games. Ah, childhood, not a care, just fun and games!"

I hadn't finished whispering "You can come out" when the plank door opened violently, nearly knocking me down and ruining the dress; the girls burst out gagging, gasping and filling their lungs with air.

"You turkey's fart!" Patricia yelled as soon as she could talk. The three said a dead lizard was a more trustworthy sentinel. They went on and on until we heard yells from the nannies that Señora Doña Mercedes had an important announcement. No matter what they planned to do to me, I couldn't tell a soul about it. Now I was an accomplice. I had to be good at something else, but what?

WE HAD TO KISS Tía Merce in her enormous satin bed. Was her important announcement that we were being punished? Or something about my parents? A chambermaid brought in many blooming vases that went out to the veranda each night and were one of Tonic's favorite spots to urinate. Their mixed scent soon merged with Tía Merce's perfume.

"Mumsy, why do you put on day makeup the minute you take off your night makeup?" If Gloria hadn't been such an asker, I'd never have found out anything. Patricia knew it all and Grace didn't care.

"*Mon petit chou,* what if someone barged in here?" She combed her hair. "There's no such thing as something a lady can do looking bad. You must look your best always. Everything one does has charm, importance; never break the continuity of well-being; that's what a good life is, my pets."

Not for me. A good life was to be uncombed in a front yard, with the smell of newspaper and the ilang-ilang tree; your father reading the paper on a rush-seat chair and handing you the comics, with flat-nosed Oscar, who loved sausages, and Prince Valiant, who saved ships, and the Phantom, who saved you, and Don Crispín, who got hit on the head with a rolling pin by his wife.

"You're going to get a governess, my princesses."

"A governess!" the three girls yelled.

"Yes, my pets. I interviewed some, and they were all so perfectly dreadful and moth-eaten. One said she'd been a nurse in the Resistance, and probably wore huge hand-knitted pantaloons; people with voluminous private parts so depress me. I never want to interview another governess. So your Tío Toto picked a good one for me, a refined French *dame* who has a subscription to *Astronomy News* magazine and once met Edouard Manet's brother. He painted—did you know that? I asked him to bring her, although your Tío Armando offered." She got up and passed naked under the arched doorway into her dressing room, a foreboding area of armoires. We followed her. "Ah, Jacques Fath!"—she put on a vest. "Ah, perfect!"—she took a scarf to go with the vest. It didn't look right with nothing else on her, but she liked it.

"But Mumsy, all the girls who have them hate them! And you say this is Paradise. There are no governesses in Paradise!"

"My pets, now we can stay in glorious El Topaz for as long as we want. Nothing's in the way. Pilar will stay, and you'll have Solita to play with. Or do you prefer those horrid nuns?

Padre Romualdo's been on my back over your schooling. These priests just kill you by inches. Ah! These pants go divinely with this!"

Papi didn't like priests either. If one came our way, he always crossed the street to avoid being on the same sidewalk with him. Mami said Papi exaggerated everything because he was Andalusian, and in Andalusia they called bats vampires and rowboats ships. Mami didn't hate priests, but didn't need them.

"How come Enrique gets to go to boarding school in France?"

"You'll have only two hours of lessons a day; the rest of the time you can enjoy your wonderful childhood, *mes choux*. The governess will be your maximum authority, of course."

Good news! Anybody was bound to be better than la Mamota.

"How will classes be, Mumsy, with one classroom or what?"

"There'll have to be three levels—upper for Patricia, middle for you twins, and lower for Solita. You have attended the best school; Solita couldn't keep up." She left for her bathroom.

The twins were my age; why should they be in a higher level? Sure enough, they looked at me from their higher level already. Maybe if I did well, the governess would treat us all the same. Then everybody, including the girls, would have to follow suit.

THE BOOK my mother was reading at the table under the terrace's grape arbor had a drawing that said "Correct Trotting" and showed buttocks on a saddle, no head or legs. I didn't ask her about Papi; I asked about the book.

"When you don't know about a subject important to someone you want to impress, my daughter, you read about it; then you can ask intelligent questions that will please him."

Mami didn't add, We are going to Galmeda now, we are going to rent a house all to ourselves. "You're very lucky, Solita. You'll have dancing lessons from a distinguished dancer, and a French governess, just like dear Father provided for us."

"Was your governess fair?"

"She was an ogre, not at all like the interesting Madame that Armando, Merce's brother-in-law, has hired. If he brings her, you and Niceto welcome him warmly, Solita. You must learn to be gracious to certain people, be a charming girl."

"How was your governess an ogre?"

"In those days discipline was harsh. You're lucky things are so easy for you; nowadays we are lenient and broad-minded, we give you rope. I never had a chance to live in Paradise, like this, when I was your age." She pressed my cowlick.

Could I ask now? "Mami, is Papi . . . ?"

She closed the book. "I thought you'd realize by now, Solita, your father can't be trusted; you're old enough. Now, go to the salon. Vicky will start rehearsing the presentation for Holy Week." She left.

I threw the rest of her raspberry-mint drink up to the grape arbor. From there it dripped down blood teardrops on the white tablecloth.

Was I going to go to the salon even if the girls didn't? The fact was, doing exactly what the girls did hadn't turned me into one of them after all. If I did very well, Mlle. Vicky would consider me the girls' equal, and so would everybody else.

As I got near, I remembered "Don't touch, it's ours" and had second thoughts. A *tenca*'s song bounced inside the adobe walls surrounding the back gardens. I hesitated, then walked in.

The boycott was off! The girls, sitting cross-legged on the floor with the faces of three prisoners in a dungeon, gave me a dark look that said partly, "This is all *your* fault." The rest was unclear. But it was clear I shouldn't enjoy the class.

Mlle. Vicky said, "We'll use *Les Sylphides.*" What was that? It was important to understand everything, in order to be able to do what would make the least number of people mad. "There's a feverish preparation going on at the palace for a big ball."

Which palace? we asked. "Any palace, girls, any palace. The king, the queen and the prince are dancing. Don't worry; we'll do it à la Isadora Duncan—very loose, very natural."

"If they're dancing before going to a big ball, they're going to be pooped," the twins said.

"That's what you do in a ballet, girls. You dance."

"And this Isadora that got loose, was she crazy or what?"

"Isadora? Never mind. Now, one of you will be the princess."

Gloria yelled, "A skull spider! Look at the skull on its back! They're poisonous! Let's get out of here!" Gloria was no more scared of spiders than she was of dead leaves.

"Sit down! Listen, girls. During Holy Week children always come to visit; they will be princesses and guests at the ball. You'll make us proud in front of your Tío Armando . . . I mean, in front of all the guests. Now, the prince dances around the princesses and chooses one for his wife."

"Just by looking at her?"

"Girls . . . Now, one of you will be the chosen princess. They dance all night and live happily ever after. Isn't it marvelous? Don't you love it?" It sounded too much to me, and, from the girls' faces, repulsive to them. Why not dance whatever we wanted? And invite the animals? Jali could do flamenco, tapping the floor with her little cloven hoofs, leaping and jerking her head this way and that.

Mlle. Vicky said, "When I play this, you're princesses at a glittery ball. Do your best; I'll choose who'll be the princess, the important one. Go on, dance."

Turning into a princess was *doing something;* this was my chance. I ran, stopped, turned, leapt, stretched my arms to fly; my legs took the music's power and became powerful; the glowing floor charmed my bare feet; the air held me up a second before I came down to leap and turn again. I had long, wavy hair, no cowlick, no knobby knees, big eyes—the prince would find me enchanting. The way Mlle. Vicky looked at me, I knew I was going to be the princess. As we left, she told me I'd done great. Papi should have seen me. It was going to make my parents proud and everyone respect me, make it more bearable to be in the lowest level in class.

On the veranda, Nanny Fresia said, "I saw you dancing so good, little girl." In spite of her rotten-potato odor, I could have hugged her. I petted Gin. But the look the girls gave me reminded me of "Don't touch, it's ours."

AS I LAY TIED with bedsheets on the play bungalow's dining table, Patricia and Grace took off my sandals and socks to do *toro.* First they tickled my feet and ribs. I leapt and twisted, trying to fall off the table. Screaming would have made me a coward. Then the two discussed when to bring the *ortiga* twigs to pass over my feet. I heard a rousing gallop and cried, "Someone important! Something important happened!" It was true. No one in El Topaz went around galloping like that. The pace at El Topaz was genteel.

The girls stopped. "Even María Cristina gallops more softly," they said, and ran out.

I wiggled free. It had to be something urgent and therefore thrilling. Had Papi changed jobs and had they loaned him a horse?

A rider, not my father, flung himself off a sweaty horse. Maids called la Mamota: "Timoteo! Timoteo, el Señor Don Jaime's second foreman's here!"

La Mamota rushed out. "What brings you here so openly, Timoteo?" she asked sarcastically.

The girls giggled and whispered that Timoteo was always chasing women in El Topaz on the sly.

He removed his hat. "My *patrón,* Señor Don Jaime, sends this message to his distinguished neighbor, Señora Doña Mercedes: her distinguished brother-in-law, Señor Don Armando, has telephoned from the capital. He will arrive tomorrow. That's the message." He seemed relieved and pleased to have delivered it in one swoop.

La Mamota whimpered with joy. "My Amito! Coming tomorrow!"

Mlle. Vicky was thrilled. "Armando's coming! Armando's coming!" Tía Merce looked angry. My mother looked glad.

Melons said, "It's not elections, so Armando's not coming to pay for votes."

The girls were visibly disturbed but tried to hide it. "So what? Mumsy used to beg him to come all the time," Patricia said.

"But now she says he's a foggy," Gloria said.

"Not a foggy," Grace corrected her, "a phony fossil. Or is it a foggy fossil?"

"Now, this thing we heard Mumsy say in Galmeda on the phone . . ." Gloria started, but finished in Patricia's ear when she snapped at her. Was that big secret related to their uncle?

Timoteo turned his hat in his hands, giving Nanny Fresia side glances. She reddened and paled like the traffic light at San Toribio Street. From leather bags on his horse, he took a net of Lady Finger grapes and a huge cheese. "And Señor Don Jaime sends news about the strikes: the Public Force set fire to a Workers' Federation meeting, and two troublemakers burned."

"Serves them right," la Mamota said, accepting the gifts.

"Ay. Almost forgot about the lady," Timoteo mumbled, embarrassed. "Señor Armando's bringing the go-vern-ess, as he promised his brothers, Señor Don Miguel and Señor Don Toribio."

The girls looked at each other with horror. "So soon!"

Timoteo made a hand gesture. Nanny Fresia's traffic light turned red and she nodded. La Mamota saw it. "Timoteo, get your horse out of the garden. Manuel will give you some maté, and teach you what to tell your *patrón,* and hand you gifts for him. Then you go on your way, and don't you dillydally." She glared at him. Timoteo shooed away a wasp as he and his horse headed out.

"Show-off," la Mamota mumbled. She turned to Nanny Fresia. "I've got a mind to tell all, girl, the Good Virgin be my witness. I told you to stay away from Timoteo, a stranger, not from El Topaz, no man for a girl who wants no trouble. I swear to Our Sacred Lady, you see that Timoteo again, and Doña Mercedes will tell Don Jaime his number-two foreman's been coming to mess with a nanny." She choked from lack of air. "And remember, any girl that gets, you know what I mean, goes back to her filthy hovel. And if you don't mend your ways, you will too, I swear."

Nanny Fresia left crying. Amazing how someone so bossy could break down like that. What had scared her so? I hoped la Mamota wasn't going to change anything. I'd grown used to Nanny Fresia.

La Mamota threw herself into a frenzy of instructing chamber girls, asking for the cook, scolding and fretting. "The Saintly Virgin had mercy, keeping my Amito's ex away, that growler. Ay, I wish my Amito wasn't coming for what I know, but Queen of Heaven, You won't let it happen. Women are always after him; such a chunky build my Amito has. Why didn't he let me know sooner! And the Señora Governess coming! So much to do! You girls go take a bath right now!" Baths were la Mamota's way of solving everything.

"I hope we won't sit on a spitting volcano with this governess," Patricia said. "And Solita, don't you start chumming up to our Tío Armando like you did with some of the grown-ups."

I knew that wouldn't do me any good. How the tables had turned. The girls were more worried than I, because a governess made children behave, and I was going to be the princess.

We were surprised to see my mother coming to the bathroom to make sure Niceto and I got our hair shampooed properly.

10

"*WHERESHEEE?*" SANG A *YOHE* BIRD. ACCORDING to Nanny Fresia, this meant someone unexpected would arrive that very same day. Everybody was waiting for the uncle with the governess, so maybe it was my father!

Mlle. Vicky cried, "I hear a car! Solita, go check!" I had to get out of the pool, drip my way to the front gardens and return to tell her that only Beethoven, the earnest German shepherd, was there.

The girls swam and grumbled, "No wonder Mumsy says Tío Armando's a drippy fossil; imagine, bringing a governess." "At least he'll bring mountains of candy." "All he says is, 'polo,' 'tennis,' 'Horses in El Topaz are oxen' and 'Are you going to church?' " "He doesn't play tennis or polo either, just talks about it." "And he pays no attention to us; he only likes huge blond children. Mumsy says that's why he married a German."

This man wasn't going to like me at all. Grace whispered something about skiing and boarding school, and Patricia said they'd have to see. It was more and more irritating the way they kept hiding their big secret, but nothing I had tried to make them respect me enough to tell me, not even being brave, had worked.

A gallop made us run to the front veranda. It was a gray-haired man without a governess riding behind him. "Don Víctor Alfonso Lamperein!" all cried. So someone not expected had come.

"He's very important. What is he, Patricia?" Grace asked.

"A justice of the Supreme Court. He makes people do what's just. He owns the lands over there, and starts to gallop when he's almost at our gate, so people think he's galloped the whole way."

I asked how she knew that. "Look at his horse, dummy. It's always bone dry. A horse that has galloped is sweaty."

While the grown-ups in bathing suits and hats gushed, "Your honor!" the Supreme man told Manuel to give his horse plenty of water, as the poor fellow had galloped non-stop since home. Manuel managed to keep a straight face.

My mother seemed terribly pleased to meet the Supreme man. Her bathing suit, which she had made herself with a flounce to cover the bad hip, was too much like having nothing on. Her carefully combed ponytail made her look very young. Someday I could have long hair too, but they said it would be brown, like my grandmother's. Grown-ups always said you had something like someone in the family, which was silly, but for some reason it was pleasant.

The Supreme man sat under the magnolia to talk to the Genius, a shriveled old man who mumbled in a foreign accent. I proposed to the girls that instead of putting snakes in the governess's bed as they were planning to do if she was horrid, they could ask the Genius, who knew everything, what to do. Patricia said I was a goose liver, that he was only interested in things that were important to the whole entire world.

Mlle. Vicky cried, "I hear a car! Solita, go check!" Again I had to run to the front gardens; it was tragic to miss so much water fun. No one there but Beethoven. On my way back, a shadow came from the end of the passageway uniting the corridors. It was the Supreme man. He moved closer and closer to me, until I had to back off all the way to the corner, behind the huge doors kept locked at night. He patted my head. "Nice girl," he said, and slid his hand between my legs, "nice girl," then under my bathing suit. My chest grew huge with fear. A crossing breeze froze my wet hair. How did you tell an important man, whom my mother was so pleased to meet, to stop something? Beethoven barked; he withdrew his hand and left.

I stood by my mother's long legs. She was telling Tía Merce, "He's your brother-in-law. Don't you want your daughters to see their relatives?" Tía Merce seemed furious about something.

"Mami," I whispered in her ear, "the Supreme man . . ."

"Solita—"my mother's voice was low—"you know perfectly well it's rude to whisper in someone's ear. At your age . . ."

Tío Juan Vicente fearlessly slapped away a bee zeroing in on his pear juice. "I hope Merce's beloved brother-in-law brings some exotic fruit from his own hothouse tropical trees."

"Mami . . ." I tried to speak softly but not whisper.

"I hear a car!" Mlle. Vicky cried. "Solita, go check!" I saw the Supreme man stirring to get up from his canvas chair.

"Mami," I said desperately, "the Supreme man, he . . ." My mother's face said, What are you talking about? My finger discreetly pointed to the Supreme man. From the look on my mother's face, it was clear I had committed the grievous crime of pointing. "He . . . in the . . . he touched me in the passageway. . . ."

My mother made her no-nonsense face. "What are you saying?" she whispered quickly. It was rude to whisper to grown-ups, but not the other way around. "We'll talk later. Don't hang around by yourself anywhere."

"Pilar"—Tía Merce kissed one of the gift puppies—"Armando better not be a foggy pest with you. Oh, did you know he paid the church to have his marriage annulled?" My mother's face turned toward her.

"How about his heart malady, Vicky," Melons said. "Actually, some love that most. Who doesn't want to be a rich widow?"

Mlle. Vicky giggled and said impatiently, "Solita, go check!"

I ran fast, fast, to make it there and back in a flash, but there it was again, the big shadow. I went back and knelt next to Beethoven, who was lying on the gravel, his eyes alert, as usual. Normally he discouraged frivolous exchanges with children, but this time his eyes turned toward me. The Supreme man came closer. Beethoven sat up. I crouched behind him. The Supreme man froze. They eyed each other. The Supreme man said, "Nice dog, nice dog." Beethoven, totally above flattery, didn't move. The Supreme man gave a stiff smile, turned and disappeared down the passageway. I hugged Beethoven, which he didn't particularly appreciate, and ran back to the pool.

I hoped the girls wouldn't notice my distress and could tell me something. I said, "He's funny looking, the Supreme man."

"True, his front and his back don't match. In back he's round, but in front he's bony, with a hooked nose," Gloria giggled.

"Maybe God got some halves mixed up, and someone out there's running around with a skinny bottom and a fat face that don't match either," Grace said, turning in the water.

"You must be more respectful with a justice of the Supreme Court," Patricia scolded them.

There had to be some hugely important reason why my mother hadn't been furious at him. Not to raise waves was bigger than anything. Mothers had their own worries, their own motives that you couldn't understand. It had been my fault for not navigating well around hidden rocks. But even if it was my fault, what the Supreme man had done was wrong! I threw cool water on my face.

"I hear a car!" Mlle. Vicky boomed. I ducked under the water.

JUST BEFORE LUNCHTIME, a big, roundish car glided quietly through the front-gardens driveway. It took all the excitement out of arrivals to sneak up like that. The chauffeur let out a stocky man my father's age, dressed in white, as silent on his rubber-soled shoes as his fat car had been. With the arms of a sweater thrown over his shoulders and tied on his chest, he held a smoking cigar and a tennis racquet. There were no tennis courts here, so maybe he was on his way somewhere. La Mamota nervously gathered the girls. People, dogs, Jali and the guanaco drifted over from the pool to greet him. Tío Juan Vicente went to put on a record of funeral music and came back to smile impishly at Tía Merce.

"*Hola,* Tío Armando." The girls planted their compulsory kisses on the man's cheek and accepted huge bags of candy. My eyes scanned the cellophane bags eagerly and, yes! yes! lots of foil-wrapped bonbons for my ball! It was needed more than ever, since my father had come and gone without us. The girls took forever to open the bags; I did little leaps in place to keep myself from reaching out and ripping the bags right out of their parsimonious hands.

I didn't like the way the girls' uncle looked at my mother in her bathing suit, nor the way he hugged her. I didn't like the way my mother stretched her neck, unfocusing her eyes the way she did when men complimented her. Mlle. Vicky hugged him so vigorously her tiny suit slid toward the wrong places. Her big hat smothered him and forced him to push back his thinning hair.

Tía Merce hummed her chuckle. "You're a little early for

votes, aren't you, Armando dear? By election time the peasants will have forgotten your big *asado* and your red-wine demijohns."

He looked at her with a round, blank face. "Mercedes, have you acquired any decent horses? I presume the priest from Las Cabras is coming to say mass Sunday?" Jali took a nibble at his tennis racket. Instead of laughing, he swung it menacingly. It made me snicker. He didn't know that when you met a goat, a dog or a guanaco, you had to let them do their greetings first.

La Mamota mumbled her indignation about everybody receiving her Amito in bathing suits. She waited by the door. "La Mamota," he said, as if none of us knew who it was, and patted her arm.

"Now, you behave yourself, Amito. Do you think I don't know why you've come? Don't forget who you are. And do something about my girls going back to Galmeda. You must convince Doña Mercedes. And why didn't you bring your brothers Toto and Miguel?"

"How can I, Mamota, my brothers are always cruising the Atlantic to Paris and back."

To my great surprise, he came to say hello to me, then patted Niceto on the head. The girls immediately gathered around their uncle. They hadn't shown that much interest in him before, except for his candy, but now they acted proprietary, asking him about his horses. Tía Merce looked angrily at me too. All four did, though I hadn't talked to him, just as the girls had ordered!

Tía Merce said, "My dear brother-in-law, are you too busy with my guests' children to instruct your chauffeur to let Madame out of the car?" Everyone had forgotten about the governess.

Madame was small and wrinkled, and her trembling fingers fussed with a faded parasol and a hat with a cluster of wax cherries. We had to shake hands while being told she was to be our final authority. Madame told Tía Merce briskly, "I wish to be taken to my rooms, Madame."

"*Mais oui, mais parlez-nous en français,*" Tía Merce said.

Very erect, Madame replied, "I speak in French only with the children I've been hired to teach and with those who know the language. From your accent, Madame, you obviously do not. Now, Madame, if you please, meet me at ten o'clock sharp tomorrow at the library. You do have a library, of course."

"Of course." Tía Merce's eyes smiled as if quite on top of the situation, but she didn't have her usually confident chuckle.

"Tomorrow, Madame," the governess said, "we shall set the girls' class schedule, which shall start two weeks to this day."

"In two weeks?" Tía Merce asked. "I was counting on, well, I thought you could rest this weekend and start Monday. After all, the school year has already started, and the girls—"

"I never start until two weeks after my arrival, Madame. I wouldn't think of taking the risk of getting dismissed by some flighty mistress before I've had my vacation. Now, where are my rooms? Good day, Mesdames." She looked at la Mamota, who seemed reassured in the presence of someone who knew how to give orders.

Under la Mamota's direction, maids had scrubbed away dust, mustiness and spiders from three rooms for the governess and the school. La Mamota grumbled, "All girls schooling at once! My girls will be held back. I wager that child's never been in school. It's all because Doña Pilar's staying around—but she won't get her way; I've bought ten candles for the Virgin of Carmen! Ten!"

Jali inspected Madame's long skirt and gave it a good taste. Seeing this, the guanaco did the same. He looked pretty with a big red bow on his long neck, compliments of a concerned delegation from the kitchen. The bow was meant to keep away the evil eye, which guanacos tended to attract because of their delicate constitutions and arcane origins. Madame felt the tugs. She turned around, swinging her parasol viciously. Both animals knew how to duck, so she hit air. We covered our mouths politely to laugh. Madame's glance said, "I'll straighten you out, all right," and she walked toward her room with two wrinkled, wet spots on the back of her skirt.

THE GROWN-UPS CHATTED in wicker chairs under the white rose arbors. My mother motioned her head for me to say something to the girls' uncle. She had told me to go to him, wait to be asked something, and if he didn't, do it myself. About what? About anything: horses, tropical birds, exotic fruit trees. All I wanted to do was to stay away from the Supreme man. My mother had said to avoid him, that I was old enough to understand these things. What things?

Marco Polo told a very famous painter with a hatchet nose that unrest in Galmeda was getting out of hand; those Spanish exiles were good socialists but stirred the pot too much. The Walrus said he didn't want to hear about strikes. Tío Armando agreed. I summoned up the courage to stand at his side. My mother smiled. He didn't say anything, so I asked, "Why don't you like strikes?"

Tío Armando leaned toward me, "Pardon me?"

My mother smiled strangely. "Solita, I know you want to talk to Armando, but he's discussing serious matters; he'll talk to you later." I had done something stupid, had let my mother down.

The girls flashed their eyes at me even more angrily than usual. Something related to their uncle made their blood boil. Before they had time to think of *toro,* I proposed we do something naughty, like smoking. We made a moat in my room, with all our wash basins and chamber pots filled with water resting against the three doors. This was an excellent way to divert their displeasure. My brother woke up and stared at the smoke with wide-eyed admiration. Grace folded three middle fingers as if they were missing, so I knew what was coming. I ran to sit on a chamber pot, holding an imaginary newspaper. "Dr. Kaplan!" the girls shrieked. Suddenly a door opened. Nanny Fresia stepped right into a basin and we scrambled out another door.

Past the big library I saw the Supreme man and my mother, her tall figure stretched to replace a book. There were hidden rocks far more dangerous than even the dirty tricks the girls played on me. You couldn't trust anything. Or anybody. You had to navigate completely on your own.

AT DAWN I WAS AWAKENED BY A DEEP, URGENT ding-dong. It had to be the huge bell hanging from the towering oak in front of the gallery. The girls said it came from an ancient church burnt by lightning from Up Above because the parishioners had been doing gross things. The previous day had smelled like crushed bees from the maids polishing all the door knobs with Brasso, so it was Sunday. Maybe Papi was coming and it was being announced!

"Santa Virgen!" Nanny Fresia said. I asked what was wrong. She sighed with relief and reached for her Nivea cream. "Nothing, little girl. Today the good Padre Romualdo will come from Las Cabras to say mass. Go back to sleep."

She still hadn't learned my name. "Why were you so afraid?"

" 'Cause the bell also tolls when terrible things happen."

"You mean like war?"

"Like what? You sure come up with strange notions, little girl. The bell lets you know if a Christian's about to leave this life, or if mi Señora Doña Mercedes' going to make a judgment on somebody."

The psychiatrist kept saying that unless Mercedes showed better judgment she was going to harm herself; had all this something to do with that?

"I was afraid la Mamota had stirred up trouble about . . . somebody. She likes to stir up trouble whenever she can."

"Oh, you mean about you and that ponchoed man from the other ranch?" Her tin of cream banged in the cool darkness.

"You wicked little girl, the Devil be after you! What have you been nosing about in, you tell me right now!"

You never knew what would set Nanny Fresia off, but it wasn't scary. Nobody paid any more attention to her than to me.

"You better forget all about that, little girl. Today you better do well in mass and not make la Mamota mad; she can get you into a hornet's nest of trouble."

"Why does the bell toll when someone dies?"

"Little girl, is your name Solita or Miss Why? So we pray for the soul while it comes out and goes up, of course."

She did know my name. "Why?"

"Ay, Señorita! 'Cause it helps the soul get a better trip. Many things can happen on that long trip, even without the body tempting you to follow the Devil; it's clear as water!"

"So why do you care what happens to some traveling soul?"

"Little girl, the Devil be too busy spreading evils to hear you. Padre Romualdo says it's what Christians must do. Besides, it won't hurt to be on good terms with a fresh soul. What if it comes down after it's done with all the business it has to do Up There? Who wants to be on bad terms with a soul you can't even see? If you're smart, the minute the bell death-tolls, you start praying." I asked what was a death-toll. "Ay! Don't you know anything, little girl? Death-tolls are eight slow dongs, over and over. Why, the bell practically cries. You better learn the bell talk once and for all, and not ask dumb questions: For fire, fast dings nonstop. For accidents, ding-dong, ding-dong. For mass, ding-ding-ding. If troublemakers are around, five fast dings, stop. Payday, three short dings, one long dong. For judgments, three long dongs, three short dings. When an earthquake's over, slow ding-dong-dings. Don't know how you managed without me before."

"Why were you upset about the mass?"

"Who said that? Mass is the best, even better than a trip to San Ildefonso, the big port full of streets and ships. At mass you get on good terms with the Ones Up Above, the more the better, and ask them what you want. I asked myself to go to San Ildefonso, and went! and saw the sailors and one . . ." She sounded happy. "Today tell your wish and you're bound to find One in a mood to grant it. Padre Romualdo can give you a hand at it."

This sounded great. But Papi said mass was shameful and priests were bad. "Why will this Romualdo person give me a hand?"

"Little girl, the saintly Padre Romualdo happens to be the most important person in all these parts. He says God Up Above listen to everybody just the same, rich or poor. And you better do well in mass; la Mamota fancies she's the good padre's right hand; she eggs him on against folks. I heard the padre's going to chastise your Señora Mamá and mi Señora Doña Mercedes and Don Armando in today's sermon! To their faces!"

This wasn't so upsetting; Mami didn't go to mass. If I did well at mass, whatever that was, my wish would be for Papi to be waiting for me right outside the chapel. But then he would see me going to mass and be mad! For him to be waiting in Mami's room. Mass could be even better than a foil ball.

"How you managed without me before, little girl, I don't know." She spread a smell of face cream over potatoes.

True, Nanny Fresia did give me good information and was concerned about me. But without her, in the freshness of this pale light, I could have been using a stick to draw pictures on the wet gravel, to knock ripe loquats from the trees and to train the dogs to run after grapefruits, then spin around the garden paths eating juicy chirimoyas.

I FOUND THE GIRLS peeking in a salon window in their usual fashion, ignoring yellow butterflies flocking to a tiled planter.

"What happened to breakfast?" I protested.

"When the padre comes, there's no eating before mass."

"How often does he come?" This could be serious.

"About once a month, unless there's a sudden funeral, storm or baptism." Patricia always had precise information at her fingertips.

"So how do you eat?"

"You don't. You better not let la Mamota hear you talk about eating. We're going to mass soon. The grown-ups are talking to the padre after their dance class. Mumsy says it drives him stark-staring crazy to see the women in shorts, not to speak of Mlle. Vicky in her naughty maillot."

I took a peek. Tío Juan Vicente and some ladies flocked around a priest in a black frock, which my father said was sinister. Niceto was chewing something and reaching for the salt. My stomach leapt at the sight of bread and melon slices left over on the side tables. Evidently the no-eating rule didn't apply here. A fight started between the formidable platoon of the girls, la Mamota and this important priest on one side, and my stomach on the other. My stomach won. As I went in, all three girls shrieked.

What buttered bread! Above music called Verdi, which sounded like a frantic cow calling for her lost calf, the priest was telling Tío Juan Vicente, "God forgives our transgressions, my son, might even get a kick out of your costumes, but there's no excuse to shun His House. How long since you confessed? The Lord keeps track of these things, you know."

Tío Juan Vicente lowered his head like a dog who has stolen an egg or barked at the wrong person. "I will today, Padre."

No one noticed me drinking heavenly, forbidden café au lait, but I saw my mother laughing with Tío Armando. I should've stayed out and starved. He hid his cigar behind his hefty middle to lean over toward her. She pushed him back. Tío Armando was a pest. Mlle. Vicky and his lady friends didn't like this behavior either. He saw the priest observing him and went there. "I'm looking forward to your mass, Padre." He didn't know he was going to be chastised. Some ladies cried, "We too, Padre, we too!"

I went to ask Mami if I was going to mass. "Of course, my daughter. You don't have to believe what they do, but we must go along. Tolerance will give you a much better life, even in a Paradise like this one." Tío Armando came back. My mother asked him, smiling, "Did you confess your wicked ways?"

Near a boat-shaped melon slice left sailing on a game table, Tía Merce told Mlle. Vicky, "You know why they wear skirts? So you won't see when they get it up watching the women in scant clothing. I bet he has it up right now, what do you think?"

Mlle. Vicky laughed like a naughty girl and said, "Merce, you're terrible!"

I was trying to figure out what they were saying when the priest said next to me, "Come talk to me, my daughter, whenever you want." I swallowed a chunk of melon. He put his hand on my head. "Don't be shy." The issue was worse than being shy; it was the chunk creeping down like the curled iron elevator I rode once with my mother, to deliver painted photographs.

"You should eat more, my daughter, fill you up a bit. Look, there's melon over there." He made an impish smile and asked me questions about my favorite games. This was a very nice man with big feet! Could I tell him they hadn't let me eat on account of his mass? Ask him to chastise Tío Armando good and hard? While I was sorting this out, he turned to tell Tía Merce. "My daughter, these girls should be going to school. What are your plans for their schooling and their religious education?"

"You haven't met the governess?" Tía Merce asked defiantly. "Now, you must honor us and stay for lunch; we're having milk-fed piglets with wild asparagus. Please?" Tía Merce smiled at him as if he were her favorite friend.

"I'd be much obliged if you'd get your spiritual food by coming to mass, my daughter," the priest told her.

I wanted to continue talking with him, but Nanny Fresia, holding a lacy dress, a ribboned hat and sandals, called me from the door. Her plastered hair hid her face, and her lipstick so magnified her lips that all you could see was an angry mouth. "By orders of la Mamota, who believe me is spitting fire about your eating, you must put on these beautiful clothes and meet her at the garden gate to go to mass." She said it as if we were going to invade a country. I added to my wish list for Romualdo to zip up la Mamota's mouth.

My mother and Tío Armando left, saying, "See you at mass, Padre." My mother going to mass! Tía Merce sneered.

LA MAMOTA, her bosom decorated with a bouquet of violets, cut through a mob of peasants milling outside the chapel, itchy in their best clothes under the hot sun. She wore a veil and two-tone pumps with a window for the big toe. We followed in a line: Patricia, each twin nanny with a twin, me, and Nanny Fresia with Niceto.

La Mamota was flustered. In a way, this was good, because she refused to hear the girls trying to egg her on about my eating. She muttered about indecent outfits on a Sunday morning, what a way to receive the saintly padre in the Day of the Lord, Doña Pilar will be sorry for this, my Amito, what fools men can be, the good padre'll set them straight all right . . .

What did my mother have to do with the dancing? Wasn't it Mlle. Vicky who was teaching people here? It seemed they had acted this elevated long before my mother came.

The peasants started a big commotion when they saw the guanaco following us. He bent to taste a gold figurine from the shiny bracelet of one of Tío Armando's lady friends. Instead of pushing him away, she screamed. A big mistake. He didn't tolerate screams near his ears. "Don't scream, lady," everyone said, "or he'll spit." Fortunately Tío Armando's friend ignored us and screamed, "Get that beast away from me! Ayyyy!" The guanaco stretched his neck, and his slimy goo splattered right on target—always a perfect aim. The dripping lady stumbled. Tío Armando and Tío Juan Vicente carried her away, while the other lady friend and Mlle. Vicky laughed hushedly as they walked behind her. I laughed, until Tío Armando said that if Arturo ever brought that beast again, he was going to shoot it. Hushed laughs went around. The guanaco decided the place was too disorderly and went back to the gardens.

We climbed the chapel's steps. La Mamota hissed at me, "Keep your finger off your nose, you bad girl. You're entering the Province of the Lord." How silly to call this little chapel a province. "You better worship properly. Confess your sins; the heathen will be punished." While I tried to figure out what this meant, the girls studied my face, maybe wondering whether I knew how to worship. What I knew was that I had to copy what they did.

The chapel had a heady smell of cool flowers, old fabric and melting wax. We sat on a front velvet bench. Everywhere the candlelight fluttered on statues, bouquets and paintings. Up on the wall next to me, terrified people burned, twisting horribly in red flames. It made me hot. La Mamota's eye spied on me.

I came up with a list of wishes, headed by having my father arrive in the next second and for the nice priest not to chastise us. Wishing was great.

Madame sat down. The peasants filled benches and aisle, fidgeting, adjusting their head kerchiefs and crossing themselves every time they scratched. They got out of the way to let Tío Armando come in. My mother came behind him!

Suddenly the priest opened his arms. He had been so still in the candles' flickering auras, I hadn't noticed him. As he turned around, his eyes smiled at me! La Mamota bit her cuticles. The girls wiggled in surprise. All four watched me fumble, copying whatever they did. After a while it got soporific. I whispered to Gloria, "Will this priest go around covered with the tablecloth all the time or just in the chapel?" Gloria giggled.

La Mamota whispered furiously, "You are both punished."

Fortunately the padre didn't notice. Now I had to be extra careful. He gave a dense talk, wrinkling his cheeks and staring at Tío Armando and my mother, repeating strange words like "lust" and "concupiscence." My mother said you had to ask about words, or you'd remain ignorant, so I decided to step forward and ask. But my mother also said, "When in Rome . . ." and the girls didn't ask anything, so I stayed ignorant. Romualdo talked about Paradise, Adam and Eve, and couples and families staying together, the most sensible things I had heard in El Topaz. In Galmeda my father came home and told stories at the table; we were together. I had to talk to Romualdo and make him set things straight. I glanced back; my mother was gone. Tío Armando looked contrite.

After some "lusts" and "concupiscences," the padre made a pitch for meekness, which was strange. He pointed to a painting of big-eyed, potbellied children and pregnant sheep standing on a meadow. Evidently he also had a thing about big eyes in children. When I was introduced, people said it was a pity I wasn't a Spanish beauty like my mother.

Then they looked at Niceto and said, "My, what beautiful big eyes like his mother!" It was his redemption. Romualdo said if we respected all God's creatures, we would go to the Heavenly Meadows after we left this Valley of Tears. La Mamota whispered, "Pray, my little ones, to Mary, Mother of God, to take you there when you leave this valley."

The girls did as told. They had to be crazy. There wasn't a thing to eat, nothing to do in that painting. Here the girls had grass and sheep too, but also trees with papayas, lucumas, satiny chirimoyas, blue figs with honey droplets, red cherries, black cherries . . . La Mamota hissed in my ear about having no respect. It turned out everyone was on their knees with bowed heads.

By the time mass was over, my long wish list was much shorter; first, never to be in a war so a bomb could burn me like the people next to me on the wall, and second, for both my parents to be in my mother's room when we left the chapel. And if Papi wasn't there, for me to find a way to talk to the padre.

THINGS WERE LOOKING UP! Children were to have breakfast with the padre. A long table with rows of sweet buns and tin cups of hot chocolate was in the middle of the yard where carts were kept. He walked around without the tablecloth worn at the chapel, his big feet erupting under his black robe. He patted some of the peasant children's heads and told them loving words.

The children, stiff or wiggly in their frazzled sweaters and blemished skin, stared at us. Oddly, they looked at me, who in Galmeda was one of the least rich in the neighborhood, as one of the rich girls. But these children were poor in a different way. They couldn't be thrown out of their own country, they owned the country, but their parents didn't have wealth in their heads, like mine. They held the tin cups with their leathery, small hands. I knew it was sad. The girls stayed away from them.

What to ask the priest? A breeze shook the *charqui* hung to dry on strings tied between some carts, and teased my cowlick. Romualdo asked Patricia a question. Amazingly, the confident, the unperturbed, the commanding Patricia looked down and mumbled. When he talked to the twins, they giggled and tried to run, but la Mamota grabbed them by their dresses. The padre lamented that our mothers had not stayed at mass, but said it would serve them well that we had prayed for them, which hadn't crossed my mind.

I inched my way to him. He talked to me, without scolding or demanding anything; it was like chatting with the refugees. He said yes, guanacos, lambs, dogs, goats and we were all God's creatures. This was consistent with Nanny Fresia's ideas about animals knowing things. I couldn't bring myself to suggest that he scold Tío Armando in stronger terms, such as, Pack and leave right now, or, Tell my mother to stop asking me to be nice to Tío Armando, or, Tell the girls never to be nasty to me again. I asked why Tía Merce and the others used so many French words. He smiled. "Well, you do come up with odd ones. Because for Latin Americans, only the French have culture." I asked why. "The French helped the revolutionaries against Spain, and the revolution's ideas were very advanced. Also the French export their culture." I wanted to talk about his chastising my mother, but asked why in this country they hated Spaniards. "They don't, my daughter. Some who aren't educated hold on to traditions going back to the revolutionary days, when Spain was the enemy."

I told him I had asked for my father to be here, but he wasn't. He said it took time, that you had to keep praying. "We'll get him here, don't you doubt it." He and I were in this together. In that case, I didn't need to ask him to tell Tío Armando to leave; I could pray for that too. He asked me questions about my parents and Tía Merce and other guests. After I answered them, he said, "Ah, *sí*. This confirms what the housekeeper has been telling me. But you, you're a good girl, not a troublemaker at all. It's not your fault your parents are reds. And even they are under God's loving gaze. There are grave dangers ahead for them. Do you want to help your parents?"

"What do you mean, Romualdo?" I said.

"Call me Padre." He pressed his lips to keep from smiling.

Probably Papi would disapprove. Among the refugees I called everybody by their first name, but I said, "*Sí,* Padre."

"All right. We'll solve this. First you must pray for them. Then you tell your mama and your Tía Mercedes and her brother-in-law Armando, and your papa when he comes, to come see me. Tell them if they don't, I will come see them. Will you do that?"

How could I tell him what Papi might say if I told him that a priest asked that he go see him? "*Sí,* Padre."

"Good girl. You do want more chocolate, don't you? That's my girl." He filled my cup and turned to the other children. Padre Romualdo would bring good things, stop the dangers he said were ahead. It was delicious chocolate.

In the bathroom I asked the girls why they wanted to go to those meadows praised in the chapel. Patricia asked me if I understood the padre's sermon was directed to my mother. I said it wasn't, that my mother had left. Precisely, Patricia said, because she had been scolded.

I told Patricia she was saying that because of la Mamota's lies, but Padre Romualdo hadn't given la Mamota much attention. She and Grace taunted me about licking the padre's shoes. Being a shoe licker had never occurred to me, but saying so sincerely would be cowardly and lead to further humiliation. Acting uppity or openly disregarding them would be foolish. I had to change the subject and hope for the best. Padre Romualdo was going to be my friend, no matter what. There were some people you could trust, after all. "Solita, wise up," Patricia said. "We don't like what's going on either. We can help you."

Berta, Tía Merce's grouchy personal maid, finished cleaning the bathroom and left. A sliver of a cobweb up in the corner of the ceiling caught the light and made a smirk, making fun of Berta, who had missed it. "She'll come around," Patricia told the twins as I was leaving.

12

DOING BATHROOM THINGS WAS PERFECTLY RE-spectable, so my mother couldn't get too upset if I spent so much time in the little bathroom that I never had a chance to talk to Tío Armando. Something interesting was always going on there; a bug or two engaged in every manner of activity in the bathtub. Some took a trip out the drainage holes. Some peered with their antennae out the faucet, deciding to come out. Some went up the tub and, at the vertical part, skied down. Sometimes things turned slippery like that. If a bug did nothing, you could bend while still on the toilet and give it a gentle nudge with your nail tip, putting it immediately into frantic action.

"Solita, Solita!" the girls called urgently. Even if Tío Armando was coming to talk to me, I had to get up slowly, for sitting for long periods bonded you to the seat, and getting up fast could nearly rip off your skin. Your behind and legs were left with a sore red circle, but it was well worth it.

The girls said Tío Armando had been summoned to Las Cabras by Padre Romualdo, so I could come out, and we had to hurry to rescue drowning kittens. Padre Romualdo's words at mass had stirred them to noble causes. We ran to the river. As we undressed, I reminded them it was dangerous, that we had almost drowned once trying to save baby mice, that the river was higher, that everybody would see us drowned in our underwear. "What's the matter, Solita, are you scared?" I was, but said no. "Solita, you know very well that we beg and beg, but they still give this ridiculous argument that they want no more than twenty cats in the houses." We made a chain, drier in order of importance: Patricia dry, I hip-deep in water. Coca-Cola whined from shore. My hand asked Gloria's to hold on tighter. The package with kittens wavered, got closer, and I picked it up.

We placed a cat with large teats with the kittens, under the floor rafters. She dried them with her tongue's built-in towel. She would keep them hidden until they blended in with the rest of the cat population. The girls had been good to meek creatures. Maybe mass worked for the rich, though my father said it was bad for the poor. Padre Romualdo was making things safe.

MADAME'S CLASSES weren't what they'd been billed to be. We didn't find out amazing things about the universe, which a refugee had said included everything from the atoms you couldn't see spinning to the Martians you couldn't see digging canals. We had to look at absurd drawings of lopsided farm animals that looked nothing like real ones. They were useful to man because of their wool, milk and hide, the book said. During the lessons Jali kept kicking the door; it was normal for a goat to want to be with girls who were her friends. But Madame was indignant; she couldn't stand Jali's odor, which was the proper smell of a healthy goat. It didn't make sense to learn about animals on French farms, instead of about the ones here in El Topaz, especially about what Jali wanted.

Madame was contemptuous of everything in this country, except Señor Armando Larraín, who had had the good sense to hire her and was a devotee of Emperor Bonaparte. When she made us read, I tried to do it like the girls, and was mortified that she noticed my accent. But Madame was pleased to learn I was born near the French border and my grandmother was French. She said Spaniards were *sauvages* because they liked bullfights. No matter how much your whole family thought they were awful, people decided that if you were Spanish you loved them. Did I think all Frenchmen loved the guillotine? That everybody in the New World shrank heads? But Madame said at least Spaniards were Europeans, sort of, and appeared reassured to have another one in the room. She made it clear that my standing was far above the girls'.

This shocked all four of us considerably.

My time of trial arrived when she ordered us, in order of size, to go to the blackboard and write the multiplication tables. The girls whizzed by, writing numbers as if possessed by demons. When it was my turn, I waited to be possessed by the multiplication tables. A *puri* bird sang. Jali kicked the door. Finally Madame said angrily, "Madame Larraín was right; you should be in a lower level." It was upsetting, but it restored the flow of things. Not knowing the multiplication tables had rescued me.

In spite of the girls' multiplication wizardry, when we wrote compositions, Madame told them that in France they wouldn't be allowed in first grade. She was glad that mine was good, because she had been instructed to make sure I could write at my age level in French schools. Three blue gazes turned grimly on me. Patricia kicked the twins, her way to warn them to keep mum, but they hadn't said a word, so this was probably related to the big secret, although I didn't get a clue. "Tomorrow we shall learn how milk is useful to man," Madame said.

Jali kicked the door more feebly. A bird outside said, *"Oui-oui-oui-o."* Even the birds were speaking in French now.

THE GROWN-UPS HEADED for the salon in hoop skirts and satin knee breeches to practice the minuet. Tío Armando, back from Las Cabras, complained that the good padre had lectured him about matters of a very personal nature. What was a personal nature? I wanted to hear more, so I told the girls it was too bad they couldn't watch the minuet. As I expected, Patricia said, "We'll watch it," and went to look for la Mamota. Gloria told her her big toe hurt. As la Mamota bent down to examine the toe, Patricia lifted a large key from a ring under her starched apron.

The key opened the door to the surplus room, adjacent to the salon. As we grew accustomed to the dark, a twin pram and a musty stuffed condor appeared, then polo mallets, a tilting toy house with all the furniture jammed into one bedroom, two stuffed hawks, trunks, guns and pistols, crocodile bags, little porcelain shepherds, cats and naked women stretching like panthers, pictures of old people with blank eyes like Tío Armando's, of horses with blank eyes like Tío Armando's, of beach houses and old houses and huemuls—strange goat-deer that existed only in the Andes—broken-stringed guitars, iron bulls, plaster ballerinas in tutus, which my father said were *cursi,* and other odd shapes. The girls took a second here and there to become reacquainted with some, but didn't lower themselves to get too sentimental.

It must have been sweet to plunge into times past like that. Everything we owned was in remote Spain. When my father had burst into the house yelling that our city had fallen to the fascists and we had to flee, my mother handed his mother a bag she'd been packing with valuables, just in case—heirlooms like photographs, jewels, ivory fans, combs and mantillas with precious stones—while she carried me. My grandmother was so nervous she had to vomit. On the way out, she took the bag, only it was another my mother had packed with unimportant papers. On the other side of the border, in France, Spanish money wasn't accepted, and vendors agreed to exchange bits of food only for valuable items. My grandmother opened the bag to get a jewel to pay for bread, and there they were—old papers. All we had were the jewels my mother had put on herself, my grandmother and aunts. Instead of being furious, my mother asked my grandmother, who was French, "Do you think they'll exchange this bag for a radish?"

The girls pushed a table against a door and put a big, then a small trunk on top, saying this was how they saw the grown-ups playing Who's the Murderer? in the dark, and in the dim light saw many guests reaching for breasts and behinds of people they weren't married to. We carefully climbed up, unhooked the trap window above the door and presto! we were over the salon! There were other observers; the guanaco peered in from an outside door.

Mlle. Vicky asked for Gunther and was told the precious girl had taken him to the playhouse. Her mouth puckered and she grabbed Tío Armando. Up on our perch, we smiled; this was fancy. Tío Armando, still in his white clothes, fled and asked my mother to be his partner. "Tío Armando's dancing the minuet!" Patricia whispered. "Mumsy's probably going to get him into a terrible smiling fight." Evidently my mother's unfocused eyes meant an acceptance, because she put her hand on his upturned palm.

The music made me want to leap, which would have made us crash with untold damage to ourselves and the girls' memories. I couldn't wait for the next dance class to be the princess.

"Elegantly erect!" Mlle. Vicky commanded.

Shoulders lifted, chests pushed forward, behinds went back; each had a different notion of what elegantly erect was. At bowing time, Tío Armando, his hair falling over his eyes, bent in the wrong direction. Tía Merce said, "How you adore showing off your lovely rear end, *mon cher* brother-in-law." My mother managed not to laugh. Then they had to do a two-way chain, but the more they tried to keep the flow, the more it got tangled, until everybody was twisting and laughing. In the confusion, Tío Armando had the nerve to sneak up and hug my mother. She stretched her neck politely with a strange smile; was that being pleased or not? Padre Romualdo had to get rid of him; he had to.

The Walrus whispered something about Tía Merce to Melons. We turned our heads, straining to hear. Melons said, "If you want to know, she's three-fourths hetero, one-fourth homo." He shook his head.

Tío Armando told my mother, "Your eyes are two black moons. Come to my horse farm." How ridiculous; the moon was one and white. My mother said she couldn't. "To Galmeda, then. I know, Mercedes won't go, but surely you can think of something she'd want to do in the city." My mother asked him to stay here, that she needed lessons from a real horseman. "There're no horses here, Pilar, only oxen. And nothing to do; no tennis, no polo. But there's Mercedes, always breathing down our necks. And that priest." The girls wiggled in discomfort. Usually men acted idiotic around my mother, but Tío Armando's way was more cocky and thoroughly hateful.

La Mamota showed up at the salon's door, shooed the guanaco away, made a face of disgust and left. "I'm stiff," Patricia said. "And there's nothing fancy." We climbed down.

"Patricia, you say Solita's mother's not distinguished, but she gets invited to Tío Armando's house in Galmeda and we don't."

Patricia seemed furious. "We do. You just don't remember."

"Oh," Grace said, reassured, "so what we heard Mumsy say in Galmeda couldn't happen either?"

For the first time, Patricia gave Grace a dirty look. "Didn't you hear?" she snapped. "Tío Armando told Tía Pilar to convince Mumsy to go to the city to visit him, because Mumsy never does."

Why were they so angry? If we went to Galmeda, I didn't want to go near their *tío*'s house. They should see the cheery streetlamps in San Bernardo Square. How to tell Padre Romualdo about all this? We put everything back, so no one would suspect that something alive and in operating condition had been in the surplus room.

I PRETENDED TO LOOK for the delicious, creamy fruit pod of the vine climbing the smoke tree. Patricia had ordered me to spy near the kitchen. We feared our rescue had been discovered. If they poisoned the mother cat, we'd have to milk a nursing dog into baby bottles, tedious work we had done for baby mice when a mother was trapped. Several servants drank maté on the kitchen's terrace. "True, now I need an extra girl just to feed more and more cats," the cook complained, her fat, blotchy legs set wide apart. "Always in my way they are, the cursed animals. My feet hurt from kicking cats all day."

"Rosalina, you're the best cat kicker in the county," the squat butler told her. "Any good soccer team would hire you."

"I just hit 'em with my broom," Tía Merce's chambermaid said. "The accursed creatures come from all over, 'cause the word's gotten around there's food aplenty in the houses."

"See? I'm such a good cook even the cats love it," the cook said, and they all laughed. It was discomforting to see people connected with me in so many ways, whom I really didn't know, displaying so many mouth gaps where teeth used to be.

"A baffling problem," Manuel, the head butler, said. Because he had worked years ago in a police station in Topotilla, he considered himself above the servants.

"Silvestre, the cheese maker, says it's the old Devil at it," a kitchen helper complained. "I won't throw packages in the river again; if they're little devils, they'll come haunt me at night."

"You'll do as told," the cook said, but she looked worried. "We'll ask the padre to do holy spraying in here." The thin pots-and-pans man, who manned the shop at the cart yard, disagreed. "Better keep the Devil occupied with cats than doing worse damage."

"The padre's coming anyway. La Mamota told him all about the *patrones;* she told me that herself. She confronted Señor Don Armando on coming courting. Just finds foreigners interesting, he said; nothing serious, he promised. But I got these two eyes in my face and can plainly see Señor Armando's got the arrow in his heart good and firm. I can see it, but men are like moths; don't mind getting too close to the pretty fire, then zap! it gets 'em. The Devil's always hard at work, I'll let you know. . . ."

"Devil's not my worry," Berta, Tía Merce's bath maid, said. "I'm praying that the Spanish Señora will convince Señora Doña Mercedes to go to the city; she's trying. I can sure use some nice rest and peace."

The cook got her soft body up. An orange cat got in her way. She was going to kick it but made a careful detour instead.

I reported back that their talk was too odd to understand. Patricia said the parts about Padre Romualdo, moths, and our mothers' trip were strange, but she was satisfied about the cats part.

"SOLITA, come out of there, we are all going for a walk." My mother stood at the little bathroom's door. "You've been as social as a mountain goat; I expect better of you. Be nice to Armando. We're heading toward Víctor Alfonso's; speed it up."

The Supreme man's ranch? I decided Beethoven should go too. Also, I could pet him to avoid having to be charming to Tío Armando; Beethoven was the only animal Tío Armando didn't insult. Beethoven had protected me, though nobody knew it. Even he acted as if he hadn't. He wanted no thanks or fuss made; that's the way he was. It occurred to me that Beethoven was a just dog. In country estates nobody, not even justices, understood a thing about justice, unlike in stories, where a valiant knight or wise king always came to put things in order and punish the bad ones.

Cocktail ran from me to Beethoven and started to flirt. The other dogs got out of the way, expecting trouble. Cocktail knew how to get himself into embarrassing situations. Although he acted like a full-blooded fox terrier, this was highly contested but couldn't be settled because no one in El Topaz knew who his father was. He acted like a female, but maids said he was confused and was male. He liked big dogs.

Beethoven didn't take flirting kindly; he was a serious dog. He did night patrol, so during the day he guarded and took short naps. When his growling failed to work, he was forced to show his teeth. The other dogs sat at a respectful distance, glancing out of the corners of their eyes.

Grown-ups, including Tío Armando, were leaving the gardens. I bent down to pet Beethoven. Like everyone else, I had failed in all my previous attempts to become his friend. He made a tolerant face but didn't wag his tail. He always let you know his position in any situation. Although he had no time for frivolities such as playing with girls (not even one who knew how to take things seriously), protecting a girl was part of his job.

The girls, with the animals flocking eagerly around them, came to hurry me. I tried to make Beethoven act as if we were friends to impress them, inviting him to go with us. Obviously he thought it beneath his dignity and above and beyond his duties to join a collection of girls, a goat, a guanaco and a bunch of scatterbrained dogs.

"Solita, don't be a silly ass. You know Beethoven's a party pooper," the girls said. "He won't even come when *we* tell him."

I persisted; I insisted. Reluctantly he finally accepted my invitation. The girls were stunned. I was thrilled.

On the road it was nice to walk with the grown-ups, but not at the risk of having to be a charming girl for Tío Armando. Luckily the guanaco didn't nibble on him. Tía Merce said, "Pilar's so *merveilleuse;* when we ate at their pensione, not two silverware pieces matched; isn't it divine?"

The girls called me to the rear and asked me to stay with them to avoid being near my mother. I asked why. Patricia said, "It's awfully dumb of you to do as your mother tells you and be nice to our *tío*. Even kittens know where danger is."

I said there was nothing wrong with being nice to people.

"It seems you're too stupid to understand, Solita. Don't you know your mother's out to catch our *tío*? You want to help her?"

I stomped on the green pod I'd been carrying, squashing it to an oozing and disgusting mess, and told them they were full of beans, because my mother always got attention from men, even from Tío Juan Vicente, Marco Polo and the famous hat man. I sped up to put distance between us. My mother made a motion for me to get closer. I asked her if we were going to Galmeda.

"No, my daughter; but Merce's been wanting me to go with her, and maybe she'll convince me." Tío Armando, with the sweater behind him and his cigar, grabbed my mother's arm, as if she, being tall, would fall without his stocky support. When my mother and father took us for walks to the outskirts of Galmeda, she sang songs, then we sat for a snack, and we looked at each other, then Niceto and I wanted to run and our parents said, "Don't go too far," and the air was fresh in our faces.

"Armando, Solita wants to ask you something," she told him.

I looked back at the girls. They observed me. After much thought I asked, "Do you like horses? Do you like Beethoven?"

He smiled, a little surprised, and said, "Yes, a great composer indeed."

"I like him too," I said, "but he's very slow, too slow, so I'll see that everything is all right," and I ran back without looking at my mother.

Beethoven hid behind a tree. Then he headed home to his patrol duty at a dignified pace. I ran after him, calling him wildly. He came back with undisguised reluctance. I kept an eye on him and caught him at his disappearing trick. He stood behind a tree, his head hidden from us, the rest of him visible, the black tail up in suspense. He thought we couldn't see him. He was surprised when I called, "Beethoven, c'mon, come with us." We laughed. Beethoven's tail moved with embarrassment and puzzlement, as if saying, How could they see me when I couldn't see them? Again, reluctantly but politely, he rejoined us, but soon enough we got absorbed bickering, and the next time I looked back, he was gone.

Luckily the grown-ups turned back long before we got to the Supreme man's ranch. They wanted to play Who's the Murderer? The girls exchanged giggles. Ultimately I had to admit defeat about Beethoven. If animals were put here to help us, as Padre Romualdo said, Beethoven had his own ideas about how. But Padre Romualdo was helping in other ways.

WE SHOOED AWAY LOCUSTS, beetles, milkweeds, around the creamery, the pig house, the camouflaged underground study of the girls' father, looking for the kitten Patricia said was missing. How nice to work as a group. Grace told me, "Reach into this hole under the rabbit house with your small hand; it's big enough for a kitten." I touched the kitten and pulled it by one furry little leg. When it came out, it was a tarantula! My arm jerked so violently it could have thrown a horse over the adobe wall!

When I stopped churning inside and shaking outside, I observed the girls. They were very quiet.

That night I asked Nanny Fresia if she could tell where tarantulas lived, but she said not to mention them or you'd fetch some from the rafters, and went on about Imbuche, the *ánima* of caves. I was beginning to realize where I stood in relation to Nanny Fresia. In daylight, although she was a bossy nanny hovering above me, she was careful not to ask anything too unreasonable; only certain ceremonies were to be ordered by her and obeyed by me. But at night, with our voices going back and forth from the same height, I understood not only that her concern for me went beyond her official duties, but that she wasn't really above me.

Being above or below someone was disconcerting. I had known about people worse off than we were, who stumbled about in a fog of ignorant confusion: yelling street vendors; paper collectors pulling their two-wheeled carts in the rain; drunks stretched on curbs like debris from street repairs; harried children delivering hot meals to workers, doing errands all day instead of going to school; women and children with matted hair stretching their arms for a peso; people who got bread or fruit from my mother and made my father make a speech about socialism and labor—people who made you sad, who made you mindful of what your mother told you, so you wouldn't end up like them. But they weren't below or above us; they were confused. Everyone in El Topaz was trapped below or above somebody, with Tía Merce way up there at the very top.

The floor boards creaked; were tarantulas squeezing through? "Nanny Fresia, when is Padre Romualdo coming again?"

"Tomorrow," she said sleepily.

The next day Tío Juan Vicente announced that he was going to be dropped at the port of San Ildefonso, where he would sail to Majorca, to a house full of balconies that belonged to the famous hat man. And Tío Armando's chauffeur took his car out! He said he was leaving because he wasn't going to put up with a priest pestering him. Tía Merce was so happy she smiled at me, and I was so happy I talked to Tío Armando as if he were a refugee. This time my mother was pleased. The way Tío Armando repeated some whisper to my mother before entering the car, and she finally nodded in response, was ugly. I wished I could take back my friendly conversation. But things were looking up.

Had there really been a kitten missing?

13

"A DIVINE IDEA, PILAR! WE'LL GO TO GALMEDA TO see the great Margarita Xirgu, the best actress of all time! Let's leave right now!" Tía Merce said. She absolutely had to get a Correa turban to go see Margarita Xirgu. They would stay at the Ritz Palace, where you pressed a button in your room and a little man appeared to bring you whatever you wanted, the girls said. They liked to press the button all day for the little man to bring them paper-thin slices of sugar-edged ham. They just ate the sugared edges. I didn't believe the little-man story, but they swore it was true. Papi had bought paper-thin ham once for a picnic. Maybe he and Mami would go on a picnic by a river. No matter how much I begged, she said she couldn't take me to Galmeda.

After they had left, there were no guests, no guanaco, fewer and fewer summer fruits in the trees or bats in the corridors at dark. The servants had a field day crying to their favorite songs, which they played loudly. Patricia bossed us more than ever. Madame was our final authority, but she only told us about farms or played Monopoly with us, with the bank on a chair next to her. She was amazingly lucky—always fell on Boardwalk and Park Place, never on Luxury Tax, which was in between, and always had money. One time I leaned to scratch my foot, and with disbelief saw Madame's hand swiping two thousand-peso bills from the bank.

La Mamota commanded everybody furiously and mumbled, "Instead of being in school, my girls are here, hostage to her ambitions. She's stringing them both along; if she ensnares him, she'll give her husband the split ticket; if not, she'll wait for another big fish to swim by. But she's going to come back empty-handed, isn't she, Holy Mother?" She forbade us to go to the cart yard to slide down the corn piles.

I asked the girls why. "Because when Mumsy's not here, the maids sneak out to meet *peones* and do dirty things that peasants do."

When la Mamota went to her siesta, I quietly followed the girls to the cart yard. By the repair shop, we heard hushed noises. We tiptoed closer. In a dark corner, a maid had her apron up and her legs apart, in front of a *peón.* They heard us and ran through the back. "We never get to see what they do; they always hide," Gloria complained. No wonder the girls wanted to come to the cart yard; learning anything about the no-name thing was hard.

While sliding the corn warehouse metal doors to go in, Grace said, "Queca Echevarría found a peephole to their servants' quarters, and she and her cousin see their maids doing . . ."—she did the fingers gesture used in their nun school—"with her brothers, and the maids open their mouths like caverns."

"What a liar," Patricia said. "I know she made the peephole herself."

"Then we should make one," Gloria said, always practical.

Someone scurried in the corn-smelling dark. I panicked; what if this was a girls-style trap? Or an army of tarantulas?

"Who's there?" Patricia asked. Nobody answered. "All right, the twins will wake up la Mamota and bring Manuel." Patricia was the bravest human being on earth.

A tall shadow emerged, saluted with a hat and left. Another shadow came forward: Nanny Fresia! She whined, "Please, Missy Patricia, please, don't tell." Nanny Fresia whining like a helpless creature! I blushed with embarrassment.

"That was Timoteo, from the Undurragas'," Patricia said. She traded with Nanny Fresia a promise of silence for one never to interfere when they wanted to do things with me. While we slid down the high corn mountain yelling and laughing, the other life of Nanny Fresia, the traitor, whirled in my brain.

DURING MADAME'S LESSON, a blanket of heavy air descended on us. Even outside, the air was oddly thick. It made the maids cross themselves, recalling horrible earthquake disasters when the sky had come down with this color and denseness. Jali kicked the door. A *turura* outside sang, *"Mitia-mitia-tia-tia."* According to Nanny Fresia, this meant someone was coming to fix things. Today it had to be my parents.

Madame said, "Now, we shall write a composition about the country." This woke me up; writing what you wanted was the redeeming feature of Madame's classes. I wrote about a spring maiden tiptoeing to make the clear rivers flow and the fields bloom. It was fun. Jali kicked the door. Madame complained of our mothers' irresponsibility leaving us here with no car, no telephone, no medicines, days away by horse to a doctor, an illiterate woman in charge of the house, peasants with typhoid, TB, rabies. She'd left Galmeda because of too many strikes and demonstrations, just as when she'd been at Herr Wagner's house in Hamburg: food riots, communist plots, a worthless mark. She thought she was over the hill then and was only thirty-three! And what if she should take ill?

When Madame read our compositions, she wrinkled her nose, as if swallowing cod liver oil. My handwriting was awful, my composition was good; it showed I had a European sort of background. However, the girls' were a *crime,* a shameful *crime*! They would be taking extra writing lessons; I didn't have to.

The girls steamed. Delight and worry struggled in me. Why should I be permitted to be one in four only when the girls decided so? Why did Mami always say I had to be like rich people? Wasn't our final authority saying I wasn't inferior? Delight won.

Suddenly the door burst open; Jali ran to the table and leapt on top. We sprang up to applaud uproariously. Madame rose with indignation, shouting, *"Quelles sauvages!"*

Jali stood triumphant on the table, accepting our applause. This performance had to be better than the great Margarita Xirgu. Nannies came running. They tried to unseat Jali from her won territory. Naturally she refused to budge. Eduardo, the gardener, had to come with a rope to take her away.

"YOU BET MARIO KNOWS all about la Señorita Madmosil Vicky and that handsome son of Zacarías Romo, el Gonzalo. Mario won't fire him 'cause he's afraid of him. Never thought I'd see the day when Mario'd be afraid of anybody," the cook said in the herb garden. "El Gonzalo's been going to meetings in Topotilla with men from Galmeda; Víctor saw him, when he went to sharpen his knives, and they mentioned those bad words: 'agrarian reform' and 'strike.' El Gonzalo's looking for trouble. And Señorita Madmosil Vicky . . ." The cook saw us, and changed the subject to the menu for la Señora Madame.

To my delight, this aroused the girls' curiosity. Mlle. Vicky, the only guest still around, slept all day and was gone all night, a mystery of no interest for the girls; they didn't have a princess role riding on it. But now we went to snoop in Mario's domain. He was reviewing some seeded flats, limping in his white suit. Mario knew everything that had happened in the past in El Topaz, unlike the servants, who knew everything that was about to happen from the hints of *ánimas,* candles, the wind, dreams and dogs. "Beautiful day, Missy Patricia." Mario lifted his hat with a zigzagging arm. The twins kept their distance. He had been a *domador,* they said, "the man who breaks the horse's will." But the horses had taken their revenge, breaking all his bones. The *yerbera,* who used simple herb remedies, and la Tomasa, the *curandera,* who used complicated ones, had cured his wounds, but had put his bones back together wrong, so nothing fit properly.

Patricia smiled with a dimple, which meant she was serious. "Mario, when are we going to have Christmas with snow, like in the movies? I bet Mumsy would love it." Patricia was a wily one. Just when I decided the girls were a total loss, it turned out there was so much to learn from them.

Mario leaned a shoulder to allow his bent arm to place a label stick on a flat of seedlings. "You'll have to ask la Mamota about having snow for Christmas, Missy. For celebrations and parties, I'm only in charge of things that grow. I'm readying to have lots of flowers blooming when your Señora Mumsy gets back; tulip poppies, wishbones, gaillardias, sweet alyssum . . ."

"I thought snow was made of petals. Mario, did you know Dr. Valdés can put you back together right again? He's coming soon."

"Well, Missy, it's one thing for a Christian to get his bones broken by animals, following the Will of the Good Lord for this Valley of Tears. But only a fool'd let another mortal, like himself, even a learned doctor, break his bones *on purpose* to fix them, with the Good Lord having not a thing to do with it. La Tomasa did what she could, and I'm still here."

Patricia was ready. "Mario, is el Gonzalo dangerous?"

Mario shifted his weight, making another arrangement of Zs. "Well, Missy, a man can be dangerous if he's provoked." Patricia waited. "Well, Missy, they say he hit his folks. They say he's the one who killed the oldest Riquelme boy. Only the Good Lord Up Above knows what happened. El Gonzalo keeps a quick temper and a sharp knife. But here he does his work and gets his meal just like anybody, and his due pay at payday just the same, and how much of a fight can you pick with an onion plant, Missy?"

"He's always alone by himself, out by the raulis, Mario?"

He looked at the grape arbor, buzzing with bees sucking the grapes split from sugary old age. "Well, they say things, that he gets visited by a guest from the houses, but, what would a man who can't even get on a horse know, Missy? It's for your Señora Mumsy to see that no harm comes to her lands and her guests."

Patricia turned in triumph, and she deserved to be well pleased with herself. I would have been scared even to try.

Bare-torsoed, toasted men with spades ran water through the furrows. The big-muscled *peón* by the onions was minding his own business, digging. None of the parts of his face under his frazzled hat was at odds with any other. We didn't contemplate him for long, because he looked up and gave us a fierce look, ignoring some orange butterflies that crossed between us. We ran back to the houses. Why would Mlle. Vicky, with her dancing limbs, have anything to do with this scary man?

"It's terrible," Patricia said in a tone that scared us. "Like playing with a peasant, with their stiff hair and knotty knees." They didn't say anything about me. Things were looking up.

"The only good thing about Mlle. Vicky and el Gonzalo is that she's always tired, so we don't have to rehearse for the stupid dance presentation. But what if other guests hear about it!" Grace worried. "If Tío Armando gets a whiff! And the governess!"

For the first time, the girls thought that something that wasn't just about them was tragic. They decided to tell la Mamota that we were riding to the glass-enclosed Virgin, half a kilometer away. That afternoon, instead, we headed for the distant rauli mountains to fetch Mlle. Vicky. This was fine with me. But on the way we got into a big fight because Gloria said writing was ridiculous, and Patricia added, "And useless. Mumsy doesn't have to know how to write. Only people who have to work at boring jobs do." This was scandalous. My mother said writing was one of the most *importantísimo* things ever. Another of the mystifying things the girls said that were hard to contradict, but I tried.

They got very hot. "Did you know that we saw your mother and our Tío Armando in our house in Galmeda? They didn't see us, and, among other things, they talked about you."

A thump like a fierce wind hit my temples. Patricia calmed down. "If you'd do what we tell you, you'd be better off. We know things that you don't." An unnecessary comment.

Instead of lifting puffs of dust, breezes went up to disturb the leaves in the trees. By the time we were at Cross Hill, branches were shaking and making scary moans, so we gave up on finding Mlle. Vicky and returned to the houses.

Papi's motor bicycle was parked under the canopied sugar pine! Nanny Fresia was right about *tururas!* Padre Romualdo was right about asking! I ran, ran, ran . . . Papi was behind streaks of cigarette smoke on Mami's bed, Niceto on fours around him, pretending to be a cat.

14

I RAN JUBILANTLY TO PAPI AND THREW MYSELF ON him. "Watch it, love! We're getting burned!" he laughed, putting his cigarette on the night table's ashtray. I beamed. He looked at me. "Is riding horses as boring as it looks?" This took me aback. I liked horseback riding a lot now. Papi was making fun of what had taken me so much courage and effort to learn. My cheeks blushed.

"Well, treasure, I have stupendous news! I have a great job, will be in Galmeda every week, and, you won't believe this—are you ready? Are you ready?" I was so ready my toes were about to fall off! "I've rented the whole pensione! All of it! Well? What do you say?" His arm under me shook me.

How could you be happy all at once about something so enormous? You could be happy about one thing at a time. Starting with the garden gate. I could open and close it anytime, without the landlady scolding me. "Are we going right now?"

"It's not so simple, treasure. I must talk to your mother. The landlady has to move out. I promised to keep two pensioners there; they'll occupy two of the three bedrooms, but they are there only at night. You children will move back very soon. So what do you think? Isn't it stupendous?" Papi always found things great. It was superstupendous. Wishing at mass did work. He shook me again. "I promise you it's going to be great, and I'll take you to the zoo. It's a promise. Would you like that, Niceto?"

"If you get me a Coca-Cola," Niceto said in his low voice. Four-year-olds were embarrassingly greedy. Papi made smoke rings for him, and he tried to put a finger inside them.

"Why is your mother taking so long to ride back?"

Papi didn't know that Mami had left days and days ago for Galmeda? It was impossible! He must have been up there where lakes collided with mountains and waterfalls pierced huge rocks.

"You haven't been in Galmeda, Papi? That's where she is!"

"I was in Galmeda." His eye on my side grew too big for its socket. I glanced down at the fabric of my—Gloria's—britches. I counted thirty-nine fabric ridges while smoke twirled around. How to tell him that Padre Romualdo had left a message for Papi to go see him? I had to say it in a way that made Papi do it. He had to.

"When did your mother say she'd be back?"

There it was, the big eye again. I told him in a few days.

"I come to tell her what she wants to hear, and she's gone," Papi said to the smoke. Then to me: "I'll be back in a few days. Tell her I'm out of the unions. No unions. Will you remember? You'll see how fast we say good-by to this place and go home."

Now home wasn't Spain but San Bernardo Street in Galmeda, a big city in America. It didn't matter; my toes danced wildly.

Nanny Fresia tiptoed in, excusing herself, and told me to put on a dress and pinafore for dinner. If Papi only knew the things she'd been up to. "Papi, did you bring me a dress?"

"Ohhh," he hit his forehead. "I forgot, treasure. Next time. It's a promise."

"And my boy doll with a loose neck?" Niceto asked quietly.

"Ohhh, I forgot, treasure. I promise you, next time I will."

"With a loose neck." Niceto inspected the scars on Papi's left hand.

PAPI TURNED UP the radio because of something in China. How could some documents on the other side of the world be more important than what I'd been trying to tell him? "Papi, Padre Romualdo says . . . he told me to tell you . . . he wants you to go see him." He still couldn't understand. The brass bell announced lunch. Papi said he'd sit with the children. Madame made a disgusted smirk. The girls were annoyed. No grown-up would sit at the old skin table. It wasn't done. They couldn't discuss how to boycott Madame's class, hide food, or plan ways to tease the grouchy maid. They said if I were smart, I would tell my father about my mother, to make him do something. Hadn't I realized I should've let them help me with their uncle, so he'd never come back? Had I seen the contessa come back? Oddly, they didn't urge me to leave with my father. What if they blabbermouthed to him? Only Padre Romualdo knew what to do. I told them if they were smart, they'd listen to my father, because he knew great stories: when he got lost, and had to spend the night in an abandoned castle, and stones from the ceiling started to fall; when he was exhausted, about to drown, and swam to a rock, and it was covered with poisonous sea urchins.

Papi sat down and rubbed his hands together, the Spanish way. This cheered me tremendously, in spite of the three finger stubs. The girls, however, looked sideways, which wasn't nice, but you couldn't scold someone for that. Niceto dropped vermicelli every time he aimed the big spoon at his tiny mouth.

Papi started to talk about cars, a dangerous sign. Vehicles usually led to "the other day" stories, which, unlike his boy stories, made me uneasy. Sure enough: "The other day I was inching my cycle carefully on a very high and rickety bridge over a river with strong currents, to get to a construction site. I was in the middle of the bridge when *crrrrr!* there was this horrendous cracking noise, and would you believe it? Two planks split and the front wheel fell through! Right through! Can you imagine? There I was, the front wheel down there"—Papi looked down the side of the table—"the rear wheel up there"—Papi looked up—"and nothing I could do! I didn't breathe for fear the slightest movement would dislodge the rear wheel and plunge me into the river!" Papi twisted three fingers to make a turbulent river. "I waited, cold and hungry. I thought, well, I'm dead; I won't get out of this one. So you're wondering how come I'm not dead, right?" I looked at the girls. They didn't seem to be wondering. But it was a good story. "Well, they rescued me with ropes! Oof! What an episode!"

It must have been very scary. Papi had told the same story with an ambulance he was driving in Zaragoza, and a jeep he was chauffeuring for a concentration camp guard in France. Luckily, this "the other day" story wasn't followed by "Wasn't it true, my daughter, just the way I described it?" I could never remember being in those stories but always said yes. He asked my mother too, and it made her very mad. Later she would tell him that was the last time she would be a "witness" to his absurd fantasies. Why did it upset Mami so? It was fun to see him gesticulating, making noises; planes, bombs, animals or a river below. In a way, I knew my mother was right and some people didn't like his stories, but he never seemed to notice, as if he had a job to do, which was to tell a story with as much energy and noise as possible. I would have let my tongue be yanked out before I would have said a story my father had told wasn't true.

I wanted to tell him about the guanaco. After two more stories about German planes trying to bomb his car, he ate, lost in thought, but he still seemed to be acknowledging the girls' disapproving presence in his mind, something a grown-up shouldn't do. He put his napkin down, said it was time for the news and left.

The girls looked mesmerized. I knew Papi would dazzle them. Did Papi have charm! I gave them a smile.

"Your father's a fool," Patricia said.

"He speaks like a Spaniard," Gloria said.

I was embarrassed to feel embarrassed and left. Papi was in the gallery, irritated because the music announcing "Copec News" was fuzzy, and when he couldn't hear the news, he turned the radio off angrily. Again I told him about Padre Romualdo. So he wouldn't think he had been singled out, I told him Romualdo had also told Mami and Tío Armando to go see him, and had scolded Tío Armando. Papi's green eyes grew large, but he was silent. I also told him he should take me and Niceto with him, then we would tell Mami. He said not to be silly, that we had to wait here. I begged him. Then I was an idiot and burst out crying. "What's this?" he said. "Niceto is acting more mature than you!" True. I wiped my tears, but the lump in my throat was about to burst. In the morning I had to make him go to Las Cabras.

I got up early. Nanny Fresia said my father had kissed us while we were asleep. He had to be at work early in Galmeda. I went back to bed.

A MOTHER AND two children rode a buggy to the public road, fast, to catch the bus before it got to the intersection with the EL TOPAZ iron letters. But the eucalyptus-bordered road stretched on and on . . . the road, cut the road to get to the bus!

The door to the veranda opened and closed; light came in the room, left the room; shadows crawled, and it was hot.

Cold hands touched my forehead; whispers left my bed; my bed was wet.

A force propped up my neck, put a cup to my lips. "Sip this linden brew." My ear filled with Nanny Fresia's voice. "Little girl, la Mamota won't let la Tomasa, the *curandera,* come to heal you; she's afraid mi Señora Doña Mercedes will find out. But don't you worry; la Tomasa'll come at dusk, when la Mamota goes to do her rosary. I arranged it. So don't you worry; you hear me?" I was worried about that road that kept stretching when we had to catch the bus with the colors Papi loved; then we were in the buggy and we rode, and the line of eucalyptus went on and on and on. . . . The door opened, and Madame's and Niceto's forms threw a shadow, and Niceto's low voice said, "Is she dead yet?"

"You bad boy," Nanny Fresia whispered. "Stay out with Señora Madame as I told you." The door closed and the horseshoes went *clopity-clop,* too slow to get there on time. It smelled of burnt herbs, cold on my neck and wrists, shuffling up and down above me; it was hot. I said I had to tell my father we'd take the next bus.

"I'll get la Mamota," Nanny Fresia said. "Mamota, the little girl wants the father." What would la Mamota have to do with it? A cold hand touched my forehead.

"Not la Mamota—Father, Father. I have to tell him."

La Mamota's voice said, "He'll be here as soon as he can, child. Fresia, she's burning up, she needs a father, she wants to confess. Run, tell Manuel to tell Alberto to race Lucero to Las Cabras and fetch Padre Romualdo. Run, don't just stand there!"

The door opened, my eyes opened; the girls were outside with pale faces; Gloria was crying. The door closed. My eyes closed.

"HOLY MOTHER MARY, I'm now an old woman, but I couldn't love Your Graceful Person more, I assure You. You know I do my rosary for You, night after night, no matter how much my legs hurt. I'm not ignorant; see the many, many of Your names and the names of Your Saintly Son, the Fruit of Your Sacred Womb, I know. Have You noticed, Holy Mary? You know I try to run the houses the best I can, and the things that go on in these houses, Holy Patrona! The worse shenanigans that Devil Satan has ever thrown this way! I had nothing against the foreign child, Sacred Mother. The padre just wouldn't hear me about the Goda woman and her designs; just kept telling me to be kind to those foreigners. And You, in Your Infinite Wisdom, would have to agree that the child was very obnoxious. She had nothing but chances to learn my girls' bearing, discretion and charm, but, Beloved Patrona, she never did, as it was written in her bad blood by the Laws of Your Divine Son for this Valley of Tears. I could've even overlooked she was a Spaniard, that's how fair I can be, but they had no right to throw this unschooled waif on my girls. I promise, Queen of Heaven, ten Hail Marys, five Our Fathers and two, better make it one—Generous Mother, You know it's long and how much I have to do—one Credo for the comfort of Your Holy Son, if You see to it that the child's soul doesn't stay in Purgatory for as long as it deserves. See Holy Sovereign, how fair this humble old servant of Yours can be? And please, Generous Queen, don't forget at my judgment time, I'm the one who sent for the padre for the child's soul, soon as she asked; it was the first time she ever showed any piety. Meantime, Gracious Mother, maybe you can do a little checking about the donation I made for You in the chapel, 'cause my legs, specially this knee, aren't any better. Amen."

"Virgin Mary, I don't know things like la Mamota; I'm not old like her; I'm still nineteen. But being the little girl's nanny, I know it's all poppycock what la Mamota says. Do you remember my promise after You granted me my wish to be a nanny and wear a green uniform? One for each of the pictures of Your Son Jesus's suffering? Remember? I didn't skip one candle—see?—not one, like some others do, even Rosalina. You grant them their wish and they plumb forget their promises. Not me, Virgin, see? I'm reliable. The chapel's closed, you can check that, dear Virgin, so here, next to the little girl's bed, I offer You six candles if You keep that nosy dragon of la Mamota out, so the little girl's Guardian Angel can protect what's left of her poor body, and believe me, You can count on your candles. Amen."

The dark was filled with whispers. The door opened and in burst a large figure, black against the shadows, followed by some pitter-patter. The room resonated with loud orders: "Open those doors, open those doors! It's stifling in here. Hand me that chair. And take this goat that's been following me out of here."

I'd forgotten about Jali—such a joyful companion. It made my throat less fiery just to think of her. A large hand took my wrist. "Nanny, push her covers back. Good, now turn her, all right, let me see her back, good, you can cover her now. Open wide those eyes, my daughter. Oh, my! What squinting! How about having a party? Mamota, bring lemonade; we're having a party in here."

It was Padre Romualdo!

"Padre, for all the Saints, the child's been practically . . . well, in need of extreme unction . . ."

"Nonsense, Mamota. The child's ready for a party and so am I; I had a rough ride to El Topaz. We want lemonade, with lots of sugar. Do you like it sweet, my daughter? Right, me too. And Nanny"—Padre Romualdo pointed to the chamber pot with purple irises—"kindly remove this before I stick my big foot in it." La Mamota was furious and scolded Nanny Fresia in whispers for not hiding the chamber pot before his saintliness entered the room.

"Sit up, my daughter, let's chitchat, this is a party. Now, what have you been up to?"

I hadn't been up to anything, it seemed, for a long time. Did he know my father had been here? Maybe he thought I hadn't given my father his message. The large black body, slowly sprouting a face with bony cheeks and a row of black buttons from the neck down, rearranged itself on the chair in front of my bed. What to ask? "Will a tarantula kill you?"

"Now, this is good party chitchat, my daughter. No, a tarantula can make you rather sick, but it won't kill you."

"Maybe a tarantula bit me; I haven't been feeling so good."

"I see; a fertile imagination. If a tarantula had bitten you, I'm sure I would've heard your scream way out in Las Cabras; you're a bit of a loudmouth, aren't you, my daughter? You also would have a bump somewhere, and all I see on you is bones. We'll fill you up with lemonade and get your appetite going. Tarantulas are God's creatures; they don't go after people for no reason."

My friend. How to ask him about so much, without telltaling? First the formalities. "Now can I call you Romualdo?"

"Indeed you can't. Now, have you been saying your prayers as I told you?" Yes, and I told him that I'd given my father his message, but my father was a very busy man. He said that my father's coming was a sign the Lord was listening. I asked if I could get up. He said in a couple of days. I asked if I could get up very early in the morning. "It pleases Our Lord that His children get up as early as possible." I told him I wanted to please Our Lord, but Nanny Fresia wouldn't let me. He said she worked very hard and needed her rest, but if I promised to be very quiet and do only what was permitted, he'd talk to her. He drove a hard bargain. I asked if I could eat chirimoyas. I could, providing they weren't green and I ate all my supper.

"Then it's agreed, Padre. I feel much better, well enough to go to Las Cabras with you." From there we could take the train to Galmeda.

"Whoa! Now wait a minute, my daughter; you ask for a sip and take the bottle. You still have fever. You may do just what your nanny tells you until your mother comes; she'll soon be here." He got up, made a cross in the air in front of me, releasing a cloud of mothballs and starch, said, "May the

Lord be with you," patted my cheek and left, making the room terribly still.

Out on the veranda, la Mamota said, "But your lemonade, Padre! It has juice from northern limes, as sweet as you like it. These are apricot tarts from my pantry, and these . . ."

"Don't spoil me, Mamota, as you have three sets of your children, so far. Mmm, delicious. See that the child drinks the whole glass, and her nanny stays with her. I'll be back for mass, unless you call me before. May God be with you, my daughter. Good tarts!"

La Mamota looked at me from the door, crossed herself and left, repeating, "A miracle! She's back to life; Padre Romualdo has performed another miracle! The Holy Virgin Mary be praised!"

Nanny Fresia came in smiling. "I knew la Tomasa could do it. With Padre Romualdo and the Virgin's help, of course."

Saying that I felt much better had been a grave mistake. How to pretend I was terribly ill so he would come back? How did he know my mother was coming very soon? What was he planning to do?

WHENEVER I HEARD a horse's gallop from my bed, instead of my parents or Padre Romualdo it was always the precious girl from the other lands. As soon as she heard that Señor Gunther wasn't here, she turned back, flushed and teary. It was strange someone that old could act that foolish. My mother didn't act that way when we went to places my father had said he was doing translations and it turned out he wasn't there.

Staying in bed was being alone in a boat in the middle of the ocean. You needed certain supplies. At first, Nanny Fresia had brought them willingly, saying everyone was impressed that Padre Romualdo had come to see me. But her attitude deteriorated very fast; she griped every time I asked her to bring me children's magazines: *El Pituso, Billiken* and the one with "The Last Days of Pompeii"; also some of the witchy black sheets that you put over a paper to trace a book's picture over it and, magic! the picture's outline came out on the paper! Or to bring the domino set for me to build a city of chips with a square for children to play in, mothers to look out the window at it, and fathers to cross it to walk four blocks to a huge street, to disappear into a mass of encounters that could lead to jobs, friendships, and unexpected wonders, which I perhaps could glimpse sometime. Then my father would feel satisfied and sit in the square, and my mother would feel trustful, and I would feel happy, and Niceto would be oblivious, as usual. Or to bring the Chinese checkers for me to tilt the board and let all the marbles race around it, bumping, running ahead, falling behind, until they were all worn out. In Galmeda I was marble rich; I challenged the boys, and they bet their best ones, thinking a girl couldn't play well, that I must have been betting my brother's marbles, poor brother. After I took them all, they wouldn't play marbles with me anymore.

Nanny Fresia wanted me only to work on a puzzle she had seen that was sooo beautiful. "The blond señorita's smiling," she explained, trying to entice me to do the puzzle. "Her hair's parted on this side, no, no, the other side, and a curl comes down over the ear, like this." I'd never noticed Nanny Fresia's ear had tremendous amounts of flesh at the bottom, attached to her jaw. It gave me claustrophobia. "And the beautiful señorita's opening a shutter, and, lo! unbeknownst to her, a handsome young *caballero*'s there, with a green hat." Nanny Fresia giggled and stared into space happily. "Now, little girl, you get working on that puzzle; it's going too slow."

I tried to work on it, but it made me yawn. From time to time Nanny Fresia came to check the puzzle's progress. She got angrier every time. I asked her to bring me scissors, paper, the Prismacolor box to draw the *almacén* for my father, the pastel set to paint a girl with espadrilles for my mother, the little gouache pots and brushes to paint the gardens in beautiful flatness for Padre Romualdo. At every request she reacted as if she'd been asked to climb the biggest araucaria pine to fetch them, instead of just going to the hobby room. Her mood worsened, her bossing increased, her complaints escalated. "Little girl, what do you think I have—four hands and six legs? Little girl, you're disobedient, a nuisance, a pest."

She was increasingly more annoying, and the worst when she brought me food, especially mashed potatoes, which tasted like your tongue sliding down your throat. "You're getting as finicky as the girls," she said. "When I come back, I want all the mashed potatoes gone. All of it." She left me behind a mashed mountain.

What would the girls do? Mold it and put it in the chamber pot? It was the wrong color. Stuff it between the wood planks? It might attract tarantulas. The only course—I had made a contract with Padre Romualdo, and Spaniards had to be honorable—was to eat a tiny bit, a tiny piece of your tongue down at a time. The bits began to stick. They got drier. They developed sharp corners. There had to be a limit to how honorable you had to be. Still, I kept at it. Time got stuck in the potato bits.

Nanny Fresia came back. One look at my plate and she accused me with her finger. "You naughty little girl, you're disobedient and obnoxious, and you . . ." *Brl-brl-brl-brl,* Nanny Fresia went on.

Something made me place a blob of mashed potatoes on my fork's handle, point its teeth toward her and hit them sharply. Presto! The blob took off through the air. To my shocked thrill, its path was abruptly intercepted by Nanny Fresia's right eye!

The room was instantly silent. There was nothing but a blob of mashed potatoes on Nanny Fresia's eye. She left, mumbling furiously. I knew that never again in my entire life would I be able to repeat so magnificent a feat. It was strange that your greatest triumphs could be accomplished when you hadn't planned them, when they had occurred to you in a sudden flash of genius.

I WENT OUT at dawn without Nanny Fresia giving me a bad time. Padre Romualdo was powerful and Nanny Fresia honorable; besides, she always woke up vomiting, and sometimes cried. I asked her if she wanted me to get help. Nanny Fresia reacted as if I had slapped her. "You better not, little girl!" I asked why. "Because, I don't want everybody to know I've been eating too many *chicharrones.*"

I wasn't allowed to eat *chicharrones,* the delicious-smelling morsels of fried pork fat that the servants ate in the kitchen. "So why don't you stop eating them?"

"Once your Guardian Angel slacks on his job and you start eating them, you can't stop. The Devil's free to do as he pleases." She got irritated when I asked her if she had seen the Devil. "You silly little girl, if I'd seen him I'd be burned to a crisp, not here listening to your silly questions. Don't you know things you haven't seen?"

I did. Millions of things: sharks, buildings in the United States that were so tall your spit, even the guanaco's, would never reach the ground, or people from Africa or Asia who were Negro or slant-eyed. I asked her how she could stop.

"La Tomasa will make me stop. You better not tell a soul, little girl."

I went out to play. It was so pleasant that all three girls felt rotten, and moaned like lambs at tail-cutting time. Nanny Fresia said the girls were just putting on a show because I had been sick. The girls wanted to be like me? Weak like me? Padre Romualdo was right again. La Mamota said I had contaminated the girls with what had made me sick. She didn't let me go near them.

As if I could care less. I threw sour oranges for the dogs, who made faces of disgust when they tasted the sour juice and wouldn't fetch them again. I threw sticks or sweet fruit, then another sour orange. Only Coca-Cola, who hated the sour juice most, scrambled to get it; her passion for fetching was stronger than her memory. Then the dogs and I watched her lift her lips away from her gums, lashing her tongue out, feeling dumb. It made me laugh really hard, which was not very nice, but so much fun. Maybe being meek would make things work, but you certainly shouldn't be a scatterbrain.

I took down all the toys in the playroom, then turned on all the music boxes. It sounded like a million birds, flying to tell my father to hurry and tell my mother the good news that was going to please her so much, so she wouldn't disappear like him, like my grandmother, the rest of my family, like Spain.

You couldn't forget things, like Coca-Cola's sour orange, like Nanny Fresia's *chicharrones;* you had to force yourself to keep in mind things that you didn't want to have happen, to avoid getting that sour taste and that nausea again and again.

15

I WATCHED WITH APPREHENSION THE ARCHED door separating the servants' dining patio from the utility yard, expecting to see Madame appear like the statue of the knight commander arriving at Don Juan's house to avenge his honor. We were boycotting the class. I was trading my exalted position as a sort-of-European and Madame's high regard for my compositions for all this fun, keeping in mind that it was far less dangerous to neglect to do what was right than to neglect to do what the girls wanted. We had jumped with all the animals into the park's tiled fountain. Now we watched preserves and treats for the winter being stirred with wooden spoons as tall as we, in copper vats over fire pits. Patricia said Madame would never find us there. I hoped so, nervously. Breezes from the creek twirled the wonderful smells. *Pinzones* raised an uproar of *pirri-pirris.* The servants hummed, "Girl with a Gypsy face / And a guitar's heart." It was joyful and congenial in the kitchen yard.

Suddenly Madame appeared at the arched door! Grimly she ordered us to the classroom. She was surprised at me. She glared at us, sitting around the table, damp and green-streaked. "You shall write fifty times, 'I'm a bad girl'—*Je suis une jeune fille méchante.*" Fifty times!

We turned our eyes on Patricia. "Madame—" she started.

"Patricia, that'll be fifty-five times for you." Patricia's leadership fizzled to nothing. The girls' eyes shone with humiliation. This had to lead to something big, but for the better? Or for the worse and suck me into it? Around her fortieth "*Je suis une jeune fille méchante,*" Patricia mumbled to Grace. "Tell you later how she's going to pay for this." My heart went fast. As I wrote the next line, my heart felt good.

When we finished, Madame said, in spite of our wickedness, she would be generous and not deprive us of our brisk little walk. She called them our recreation and reward. We called them our funeral marches. "Perfect for *the plan,*" Patricia whispered as we were leaving, and my heart pounded.

We carried a rush-seat stool to use as a bridge for Madame. Instead of putting it in the shallow spot where we normally crossed the creek, the girls continued upstream, and gave me such a look that I followed them.

"Where're you going, girls? We must cross the stream," Madame said.

"Ay, we forgot," Patricia said, but she didn't go back. Grace leapt to the other shore, and both held the stool above the water. I could tell by the color, the flow, and the absence of weed tips that the creek was deep there. This was thrillingly scary.

Madame handed me her parasol and held on to me and Gloria, saying she liked the regular spot better for next time. She stepped on the stool. Patricia and Grace let go. Madame went down. She howled, "*Sauvages! Des primitives!*" while we helped her out. She rearranged her hat and yanked her parasol back from me.

We watched her going down the road, making a steady beat with her parasol, the muddy skirt stuck to her legs, the cherries bouncing menacingly. We held in what we felt until she was out of hearing range. "She learned her lesson," Patricia said, and we started to release the reserved laughter until it became uproarious. I was included in the self-congratulations.

But Madame's back spelled war, no doubt about it. If by a miracle we got away with this, I should definitely accept their offer for help. It was possible that sometimes you were better off aligning yourself with your enemies. The stool flowed downstream and stopped at the normal, shallow crossing spot.

THE BELL WOKE ME UP at dawn. It spoke of death. Each slow chime hit the heart. Niceto wiggled; he was alive. Was this the terrible thing that my mother said might happen in Galmeda? Had war started, even though my parents said we had left Europe to come to this end of the world knowing no one because this country hated fascists and Nazis? After years of owning Spain in his little boots, had Franco finally died? Did I need to grab my brother and escape? Escape where? Nanny Fresia leapt out of bed. "I knew last night someone would die; the dogs were at it all night."

"What do the dogs have to do with it?"

"Dogs can see Death, little girl. Please, please, Virgin Mary, don't let it be my mother or my sister Teresita, Audolina, María . . ." She retched. We could have spent the whole day here naming her relatives. If the bell tolled for one who'd died already, it was unlikely that the Virgin Mary'd be willing to switch the body for someone else's at this point. It turned out that the unlucky Christian done in by Death was el Francisco, her cousin, who had always lifted a hand grown yellow with tuberculosis as we rode horses by his adobe dwelling.

Nanny Fresia said all her friends and relatives would ask permission to be with her cousin, the Lord have him in His

Glory, when his soul rose out of the body to go to his judgment, which was no picnic, and the more company the better. She said Padre Romualdo would come bless the box. I wanted to be there! I'd never seen a soul and wanted to check with my own eyes whether Nanny Fresia was making these things up. Hopefully the soul would make its departure before my bedtime.

I told the girls. They were scandalized; people from the houses didn't attend events in the peasants' dwellings. Just in case, they asked la Mamota. "All the Saints forgive you, you naughty little girls. You know there's going to be wild goings-on all night at el Francisco's. Every last *peón* will get drunk, the dirty pigs, and will say scores of offending things to the Good Ear of the Virgin. Who knows what will happen out there; you tell me, is that a proper place for little girls from the houses?"

This soul-raising event sounded like the party of the year, even topping the one for the very, very famous pianist. The girls were keeping a secret from me, so I could keep one from them. I begged Nanny Fresia to take me. She said if la Mamota found out, she would be banned for sure. But not feeling so well, she was vulnerable to my pestering, so she finally agreed.

El Francisco's house was all lit up with candles and sad guitar songs. Everyone, in their rubber-tire sandals on the dirt floor, received me warmly. Padre Romualdo was busy, but came to bless me. Nanny Fresia said tomorrow he would take el Francisco to a beautiful cemetery, far away. What would Papi say? He said priests exploited people. El Francisco was a dead old man, so how could Padre Romualdo possibly exploit him? Mario, making Zs as he changed postures, talked about things that had happened long ago.

In a corner la Tomasa, the *curandera,* not a fiery-eyed old woman, but a young one with permed hair and bony shins, gave Nanny Fresia a small bag. She cried. She had a secret life. She then explained to me why funerals always turned happy. It seemed la Rosalia's parents wouldn't let her marry cousin Pancho, even after he'd gotten la Rosalia in an interesting way four times, because he had before gotten la Matilde, la Rosalia's sister, in an interesting way. As for la Filomena, the lady drinking *chicha* over there, and el Juancho, they couldn't get married because she used to have a husband who married her legal, and who'd gone to a ranch near Rancalca to shear sheep, and instead of bringing back a medium-size, porcelain-coated cooking pan, as he'd promised, he never came back. And now, while he blessed el Francisco's box, the padre was going to talk about Up Above and Sin, and scare the daylights out of everybody who'd been fooling around with the apple without his blessing, so a lot of happy weddings and baptisms would follow. I asked what apple, but she didn't answer. You couldn't insist, you had to let her talk.

It had been fun, although Nanny Fresia said the soul had already left. She was right about how important she was to me. Now I was part of a big side of El Topaz that the girls didn't know, no matter how much they owned it. I had a secret life too, and I could never give it up.

MY MOTHER'S BLACK CHIGNON at her white neck traveled in the rear seat of the car, through the front-gardens driveway. Melons' gray head blocked my view. Papi wasn't in the car. But I had millions of things to tell, show and ask my mother! Right away!

Around the toy room's small table and chairs, my mother and Tía Merce laughed, teasing each other. It put Mlle. Vicky—just out of bed in her useless, filmy bathrobe—in a sour mood. I had grown accustomed to the servants' slower speech. Holding my drawing of the girl with espadrilles, I stood next to my mother's elbow, where the white curves born at the wrist and the shoulder joined smoothly. Everything about my mother was smooth. The psychiatrist whispered to her, "Congratulations, my dear, you've made history in the annals of psychiatry."

"I knew this would happen all along," Melons said.

What had made history? Everyone listened to Dr. Kaplan, because he was supposed to know everybody's secrets, but he used strange words. Melons was unimpressed. "When you're feeling great, forget that you'll feel rotten again. When you feel rotten, remember that you'll feel great again. That's happiness." Melons said more sensible things than her husband.

"Each person knows what he or she must do to keep happiness flowing," my mother said, her long arms picking up Niceto.

"What nonsense, all of you," Tía Merce said, transferring packages from Evaristo's arms to the girls' arms. "Happiness is being in love all the time, *mes chers.*"

Madame appeared at the door in her long skirt. She said hello and left without a word, but her glance to us meant, Just wait till I tell, and I will. Patricia shrugged. In anticipation of Madame's report, she had been pouring a little dog urine in Madame's white wine glass at every meal. Madame said white wine was the only good thing in this country.

My mother stroked my hair. "So in the short time I was gone, you got sick? But you look fine; you're a strong girl." A short time! It had seemed forever! Did she know about renting the whole pensione? And the no-unions? People here didn't like that word. My mother gave the girls three slim dolls with matching red sweaters and plaid skirts, like bourgeois dolls, imported from some advanced country, maybe the United States, or maybe Switzerland; the last word in chic dolls. I got a potbellied, red-cheeked doll with eyes permanently side-fixed, so that you had to get on one side to look into its eyes, as you did with a cat, because cats always avoided your direct gaze.

Dolls weren't good for much, except to keep their heads away from Niceto and put them up somewhere, because a girl had to have a doll. Still, I wanted my mother to give me a chic one, like the girls'. My mother whispered, "Solita, be sensible, we couldn't possibly afford a doll like those. We owe Merce so terribly much; the least we can do is give her children a tasteful gift." I watched the girls take off their dolls' skirts and sweaters. My doll could grow big and invite me to go to Charley's. I accepted. I stayed sensible. I licked wounds.

Back in our rooms, my mother told me about the elegant Ritz Palace Hotel, and the great Margarita Xirgu. And Papi? She had been so busy she hadn't seen him. Too busy to see Papi? I told her about his visit and the no-union message. She didn't say, Let's pack and go, as Papi said she would. She was silent. She asked if I had been conscientious about taking my cod-liver oil.

IN PENSIONES it wasn't customary to hold meetings in the bathroom, but Tía Merce did, in the blue alcove of her sea-of-perfume bath. The psychiatrist said Mercedes' bathroom was El Topaz's reception room. Veins branched without rhyme or reason through her big, floating breasts. Were we going to get punished about Madame? "*Mes petits choux,* you must be nice to Madame, otherwise she'll leave and then you'll have to go to nun school." We gave each other invisible glances, which included me, even in the presence of their Mumsy. "But let's talk about lovely news." Tía Merce's brick nails dropped a cube of sugar into the cup of tea sitting on a tray bridging the tub. "It turns out I had a divine, divine time with your Popsy! We dispensed with his gruffy chauffeur, and even took the trolley once!"

"We want to take the trolley," Grace pleaded. "A chauffeured car's so boring." I wanted to brag that I'd taken the trolley with my parents several times, even the open wagon.

"Close that door to the bath's garden, one of you, the sun's too much. Your Popsy's coming this weekend. Who would guess you could get a kick out of a dull man who's your own husband? Ay, life's divine! Surprises, surprises." This news made me more excited than it did the girls. I was full of curiosity to see this man whom my mother said was the toast of the ladies. "Armando's bringing him." Patricia elbowed me. I looked up at the louvered skylight. "I have to admit he, and Pilar, proposed fun things for Miguel and me to do; he even got the theater tickets." A bird bumped against the frosted glass door. "You know how your Popsy is; incapable of thinking of anything but silk screens."

"So, Mumsy, you like Tío Armando now?"

"My darlings, one must 'like' one's relatives. The only charming one in the family's your father's twin, Toto. He plays the guitar too, you know. One of these days he'll find me interesting." She looked at me and smiled. "So, you were sick, little sparrow?" I nodded. "My poor dear, don't get wet, you mustn't get cold." Even Tía Merce was treating me as a person of importance! Now I was sure they were nice to me when I was sick, weak and meek. Being proud like the guanaco wasn't of any help.

"How come Tío Armando's coming again? He never used to."

"My pretty, if you knew how many people are foaming at the mouth about your Tío Armando suddenly finding El Topaz so attractive. Hopefully it's just a case of him trying to profit from our guest's marital problems, *mes choux*. But in any case, I've been writing to María Pía Ycheñirre, Jorge's old fiancée; at this point she's probably tired of the old baron, and this may lead to solving all the problems; well, you're too little for these things. Ay, I wish I could tell Juan Vicente how things have developed! But he and Claudio Correa are going to Venice. That's where I should be—gliding down the canals at sunset; I don't know why Miguel doesn't think of taking me to Venice. Here, a letter from Juan Vicente." She handed Patricia a violet envelope. "Read it."

"We can't understand Tío Juan Vicente's handwriting. It's like blackberry bushes tangled all over the page," Gloria said.

Tía Merce chuckled. "Poor Juan Vicente; he's dedicated more time than anybody to develop his very special penmanship. You haven't read the other letters? He's been a hit everywhere."

"Why, Mumsy? Do they love his patches in Paris?"

"Listen: 'My beloved Cleopatra' . . . He says he's shocked to hear about Vicky taking up with a *peón.*" Our feet nudged one another out of her sight. "He's pleased about Congress' new health and eight-hours law. Ay, Juan Vicente can be a bore. Oh, here! He says when he went to Maxim's in a turban and habit, everybody thought he was an exotic prince. He ordered the best champagne—d'Épernay 'forty-five—then, pretending to get drunk, he announced that he wanted everyone to have a jewel from his mother's imperial collection. He then threw handfuls of rhinestones and colored glass to the dance floor. And when the *haute société* of Paris was on all fours fighting for the empress's jewels, he and his friends scooted out of Maxim's without paying the bill! Ay, darlings, Juan Vicente's such a marvelous character. It ought to occur to your Popsy to take me to Paris. Ay, horror! Patricia, look at your hair! La Mamota's getting too old; go tell Ema to do your curls properly. Go on."

It seemed that Tío Juan Vicente had done something very wrong. Even my mother, who always talked of Spanish honor, now laughed at these things. Elevated people considered you one of them when you agreed their wrongdoings were cute. Was that what Padre Romualdo meant about the meek winning at the end? After all, the kittens and the baby mice had been rescued and survived.

Outside, the guanaco was so ecstatic to see me, he ran pretending he was going to ram into me, then leapt to one side at the last minute. I was so ecstatic to see him, I pretended to be scared, even though it was one of Jali's favorite tricks.

Patricia said to me, "Did you see how much we were punished about Madame? When our Tío Armando comes, we'll help you to do something that will get him really mad, and keep him at arm's length from you and . . . you know."

I nodded.

THIS IS GOING TO BE IMPORTANT, MY MOTHER'S fussing said. She redid her bun. She tried earrings. She had Fresia do this, do that: wash my sandals, iron her special-occasions blouse with its embroidered pansies gathered by a silk string.

Preparations for the arrival of the girls' father, Señor Don Miguel, rippled through the houses. Every servant, from la Mamota down to the last aproned girl in charge of washing combs and brushes with ammonia, was either giggling, barking at someone or crying because someone had barked at her. I assumed Señor Don Miguel was to stay in Tía Merce's scented room, but a beehive of servants opened and rubbed and slapped and spanked clean a part of the houses beyond its elbow, which the girls said was their Popsy's quarters.

The dogs—except Beethoven, who showed his teeth in no uncertain terms—were shampooed. The guanaco's neck flashed a fresh red ribbon. Madame planned a serious conversation with the coming owner about his daughters and the lack of seriousness in this place. This in spite of the girls' good behavior in class, to make Madame totally unprepared for their next trick. They had to spend hours getting curled and ribboned, so they couldn't inform me of their scheme for their uncle. Papi had said he would come back in a few days, so maybe it was today. I wished it were he coming, not the girls' father and uncle.

My mother went to work on my cowlick. Looking your best had inexplicable advantages that you had to take on trust. She gave me an evaluating look, which was never reassuring. Not all the things revealed by her face were clear, but one was that she wished for me to appear somewhat prettier, bigger-eyed, like her and Niceto, not like my father so much. Regardless, my mother was brave, nothing got her down, she tried her best no matter what; today she expected me, her oldest child, to make a great impression. I would kiss forcefully, so it seemed willing, answer questions promptly, without prefacing them with *aaah.* And what else? I would have to fake it. "My daughter, these coming visitors, well, their children aren't very warm toward them; for Armando it's a sad disappointment. So you be extra charming and affectionate." What would the girls say to this? I couldn't tell them. I was having a secret life all around. "People love a charming girl. Nothing's worse than a girl who stands there like a piece of meat with eyes." How about the three girls? It was no use asking; my mother wouldn't say a thing against them no matter what. Once she had done all she could for me, she checked that Niceto wasn't munching *espino* seeds, a habit he had acquired since he was barred from rose petals or green gooseberries. The seeds tasted all right but made your breath smell like decayed carcasses. An irresistible perversion drove you to munch *espino* seeds.

Again we were subjected to sitting so we wouldn't get dirty. All we could do was put our hands under our thighs, swing our legs up and down, and watch leaf shadows wading in the filtering sun outside the gallery's windows. It was criminal. There wasn't the remotest possibility of a striped caterpillar or a designed spider having escaped the chambermaids' fanatical brooms.

It suddenly occurred to me that I couldn't just imitate the girls in front of the imposing owner of all this, the handsome toast of distinguished ladies, because he was their father. Perhaps behaving in front of him had a special twist I should know. This worried me for a second.

After ages, two cars entered the front garden. One was Tío Armando's gleaming, silent job. The other was old and sputtered over the gravel.

Instead of jumping, ablaze with excitement, the girls stopped swinging their legs and groaned, "Ugh, Popsy still has that awful old car. When is he going to get a new one?"

Out of the old car jumped a man about my father's age, his blue uniform gleaming with gold tassels, buttons and leg stripes. I told the girls no one had ever mentioned Señor Don Miguel was in the military. A lash of anger hit me back. "How can you be so ignorant! Can't you see Maximiliano's a chauffeur?" Being a chauffeur sounded impressive to me. The uniform was spectacular, the name majestic, the mustache imposing. The girls read that in my face. "A chauffeur has a chauffeur's face, stupid. Look at his color, his sinking eyelids and his stiff mustache." At least they hadn't said anything like that about my father.

El Señor Don Miguel had a round middle, a bald head and round blue eyes that sagged benevolently. He was old for a father. This was the man who was chased by hordes of women in Galmeda and breezed through the elegant spots of Paris? The man for whom Tía Merce was going to throw herself into the San Jorge Canal? Who'd sired those three gorgeous, dimpled-kneed creatures? Facing my mother, he whispered with some emotion, "Thank you, Pilar. I never thought I'd get my wife back. And don't worry, the strikes are over, at least in the textiles."

While I was trying to recover from my double surprise,

the girls gave their father a perfunctory kiss, then rallied around and followed an old suitcase carried with martial dignity by the tasseled chauffeur. I did too. He took a good look at the nannies and maids. The aproned group twitched or blushed. La Mamota reprimanded us. They hadn't asked their father about his visit in France with their brother Enriquito, and there was more kissing to be done. She received a feeble hug from Don Miguel. "About time you came, Miguelito; your little brother's been here more than you, and for the Holy Virgin, you better do something about him. I know what's up; you better put an end to it; you're older. And why didn't you bring your twin, Toto?"

The foggy fossil, as Tía Merce called Tío Armando, didn't give my mother the same blue, dead-cow glances as before, but treated her more naturally, which was better. He gave Tía Merce the required peck and handed her a shiny book with famous paintings, saying, "My dear sister-in-law, El Topaz will finally get some tennis courts. Pilar persuaded Miguel; I'll talk to the foreman this very afternoon. Isn't that right, brother?"

El Señor Don Miguel nodded, uninterested, or resigned. Tía Merce muttered, "Pilar chose this book for him, obviously."

To the girls' outrage and my distress, he didn't give them candy. "I've been told you girls get too many sweets" was his lame explanation, something my mother was always saying. There went the foils for my ball. Then he came to ask me if I was feeling better after my sickness. He said that later I could ask him the questions I had for him! He looked at my mother, and she smiled. He patted Niceto's reddish head. The girls stood regally, their blue gazes full of messages. Mine was full of questions.

I didn't remain surprised very long, because a vision emerging from the car electrified us: after the painter with the hatchet nose came a willowy young man in a black three-piece suit that revealed enchanting narrow hips. He glanced up with eyes droopy like honey drops. "Meet Reginaldo

Bravo," Don Miguel said, "the son of sculptress Tina Rokosky. Pablo says the boy has talent and asked me to look after him. So here you have him." To his discomfort, the young poet was soon covered with a variety of lipsticks. We froze, mesmerized. I even forgot Papi hadn't arrived. Following the path of his hand over his bushy hair, Patricia said, "He must be important. Pablo is the number-one poet in the world. Popsy has superimportant friends. We'll do something about *him*." We had no idea what, but we agreed eagerly. Did this mean they thought doing something about their *tío* was no longer necessary?

ON A TABLE with lion feet, the chauffeur deposited the crinkled suitcase. It had something sacred about it, judging by the girls' faces. Señor Don Miguel was taking his time, so we inspected his quarters, striped from the sun filtering through the wooden rollers. Masses of the same painting were stacked over rattan furniture and against the walls, up to the framed pictures. We climbed, sat and stretched on them, as if they were stairs, chairs and beds. "Where's your father?" Patricia asked me, as if their father had been here all along. Or maybe she meant I shouldn't be in their father's territory?

"He'll be here soon." Saying that my father'd been here more than theirs would have been unmeek and unwise. Ruffling them would have distanced me from the suitcase and from meeting their father, whom I found oddly attractive, and sent me outside, where I might run into Tío Armando. The girls had been pushing for a confrontation with him, whatever they meant by that. We helped each other climb the tall bed in the bedroom. "Mumsy and Popsy are together. Of course, they've always been very good friends," Grace said in a certain firm way, as if she should get credit for their togetherness and their friendship. The girls were experts at taking credit for anything they could. I didn't brag that my mother and father would be in the same room when he came.

Finally Señor Don Miguel stepped in, stirring the hot air with a breeze from the veranda. I'd been told to call him Tío Miguel, but Tío Popsy went better with his roundness and benevolent sagging eyes. We gathered around the suitcase. He chuckled softly, not in Tía Merce's disquieting way. He removed his jacket, smelling of lavender and liquor, and observed us. "I didn't know there was another bunny in the burrow. Everything will be divided in four equal parts, my little bunnies."

The girls were displeased but had to agree. My throat closed. I wanted to put my face on his fat middle and let out tears. No one had ever said that before. But Spaniards didn't cry, especially not in front of a mysterious suitcase. I smiled.

"Well, shall we open this crocodile's mouth?" Tío Popsy asked, opening the suitcase. A cry escaped me. He chuckled. A dizzying sight brimmed with unthinkable treasures. He handed me and the twins a cluster of see-through candy grapes; Patricia a glazed pomegranate that opened in slices filled with little red peppermints; then licorice baskets with marzipan in tiny watermelon slices, carrots, oranges, cabbages, avocados; I liked the tiny bananas best. Then packages of nougat; long boxes of "little tongues," chocolate kittens sticking out their tongues; *negritas,* big balls of chocolate filled with meringue; *camotillos,* made of yams, crunchy on the outside, creamy inside; cellophane wrapped petit fours with tiny animals; round boxes of mint pills; marrons glacés floating inside bottles, like Lolita.

Then he handed out wooden men who danced; bouncing balls; elephants who lifted their trunks when wound up; periscopes; a cradle with a tortoiseshell baby; a doll with four faces and costumes: one white in front, one black in back, then, turned upside down, one Chinese and one Indian; a musical china chapel . . . Tío Popsy's suitcase was the magic trunk in "The Caliph of Old Damascus" story, and the biggest magic was that he made my share as legitimate and abundant as anybody else's.

"I HAD THE MOST divine time in Claudio's itsy apartment in the Île Saint-Louis, as bitsy as a charming cricket's cage, and you can see Notre Dame from the diminutive window! Ay! The sun here's too much. Ay! that romantic fog in Paris! And the wintry wind crossing the Pont de l'Alma; it was divine! Claudio was perfectly beastly; he ran around with practically everyone without the slightest regard for my feelings; it was miserable." Well, was Tío Juan Vicente happy or miserable? And how could a cricket's cage with a small window, or cold fog and wind, be divine? Drinking café au lait in their wicker chairs, the grown-ups, except for the stony painter, who had lived in Paris and knew all about it, couldn't hear enough of this. Maybe they were a lot like the parrots in the Doña Pepa stories. My mother had predicted Tío Juan Vicente's return when he had written that the famous mountain in southern France painted by a revered painter was no mountain but a molehill, that Europeans had to come here to see a real mountain. He's ready to come home, my mother had said.

I peeked from behind a column, making sure Tío Armando wasn't with them. Even the Genius was there, but no Tío Popsy. He usually slept till high midday and then vanished into his secret room beyond the grange. He was generally ignored, even by his own daughters, as my mother had hinted. The tasseled chauffeur walked up and down the veranda in his gold buttons and imposing mustache, causing the maids to drop feather dusters, candle-holder cleaners or floor mops in a daze.

"Solita." My mother startled me. She had come from the other corridor, with Tío Armando. They were usually out for more riding lessons. What good could it do her in San Bernardo Street? Even vendors wouldn't venture in, not wanting their horses to slip on the cobblestones and overturn their carts. The girls kept saying the lessons were excuse for . . . but I always interrupted with some story. "Solita, since you are so interested in learning to ride properly, Armando has generously offered to give you horsemanship tips. He's the most superb horseman, you know, you lucky girl."

"How encouraging to know some children are interested in perfecting themselves," Tío Armando said. "At what time are you free from Madame's classes for your first lesson?"

Recklessly disregarding my mother's expectations, I mumbled, "But I already know how to ride."

My mother barely moved her head forward, a frightening omen, understood fully by me and dimly by Niceto. She demurred. "Don't be embarrassed about not knowing everything perfectly, Solita; Armando doesn't mind."

"I'm also going to have dance classes," I persisted.

Tío Armando frowned impatiently and sat down. I didn't look at my mother. She said, "Solita wants to learn everything," and sat down too, releasing a heaviness that glued me in place.

"Ah, my dear brother-in-law, I just received a letter from Europe. Have I got a huge surprise for you!" Tía Merce smirked, then watched the hipless poet go by. "Mmm. Intriguing creature."

"Have you seen how he looks at María Cristina or Pilar, with the 'eyes of a slaughtered cow'?" the Walrus laughed, lifting his shoulders to where his neck should have been.

"What makes you think they're the only ones he looks at," Tía Merce said angrily. "And, I can tell you, that phrase is from a Greek poet called . . . now I forgot." She turned to my mother.

"Homer," my mother said.

"The poor young man's full of longing," Melons said. "I know he lies in bed listening to the echoes of snakes, frogs, pumas and ranch animals mating out there. That's Paradise for you; Adam and Eve and all other creatures; it heats up your bed." The psychiatrist looked at his wife, surprised.

"And beware, Paradise dwellers; remember that after that apple comes mortality. Death."

Tío Armando leaned toward me. Just in case, I leapt up and went after the pink uniform of Evangelina, who was carrying Tío Popsy's breakfast. She, I, the guanaco and the scent from the witch vine entered his room. Evangelina deposited his tray and told me to get myself and that beast out of there. "It's all right," he told her.

Up in his bed, Tío Popsy drank from a glass cut like a huge diamond and drew with colored sticks on a cardboard, ignoring his breakfast. His eyes smiled. The chuckle that seemed to be chronically churning in his stomach almost came up. "You want to know about my study, what everyone calls the secret room, right?"

It was disappointing that, like other grown-ups, he thought he knew what I was thinking. "No," I said.

"Never be afraid of anything, little hummingbird."

I took him at his word and asked why he furnished his rooms with pictures. The chuckle came up. "They have to go somewhere."

"But why so many of the same painting?" I said, pushing the guanaco, who was tasting one, since he couldn't understand it.

"I did those silk screens." He drank from the diamond glass. How strange. I remembered my mother saying that everybody in the New World fancied himself a writer, poet or painter. Many were true artists, but many more didn't know the most elementary grammar and didn't study the great masters, just talked about them. They have no craft, she said. "You see, galleries and critics don't understand what I paint, so I print them and, here they are." This confused me even more. It occurred to me that pictures didn't just happen as if by magic. Yes, there were many pictures exactly like the ones I knew, spread around in unknown parts, but it was baffling to find so many together in one man's room, proliferating like mushrooms in dark places. I asked him if he could sell them. He could be rich, this could be as good as my foil ball. Except he was rich already. The chuckle didn't come up. "I'm a painter, not a salesman, little hummingbird."

The whiff from his glass was pungent. I asked him what did his paintings mean. They told a story, he said, and what kind of stories did I like? Gaucho stories, I told him. Such as? The one about the majestic ombu tree that was always making fun of the puny reed at its feet. During a hurricane the defiant ombu stood rigidly, but the reed bent down to let the wind pass. The ombu was ripped off its mighty roots, but the meek reed survived. This story would please Padre Romualdo. He liked it too. I asked if he was going to stay here for a long time.

"Why, little hummingbird, you too? I just arrived and you want me to leave?"

"No. I would like you to stay."

The profile that looked at me from the high bed had a hint of disconcert. "Why, little hummingbird, yours is the only request I've had to stay." He sipped from his glass. "You see, to others I'm just a confused, a failed everything, a failed artist." He put the color sticks on the night table. "My wife, first she wants me here, then . . . my brothers, total philistines, everybody disapproves of me." He took his pajama-clad figure with naked white feet out of bed.

"Do you know my father?"

"I met him at the house of socialist Senator Barros. Very charming, and passionately in love in the same way that my brothers are; with himself. Don't you want to go play with my daughters?" He went to the bathroom. Water ran in the tub.

It was I who was confused. Wasn't it that hordes of women ran after him? I should have asked him if he had craft, whatever that was, and he would have been so impressed he would have stayed. But it was scary to use important words; they had a scary power. The girls wouldn't use them, not even Madame did. Then I remembered I had to be a charming girl. But my mother hadn't really said how. It didn't matter. I, with the guanaco, would be back. There was no one outside; it was safe. We were in high spirits.

NICETO WAS STANDING near the play bungalow by the gooseberries. He said Nanny Fresia was down there with the man, and pointed to the calla-lily field. I went to the slope's edge and crouched. By the creek, in the elongated shadow of the play bungalow, was the dashing foreman from the other ranch, talking to Nanny Fresia. She cried with her head down. He put his hand on her shoulder. "Why haven't you gotten fixed by la Tomasa like we agreed? Those herbs are no good; she's got to do it. Then we'll get married." Married! Nanny Fresia was bossy, arbitrary and obnoxious; she forced me to wash and change clothes all day. But she was straightforward, she was with me in everything essential, we had a secret life together. She was right; without her I'd have a hard time managing, not that I would ever admit it to her. It was unthinkable for her to go to the other ranch.

"You won't marry me," Nanny Fresia said, wiping tears.

"Yes. Word of honor. Go to la Tomasa tonight. Tomorrow you'll be good as new. Promise me. Tonight." She nodded.

"I'm about to pee!" Niceto yelled toward them. Beethoven growled; the other dogs barked at his command; I ducked. The man rushed up the bank toward the road to get on his horse, scaring some coots away.

Nanny Fresia was bending like the reed. Was she trying to survive something? When I asked her to take me with her to la Tomasa, she was angrier than she had ever been before.

WE STILL DIDN'T KNOW what Patricia meant by "doing something about" the hipless poet, but we stared at him in rapturous unison. He was fascinating, no doubt about it, wandering as if forever lost, maybe looking for inspiration. Leave it to Tío Popsy to bring an interesting human being. He seemed to see us as a lump of anonymous pinafores.

This anonymity gave us confidence, made us bold, but the girls said he was beastly rude, hiding in his room every time they followed him. This was reassuring; if I got sucked into doing something my mother considered beastly rude, it'd be tit for tat. It was selfish of him; we badly needed to know things about young men, the most intriguing of all human categories. What other chances would we have? Perhaps none, or it would take forever. Nanny Fresia wouldn't be of any help in this. The twins and I had no legitimate reason to have an interest in young men, but Patricia did, being big for her age, beautiful, self-assured, and a stepping-stone between us and the grown-ups.

Mlle. Vicky, who had stopped going to the rauli mountains, said he was probably writing love poems to her, as poets were entranced by the beauty of dancing. Instead of rehearsing with us so I could be the princess, Mlle. Vicky danced for the grown-ups herself, then fluttered around the hipless poet.

It turned out his poems were for the precious girl. This caused the German photographer to stop taking pictures and pout. First the precious girl said her father didn't let her socialize with the likes of the German photographer, but when he threatened to hit the hipless poet with his tripod, she stopped saying anything about her father. Who could figure her out?

Then we found out the hipless poet wrote a poem to my mother and slipped it through her window at night. Tía Merce and Tío Armando cried that this was vulgar. The girls taunted me, wanting to find out if it bothered me. It didn't. These were things poets did. It was in the old songs and poems sung by the refugees. It didn't bother the girls either. We weren't interested in his poems, but in his body. We developed a thirst for knowledge of it, beyond his droopy eyelashes, his stretched neck that blossomed into wavy hair, his long limbs. We meant to find out.

In the morning we walked up and down the veranda taking a discreet peek now and then through his window.

But soon we found the shutters for both his door and his window closed. How rude. I asked them if they knew any secret ways to look into his room. This inspired the plan to make a human pole up to the trap above his door. What would my mother say? Now I had to be nice at all times more than ever. "I'll be at the top," Patricia ordered. "It's better for an older person to see him undressing first. Solita, hold your hands together for Gloria to climb on you."

I couldn't say it wasn't fair, but I could be weak. Every time Gloria climbed on me, I folded over. Patricia, exasperated, finally gave up. "Gloria, you'll be first." Gloria complained. Finally she agreed. I was moving up to the next echelon!

We held on to the door's locking bar, kicking away the dogs, Jali and the guanaco, who wanted to participate. Patricia was about to look in when a nanny screamed. The pole collapsed all over the animals, who tried to scramble out, scandalized. We got up with a few scratches, some torn flounces or pockets and messy hair. The nanny rounded us up to go face la Mamota. The animals licked themselves and followed us.

LA MAMOTA WAS APPALLED, but, surprisingly, she didn't blame it on me; it turned out it was the fault of someone called Lucifer. She rounded us up to go face Tía Merce. We had never done anything before requiring such drastic measures.

Tía Merce left her card game to hear la Mamota, with Lucifer being blamed throughout, and rounded us up to go face the grown-ups at the game tables. Things went from bad to worse. "It seems this motley crew"—Tía Merce pointed to us—"tried to see our young poet in a state of undress." Judges stopped playing cards to look at us. My mother wasn't here, but my face heated up when I saw Tío Popsy holding his diamond glass.

Melons said, "When one's little like you girls, frogs turn into princes. When you're my age, princes turn into frogs."

The curled-red-bangs, poetry-writing lady said, "Ay, he reminds me of Chateaubriand." Tío Juan Vicente agreed.

Mlle. Vicky whispered to Melons, "Leticia, you're sure he's not too young for me?"

Melons said, "My dear, true love knows no numbers; love is a soufflé—always has the same ingredients. But one will overflow, one will be flat; it's all in the timing. Don't open the door before it's done, my dear, or it will collapse." No wonder the girls said she was crazy.

My mother came in with Tío Armando, and my chest became too small for so much jammed inside it. Had I ruined all her plans?

"Ah, Pilar, Armando. We're talking about our young poet," the psychiatrist told them, saving our skins for the time being.

"He's just a child," my mother said; as if she were talking about Niceto, who came to lean on her legs.

Tío Armando made a face of impatience. The psychiatrist said, "I hope we don't end up with another Werther." Mlle. Vicky asked him why, maybe also wondering who Werther was.

"Werther's the quintessential young, impossible love," he said. "He kills himself, talking to his beloved as he dies."

Tío Armando smoothed his thinning hair with discomfort. "You guys come up with the weirdest things."

He got slapped on the knee by one of the curled-bangs ladies who wrote poetry. "Silly," she told him. "You must develop an interest in things other than horses. He's Werther. Ay, *tellement romantique!*" she sighed.

Patricia turned slowly, giving us a look of We might as well leave; let's go quietly. But Tía Merce held her and related la Mamota's report, including Lucifer's contribution, and the grown-ups roared laughing! Even Tío Armando! He said Tina Rokosky's son was a cream-puff fairy who had less guts than we. Tío Juan Vicente said, "Ay, I adore these little girls!" We smiled with relief. Patricia's face intimated even bolder plans. Now I could go along in comfort. You could do wrong things if three in your group were colossally rich and you were meek.

Things were great, but then my mother told Tío Armando, "Solita's anxious to have the riding lesson you promised."

I hung on to the guanaco's neck as if he could save me.

"Yes," Tío Armando said. "Meet me in the cart yard tomorrow around five, after siesta, but first get that disgusting beast out of here. I say, Arturo, why don't you get some purebreds, instead of that useless, spitting piece of fur?"

My mother's smile had a perfectly clear message for me to do things right. A nudge in my elbow let me know Patricia was well prepared for tomorrow after siesta. The animals crouched quietly. The only one who was thrown out was the guanaco, because he stretched his neck up so proudly.

NOT FINDING TÍO POPSY ANYWHERE, I WENT TO the dining room to steal a sugar cube. I expected to find the air sinking heavily over the big carved furniture, as if no one had ever been there, or ever would be. And maybe a few fat flies agonizing in a low buzz from the Flit bug killer that the maids sprayed with a vengeance before going to their siestas. Instead, I found Tío Popsy! He was having a meal, all by himself, at such an unnatural hour. I approached the table and stood next to him, a fair man, a calm man, and waited for some signal.

His back slouched comfortably as he munched on a celery-and-onion salad, making a steady and impressive racket. I had met his left side, facing his enchanted suitcase and his bed. His right cheek had a pink wart, an exact miniature replica of his bald head. The tiny bald head went up and down his cheek as he chewed. Something reminded me of oxen pulling carts. Evidently the amusement in his round blue eyes was the acknowledgment of my presence, but he said nothing.

And what could I say? How's the celery-and-onion salad? The hour was still; words might have turned into echoes. I waited. He could answer a few things. For instance, had he told me to play with his daughters for a special reason? Why couldn't he notify everyone to give a share of their nice words and attitudes to me, as he had told the girls to share his presents? Why didn't he invite Padre Romualdo to come more often (although I couldn't say that Padre Romualdo was going to help my parents; you didn't say those things)? I couldn't ask why the girls were more proprietary about their uncle than about him, or why he squeezed sour orange juice on his salad—the juice that drove Coca-Cola to despair.

He turned to his asparagus. I wanted to tell him that, for some reason, nobody started eating asparagus at the bottom, always at the tips, so it was all downhill with no hope of a pleasant surprise at the end. Some things were like that. Maybe he would tell me why he put green chile on his asparagus. As if reading my thoughts, he offered me some chile with a twinkle in his eye. No, thank you, my head motion said.

A churning chuckle shook the napkin covering his big belly.

A serving maid entered with a soup tureen. "What are you doing here, you naughty little girl? Go to your siesta or I'll wake la Mamota." This would get me and Nanny Fresia into trouble, and Nanny Fresia said she couldn't afford any more of that. I put one elbow on the table, claiming territory, and waited.

Tío Popsy's smile seemed to say, Aren't these servants a pain in the neck? But you must understand, they're only doing their job. He didn't tell me to stay. After a moment I left. Not a word had broken the spell of that time when everything was suspended in inattention, but it had been sweet.

A picture in the shadowy parlor showed a room with a picture of a room, which had a picture of a room with a picture, and so on, forever. In a dark corner sat Tío Popsy and Papi. Fathers mostly talked to each other, not to girls. They told me to go to my room and pretend to sleep, so I wouldn't have to have any mortifying riding lessons. Everything could be enchanted, like Tío Popsy's suitcase.

AFTER PUTTING Niceto down for his nap, Nanny Fresia had left a cloud of potato smell, mixed with the violet perfume she wore on Sundays. I fled to my mother's room. On the windowsill an envelope said "Pilar Prados" in my father's handwriting. Without moving a paper next to it, I could read, ". . . understand why I can't go right now. I can't use levers for a position at the Ministry of Labor as a negotiator and advisor until I have experience with the unions. In a law office, I would be just another legal worker without a recognized degree. I shall make it big; you and the children will be proud of me. When I get to be the biggest labor . . ." When had Papi written? Who cared if he was the biggest anything? It would make me proud for him to come get us. But Papi was a busy man. Sometimes you felt a hurt inside, like a frantic wasp trapped in a shoe box.

THE CROQUET LOOPS made imaginary tunnels through which balls were sent touching, rubbing or crashing against each other, amid shrieks and laughter. "Armando, I have a huge surprise for you," Tía Merce kept saying.

Someone asked, "Do you suppose it's about that beautiful heartbreaker María Pía Ycheñirre? You know, she was engaged to Jorge Echaurren but married a baron. Merce's been writing to her for weeks, and she just got a letter from her."

"Does Armando know? Remember, he's been crazy about her since he was a boy." I prayed this went on until dark. Manuel passed a tray with fruit drinks, bending down to display his movie-star hair waves—needlessly, as he was very short.

My mother sat to take off her hat. She smoothed her black hair and called me. Before she could tell me about a good horsemanship lesson and what a lucky girl I was, I put my knee on her bench and asked, "Mami, the girls say I should be ashamed of my ancestors. Their teachers say Spaniards were cruel and bloodthirsty to the Indians."

She gave me a sip of her drink. "My daughter, tell them those cruel and bloody Spaniards were *their* ancestors. Yours stayed in Spain minding their own business."

"Mami, if we go to Spain and live with my grandfather, they might kill Papi, but not you, would they?"

"Probably not, but jails are still full of Republicans who opposed Franco, and I did leave with your father. Always stay out of politics; it brings nothing but grief. Now go put on your breeches and boots for your lesson with Armando. You're such a lucky girl. And Solita, it's been so disappointing for Armando that his children have been soured about riding by their mother. Show enthusiasm; it will bring him such comfort."

The girls were outraged when they saw me heading out in my riding outfit. Why hadn't I called SOS, as agreed? I was upset enough to lower myself to make excuses. They took me to the park and pointed to a luxuriant broadleaf bush. I demurred. How could I do this? My mother had been serious and worried for too long, about too many departures, too many pensiones with bedbugs and wild children who played with knives and threatened to kill Spaniards, too many long walks from the outskirts of the city loaded with food bought from farmers because we had no money for the bus, too many people condescending to help us if it pleased them. The girls pushed me in and rearranged branches while fretting because Melons had said the hipless poet might be leaving. Gloria said it was Mlle. Vicky's fault for hounding him, but Grace was optimistic. "Mumsy says she won't let him leave."

"But stinky-feet Gunther howls about his poems to María Cristina Undurraga," Gloria complained. "Men have moldy brains. Imagine, getting all out of shape about some drooling words."

"Shh!" Patricia hissed, "he's coming! Maybe he'll write his last poems." They dispersed to blend into the forest. Our sudden love of green clothes baffled the nannies, but we knew it was the color used by soldiers to avoid detection in order to spy on their object of interest. His last poems; it sounded grandiose, much more so than the songs the maids loved to cry to.

Werther walked in the forest of light descending between the treetops. Anything could happen now. He could run into Genevieve de Brabant and her baby; or a gallant robber; a gnome with tiny bells on his pointed shoes; a pale hermit; a dragon killed by a beautiful knight; a wise old woman with dirty hair; a white snake who was really a bewitched girl. He picked a dead leaf from the fountain, then sat on a stone bench to write in a notebook. He *was* a prince. Fairy tales were true.

After a while he stood in front of my bush and looked around. He spread his legs, opened his trousers and took out his fig-leaf stuff. A stream glistened in a ray of light. What I saw was so shocking, I didn't even scream when I was sprinkled; it was a slovenly jungle; a tangle of pink and brown and coiled hair and a spout, and shifty walnuts. It could only be compared to the description the girls had given of the time they had accidentally witnessed the slaughter of the pink piglets.

It embarrassed me to have been dazzled by someone with the convoluted parts of a dog or a horse taken to its most ludicrous extremes. A prince indeed. A prince was a graceful statue with a smooth surface reflecting his valiant and genteel nature. So far as I was concerned, he could leave. The death of Werther was true after all.

I sat inside the bush until the girls came to tell me the grown-ups were at tea and their *tío* planned to give me a lesson the next morning, during a cart expedition to the volcanic mountains. "It's absolutely essential that you don't have that lesson in the campsite; we can't tell you why, but it can lead to terrible things for you."

I didn't trust Patricia but I did Gloria, and she agreed. "Don't worry, Solita, there're great places to hide in the volcanic mountains."

With all the things they'd told me about them? Ravines with silky dust that slid you down into volcanoes; caves with thirsty, big-fanged mountain bats and sudden holes; *litre* trees that gave you a rash so you looked like a burnt salamander, and leeches that got fat with your legs' blood. Plus my mother. I'd think about it.

When I told them about seeing Werther from the bush, Gloria was upset. "Everybody gets to see everything; Grace gets to see an ostrich, Solita gets to see a dong."

INSIDE OUR CART, turned into a wagon by a canvas that filtered a cozy red light, we bounced excitedly on the mattresses covered with Indian loom rugs and strewn with pillows. The *aromo*'s yellow pompons sweetened the air. In front the oxen's tails slapped away flies from brown streaks on their bony asses. The *cuchillero,* the dashing and serious knife man who killed pumas and wolves by rolling a blanket around one arm and holding a knife with the other hand, led Lucero and Rabelais by the reins for my lesson with Tío Armando. I had to decide what to do. I crawled out to get fresh air, ignoring Nanny Fresia's objections.

I marched next to a tan ox for a while, seeing myself tiny in his brown eye. The beast tried to turn its head, the way shy animals said hello, but was frustrated under the yoke. His pace was resigned. What could I do? The huge wheel turned and turned over its shadow. We passed a peasant house surrounded by musty little bushes spreading an orchestra of perturbing odors that reminded me of my illness. The nannies stuck out their arms to wave. "Good day, Doña

Tomasa. The *boldo* brew worked fine for my jaw." La Tomasa made a gesture of covering the sun, maybe to indicate nighttime, to Nanny Fresia. She agreed with her head, then looked very sad.

From the grown-ups' wagons came crisscrossing chatter. I heard my father's name. "You think Armando and Julian are different? How about him and Miguel? It's like the old Spanish saying: 'They are so different you'd think they were brothers.' " "You mean Armando went to Germany to marry Helga—that unchic Teutonic tank—for breeding purposes, then divorced her?" "Doesn't he have a horse-breeding farm too?" "Not true, it was her passion for electrical appliances; she fired all the servants and went about efficiently pushing buttons, and wanted him to do the same instead of being served. It drove him out of his mind and out of her house." "No, no, he was dazzled by her huge feet, broad shoulders and blondness, the vision of all that grandeur passing on to his children." "Then why didn't he marry one of those girls from our German settlements? They are just as big and blond." "Ay, my pretty, really," the Walrus voice scolded, "whoever heard of a man from a good family marrying one of our Germans!"

If I got near the other wagon, maybe they would be talking about the people in this wagon. I wanted to hear why people married. Tía Merce said, "María Pía Ycheñirre's coming tomorrow. She left the old baron, you know." "Reaaally? Jorge was right, he had no title, and that's all she wanted." "The minute Armando sees her, he's going to flip!" "Merce, you naughty girl, you planned all this."

Nanny Fresia called me. Every time you were about to learn why grown people did things, you were left with unusable pieces.

TOWERING MOUNTAIN PEAKS with occasional perpendicular walls of many pale colors, bigger than the ones that gave Tartarin of Tarascon such problems, rose magnificently around the campsite. Servants spread the hand-loomed rugs in a shaded oak grove and labored in a make-shift kitchen. Tía Merce sang about the cinnamon flower. "Be patient, Solita," my mother said. "After we stretch our legs on a walk, Armando will give you a lesson."

We frolicked in a lagoon between pebble beaches. The nannies called us to check for leeches. Patricia said, "Who-ever can't follow me is a stinking swine," and while the nannies shouted about pumas and wait till la Mamota hears about this, all three headed up the river, with me behind them, climbing up and down slippery rocks until there was no trace of the smell of tomatoes, onions and cilantro herbs, or wood burning to roast the calf. "They'll never find you," Patricia told me. What if my mother wanted Tío Armando to help us and also my father? How could you decide about things you didn't know much about? Past some trees with glossy leaves, which I carefully avoided, we climbed up a ledge. On the other side of a huge ravine, Tía Merce took the hipless poet by the hand and led him under a water fall. Tío Popsy looked sad and headed back to the campsite. The girls said nothing.

We followed a winding ledge through a city of jagged towers with violet or orange-gray faces. I was first, keeping a close watch for slippery caves. I stopped; somebody was past the next corner. "Who could it be?" Grace breathed. "Solita's mother and Tío Armando left first." Patricia made a gesture for me to go on. I turned to go back, but faced a line of three rigid girls. Anyway, they were always saying dumb things. And I had no choice. I stepped on the other side and came face-to-face with a gigantic cat! He looked up from a bloody carcass, as surprised to see me as I was to see him. The girls turned the corner and screamed. We ran out until we were sure we were safe from being torn apart. "It was a puma," Gloria and Grace said, scared.

"It was a *guiña,* and that's final," a pale Patricia said.

I was that close to being able to tell I'd been nearly torn apart by a puma, but I had to say it was a *guiña.*

Back at camp, we sat on rugs under the oaks. Tío Popsy painted on a cardboard. Melons, with Lolita in her jar next to her, tried to communicate with the spirits, who ran freely at such high mountain altitudes. After Tía Merce's song, a maid served *chicha,* a fermented grape juice which made you giggle at everything. Tía Merce lifted her *chicha* glass. "*Salud!* Our great poet has agreed to do a reading tonight, right?" The hipless poet looked ill at ease. The girls looked serious.

My mother said, "Merce, why don't you ask Miguel if he wants to join us?"

Tía Merce ignored her and made a toast: "To the great surprise I have for my dear brother-in-law!"

My mother and Tío Armando called me. I finished my *chicha* and went to their rug. The fallen oak leaves were ferocious man-eating coleoptera turned powerless under my invincible tennis shoes, but I still had to follow Tío Armando to the horses.

"Control, control," Tío Armando kept saying from Lucero. He wanted me to command the horse with my seat without stirrups! I finally told him my bottom wasn't any good at giving commands. He got impatient. "No, no! Increase impulsion from leg pressure, no heels!" He said my little finger wasn't doing its part with the reins, nor my wrist. I saw us not as a girl and a horse, but as body parts strewn in confusion. "Even an ox like Rabelais deserves better. At this rate we'll never get to diagonal moving." Surely Rabelais was as uninterested in diagonal moving as I was. While practicing backing, I put the wrong pressure somewhere and Rabelais's back collided with Lucero, pushing him against an ash tree and nearly throwing Tío Armando off. I had Rabelais freeze until I realized Tío Armando was livid, ordering me to move forward so he could get unpinned. The girls laughed hysterically from the oak grove. Tío Armando slapped his boots and said we would do this some other time. I shouldn't have been pleased to have squashed his leg, but I was. But my mother's eyes were reflecting the roasting fire like it came from within. Why couldn't I manage to make things happen the way I wanted, without making my mother suffer, after all she had been through? Ruperto started a ballad about glum moonlight and longing lovers. The crisp smell of the roast, the chords "Oh river, oh river" spread beyond the oaks. I watched the poor calf being turned over the fire.

18

NICETO AND I HAD TO HAVE TEATIME WITH TÍO Armando. Where was El Zorro? El Cid with his volunteer army? Jeff King, thunderbolt of the air, destroyer of Dr. Vulcan's evil plot to crush Earth? The serving maid pushed her braids back as she put empty cups on her tray. Wasn't she furious about living here? She went back to the kitchen to join people who weren't more noticeable than tree shadows; who said things about others, as the guests did, but we weren't to consider any of it, since it was just "kitchen talk"; who had information that was useful to us, such as how to make croquettes, but were considered totally ignorant; to whom things happened, but we weren't supposed to find out what; who lived with us, but would have no contact with us in the future. For whom did the serving maid wait? For her father? For Padre Romualdo?

Tío Armando asked me what grown-ups asked when they

didn't know what to ask, starting with "What's your favorite subject in school?" followed by "You like math, don't you?" I didn't confess about never having been in school, or my lack of rapport with the multiplication tables. I nodded. You had to do what your mother wanted you to do. She looked impatient; this was not being charming. Tío Armando launched into a speech about the value of mathematics in this changing world. I turned a eucalyptus seed in my hand; the buds were jewels and I, the jeweler, appraised them; the tiny hairy blossoms were powder puffs and I, the famous actress, powdered my face; the seeds were dice and I, the daring gambler, played millions in a casino. He said, "So you like tennis. I'm delighted." Tío Armando launched into a speech about the value of tennis, tapping his cigar. The guanaco approached him gently and grabbed it. It gave Tío Armando such a start, his hat fell on his ear. He turned around and saw the guanaco quietly eating his cigar. Manuel and I couldn't suppress a laugh. Tío Armando said it was impossible to have any peace in this zoo, and ordered Manuel to take away the guanaco, who loved teatime, most of all eating cigars. I noticed Tía Merce spying with a smile behind one of the corridor doors. She made a motion to someone behind her. A woman with thin chestnut hair joined her. Tía Merce gave her a push happily, and the wispy woman strode toward us, moving her hips forward with pumalike motions. She stood behind Tío Armando and called in a voice barely audible, "Amito."

Tío Armando leapt. My mother looked at her with shock. He scrambled up and cried, "María Pía!" then fell silent, flushed and misty-eyed.

AT DUSK Nanny Fresia didn't put Niceto to bed, so I did. He started to whine. I went to get my mother. "Where's Fresia?" she asked as she tucked him in. I wouldn't tattle-tale about Nanny Fresia. "Solita, we've had enough debacles, haven't we? Next time ask Armando about his tennis courts.

Tell him how much you wish to learn to play, as I told you. It's more important than ever, my daughter. My sisters and I loved tennis."

Niceto said, "The *chicharrones* make Nanny vomit all day."

"That's not true," I said in her defense. "Only in the mornings."

"She vomits in the mornings?" my mother asked.

"It's her liver. Mami, if Nanny gets married, can't she still stay with us?" I didn't say a word about the foreman.

My mother's face set as when things were serious. She forced me to tell her everything I'd heard, which turned me into a squealing, double-faced betrayer, but what else could I do? We tried to tell her that the servants kept saying an earthquake was coming, but she left in a hurry, filling the dusk hour with calls that a woman they called la Tomasa was about to murder a maid. Everyone thought my mother was crazy. I almost thought so too, but you always had to give your mother the benefit of the doubt. After a lot of arguments, Evaristo brought the car and my mother left with him. La Mamota fumed. Taking a car for a servant on those godforsaken roads at night!

I went to bed. Owls hooted. Dogs barked. Bats whistled. *Ánimas,* or whatever they were, made their hoarse hisses. A long time later, the car rumbled back. I got up and cracked the door open. A white owl looked disapprovingly from an eave. The floor was cold. The moon lit half of every lemon leaf on the landscaped hill. Tía Merce and la Mamota met my mother at the veranda. Nanny Fresia cried on and off. "Got there just in time," my mother said in her firm way. "That woman had her on a dirty bed and was just about to insert a jagged broomstick, which she uses for this purpose. There was no water, much less soap, in that hovel. Let's go to bed. Tomorrow, Merce, you should go settle things with this man, and demand that he fulfill his obligation."

"Ave María Santísima!" la Mamota cried, and mumbled prayers.

"My *chère* Pilar," Tía Merce chuckled, "it's not done—"

"Mi Señora Doña Mercedes," la Mamota burst in, "that Timoteo has gotten into the *interesting* way at least thirty girls from these parts. He's got blue eyes, you see, so girls just fall for him, like he's decent folk." My mother had explained that "decent" in the New World meant having money, and being blue-eyed was considered being decent, because many of the poor, industrious northern Spaniards who settled here and prospered had blue eyes.

Guests asked at their doors what was going on. Tía Merce whispered to them. The men mumbled sleepily, "Oh, women's matters," and went back to bed. Tío Armando said, "You girls are crazy; one can't get any sleep in this zoo," and closed his door.

"Surely, Señora Pilar," la Mamota said, "you don't think Timoteo's got to marry all of the girls he's gotten into an interesting way. . . . The fact is, Señora, I told Fresia, I told her a hundred times; it's her fault, she has no excuse. . . ."

"Yes, Mamota," Tía Merce said, amused. "Pilar, *ma chère, chère* Pilar, you have to face the realities of these people."

"Merce, the reality is, You get her pregnant, you marry her—that's what the reality should be."

"Ave María Purísima!" la Mamota cried. "It's a good thing the girls aren't hearing this!" I would have bet my foil ball the girls were at their door listening.

"Pilar, really, I can't imagine what Jaime Undurraga, another superfossil, would say!" Tía Merce laughed.

"If you don't go, I will," my mother said. "Fresia, you go to bed. And don't you ever leave little Niceto alone again."

When Nanny Fresia entered the room, I was jumping joyfully because she was staying, my nightgown flying up to my waist every time I came down on the bed. "What happened? What did la Tomasa do?" I asked out of breath, my happiness making me bold.

"Nothing, little girl. It's my liver; I needed some *boldo* leaves, because . . . el Trauco got me. Stop jumping, you bad little girl! You're ruining the springs!"

I STAYED WITH Nanny Fresia in the mornings. I watched her dip the turtle comb in the basin's water, glide it easily near the scalp on her new straight hair, then struggle all the way to the ends of the permed little waves, going "Ay! Ay! Ay!" She told the Saints she needed five pesos. For a permanent for her sister Felicia, she told one. For a safety pin to reunite the strap of her slip with the bodice, she told another. To get Rita the seamstress to make her a bigger uniform to hide a few unwelcome spreads, she told a third. She got angry when I said maybe the Saints talked to one another and knew she was asking each something different.

During Madame's funereal march, Patricia said, "Mumsy's furious at your nanny and is going to banish her. She instructed la Mamota to find another nanny for Niceto and you. Probably Berta." Berta, a chambermaid who was chummy with la Mamota, also had a foul attitude toward me. I had to go on seeing Nanny Fresia, her apron, her big teeth, even her odor and showers of complaints.

When we got back, I begged my mother not to let Nanny Fresia be banished. She said I had big ears and not to worry, she had a good plan. The girls observed her, then headed for the gallery to find out what was going on. They heard my mother was fuming because Tío Armando was falling all over María Pía.

Passing the herb garden, I heard the cook's voice. "The cook's saying something fancy," I invented, hoping to divert them. They fell for it, and we hid behind the dry herb shed.

"Chela, get some basil from there. Yes, Fresia has no end of foolishness, like all you girls. Imagine, sending a message to Timoteo that she was doing what he'd asked." The fried-onion smell that clung to the cook was even stronger than the herbs. "Of course, Timoteo told Fresia he won't marry her anyway, after she asked la Tomasa to take the eye out of her potato." The cook giggled, sounding like sizzling onions. "By the time you girls learn about men's crafty bamboozlement, you're saddled with a couple of little bastards. Carmen, you throw away that garlic you dug; get some from a plant with yellow tops. You girls never learn, never learn, about garlic, about men . . . Chela, get a bunch of cilantro. It's earthquake weather, I'll have you know."

"But the Spanish señora says she's going to have el Timoteo marry Fresia," Chela said. "Saintly Virgin! Wouldn't Fresia be the luckiest girl in El Topaz!"

"I'll sleep in a bed of thistles if el Timoteo marries Fresia," the cook said. "It'll do nothing, the ruckus the Spanish señora's raising with el Timoteo's *patrón,* Don Jaime. Whoever heard of such a notion! A man has his bit of fun in strange territory, then his *patrón* gets hounded by these foreigners to force him into the eternal bonds of matrimony! In this world, between the Saints and the Devils doing their work, you get to see everything. See, if you girls are foolish enough to fall for Satán's tail wiggling at you, well, then, you got to suffer the consequences. Ayyy! My back! This picking beats my kidney to a pulp. Carmen, go to the kitchen, boil water, it's my maté time."

Carmen left, mumbling that the cook had followed the Devil's tail herself; Martita, the cook's daughter, was proof enough.

Whatever my mother was doing, I wished she wouldn't do things that raised big waves, even in the kitchen. When you went against the rules, it didn't do any good. You had to surrender, you had to cooperate. Nanny Fresia was wrong to defy things.

The next day, the *peón* José was summoned. My mother asked him if, after what had happened, he still wanted to marry Fresia. He turned his hat round and round in his hands, and nodded shyly. My mother asked Nanny Fresia if she would marry José. Nanny Fresia cried and cried, and nodded shyly. Then my mother told Tía Merce that, as soon as it could be arranged, the priest should come to marry them in the chapel.

"Bizarre!" Tía Merce cried. How could they possibly have a wedding for a couple of peasants! And in the bride's condition! Preposterous!

María Pía let out an airless laugh, bent like a daffodil stalk, and in a whisper said she wished to see a rodeo. "Wonderful, me too!" Tío Armando said. Tía Merce agreed.

"A country wedding would delight a sensitive young poet," my mother said.

"A divine idea!" Tía Merce said. "We're tired of rodeos. You can't go to a country house but they force one on you."

So this was my mother's plan for Nanny Fresia. Why was a wedding such a big deal? The important thing was for Nanny Fresia to stay with us until we left. You had to trust your mother's plans, but it was getting very difficult. The good part was that Padre Romualdo was coming. He had ways to make things work right.

ONE SENSIBLE THING about Tía Merce was that she always wanted to do things right away. Every guest and peasant was in front of the chapel waiting for Padre Romualdo, except el Gonzalo. The precious girl said her father knew she was at a wedding, but wouldn't dream it was a peasant one. María Pía, in flowing gauze and a much-admired big hat from Paris, smiled delicately. José wore a suit, retrieved reluctantly and furiously from Tío Popsy's armoire by la Mamota. It made his thin shoulders and short legs look permanently bent. Everyone laughed, but José was a nice man and smiled shyly, advertising with dark gaps in his teeth the lack of calcium in El Topaz's soil.

Peasants didn't have big weddings, much less with a fancy dress, but my mother persuaded Tía Merce that it wouldn't be a wedding unless it had a big, white dress in it. Rita had sewn one with a barrage of complaints and la Mamota's total sympathy. The servants heatedly criticized Nanny Fresia for wearing a white dress. They said she'd look like a fly in milk, that she would commit a mortal sin because she had already ordered the goodies. All my attempts at finding out what this meant proved fruitless. They said Fresia always put on airs and wanted to marry someone highfalutin, like a foreman; a chauffeur even! And look, she ended up with not only a *peón* with no hope of work near the houses, but an *ilegítimo,* from one of El Topaz's poorest women. I was very upset; Nanny Fresia never bothered any of them.

I ran to welcome Padre Romualdo, but stopped short of his black robe, which my father called sinister. It seemed you didn't hug or kiss a priest, but nobody explained why. He put his hand on my head. "Have you prayed, my daughter?" I couldn't talk to him because he went inside the chapel.

After Fresia and José were married, the women covered them with locust blossoms, so they would have lots of children, the cook said. Fresia and José seemed worried it would damage their clothes. What would locust flowers have to do with children? It was clear—mostly from Patricia's insight—that Nanny Fresia would have a baby sometime. After weddings came babies. But there was much confusion about it. Asking Nanny Fresia was useless; she got mad or sad, and talked about Trauco. My mother told me she'd tell me later. Tía Merce told the girls she'd tell them later.

The bridal couple, followed by family and friends, strayed toward the cart yard, where accordions, guitars and happy songs announced a fiesta. Instead of joining them, Tía Merce and her guests laughed at what they wore or said. It didn't seem what good-mannered people should do, but they were having great fun at it. Then they flocked around Pablo, the world-famous poet, who had arrived for the weekend with sad eyes and a beret. They talked to him about young Werther's poems. "Such a tremendous spiritual tension, such intensity of texture," the spiritual lady who wrote muddy poems said. The Walrus was impressed and smiled at her.

María Pía sighed. "Ay, Pablo, I think Werther's so ideeal!" Everyone who had gone to Galmeda's good schools said "ideeal" all the time. The girls didn't, because nothing was ideal to them.

Pablo told María Pía she was as languid and lovely as rain at dawn. I stood next to him, to see what he would call me. Those who wore lilac dresses were Violet; yellow ones, Dandelion; pink ones, Rose. "Hello, Mushroom," he said.

Melons said to him, "Haven't you noticed that when you die everyone drops you from their list of friends? They even erase you in their address books—haven't you noticed? They don't put Cemetery of Our Blessed Lady, or wherever you are, but someone else's name and address instead."

Pablo looked at Melons with his big, sad eyes without answering, so she went to look at Mlle. Vicky's bruises. "That brute's apt to kill you, my dear. I get these vile vibrations."

The psychiatrist agreed. "My dear wife's right, Vicky. The man exhibits clear signs of criminality."

Mlle. Vicky opened her dancing arms. "How long am I supposed to wait for an *acceptable* man? Leticia, what's this? I'm young, I'm attractive . . ." True, she was attractive, but definitely not young; the girls said she was nearly twenty-six.

"Vicky, I keep telling you; you come on like runaway Percherons and scare men. Can't you be skittish? Just a bit?"

When I grew up, I wasn't going to scare men by acting like runaway Percherons.

My mother talked to Tío Armando. He left María Pía and came to me, absentmindedly disgusted at the lacerations of the *capataz*'s dog, whose scabies made him the same pink as Mlle. Vicky's sweater. Going around the dog, he said to me, "I hear you love my tennis courts." My mother gave me a significant look. I watched the dog throw himself on the ground as a signal of total surrender. He was accustomed to being kicked out of the way, and managed to have his life spared because he was so flashily obsequious.

Instead of saying something, I bent down to pet him with a stick, so my skin wouldn't touch him. I felt my mother's eyes on me. The dog closed his eyes and clenched his teeth, expecting a blow. He opened his eyes with surprise and waggled a grateful tail when he realized what I was doing. I straightened up. My voice came low. "I think it's going to be a lot of fun to play tennis." Tío Armando's round face flashed a smile. I looked down to hide my wet eyes. María Pía came, and Tío Armando held out an arm for her to avoid the *capataz*'s dog, who threw himself down once more then left, satisfied of his good performance.

I moved near Padre Romualdo. Could I ask him about the locust blossoms? About my parents? I needed to know, but a polite girl had to be careful about her questions. He asked me what I was up to. "I'm going to be the princess in the dance," I bragged proudly.

"Good. Make sure you're a kind princess with everyone."

Fair enough. "But if someone has bad power over someone else, the princess can punish them," I said.

"Only God can punish, my daughter."

This was bad news. "But, Padre, what if God doesn't?"

"Victims are not scarred if they refuse to cooperate and are victimized forcibly, my daughter. You be a good princess and also say your prayers." He went to talk to the bridal couple, then left in a swing of two big wheels of his buggy. I was so preoccupied with what he had told me, I let him get away.

19

CAVERNOUS NOISES SOUNDING LIKE GIANT TARANTULAS came from the ground. Berta's yells cut my dream, right when I was about to throw a bucketful of goo on a pack of huge ostriches coming at me with stretched necks. My bed rocked away from the wall. Berta screamed, stumbled, pulled my brother, grabbed my hair, yelled, "Little girl! Wake up! Get up! Get out! Have mercy, Santa Rita, Santa Lucía, San Gregorio, Santa Catalina, *mártir y virgen,* have mercy! Little girl! Get out!" She stumbled toward the door carrying my half-asleep brother.

My dream bucket of spit turned into a real bucket of iced water going through me; I headed after them. Was this war? Walls moved like giants; dust showered from the ceiling; my bed followed me creaking, as if angry at me for leaving it before morning; the night table opened its door, letting out the chamber pot; the dresser danced to the music made by the basin and the pitcher banging against each other. While I was passing through it, the doorway moved sideways. I leapt across the veranda to the front garden.

Near and distant screams, people and shadows poured out of doors and corridors. A creamy moon spilled eerily over the front gardens. The cook and some chamber girls hit the gravel on their knees, like ghosts in their raw cotton gowns. Young maids cried; older ones punched their bosoms with their fists, looking up and yelling, "Mea culpa, mea culpa, Lord Father, forgive, mercy, have mercy!" Half-dressed gardeners, butlers, chauffeurs and helping hands leapt over bushes, staying away from creaky trees. Maximiliano ran buttoning his tasseled jacket, not nearly as impressive without pants. Gabriel, the back-gardens gardener, ran naked with a burlap bag clumsily wrapped around his middle to the huge oak and started the bell talk: fast ding-ding-ding-dings, for disasters.

The girls came out in their ruffled nightgowns, pulled and pushed by la Mamota, who crossed herself with frenzied eyes. Someone tripped out of Tío Juan Vicente's room, removing a chin-to-head contraption.

It was he. María Pía floated like a ghostly puma wrapped in silk. Mlle. Vicky erupted in her filmy nightgown, her face a white skull, yelling, "Save me! Save me, someone! Don't let me die unmarried!" Men came out trying to act composed. At the sight of them, Mlle. Vicky wiped off the white from her face. Ladies with curled bangs and the Genius avoided the dogs, who howled at the moon, maybe imitating the servants. Beethoven pranced, wagging his tail and barking gently to reassure everyone he was on top of the situation.

Madame ran up and down the veranda screaming, "*Au secours! Ce pays sauvage!*" Tío Juan Vicente grabbed her and brought her down. Madame fidgeted frantically with a bathrobe, furious at us, as if we had planned the event just to scare her to death. She mumbled about civilization as if earthquakes were the result of backward governments.

There were none in Paris, ever, she cried; presumably the Parisians simply wouldn't stand for it.

Tía Merce, pulling the frightened hipless poet by the hand, wobbled, bemused by the screaming scene. "Thank Goodness Pablo left, this would have given him a dreadful impression."

"Watch the ground for cracks, little girl!" Berta warned; you fall in one and it closes, and it'll make flat *charqui* out of you, mercy, mercy, San Gregorio!" I told her I had to tell my mother to come out, and rescue my foil ball. "Don't you dare, you foolish little girl. The houses can fall any second! Señora Pilar'll come out. Protect us, Santa Rita, Santo Tomás!"

As if the prayers had worked, Tío Juan Vicente stumbled to my mother's window. "Come back here!" la Mamota shrieked. "What if a loosened roof tile decapitates you! Remember what happened to Elias Cabezón, the cheese maker!" He came back saying Pilar refused to get up. Terror hit me. I remembered a refugee saying that Pilar ignored the sirens and never went to bomb shelters.

When I started to whine, the tremors subsided and suddenly the earth was still, as if bombing planes had left. Voices yelled at my mother to come out. With a candle, she looked through the window's ironwork at us as we shivered in the moonlight, now more frightened than when the earth was shaking. "Can't a person get any sleep around here?" she asked.

Everyone was dumfounded. Tía Merce chuckled with delight. I wished I could be brave like my mother, like a Spaniard had to be. Niceto was like her; he slept on Berta's lap.

"Pilar, come out, come out," Tía Merce ordered. "First tremors aren't always the worst. . . ."

The psychiatrist shouted, "Pilar, enough of this bravery nonsense; we aren't under siege from the Moors or the fascists; this is an earthquake, you know."

"I don't want to catch cold," my mother said. "If it gets bad, I'll come out."

Tía Merce laughed happily and ordered the men to go inside, grab blankets from the beds and bring her guitar. She talked to Werther secretively. The men came out, and everybody wrapped themselves and prayed. Tía Merce and Werther went toward the bungalow playhouse, and one of Tía Merce's songs could be heard.

There was another tremor, more wailing and chest-pounding. What would my father say about all this? A good thing he was safe in Galmeda. Or was he? "Make the sign of the cross again, my little ones, don't falter, Spaniards always bring bad luck," la Mamota told the girls. In the moonlight, their heads were wild escarole plants, appearing less powerful and more dangerous at the same time. No wonder it took so long every morning for the nannies to tame that flaming chaos into their magnificent curls. "Promise the Good Virgin," la Mamota ordered, "to be good girls, if She prevails upon the Heavenly Father to stop for good."

Grace, the closest to me, prayed. The tremor stopped. There was an opportunity here. I asked Grace, "Did you promise to be good?"

"Of course, you dunce; didn't you see that after my promise the tremor went away?" There was no doubt that Grace had unlimited confidence in her power. So much the better.

I asked if that meant good to everybody. She thought for a moment, then said with reluctance, "I guess so," but added, "I'll do what la Mamota says." That would be of no help to me.

I asked if being good meant being nice and sharing things, including secrets. She agreed. "Well, then, you have to tell me those things you know about me." She was appalled. I had to try it with her sisters. It was like a field of flowers to think of three meek girls.

Patricia said, "We don't mean just anybody. For instance, we don't pray for the peasants. And anyway, we're very fair and always give people what they deserve."

Gloria agreed to be good. She took me aside; she could let

me know one secret. They had heard their Mumsy confide to her friend Mónica on the phone that she was taking Pilar to El Topaz to get her away from her brother-in-law Armando, because she feared Pilar could catch him, then Pilar would have no use for her. As for the other secrets . . . another tremor started. Grace shouted to her, "If this one keeps up and Madame's study falls down, we won't have to have classes."

Finally my mother came out, tripping on the shifting veranda steps, her black hair down to her waist. The men helped her once she was away from falling roof tiles. Something crashed noisily in the dark. The air sponged up noises from underground. In the salon, furniture traveled around as if having a dance class, or banged against the walls as if complaining about the noise from next door. Several walls cracked; our room's wall crumbled. I wished the houses would be swallowed forever by a crater, even if my foil ball disappeared. Then, abruptly, there was an eerie calm.

"Ifigenio, see if this's the end of it," la Mamota told him. A small man who worked in the hothouse put his ear to the ground. Everybody watched him. Would my father include this in what he called "bizarre religion"?

As if reading my thoughts, Tío Juan Vicente said, "Ifigenio learned to be an underground noise expert from my *viñas'* expert, who's never been wrong yet."

After a while Ifigenio said, "It's the end of it. Won't be another one this night."

Everyone got up, hugged, cried, thanked a list of those Up Above and discussed where they should go to drink something hot.

Tío Armando grumbled, "A poorly built house in an earthquake zone; I'm never coming back to this godforsaken place." The earthquake was bringing good things!

The Genius said he liked this country because they left geniuses in peace and didn't expect them to discover anything. The guanaco nibbled on his collar, and he slapped it away.

Tía Merce arrived back from the play bungalow and announced, "This divine tremor will change everything. Come inside; wait till I tell you the news!"

Gabriel went to the huge oak to toll the bell; slow ding-dong-dings told everyone in El Topaz the earthquake was over and they could go back to bed. If there were beds to go back to.

LA MAMOTA GAVE instructions about debris and beds.

"Mamota, how's everything going to change, like Mumsy says?" Gloria asked, true to form.

"None of your concern, you nosy child; none of your concern. You better thank the Good Virgin, who prevailed upon the Almighty Lord to lift only one finger this time," la Mamota sighed.

"One finger?" Grace disagreed. "It seemed like three to me."

"No, child, that was one finger He lifted; two at the most. If He had lifted three fingers, the houses would have flattened."

Berta carried sleeping Niceto on her shoulder. She was glad the Basilisco hadn't gotten away with anything. That featherless, roosterlike *ánima* slid through canyons on its snake tail, promoting earthquakes in cahoots with the Devil, so he could expand his territories. In the moonlit dust, all those things you couldn't see seemed more plausible: the *ánimas;* the crowd Up Above; the floating souls who influenced humans; the girls' rules. In El Topaz, bad, evil and the weird weren't in mad political parties, in deranged tyrants, weren't remote and clear-cut, but confusing, unpredictable. Would the twins keep their promise to be good, and Tío Armando his to never come back?

La Mamota told servants to make maté and be ready for anything that might be requested. They headed for the kitchen, repeating to each other, "I knew this morning there'd be trembling. First such heavy air, then that wicked moon. Can't say the Saints didn't warn us plenty . . ."

"I knew yesterday! I told everybody, remember? I said . . ."

"That big one that crumbled half the houses in El Topaz; I warned everybody for days. But not a soul listened, nobody ever listens to me, then they're plenty sorry. . . ."

"A day like this, back before Terencio, the old butler, died, remember? And I kept saying, 'It's earthquake time,' but nobody paid any attention, but I was sure of it. . . ."

". . . and the wall fell over María Quiñones' baby, remember?"

". . . and that big elm just crushed the poor boy, remember?"

". . . and Victorina Soto was swallowed by that ditch that's still there, near the sheep's bath, pregnant and all, remember?"

". . . and the entire room collapsed on me, but I stood right under the doorway, and that's how I'm here to tell the story."

Their chatter drifted past the corridor.

My mother and the guests waited in front of the salon for servants to clear away debris and broken glass. I sneaked toward them, anxious to find out whether Tía Merce's big news was that my father was being invited to live here, or that now the houses were unlivable and we had to leave. Maybe it had to do with the other big secret the girls didn't want to tell me.

The salon's door was blocked by furniture packed like animals trying to get out. The grown-ups settled in the gallery. A couple of chamber girls managed to light two candelabra with their shaky hands. Tía Merce grabbed my mother's arm, whispering, "I did it! I did it! A double coup! At last, I got my lovely bard, and what I had long wished for, a workout during an earthquake!" She chuckled. "And I managed to keep that lovely slim body going—la Madre!

what leaps!—and he threw a torrent like the Mapu-Mapu River, right up to my lungs. I'll drip for a week. . . ." She saw a chamber girl nearby. "Tell Manuel to come light the fireplace."

The chamber girl started to leave, then mumbled to another one, maliciously, "There's no lack of kindling around."

Judging by her manner, Tía Merce had said something naughty. Someone had nearly drowned her, but she wasn't angry. I couldn't ask the girls because it had to do with their mother, and you didn't do that. They did, but it was wrong.

Manuel lit a fire and a chambermaid threw a basket of chestnuts on it. Sofa chairs, with figures wrapped in sheep-smelling blankets, like mummies, moved closer. I hid in a dark corner. "What do you think happened out in the mountains?" Mlle. Vicky cried with agitation, but no one answered.

"Europeans criticize us for being lazy," the Walrus complained defensively, "but what's the point of building great things when we know they're going to crumble periodically?"

"Then you rebuild; you have a rebirth; build something better," the psychiatrist said. This was a cheerful idea.

"That's exactly what I wanted to tell you," Tía Merce said.

"I kept wondering *où* Mercedes was." Tío Juan Vicente readjusted his satin pajamas. "I feared she *and* Werther'd been swallowed by an earthquake ditch." He looked impishly at the hipless poet wrapping his blanket up to his ears, then motioned to a chambermaid. "Bring *cedrón* brew for Mlle. Vicky, my dear, to calm her nerves, and bring me some hot chocolate."

Orders came from everyone. I badly needed some hot chocolate, but if I didn't keep quiet, they would send me to bed.

A chambermaid asked Tía Merce shyly, "Should I send a couple of girls to do some cleaning up?"

"No, no," my mother said. "It's more interesting this way. This is like penetrating inside an ancient pyramid."

Tío Juan Vicente kissed my mother's hand. "Divine Spaniard, you find enchantment even in a roomful of earthquake dust!"

Tío Armando fretted, "We're right next to a volcano-ridden ridge, a perfect place for earthquakes." His bald spot was dusty. I wished a brick had fallen on it. He said to María Pía, draped over the sofa as if she were an empty silk bathrobe, "And for you to come at this time; I shudder." He removed his blanket and put it carefully over her.

Tío Popsy appeared at the door in a bathrobe. I almost leapt to my feet. "I need a chambermaid to redo my bed," he said sleepily. "It's full of dust. Goodnight, my friends." He left. The gallery felt empty.

"He slept right through," Melons said. "Whiskey turned the rocking into la Mamota's young arms, and noises into a lullaby."

Tía Merce clapped, "*Mes chers amis,* permit me to make my wonderful announcement. This tremor caused me to realize I've been acting too much like a matron. I'm young! Really, I'm just a girl enchanted by life . . . and poetry. And—"

"Naturally," Melons interrupted. "An earthquake makes one think about one's life." Melons should have thought about shutting up.

"I'm revitalizing El Topaz," Tía Merce exulted, "turning it into a creative force, a haven for poets! We'll have readings, unveil young talent! Isn't it the most divine idea?" She looked at the hipless poet, who observed the fire gloomily.

So, these were the big news and big changes announced by Tía Merce with such fanfare? Who cared about poetry! Wasn't Tía Merce going to release that terrible power she had over my mother so we could leave? It made me so angry. . . .

When I woke up, I was in a strange bed. Outside, the sun appeared feebly between clouds as heavy as the bottom of ships.

WITH DEBRIS EVERYWHERE and the guests changing rooms, the confusion was wonderful, but the girls had gathered no news about what was going on, except that the hipless poet had announced he would leave with the first departing guest. We had too much important detective work to do to worry about him. We met at the avocado orchard. "Solita, did you see or hear anything about your mother and Tío Armando? We haven't seen them together since María Pía showed up."

I would have eaten a prickly pear, skin and all, rather than tell them anything about my mother. I asked, "Do you know about a torrent like the Mapu-Mapu River near your play bungalow?" They didn't, or weren't telling either. We would get nowhere this way. We ate fallen avocados, whose black skin peeled out like a satin glove, leaving a dark, almond-tasting aura around the juicy flesh, the perfect gateway for the guarded sweetness that followed.

"I heard Tío Armando and Tío Juan Vicente talking, and maybe it was naughty," Gloria said. This was a word that made you pay attention. "Tío Armando said he was fed up with hard-to-get dames. He said, 'Our own women are far more sophisticated; they get to a romp as fast as we do.' " She ground an avocado pit with a rock.

"Well, go on, that doesn't say anything."

"Tío Juan Vicente said, 'They are also fickle; your wispy beauty has left you twice already—first Jorge, then the baron.' "

"And?" Patricia packed her pipe with the pit grounds.

"Then he said something and laughed his way that's so funny, knotting his face with teeth in the middle, you know?"

"But what did Tío Armando say?" She burned the grounds.

"Nothing. I laughed so hard at Tío Juan Vicente's face,

they noticed me and stopped. That's how I know it was naughty."

"Gloria, you turkey, you always gather useless info."

All we got was a sore throat and a raspy voice from smoking avocado pits. The Genius was consulted about our throats and said it was due to the climatic and air-pressure changes brought about by the earrrthquake. Everyone was impressed.

MADAME JOLTED US by handing me a new book with pictures, saying I would do work for my age. The girls would stay in remedial, but although she had recuperated from a *crise nerveuse* due to the *sauvage* earthquake, they wouldn't write compositions, as her nerves couldn't take it. The new book showed Earth with layers, all the way to a pit of fire! Having me on a higher level made the girls sit on a pit of fire, and me happy. But jumpy.

Depending on her mood, Madame made them write twenty "*Je suis une fille paresseuse*" or "*lente.*" The next time we went on a funereal march, Patricia dallied, so we arrived at the center of a field just at the time the irrigation water was let go. We ran to a hill, then watched Madame calling us, until the water hit her up to her calves. She held her skirts up to slosh through the field. This cost us one hundred "*Je suis . . .*" After we started, Patricia made a special nod, and all three bounced their legs against the table, making the floor tremble. Patricia gave me a kick; I joined them.

Madame stiffened up, then stampeded out of the classroom and down the veranda, screaming, "Earthquake! *Au secours!* Help! Help!" After screaming up and down the veranda a few times, she realized everyone stood looking at her as if her brains had crumbled. She was mortified. We observed from the classroom door, thrilled.

Thereafter, when we made the floor tremble, Madame never knew whether it was for real, and tried to act calm. We kept it up. She continued to tell the girls about farms, but sooner or later her nerves piled up and she rushed outside in a cold sweat. She couldn't punish us with one hundred "*Je suis* a treacherous earthquake fraud and sadistic savage," because it would be a recognition that she had swallowed our bait. It made me happy to see someone else scared.

Patricia told Madame not to worry about the tricks the twins and I played on her, because in El Topaz earthquakes came only every three months or so. Madame called la Mamota and told her to go directly to Madame Larraín and inform her she was leaving as soon as a car could take her back to Galmeda. Fine, Tía Merce said, she'd bring the real governess. It turned out that this Madame was not the one chosen by Tío Toto, the one who had a subscription to *Astronomy News* and had been a friend of the famous painter's brother. Tío Armando had decided that that one was a screwball and had taken it upon himself to bring this one instead. We didn't know how Patricia came up with such brilliant ideas.

PAPI GULPED his coffee while standing up. He handed back his demitasse to a serving girl. Instead of hugging me, asking me where Niceto was, or taking me with him to the park, where the grown-ups were, he rushed out, telling me to wait in my room. The front wall to our two rooms had collapsed. The little bathroom had crumbled; only the toilet was left, presiding over the calla-lily field. I sat on a step at the people's entrance, closer to the park than the vehicles' entrance, feeling like an earthquake aftermath. But it was thrilling; everything would be fixed now.

Under la Mamota's command, the houses were being assaulted by repair brigades. Broken glass, knickknacks, branches and debris disappeared, furniture pieces went back into place, cracked adobe walls closed up. Dusters, sweepers, patchers, painters and trimmers cheerfully shared what they'd been thinking right before the tremors started, and what they did next. My nose was tickled with a barrage of exotic fumes.

I got tired of waiting and went to the park. Through the trees I spotted my father by the tiled fountain. He seemed very upset. Everyone looked at him and at Tío Armando, who one minute had a neck like a fighting rooster and the next a superior goose smile.

My mother came closer to the fountain. "Of course, Julian, I'm very pleased about your job offer with a lawyer, but I have no intentions of leaving for the time being." The fountain's waterfall drowned their words, but his body was angry. She said something. He turned around and headed toward the houses, his eyes and jaw about to pop out. Everyone looked at him; some seemed amused.

Tío Juan Vicente, his patches bouncing, followed him, distressed. "Congratulations on your job, old boy, but you are truly mad; most roads are impassable. Stay awhile, Julian."

My father didn't slow down. He jumped on the motor bicycle and left before I could catch up with them. I was greeted by the dry smell of dust settling on the road.

I swung the white chains flanking the entrance steps. Underneath, some vicious scorpion flies sucked the defeated body of a millipede with their long mouths. The millipede squirmed in pain and despair. After a while the crunching of pine needles and voices got near. "It takes an earthquake to have Julian come see his family." "You know very well that other earthshaking news brought him here." "Ironically, he hadn't heard the last one."

Earthshaking news? And he hadn't told me? The millipede died. One of the two white chains made a rusty sob as I swung it, and swung it, and swung it.

MADAME SHOWED UP at the veranda, jerking her parasol, followed by a butler with her suitcase. "I'm not surprised to be leaving so soon," she said haughtily. "Nobody in this country takes education seriously. Or anything else, for that matter." When the girls saw Madame's hat with the cherries settled in the back of Tío Popsy's car, they ran up and down the gallery a hundred times, yelling, "*Je suis* a happy girl!" I ran too. The German photographer promised to bring back the new Madame.

The guanaco, on the rear seat of the Walrus' car, and Tío Popsy's bald head were being removed from us. His departure didn't cause the girls any visible grief. It was a cruel blow to me, although nothing had really happened with respect to Tío Popsy; what I expected of him wasn't even clear. The maids couldn't reconcile themselves to the loss of the tasseled chauffeur. La Mamota wiped tears, waving at her Miguelito. Tía Merce waved a perfumed handkerchief, mumbling, "Good-by, my poet, *mon beau* Eros . . . ," then turned to my mother: "I must say, Pilar, it's all your fault for having a consort who drives everybody away with his maniac macho scenes. Well, my revenge is that now you have neither one and will have to stay here." My mother had the same face as when she'd tell Papi, "You're wrong, just wait and see." Whatever it was, my mother was always right.

That night Tía Merce and the girls went to their well-lit quarters, the only ones fully restored. My mother, Niceto and I were given rooms next to the salon, which had been cleaned but still needed repairs. I checked on my rescued foil ball under my pillow; it shone like a moon. The wall between my mother's room and ours had a crack. I could hear her breathing, awake. What was left here was the wreck of our part of the houses.

On one side of a big earthquake ditch was my mother, and on the other side my father; they refused to jump across, and I was too dumb to convince them with my begging and crying, so I decided to show them by jumping myself, but I fell inside and the ditch closed forever.

20

"GOOD THING I OWN ONLY ONE SUITCASE; I HATE packing," my mother said, reaching for a shawl behind her terrace chair. She didn't apologize for owning so little, she flaunted it. She didn't remind Tía Merce overtly that we were leaving, she gave gentle hints. It made me just as happy.

Tía Merce's peach fuzz underneath her chin trembled against the garden's light. "I still can't believe it, Pilar. Back to live in a pensione? You can't be serious." Her teacup stayed in front of her lips, as if what she was saying weren't that important to her.

"Merce, I told you, it's no longer a pensione. There'll be a lot to iron out, of course, and it still may not work out."

"You can't, Pilar, you can't leave me here alone." Tea from Tía Merce's cup fell on its saucer. Every cup in El Topaz absolutely had to have its matching saucer.

"You're not alone, Merce," Mlle. Vicky, back from the rauli

mountains with a bruise on her chin, said morosely. The old and pretty brown eyes of Mme. Chanel, the imposing new governess, smiled: I'm here too. Aside from her nauseating breath, she was fun. She liked this country, even goats. She filled the study with books, an old organ, fossils, maps of the heavens, and a wall-size nude picture of her younger self on a couch, done by the famous painter's brother. It was spooky to sit under it, with glaring breasts, and hair in naughty places. She assigned me more advanced books than the girls, but was gentle and patient, and didn't insult them. Still, it wasn't enough to make me want to stay; I fidgeted, eager to get to the public road and the bus.

Tía Merce ignored them. "Remember what I can do, *ma chère;* remember my brother-in-law? Don't ever underestimate my power. . . ."

"Merce, you should know better than to threaten me." Threaten! It sounded like a spy radio program. "But if you were planning a long get-together, with lots of new guests, I might be persuaded to stay longer and help you."

Tía Merce's back straightened up. "Why, yes! I'm planning a week-long *fête,* with *la crème de la crème* from Galmeda; many interesting men, and children your own should meet. I need you to help me, Pilar!" A defeated vine leaf lay on a paving stone.

Mlle. Vicky stirred. "How wonderful! Single men? Well situated?" She giggled.

"Naturally, available men of means, *ma chère* Vicky."

"Mumsy, is Jaime Idarrázabal Ochagavía coming?" Gloria asked, and the three looked at their Mumsy expectantly.

"Of course, my pets, we're inviting the best families."

The girls whispered happily, "He's dreamy. And the same age as our brother Enrique." As if I could have cared less.

"Well, Pilar?" Tía Merce looked at my mother. Niceto observed milk's steam passing under the serving maid's chin.

My mother nodded. "All right."

Tía Merce churned a triumphant chuckle. Mlle. Vicky

cried, "When is the party, when? I promise never to see that kicking animal again." Madame patted her arm. A wisteria dropped a petal.

My mother proposed a piñata, Madame a confectionery animal hunt for the children. The girls smiled. Mlle. Vicky proposed several very good dance solos, and a children's dance. The girls frowned. My mother proposed a ship theme: dances, banquets, deck games, with stops in exotic ports, decorated so the gallery would be Tahiti, the parlor Antarctica. . . . "Divine! Divine!" Tía Merce kept crying. "How long do we need for the preparations, Pilar?"

"A couple of weeks," my mother said, "considering that getting anything done here is like getting twenty cats to walk down the road with the aid of a little stick." They laughed as Tía Merce took my mother by the arm to go make a guest list.

Three weeks! That was forever! We were staying forever! Was my own garden gate, that I could open whenever I wished going to turn distant and legendary, like Spain, which was now dim centuries distant with faraway people who had feverishly reigned and written and defended and painted and built and signed agreements and made *churro* pastries, and became less and less connected with me, because I was still here? Naturally they would invite my father. He knew a lot about ships, mostly dockworkers. Back in Galmeda my father had been a train coming in and out at high speed, but on track. Now he was a ship barely veering this way, not stopping long enough to pick up passengers. We were in the wrong port.

María Pía and Tío Armando returned from the tennis courts, and she came to our table. Mlle. Vicky happily told her about "Pilar's wonderful idea" for the party. "I wonder what the Spaniard's up to?" María Pía said, barely breathing.

EVERY ROOM in the houses had to be readied. There was a traffic of decanters, flowers, ashtrays and a hundred other proofs of la Mamota's unsurpassed housekeeping. The dining-room table expanded until it looked like an airplane landing strip in the movies.

La Mamota said the decorations, directed by my mother, were ridiculous. Garlands hung between the veranda's columns, as in a ship about to sail. From the shops at the end of the cart yard came wooden portholes for the doors, and half lifeboats hung near the ceiling. From the surplus room came old pictures of ships Don Miguel or the girls' grandparents had sailed; Chinese figurines, lanterns and Buddhas, as well as cardboard pagodas on the walls, turned one room into the Orient. White bedsheets turned the parlor's stacked-up furniture into Antarctica. Thatched huts and canoes made from reeds from the big lake, and loud prints of tropical plants from Rita's sewing room, turned the gallery into Tahiti. A hunting horn from the surplus room that Manuel stuffed with straws sounded like a ship on a foggy night. We waded through the front gardens, now an ocean, looking at all the activity. I almost forgot about Galmeda for a while.

La Mamota was beside herself about the coming Ochagavías, Echaurrens, Idarrázabals, and Larraíns, known personally by her, not quite from the time of birth, but soon thereafter. She recalled a mess of baptisms, weddings, trips and events she had witnessed herself, personally. She described their *nanas,* now old, some dead, but none could hold a candle to la Mamota in competence.

The girls' rooms were a frenzy of comparing ribbons, dresses, pinafores, camisoles, socks, panties and hankies, so everything "matched," as if the girls were a color machine that wouldn't work unless every piece did its job perfectly. No doubt I'd be stuck with my old panties with unreliable elastics, but with so much turmoil, who would notice me tucked away in the library, reading up on how to sculpt a bear out of a soap bar? I had to change my plans, however, because my mother kept insisting I was to be charming to the children from such well-situated families, and Gloria confided that she couldn't tell me why, but there was something significant about how I got along with the children.

I DREW A TREE TRUNK on a brown piece of paper. The girls discussed what to do about games and contests, because they never won. They decided to have them at the end, when the children were happy and it wouldn't matter whether they lost. But their main topic of conversation was Jaime Idarrázabal Ochagavía—Ochagavía on one side, which evidently needed no explanation, and the great-grandson of a president on the other. He was brilliant and read voraciously, his mother said; he had dimples and only one drawback—a bratty sister. They were mortified to have to dance in front of him.

"Again, it's Tía Pilar's fault," Grace complained. "La Mamota says it's going to be embarrassing to have to lug Solita around when they come. What are we going to say about her?"

Why did they have to say anything? Maybe I would collect the most confectionery animals and win the prize, a picnic basket with dishes and everything inside. I would save it all, and when my father saw the basket, he would want to take us picnicking. And if I didn't win, I'd still harvest candy and lots of foils. "I wouldn't embarrass you." I drew an apple on red paper and cut it out.

"You wouldn't? Look at you, Solita. You sit on the floor with slovenly panties, showing parts that are impolite."

"I don't." The apple put a joyful red on the tree. "I can make friends with those children who are coming just as much as you." I said it. If we played marbles, I'd be a hit.

"You think just because you learned the planets in the book Madame gave you, you're the last Coca-Cola in the desert."

The scissors disobeyed me and cut an apple lopsided.

"Solita, the coming children aren't Italian button makers. These children go to the best schools." They were nervous.

I cut another apple. You had to keep trying.

"If your father shows up in that rattling eggbeater, we'll just die." They were frantic.

"Solita rides English," Gloria said.

"Ugh, Gloria, you dunce. We're not talking about horses."

Jaime Idarrázabal Ochagavía could be more like a prince than Werther. When I danced the princess, they would see. A princess had rough times, but at the end she didn't have to be like others, cry inside for protection, get terrified by pretending to be brave, or have to go along with things that were wrong. She got her own kingdom with her own prince. My mother wanted me to make friends with these children, and that was fine with me; they weren't Tío Armando. Four apples were enough for a tree.

THE CART YARD filled up with cars; the veranda resonated with loud music and fog horns; I kept hearing motorcycle roars; we kept kissing odd cheeks. Dr. Valdés arrived with Werther and Marco Polo. The straw woman ignored my mother and displayed proudly a Romanian count and his beautiful wife. Tía Merce went crazy about them. Werther moped, went walking to the main road and took the bus back to Galmeda. Two men, one in a fancy car, who kept one hand in his pocket, and a senator with a silk neck scarf, went crazy about my mother. The German photographer fiddled with his tripod. Soon the precious girl arrived, gushing about the ship. A swarthy young Persian was Madame's guest; the girls overheard that Madame was in love with him and he took all her money. Mlle. Vicky said nothing will ever change and left, leaving my princess role stranded. No one asked about Tío Popsy. The twins, worn out from running down the veranda, asked Patricia what the straw woman was up to. "Topsy-turvy," she said.

"Let's drink to the ship that will give us a rebirth." Tía

Merce lifted her glass, chuckling at the Romanian count and his beautiful wife.

"To rebirth!" They all lifted their glasses.

"Reminds me of the *Titanic,*" Melons said.

"YOU GO HERE, you here, and you . . . no, not so close, on the other side . . ." Mlle. Vicky moved us by the shoulders around the back veranda. She had come back from the rauli mountains with a limp, saying she had fallen off her horse. "Solita, you stand here." My legs twitched with anticipation. It was amazing to turn from a skinny girl with messy bangs into an admired princess by plunging into floods and splashing and stillness—anything the music was. The perfume of the jasmine in the fat-bellied pots underneath the windows was auspicious. "Patricia, you'll enter later; now hide behind the bougainvillaea around that column." To think I had been so afraid the girls would boycott the rehearsal.

"This area here is the stage. The audience sits out there, where Madame is watching, between those tiny white flowers . . ."

"Baby's breath," Gloria said patiently.

"Yes, and those big whatchamacallems."

"Dahlias," Gloria said, not believing such ignorance.

The veranda was a great stage because everyone going by saw us. "Each time I clap, like this—*clap!*—one of you arrives. First Gloria, the queen, and you, Solita, the king."

Solita the what? There was a mistake here.

"Grace, you're the prince, and you enter next. Patricia, when I clap twice, the princess comes from behind the bougainvillaea and dances over there. Now! Gloria and Solita, start dancing!"

Gloria moved around like an elephantiasic queen. "Solita"—Mlle. Vicky's voice entered like a nail—"dance with your queen!"

I didn't know the first thing about how to be a king! A

king sat on a throne with huge rings on his fingers! How could you dance sitting down! The choke started. "I'm too skinny," I said.

The girls stopped to giggle. Mlle. Vicky stiffened up. "Solita, I'll tolerate no jokes during rehearsal. We'll pad you so you're fatter than a hippo after his dinner. The important guests with their children are coming toodaay. So dance!"

How? Tears, plans revolved in my head while Gloria and I moved around each other. Mlle. Vicky clapped for the prince.

"Hey, Prince, come here!" Gloria yelled. Mlle. Vicky's limber body stiffened into an awesome weapon. Gloria got serious. After more nonsensical revolving, Mlle. Vicky said she would rehearse with Patricia because the princess role was the most complex.

I spotted my mother going to the aviary with the silk-scarved senator. I ran. "Solita!" I ignored Mlle. Vicky.

"Mami, Mami." My legs wouldn't stop jerking up and down.

"Ah, Solita, what a lucky girl you are; today you'll make wonderful friendships." She pointed at the sad old condor.

"Mami, she gave her *my* part, she's bigger than the prince and his father, and she said I'm the one who did very well!"

"What on earth are you talking about?" She pressed my cowlick while she looked at the senator apologetically.

I had talked like the dumb giants in stories. I explained.

"Oh," my mother said, as if remembering. "Yes, Vicky said how well you danced. But Merce told Vicky she wanted Patricia in the princess role. What difference does it make, Solita?"

"But it's not fair! I tried the hardest! Mlle. Vicky said . . ."

"My daughter, don't be petty; Vicky is Mercedes' guest. And so are we, Solita; you seem to forget that."

"I don't!" My voice came out too loud. My mother took me aside and whispered sternly, "Let's not have melodramas, Solita. We all have roles to play, and not always the ones we want. Don't let me hear you're not being cooperative. How many times must I tell you; the best way to get where you want to be is to please those who own the road. Now, go do your best." She came back to smile at the senator, who smiled at me, and they left.

I opened the gate to a pen with an exotic palm tree and rare flowers. We weren't allowed inside. The guanaco stood at the fence. I rested my back against the warm palm trunk, by some strange orange blossoms sucked by a hummingbird. People who were supposed to help you didn't know certain basic things. Padre Romualdo didn't know about princesses, because to punish the bad was good. My mother didn't know you could cut cross-country to get somewhere; I would rather cut through puma-, black-lobo- and *litre*-infested brush; through lakes with leeches; through volcanic mountains. We could walk to the public road and hitch a ride back to Galmeda if she wanted; we had done far more difficult things before. Why, why did she want to get to a place where she needed to use these people's roads? I detoured an ant who insisted on coming on a path toward my sandal. Stupid ant; I could squash it in a flash. She should have chosen another road.

THE MINUTE THE CHILDREN ARRIVED, the excitement started, because a boy with long hair, legs and nose disappeared. We were thrilled. We were envious. Men on horses went to comb fields, woods and mountains. The long boy's mother was a something-or-another, one of those names that here meant you came from Spanish noblemen but which my mother said belonged to poor Spanish landworkers. You couldn't tell the children that, however. The long boy's father was a very, very famous poet in Galmeda. Women with something-or-another names didn't marry poets, so this made the boy even more noteworthy.

At dusk the long boy was found past the big lake. He said he'd been kidnapped by maniac zoologists and put in a cave under the lake. Under the lake! They almost opened his skull with huge silver machines to put his brain into a giant lizard. They had the lizard ready, right there, to take his brain. I was nearly hysterical; then I saw my mother's face, which said, What a liar this boy is, what a spoiled troublemaker. So I relaxed. The other children had decided to consider him the leader of the younger set until they saw their parents' faces. It was very comforting to know you weren't in danger of having your brain put into giant lizards. It was even more comforting to know that among the new guests it wasn't considered cute to be a liar and a spoiled troublemaker. Things were looking up.

The next day, Jaime Idarrázabal Ochagavía—Ochagavía on his mother's side, etc.—wanted to know where the games and contests were, but Patricia quickly proposed that we go boating, and he agreed. With the long boy discredited, everybody took it as a given that he was the leader of the younger set. He started large at the top, with a big head and a plump, freckled nose. At the bottom he petered into skinny, gray-socked calves, which sneaked out of his knickers, like drawings in old books. He stretched his lips constantly to flash his famous dimples, and in a toad's voice, if he was acting generous, he said, "For Bercebu, how wrong are you!" If he was acting superior, he said, "Gad, you're a turd!" He considered "For Bercebu" the height of cleverness, and "turd" the most useful word in the human language. His mother called him "Jaimito, my precious." He was no prince. His pretty sister, just as superior and freckle-nosed, was always crying and storming out to tell her mother. This made her unworthy of consideration.

Whatever Jaime Idarrazábal Ochagavía wanted to do, everyone agreed, eager to have him acknowledge their existence. They gladly heard him call them turds and tell fantastic things that had happened to him. These sounded suspiciously like the bloodthirsty pirates and evil-alien invasions in *El Pituso* and *Billiken* magazines, which weren't that interesting anyway. Being a princess would have been a total waste on him.

The girls boasted about the quick mud near the lake, where cows sometimes drowned. Fights broke out because some children wanted to go on the same boat with certain other ones. As we turned on the reed canals, the *peones* manning the boats bumped into each other and the children laughed. None could be called friendly. They mostly bragged about Paris hotel rooms or their parents' ski chalets in Llotera and yachts moored in Tilipulli. Some children were more superior than others. It became known that one of the girls didn't have a beach house in Tilipulli, but in Bedsagua, the next beach. No one gave a fig after that whether she acknowledged their existence or not, and she returned any insult with gushing acceptance. Like the other girl guest, she wore gold and diamond earrings given to her by her godmother at birth, and lifted her shoulders, bending her wrists under her chin anytime a dog, the guanaco, or Jali got near, as if they were going to bite her neck. They complained the animals stank, which wasn't true; they smelled normal.

A girl whose grandfather had also been president of the country, a more recent one, said she was tired of boating and wanted to go swimming in the pool. She was the only person, other than Jaime Idarrázabal Ochagavía, permitted to propose things. He didn't tell her, "For Bercebu, how wrong are you!" much less that she was a turd. Whether because of her grandfather or other reasons, the president's granddaughter believed—and everyone agreed—that she held a perfection unattainable by others—the way she strode, shaking her long, ribboned hair; the way her fat cheeks ballooned from underneath her bluish eyes; the way she looked at things with disinterest; the way she dove to the bottom of the pool, just like the little Jantzen woman on her imported bathing suit—all of it was indisputably superior, and everyone was grateful for any acknowledgment of their existence on her part. The president's granddaughter mostly wanted to go dive in the pool, especially in front of the German photographer.

I had zero aspirations to be acknowledged by the superior

group, but being respected by all the children was necessary and weighty. Aside from what Gloria had said, aside from being in their country, my mother had told me these children would be my friends for life. You never knew when people of money and influence could get you out of a country at war or a concentration camp. Being respected was weighty, no doubt about it. Luckily I didn't live in their houses, so there was a limit to how much I had to go out of my way to get along. Maybe the children would find me interesting. The painter with the hatchet nose said my nose stuck out and this was interesting. What a pity we didn't have classes with Mme. Chanel during Holy Week; it would have impressed them how much she liked me, and my mother would have been pleased, and realize that I wasn't bad; I just didn't like Tío Armando. The children didn't ask me about my street or my school, so I just followed them, getting along. They complained mightily about having to walk back from the lake to go to the pool.

As we passed by the classroom, the long boy asked, "What's in here?" I was surprised to see Patricia panic; what if they saw the nude portrait! She scooted everybody to the play bungalow.

During the dance presentation, I was mortified, prancing like a drunk pigeon, stuffed so I could barely move. Afterward, Jaime Idarrázabal Ochagavía accused me of getting the king's role due to my mother's leverage with the girls' uncle, which he had heard his mother mention to a friend on the phone. I blushed and looked at him in surprise, which he took as confirmation of his clever suspicion. The others looked at me respectfully. You never knew what would give you prestige! But this made Patricia and Grace very upset. Did these children know some of the same secrets that the girls were still keeping from me?

"TONIGHT I WANT you to be very helpful." My mother cut the corners of a velvet piece on my front and sewed quickly on my back. "This ship's first port of call is going to be back into history." She sighed. "There's no end to the things I have to dream up. Solita, be helpful, show you're a girl with charm, with personality." Charm and personality; you probably didn't have to be beautiful or cute to have it. But how did you get it? "Do you have pictures to show me?"

"Pictures of what?" She cut Niceto's bolero and kissed him because it looked so cute on him.

"Of charm and personality."

My mother smiled. "Ask pleasant questions; add something when they talk to you, not just yes or no. And, well, talk to Armando; really, you must make more of an effort. I told you it's very important." I pressed my cowlick.

She left for the sewing room, which had been a beehive, with Rita bent over the sewing machine, instructing the chambermaids assigned to help her, and la Mamota complaining that all her girls had been taken over for this folly, and guests bringing pictures of the characters from history each had chosen to portray, with stories about their lives, so they would know how to dress and stand, and what to say. My mother reminded them they weren't wearing costumes; they *were* their chosen person; they were stepping into history. My mother knew how to make guests excited about parties. When two ladies with curled bangs wanted to be Marie Antoinette and started a fight, my mother convinced one that Catherine the Great was far more sexy. Children weren't given any choices; we had to be pages in velvet breeches and play the cithara, except they didn't give us any.

That night the salon was invigorated by Aladdin lamps and music from the Espinosa brothers, who had come in their striped mantas from the town of Llotera. La Mamota and Berta were at the entrance, pinning on each guest little bouquets of gillyflowers and jasmines, which made you dizzy with their perfume. The precious girl was Helen, the face that launched a thousand ships. So why had my mother chosen Queen Isabella, who had launched just three little caravels? Tía Merce was Cleopatra. "I'm Venus." "I'm Van

Gogh." "I'm Victor Hugo." "I'm Socrates." "I'm Madame de Récamier." "Who are you?" No one was from this country, as if it had no history. The way guests talked in El Topaz, only three things had happened in the world: Cleopatra, the Greeks and some Frenchmen, mostly painters called Impressionists; and only two places existed now, a foggy Paris and a vague Orient.

The justice of the Supreme Court arrived galloping, wrapped in bedsheets. He said he was King Solomon. I stayed out of his way. Pablo, with a beret, said he was Earth. My father could come as Saint James, who killed the invading evil and saved Spain. The guanaco, Vodka and Coca-Cola slipped in unnoticed.

When I tried to enter, la Mamota stopped me. She said I wasn't dressed properly. The children looked at me from inside.

I told her my mother had made my outfit. "It figures," la Mamota told Berta. "Go tell Rita to put a proper hem there on those jags, and a seam on that chicken's ass you have in the back of your costume." I looked at Berta; she stared at la Mamota.

My face turned away just in time to hide my eyes. I went to the sewing room, playing tug-of-war with my throat to keep tears in. Rita wasn't there. It was too shadowy to read in the little library. In the pensione we had a cheery bulb hanging from the ceiling that spread the most spirited yellow light at night. When crossing the corridors, I kept a lookout for shadows. Every time I approached the salon, there was a rush of music, chatting and laughter. I sat on a veranda bench. A tree trunk behind some viburnums turned out to be my father. His red hair glowed in the last light of dusk. He hated these parties; he shouldn't blame my mother; for some reason she had to show all her teeth laughing now, but she was very serious. My father and I sat on the bench and talked. The gardens faded—grayer, colder, scarier. A Chinese emperor came down the veranda. "Why, little page, what are you doing here in the dark?" What could you tell a

Chinese emperor? Not the truth; my mother had done my outfit. I pressed my lips to avoid a wet deluge and tried a smile. "That's what I adore about little girls, always smiling. C'mon, little page, hurry, dance, play the cithara, bring me something exquisite on a velvet cushion." Tío Juan Vicente took me inside by the hand. La Mamota didn't say a word.

I STAYED AWAY FROM Patricia and Grace; they were upset about the prestige I'd gained with the king's role. Melons scolded Mlle. Vicky, calling her Monsieur Chopin. Mlle. Vicky, in a dark old-fashioned man's suit, played a chord like a sob and said the bruises were from her tuberculosis. Well, was it a horse or was it tuberculosis? "Tell me, Cassandra, why does she get them all?" she said, looking to one corner. With my mouth full of anchovies and olives, I looked in that direction; my mother was showing her beautiful teeth at the sheet-covered senator, who smoothed his wavy hair, looking gratified. My mother wasn't out to catch anybody, she had to play games; everyone in country estates did. In San Bernardo Street, people went to work, women went to market with their fishnet bags, children went to play in the square. . . .

Tío Armando appeared in an old-days uniform that displayed his belly, one hand under his vest, the other held high, leading María Pía in clingy gauze tucked under her bosom. She said she was Josephine. My mother pretended she hadn't seen him, but I could tell she had. The Supreme man went near Gloria and she ran to me. "You have to be careful with His Honor," she said. "He passed his hands on my bottom. We told Mumsy; she said he's just a dirty old man and to stay out of his way. He's very important." I pondered that and decided they were all dead wrong to invite him.

Tía Merce, the Romanian count and his beautiful wife were latched on to one another, like Siamese triplets. The straw woman had been pleased at first, but instead of being mad at my mother, now she complained to them: "What happened at siesta? I won't permit you to leave me out, darlings."

Tía Merce said, "My peach, three is divine; four is a crowd," and the three giggled. The straw woman stormed out, and without the girls having to do a thing about it this time, went back to Galmeda.

It seemed the children didn't know what to make of the historical party; they wanted games and contests. This bothered Patricia and Grace a lot, and they kept mentioning the confectionery hunt to gain clout. It was the proper thing to try to make children take you as wheat rather than chaff, but it amazed me to see how hard Patricia and Grace worked to keep their position in the superior group, which—to my astonishment—was tenuous. Although they had a ski chalet in Llotera, they had a distinguished last name only on one side, and maybe didn't have a beach house, or a yacht in Tilipulli, but Patricia and Grace put a muzzle on Gloria and were clever about avoiding issues. Could I ever toss a head, drop a phrase, throw a fruit to a dog to change the subject so well under duress? As hostesses, the girls could give many amazing reports, but they had to keep it up, and it seemed sooner or later they would run out. How could they top a cow drowning in quick mud? Their father's secret glass-roofed study? The sinister *despacho* where people were heard crying or begging when Tía Merce gave sentences from her carved chair? The overly excitable ladies with their curled bangs dripping guanaco spit? No matter how high elevated people were, they felt they had to be even more so. I was watching María Pía when Patricia came to tell me I had to do something when the children complained about being bored; I was here to entertain them, not to just stand there looking stupid. Do what, I asked her, but she turned to watch María Pía follow a man with red whiskers and one bandaged ear who had asked her to lean on the grand piano so he could sketch her.

Tío Armando also followed María Pía with his eyes, then

looked at my mother and the senator, who were laughing and acting idiotic. He took his big hat off to scratch his balding crown and frowned. A man with a smock and a palette told him, "Emperor, this is the best party I've ever attended. Now I see why you told me you had found someone who really amused you. But I see she's now occupied elsewhere. . . ." Tío Armando looked down. "And are things serious with the baroness, Emperor? Frankly, I could not see you tying the knot with a Goth, a Bolsheviky one at that. However . . ."

"Monsieur Renoir, Peninsulars are all barbarians; if not, would they have had a civil war? Would they need a strongman?"

"But Emperor, you told me she's from a well-placed family."

"I wonder; how about the *mésalliance* with that labor maniac? I tell you, Monsieur Renoir, we're sure only with our own women."

The smocked man went to listen to Pablo recite a poem about wine. Tío Armando kept observing my mother and the happy senator. He finally walked resolutely to where she was, took his hat off and bowed to her. I swallowed a caramel-coated cherry.

21

EVERY TIME THE CHILDREN GRUMBLED THAT THIS country estate was boring—no movies, no teahouse with ice cream, no slide, no Maypole, no organized games, no anything—Patricia's and Grace's eyes sagged in their sockets, like cats upon seeing a new dog nearby. Then they looked at me, as if saying, Do something! In San Bernardo Square, nobody organized anything; for as long as we were allowed outside, we played at a feverish pitch, our hearts going pitter-patter, our faces streaked with dusty sweat. It was a problem to agree what to play because there were so many choices: "rice pudding," pebble-throwing contests to hit a dust mark, hopscotch with a piece of broken pavement, "bate, bate chocolate," forbidden palm-tree climbing (only very early before grandmas arrived with babies and toddlers), tic-tac-toe on dirt with sticks. If the gear was available, we played marbles, jump rope, blind chicken—with a handkerchief, although a small sweater would do in a pinch. Past dusk, a time especially intense and inspiring, mysterious, a time that made you tenderhearted about the shadows created from the newly lit streetlamps, we played hide-and-seek, in constant fear of being called to go home. "How about playing marbles, or jump rope?" I proposed.

"What's wrong with you? Those are icky street games for low-class children," everyone around the billiard table agreed.

I observed my dress's little yellow squares. Bragging about ancestors seemed the thing to do. I told them my grandfather was Ignacio de Prados. Nobody knew him. "He was important. He helped the Madrid Philharmonic. He was invited to the palace. The king gave him his portrait, signed." I didn't say that my mother and her sisters always turned the king's signed portrait upside down because they were Republicans. Having Republican daughters and the king upside down got my grandfather so worked up they had to give him a cold bath in the big tub upstairs, then they put a "draft protector" over his chest to fend off pneumonia.

"What king? What palace? How incredibly ridiculous; that's in history and fairy tales. That's no distinguished name. What street is his mansion in?" Jaime Idarrázabal Ochagavía asked.

These children wouldn't understand that I would live in his big, drafty house if Franco was kicked out. "It's in Madrid."

"In Madrid! That city's a turd. Nobody in Galmeda knows him, and he doesn't live in Paris, so he's not important."

Bragging didn't work for everybody. But having things did. "I have a huge foil ball. Do you want to see it?" I offered.

"A foil ball?" Jaime Idarrázabal Ochagavía put his billiard pole back on the rack and flared his fat nostrils. "That's for little kids."

"It's not. I'm going to sell it. Maybe in the United States, for lots of money." Patricia and the twins looked at me with surprise. Jaime Idarrázabal Ochagavía laughed. "Gad, you're a turd. That's what nannies tell little kids to keep them busy." Nanny Fresia had told me no such thing. And now she wasn't even here, but out there with José and his mother and her many children.

I started to get furious, but a girl who slid a gold bracelet up and down her arm made me more alert than angry by asking Patricia, "Is it true that you live here all year round now?" Was this considered enviable or not? The bracelet swinger was definitely of the superior kind, a something-or-another on both sides, and, additionally, had an imported Jantzen bathing suit, so Patricia was obliged to answer.

"Yes, we do."

"Ayyy, how boring; you don't have anybody to play with!" Jaime Idarrázabal Ochagavía's sister commiserated.

"Oh, yes, we do," Patricia said. "Solita here was brought to play with us." They all looked at me. I looked down. Did I pass the test?

"Solita rides English," Gloria said. "Do you know Lucero?" My gaze moved away from my feet and covered the ground to Gloria's feet, then legs. Her knees looked better to me than her sister's. Maybe due to her having a better brain, regardless of what they said. For the first time ever, Patricia and Grace approved of her defense. Like lightning, I was suddenly fused with them into El Topaz! For all the times I had summoned knights to throw them into dark and dank dungeons full of spiky, crawly creatures, I repented.

"It must be boring to play just with her all the time."

Patricia paused. "No, because she must do what we tell her." The grown-ups went by to play Who's the Murderer?, ignoring Tío Armando's protestations that immoral things went on, and still, all eyes fell on me.

"Isn't she here because her mother knows your uncle?" the president's granddaughter asked.

"Isn't she the one whose father's a troublemaker?" the girl with the French name asked.

"There was something about her and a French boarding school," said a girl so round and petite she seemed to be made of Ping-Pong balls. Surprise made me expel air the Spanish way, throwing wet matter into my upper lip. I had no little embroidered hankies at my disposal, so the mess had to be wiped as delicately as possible with bent wrists. When I grew up, I was always going to have handkerchiefs. So the children did know about the secrets.

"Then it's true what Grace says, she wears your cast-off clothes?" the long boy asked. I felt suddenly naked, the yellow dress yanked off my body. My father was bringing me a dress.

"You girls are so lucky to have someone who always does what you want." Everyone agreed.

"I don't care if she wears my clothes, she's my same age," Gloria said. Everyone ignored her.

Her confidence restored, her imagination flowing again, Patricia proposed we jump across the river on willow branches and then float on a raft. The river carried dead leaves floating sadly. The raft sank, so we sat to dry under the willows. Jaime Idarrázabal Ochagavía announced, "Let's play Who Stole the Card?" Someone giggled. "Everybody knows how to play?"

I didn't. He explained, "One of us hides a card. Another one has to guess who has it. We take turns. You haven't played it," he told me, "so you'll guess first. Walk around that patch while we decide in the rustic playhouse who stole the card."

"That's no patch; it's a green-pepper bed," Gloria objected.

Being singled out could be a mark of distinction; in any case it was a way to be considered. I walked around the green peppers, then headed for the playhouse. Voices said, "Come in!"

The door was ajar. I pushed it; I was buried alive! Exultant laughter burst all around while I removed a bucket from my head. My lashes, mouth, ears, hair were full of dirt. "It was on top of the door!" voices managed to shout, laughing. Why? Why this? I hadn't bothered anyone, hadn't been a pest, taken anything from anybody. What could you do with people who had to be stopped from doing evil things, like the ones in the cartoons: Franco, Hitler, Mussolini, Hirohito? In country estates no one took notice of them. We had been hunted out of Europe and had landed here with elevated people. I didn't have the right to be like other children. All of me had turned into dirt; tears muddied my face. I was going to be dignified like the guanaco, but at some point even the guanaco had the courage to spit. I would go to the mulch pile in the grange to bury myself, no, to bury the bucket there.

THE CONFECTIONERY ANIMALS were distributed throughout the front gardens in the secrecy of night. We couldn't go on the hunt until we had had breakfast. All children got up the minute the roosters sang and were demanding breakfast at the dining room when the sun was a flicker of pink light in the bay window.

The children fussed and used the same tricks the girls did to hide food; this knowledge spread in mysterious but precise ways. My mind went through the gardens trying to guess what the kitchen maids would consider good hiding spots. Since it would be a while before we could eat the hunted sweet animals, and we didn't get papaya crepes with palm honey every day, I ignored the disgusted looks from the other children and ate to my stomach's content. I was willing to go to great lengths to ease my distress and regain respectability, but there had to be a limit.

We were each given a harvesting basket. My heart beat fast. I devised a plan to win the prize. This was going to be great not only to go on picnics with my father and make my mother proud; a picnic basket was as interesting as having a ski chalet, a yacht or a beach house in Tilipulli. Probably more. You could mention Tilipulli, but could you carry it? I made Gin and Tonic, who had the finest noses and heads small enough to fit in any nook or cranny, smell a chocolate I had saved in my pocket. It was one of those cream-filled ones the girls said no self-respecting guest would give them, but some sneaky ones did. By now, lint and debris crusted the fleshy cream oozing from several cracks. Gin and Tonic sat, lifting their little behinds enough to wiggle their stub tails, letting me know they understood and wanted to know when to go find something with that smell.

The dining-room brass bell announced the hunt. I made Gin and Tonic smell the bonbon once more, and tossed it on some blue columbines, next to the aviary. My scouts took off. I ran after them in a frenzy, but none of the places they were sniffing had anything. I started to panic. Then all the children shouted that there were no candied animals anywhere. La Mamota summoned Tía Merce. She arrived with the Romanian count and his beautiful wife, and so did my mother and other guests, including the bald conductor of the National Philharmonic Orchestra. They all went hunting candied animals, shrieking and guffawing. Mlle. Vicky chased the man with the fancy car. Tío Armando alternatively chased María Pía, who floated gracefully with a flowing veil, then my mother, who ran in big strides in front of him and the scarved senator. The bracelet swinger pointed to her and whispered, "Look at *that* hunt; my Mumsy said she's on the prowl." It oppressed my chest, but Patricia fixed things by reminding her that this had been organized for all, even for grown-ups. Patricia had her own reasons for wanting to erase evidence that their uncle had anything to do with my mother, but it was opportune, because I was in no position to defend her myself. The only candy found—among the blue columbines, by the long boy not kidnapped by maniac zoologists—was my messy bonbon.

Finally, numerous small, barefooted prints led Mario to deduce that peasant children had descended upon the gardens at night to loot the candied animals. The cook said Mario's head had been hit by horses too many times, because the disappearance of the candied animals was obviously the work of *ánimas.* I was sad, but not surprised. If you left half a candy in San Bernardo Square at night, you wouldn't find a hint of it the next day. But the guest children were indignant, and Patricia and Grace mortified, as only these children could make them.

Patricia staged a one-woman daredevil act by pouting and announcing she was going to stay in her room for the rest of the week. La Mamota was busy running things, and no one else paid attention to it, so in a few minutes she came out.

Then the long boy displayed my mangled chocolate bonbon, claiming he was entitled to the picnic basket because he'd found a chocolate snail. This had to be the height of unfairness. Jaime Idarrázabal Ochagavía took a look at my bonbon and pronounced it not a candy but a disgusting, squashed snail that had eaten a bit of chocolate. Everyone agreed. Tía Merce said the picnic basket would be given to the winner of coming games and contests. I could be good at games and contests. It went to show that even if your mother was a something-or-another and your father was a very, very famous poet, sometimes nobody paid any attention to you. Things were looking up.

PATRICIA AND GRACE vetoed Manuel's suggestion that games and contests be done sooner, but considered it a catastrophe that instead we had to listen to curled-bangs ladies read poetry with soft background guitar. I agreed. Fortunately, many of the grown-ups whispered to each other in the park gazebo, so we didn't have to hear the poems. The count pointed his manicured nail at a photograph. "Gosh, don't I look young. The one in the middle is King Carol. I was in his personal guard, you see."

No matter what he and his beautiful wife said, Tía Merce chortled, "*Merveilleux!*" "Let me tell you what she just did!" she told one of the guest mothers. "She wouldn't wait for the chambermaid to bring her toilet paper, so she used a hundred-peso bill from her pocket! Isn't it divine?"

Dr. Kaplan told my mother things had run away again with Merce. "She's clever, clever." He shook his head. "Now she can conveniently seduce her mother and father at the same time." The girls also seemed to wonder what he meant, but said nothing.

Another mother leaned over Tío Juan Vicente. "If only the dancer would learn to flirt the way María Pía does, ever so genteel, no?"

The man with the fancy car said, "True, but Armando can't make up his mind, you know." "María Pía doesn't look up to him, that's why." "Perhaps she's just too much a wisp of a woman for his taste." "She has awfully skimpy hair, don't you think?"

The children yawned. The girls agonized. I sympathized. We were saved when Tía Merce announced, "Children, why don't you go recite your own verses, my pets?"

A father stood up. "Yes, you young ones go recite poems you learned at school."

We scrambled out of the park happily. If I recited a poem about young Count Olinos, who sang so sweetly that ships sailed in reverse, perhaps my lost prestige would be restored. Outside the play bungalow, Jaime Idarrázabal Ochagavía announced he would start. He flashed his dimples. "Ladies and gentlemen, I will read a lofty poem written by the senior class of the French Brothers, as you all know, the best boys' school in our country." Maybe he would redeem himself by reciting a soft-sounding poem from *The Treasure of Youth,* about maidens dressed in flowers who lived inside rivers, bees buzzing for your contentment and birds flapping their wings in your honor. "It will be in her honor." He pointed to the girl with a beach house not in Tilipulli, who blushed, confused. There were murmurs of surprise. "The title of the poem is 'Farts.' " There were giggles. "First 'The Fart's Lament,' written by the very sensitive senior class of the French Brothers, which I dedicate to her because she's a colossal farter, I'm told." Giggles. She smiled.

I wanted to tell her that accepting untrue insults meekly

didn't work, but you didn't say those things. "What you said about her isn't true," I asserted. Not only did they all get mad at me for interrupting and being contrary, she did too!

"We farts have innumerable grievances against you humans. We do not have our proper place in society. We are an important part of your daily lives, yet you shun us, pretend we don't exist, ease us out with deceit and in shame, then pretend others have authored us. This is made even more intolerable in view of the high position accorded to your solid waste, so highly esteemed by the medical profession, so royally treated in your homes, with thrones in luxurious rooms. Turds are bestowed grand honors, while we languish in neglect and opprobrium. It is high time something is done about this explosive situation. Frankly, ladies and gentlemen, it stinks."

Jaime Idarrázabal Ochagavía was exceedingly proud of his lament. He dimpled once more and recited:

> "Some are boisterous and happy, some mournful and
>   sad,
> some are shrill and imperious, some quiet and shy.
> But whatever they are, they'll be here for life,
> so don't get so serious, don't get so mad,
> have a heart, smile! Smile at your fart!"

There was applause. The poem wasn't as good as he thought, but not bad. Smiling seemed a lot better than getting red-faced, in general. I decided Count Olinos wouldn't go over very well here.

The president's granddaughter whispered to Patricia, "Jaime Idarrázabal Ochagavía has a thing about farts. At a costume party once he came dressed as one." I wondered how you did that.

The girl with a beach house not in Tilipulli tripped. "Oops!" Jaime Idarrázabal Ochagavía said, removing the leg he had put in front of her. "It was an unfortunate accident."

THE CHILDREN LEFT me alone while they insulted the girl with a house not in Tilipulli, who was all smiles. She should learn about dignity and pride from the guanaco. When a girl with blond curls and a French last name addressed herself in a whisper to me, the president's granddaughter and Patricia, I prepared myself; maybe she was going to say something about my parents. Having a French last name was as good as a famous grandfather, so she was definitely in the superior group. "Did you know that Jaime Idarrázabal Ochagavía has, well, you know, that grows? In Tilipulli my cousin María Angélica saw it."

What a relief. What had I done right? Or had something happened about my parents? Patricia looked at me somewhat offended because I had been taken into the confidence of the president's granddaughter as much as she. In the games and contests, I was going to win and cinch my respectability.

"What do you mean? What grows?" Patricia asked.

"Shhh, not so loud. A carrot, you know. Have you seen one?"

"Oh, a boy's carrot. Yeah, it's like a faucet."

"Well, have you seen a real one?"

Patricia was noncommittal and looked at me, who had seen an extravagantly real one, but I indicated I didn't wish to discuss the matter. The president's granddaughter insisted, "Jaime Idarrázabal Ochagavía's grows!"

"Well, of course, otherwise big men would go around with little babies' carrots."

"No, you yokels, I mean grows instantly."

Patricia didn't like the "yokels" part, even coming from the president's granddaughter, which gave me a sensation of impending thrill. We could stand together, not accept insults, then no one could assault anybody.

"Jaime Idarrázabal Ochagavía's grows like a balloon and

gets huge. Ask my cousin María Angélica." We were suspicious.

"If you don't believe me, find a way for him to show it. We have to convince him. We could ask one of the other boys, but I know nothing about theirs. But we have to touch it. It's the only way he'll agree to it."

"Ugggh!" we all said.

"Well, do you want to see it or not? We'll take turns." The president's granddaughter took her important stride toward Jaime Idarrázabal Ochagavía. "Let's go upstairs," she proposed.

"For Bercebu . . ." he started to say, but realized who it was. "Sure."

We sat on the beds in silence until the president's granddaughter said, "My cousin María Angélica, you know, from Viñas Astaburuaga, and that shiplike blue house in Tilipulli? She says you showed her and her cousins something."

He looked at us over his freckled nose. "Yeah."

"Well, the girls here don't believe it."

"Anyone who doesn't believe it is a turd. You want to see it?" he asked. We agreed. "You have to touch it." We knew, she said. Jaime Idarrázabal Ochagavía stretched out and unbuttoned his trousers. He took out a little fat finger and started to caress it. "You do it," he told the president's granddaughter.

She leaned over, very dignified, and moved the soft finger with two fingertips. Amazing! It started to grow! We took turns. They let me do it without a word. It was boneless. Grace refused to go near it. "C'mon, it's not a bear, it won't bite you," he prompted her. "Go on, you'll see all sorts of amazing surprises."

After a while the president's granddaughter said, "Jaime Idarrázabal Ochagavía, it's staying the same and doing nothing."

"Go on, you can't stop, you have to keep going," he said.

"Is this as big as it gets?" Patricia asked. The president's granddaughter tried harder, attempting to save face.

The bracelet swinger slid her bracelet. "Big deal!"

"Let's go see about the games and contests," the girl made of Ping-Pong balls proposed.

In spite of Jaime Idarrázabal Ochagavía's insisting that we do that later, we left him with his knickers opened and his carrot pointing up to a knot on the pine ceiling. We went down the curved staircase. "Girls! Ahem, girls! You must go on!" he called from upstairs.

"What for? It just grows a little and stays that way."

" 'A little'! What do you mean, 'a little'!"

We all left.

22

THE SOCCER FIELD VIBRATED WITH IRRESISTIBLE accordions and guitars, wind-blown banners, flags and peasant fiesta attire. Dancers swung handkerchiefs up in the sun and air; the women's printed roses flowed on their full skirts; the fringes on the men's knee boots wriggled. Guests in their lawn chairs clapped with the music. The silk-scarved senator left the bald conductor of the National Philharmonic Orchestra and came to tell me he liked the lively peasant dances. He was nice. He said he knew my father and he was an interesting man. When my father came, he would bring me a dress. My mother got in the rink and danced with a peasant; the other ones laughed. The senator congratulated her. From what I could see, the children didn't find it amusing. Some guests said, "How eccentric." María Pía smirked elegantly. Tío Armando told my mother she was a character, and it was better if she danced with him. María Pía got up slowly and slithered away looking offended. Tío Juan Vicente said every peasant there was going to get drunk.

The guanaco-shaped piñata intrigued everyone, because piñatas were unknown here. Niceto gave it the biggest slam-bang and split it. This country air had made him strong! The guanaco, Jali and children rushed to pick strewn goodies and tokens.

I asked Manuel, who having worked in the Topotilla police station fancied himself a great leader, when were we having games and contests. He took a cymbal—"Attention, attention, young ones!"—then organized the musicians. Patricia and Grace directed angry looks at me. We went around and around a circle of seats. The instant the music stopped, I plopped on a chair as if it were the last raft in the Pacific Ocean. But again and again, Jaime Idarrázabal Ochagavía kept bumping me off. Everyone was enjoying it but me. I seriously considered party poopery and going back to Jules Verne in the little library, even if it disgraced my mother, me and my brother for life. The next time he bumped me, instead of hitting my chair, his behind hit the ground! It astonished me to see him down there, and to feel a chair put behind my legs. I turned and saw Padre Romualdo release its back and go with his big feet toward María Pía.

Jaime Idarrázabal Ochagavía got up slapping his knickers. I offered a big smile from my seat. After his nose regained its normal freckles, he said, "This is a girlish game," and went to talk to his mother. She talked to Tía Merce, then to la Mamota, who talked to Manuel. He stroked a cymbal on his tippytoes. "Attention, young ones! Attention! I will now announce the winner of the picnic basket! The winner is"—he motioned to the accordion man, who played an arpeggio—"Jaimito Idarrázabal Ochagavía! Applaud, children, applaud!" The applause was weak, the grumbles audible. "Congratulations, Jaimito!" la Mamota gushed. "Ay, Jaimito, I can't believe how big you are; I was at your baptism, you know." The winner accepted the prize graciously and flashed his dimples.

I looked beyond the soccer field to a harvested cornfield stiffly enjoying the breeze. If you wanted to get somewhere, you had to please those who owned the road, my mother said. If you were meek, you'd be rewarded, Padre Romualdo said. There had to be a less infuriating way. Suddenly, a storm hit my brain. If I found an ear of corn on that field, I could plant the kernels and have about one hundred plants, with five or six ears each. That would make, oof! about five hundred ears! Each of those five hundred would give me one hundred more plants. This would be . . . thousands! Millions! I was rich! Rich! Rich! This was so thrilling, I ran to tell Gloria about my unexpected good fortune. She was amazed. We went to tell Manuel. How come he hadn't thought of it? Manuel bent down to show his waves. "And how are you, corn millionaire, going to buy land to plant corn?" He left to tell the young women serving empanadas elaborate compliments about their beauty. I had lost a fortune. Maybe corn wouldn't work, but something else would. You had to keep trying.

Tía Merce clapped twice to command food in her imperial way. The dance stopped and three men with guitars sang quiet songs. Several young peasant girls with red waistbands distributed hot empanadas from big baskets, spreading the air with mouth-watering smells. Empanadas were magical; a crisp, smooth crust hid juicy surprises: onion bits, olives, meat, plump raisins and some other chewy or squeaky enigmas. We never got any in the dining room, although it was the country's typical food, they said. Near me, Tía Merce, the Romanian count and his beautiful wife nibbled the edges of the same empanada, as if there weren't hundreds for everybody.

Big silver cups from the *despacho,* won in soccer games against other ranches, were passed around full of wine. I waited for a chance to get *chicha,* whose smell tickled my nose sweetly. Tío Armando took my mother out to dance. María Pía told her something and she answered. I went there, but couldn't hear with the music. The bracelet swinger's mother said, "Did you hear María Pía's catty remark? And the Spaniard answered with a compliment! I think María Pía ended up the loser, don't you?"

"I wish to see all of you at mass tomorrow," Padre Romualdo said loudly above the noise. "Let's not forget it's Holy Week." He saw a basket and rubbed his hands. "Bring those empanadas this way, my daughter."

Manuel stroked the cymbal. "Attention, young ones, we're now playing ball and base! Choose your captains to form two teams!" Jaime Idarrázabal Ochagavía and the president's granddaughter, as obvious captains, chose their teams. The girl with a beach house not in Tilipulli and I were last. Both captains wanted her. She beamed blissfully. I kept looking at my feet, ordering them to take me out of there, but they weighed a ton. Then the two huge feet of Padre Romualdo came into view. "What's going on?" he said sternly.

He was showered with explanations: who suggested the game, who had the right, who chose first, who didn't want me on their team. "Is this Idiot's Day or what?" Padre Romualdo growled. He glared at the captains. "Since you're such infants and can't settle this like sensible young people, you'll do this: she's on your team this game, on yours next." He poked both with a finger.

As a roar of protest started, Padre Romualdo glared. "Anybody who says beep is coming to confession at seven. Is that clear, my young friends?" There wasn't a beep. He went back to talk to Dr. Valdés and eat more empanadas.

That was the last thing in the world I wanted Padre Romualdo to do. I just wanted him to see that my feet got me out of there.

One by one, Jaime Idarrázabal Ochagavía's team—mine by default—barely made it to first base, was hit between bases, or tagged. A disaster. I was last. They gave me the ball.

Jaime Idarrázabal Ochagavía asked me, irritated, "You know what to do?"

"Yes. Throw the ball as far as I can and run to home base."

"Oh, turd," he said. "This is the end." How had he guessed I threw poorly? But I was fast. He gave me the go-ahead morosely. I didn't throw the ball the way girls did, but over my head, and took off. My legs ran so fast I forgot to check on the ball, but soon leapt to home base. There was a silence. Then my team moved, jumped and screamed, "Home run! Home run! We made a home run!" and mobbed me to dust my pinafore and legs!

It happened again, and my team went wild. We won. Jaime Idarrázabal Ochagavía said we were going to ask for El Topaz's pastries and papaya sodas to celebrate our victory.

"Not so fast," the president's granddaughter said. "It's our turn to have her in our team." I was a hero in demand. But they didn't know my name. A glorious war started. Again Padre Romualdo came and said it was the other team's turn to have me.

I didn't make as many home runs on the president's granddaughter's team because I was tired, but enough for us to win. An exulted cloud followed me.

THE BEST DANCING COUPLE in El Topaz did some intricate footwork. The scarved senator whispered something to my mother. Tío Armando saw him and went to grab her by the waist to dance, holding his big head up and giving the senator a dirty look.

My mother had been playing tennis with the senator while Tío Armando sat to watch. Sometimes they acted nearly as silly as the twins during meals. It was disturbing, because my mother had never acted flighty like the other women in El Topaz. Once Tío Armando hit my mother's bottom with his racket, and instead of hitting him over the head with hers, she laughed and told him he was naughty! It was incredibly unpleasant. While they danced, he seemed to keep asking her something, but she wouldn't agree.

I hoped Padre Romualdo would talk to them, but he was busy listening to the precious girl from the other lands. Her face was partly hidden by a chamber-pot hat, while tears ran under her dark glasses. She didn't want her father to know she was here.

My mother made faces at me to go to her, where Tío Armando was. I took Niceto's hand and went there reluctantly. What could I say that would please her and not hurt me?

"I was just telling Armando how much you love birds, Solita. Armando has the most stunning exotic bird collection."

Were they waiting for me to say, How great!

"I own seven tropical stuffed birds, not ordinary birds like around here; more valuable than the ones in El Topaz's aviary. They're just like in the movies. So you like tropical birds?"

I couldn't say that I thought "tropical" meant "hot" and knew nothing about hot birds; or that birds in El Topaz—in and out of the aviary—seemed the most beautiful in the world to me, and I couldn't care less about stuffed ones; I had to say yes.

"Great, that's great. You're a girl of good taste. You must come and see them."

"May I go and join the children's games?" I asked quietly.

"Indeed," Tío Armando told me. "Excellent of you to make good friends with these children." He said to my mother, "How hard it must have been for her to live in neighborhoods with no one to play with."

Oof! Was he wrong about that! I told him, "We played many games in—"

But my mother interrupted me: "Yes, this week Solita has made close and lasting friendships." Her smile indicated this was terribly important. Tío Armando approved. I turned and saw Patricia and Grace looking at me angrily.

WE DRIFTED BACK to the houses, which were as empty as an abandoned cruiser with everybody at the fiesta. "Good thing someone here knows how to play a decent game," Jaime Idarrázabal Ochagavía told Patricia, pointing at me. The games had given me respectability after all.

"We're going back to Galmeda tomorrow," the French-name girl told Patricia. "You're going to be so bored."

"Bored! We do as we please all the time," Patricia said. "We have only two hours of classes a day, that's all."

"And no homework," Grace bragged. "This is Paradise, ask Mumsy."

"And she has to do what they tell her," the bracelet swinger said, pointing at me.

I went to pick a puzzle. When I looked back, they were all observing me. Jaime Idarrázabal Ochagavía told Patricia, "For Bercebu, how wrong are you. She got the king's role, not you."

The Ping-Pong girl told her, "I don't believe you."

The French-name girl said, "You're just bragging."

The bracelet swinger told her, "She's never done one thing you've told her."

"That's because I haven't asked her," Patricia said.

"Why should she? Who'd want to have you on their team? And I heard my father say her father's been seen with the daughter of a very powerful senator."

Gloria shrugged. "Solita's faster, so what? It's fine with me." She shrunk under the murderous glance Patricia gave her.

"Gad, you're a turd," Jaime Idarrázabal Ochagavía told her.

Patricia's curls shook like a lion's mane. She took the tea-set tray, went inside the armoire, and told me to get in. I assumed she wanted to brag about having an empty armoire all to herself. I got in. There was plenty of room for more. Patricia closed the door. "What are we doing?" I whispered.

"See this?" she said loudly, putting the toy tray in the sliver of light from the doorjamb. "I'm going to spit on it and you're going to eat it."

I couldn't figure this out. "What?"

Voices said, "See? She won't do whatever you tell her. You were just bragging." Patricia's neck tensed defiantly. She cleared her throat and spat what she had dislodged on the toy tray. "Eat that!"

I felt cold. I tried to get out. Patricia slammed the door and covered the latch with one arm. "Eat it!" she yelled, holding the toy tray the way Padre Romualdo did at mass for the wafers, which the girls said were the flesh of Jesus Christ.

"No," I cried. The yellowish, gooey mass trembled and a wave of nausea hit me.

"You won't get out of here until you eat it," Patricia said.

"I won't, I can't," I said, feeling very sick.

A slap hit my ear, rattling my brain. "Do you want me to tell Mumsy you've been making us look horrible? Eat it!" My ear felt in flames, I felt dizzy, but I wasn't going to do it.

"For the last time, do you want me to tell the children about your mother?" What would the guanaco do, he who spit on others when they hurt him? The guanaco was free, because although no one protected him, he had no one to protect. I saw Padre Romualdo's buggy leaving, maybe to some old peasant woman who was dying—important things. What would he do? "Victims are not scarred if they refuse to cooperate in what's wrong or are made victims by force," he had said. What did it all mean? People liked fancy ideas sometimes, when the thing to do was not use their road, stay away, far away, even if you were inside an armoire. Patricia grabbed my hair to push my head down, then her fingers pierced my neck like an iron tarantula. "Solita's mother . . ."

I closed my eyes and took her spit into my mouth. At the same time, Patricia opened the armoire's door for all to see. I tried to swallow it, but a wave of nausea clogged my throat.

Then the spit slid down inside me like an animal who had gone limp and died after being subdued.

Patricia triumphantly showed the empty toy tray. "See? I told you."

IT WAS DUSK OUT, and the girl with the French name came running to tell us that two men had gotten into a nasty argument; one was the girls' uncle, and the other an odd man with a Spanish accent. Then the girls' uncle had left in his car, furious, telling his friend that he was through with her, that he didn't need any Iberian Othellos. What were Iberian Othellos, everyone wanted to know. "A dessert, I think," Jaime Idarrázabal Ochagavía said. We ran to the fiesta. Papi was there!

He said we would be going home very soon. Mami wouldn't talk to him. He had forgotten to bring a dress for me, or a soldier for Niceto, but promised next time. He said he could only stay overnight. And Padre Romualdo was already gone.

My father left.

After Jaime Idarrázabal Ochagavía bothered the girl with a house not in Tilipulli for a while, and she kept acting meek, he poured cumin in the book I was reading. I couldn't stop sneezing and he laughing. Later he bumped into me every time he came near. The next time, I didn't move out of his way. He collided with me and I lost my balance, falling from the edge of the veranda into a reseda alba plant. It had fragrant flowers, but this didn't make it any better. "Oops! It was an unfortunate accident," he said. Everybody giggled.

I looked at the guanaco. I went to the chirimoya tree and rummaged in the flowers underneath it for one with brown spots, revealing superbly rotten flesh inside. I walked back with it. I stood in front of Jaime Idarrázabal Ochagavía, looking at his skinny calves, because seeing his plump, freckle-shielded nostrils would have scared me. "You're a coward," I said.

"Whaaaat?" He dimpled, shocked. Everyone else froze.

"You're a mama's boy!" I looked at the guanaco, trying to extract strength, because my legs were weakening. "And you wear knickers like the jackass in the Julius cartoons!" He grabbed my neck. I pushed the chirimoya up on his chin.

"Ayyyyyy!" Jaime Idarrázabal Ochagavía howled with outrage, with a chirimoya beard, his freckles gone. Suddenly, what looked like a rotten chirimoya flew through the air and splattered on Jaime Idarrázabal Ochagavía's face! He stopped yelling, trying to remove yellow goo from his mouth.

I turned; the guanaco lifted his neck with an expression of justice having been done, and the sanity of his ears being restored. The children stood in amazed silence. Jaime Idarrázabal Ochagavía pawed his face, stumbled and whined the way his sister did. "Wait till I get my mumsy! Mumsy!"

My amazement was as big as anybody's. A twinge of fright was erased with jubilant shock, huge delight. I was leaving El Topaz soon. Pride in myself and gratitude to the guanaco took over other important considerations, such as lifelong friendships.

FINALLY THE WEEK was over. A line of cars went past the veranda. Tía Merce promised the Romanian count and his beautiful wife the money they needed. They kissed her hands and face. Dr. Kaplan told my mother he was mistaken to have recommended country living for Mercedes, that she was clever, too clever. Melons, holding the bag with Lolita, said she knew it all along. The senator patted my head and said he hoped to see me again. He was nice. The children said good-by politely, in their suits and flouncing dresses. "A band of angels," la Mamota sighed. As the cars disappeared, the girls didn't say a word about Jaime Idarrázabal Ochagavía being dreamy. Not a word.

23

"MY MIGUEL ALL ALONE IN THE MANSION, WHERE my girls should be this time of year, in school, such lovely friends that came for Holy Week, such lovely toy porcelain tea sets . . ." la Mamota bellyached, trying sweaters against the girls' backs. She turned to me. "What are you and your brother doing here, child? You have the rooms that mi Señora Doña Mercedes lets your mother use."

As I was leaving holding Niceto's hand, Patricia said, "Look, Mamota, this is *my* room, and I'll have here anybody I please. It so happens I find the children that came for Holy Week horrid, and I never want to play with them again."

The twins and I froze in amazement. La Mamota went on trying boots on Gloria with trembling hands. She pretended not to hear, but looked as if a bee had stung her ear.

A car was heard outside and we ran, forcing la Mamota to

go after the girls while she carried boots, complaining that the foreigner had undermined her authority.

The German photographer seemed pleased to arrive driving a car with the precious girl. She swung her mahogany hair. "Mumsy lets Gunther drive her car," she confided in a duck's voice. "The Gypsies who just left our lands, and are headed this way, told her that a man who took pictures would bring good luck. Mumsy thinks Gunther's sooo ideeal. Ay! Did you hear that María Pía Ycheñirre left with an Australian sociologist? Imagine that!"

"Gunther," Tía Merce asked anxiously, "did you give the counts my message? What did they say! Are they coming?"

The photographer looked embarrassed. "Yes, they did receive your gift, but they can't come. I'm sorry."

Tía Merce grabbed his arm nervously. "*Mon vieux,* you're the only friend I have now; you must help me. You see, everyone else has turned into a rat; even Juan Vicente won't come, just because they don't like my friends the counts."

"I'll be coming this way often—I mean to the Undurragas' ranch," he said, uncomfortable.

The precious girl smiled. "Mumsy convinced Father that it's practical to have a photographer in the family, considering the many weddings he's going to be paying for in the next few years."

"Not to speak of baptisms," he added seriously.

Tía Merce sent them off with presents and yelled down the veranda to Manuel to tell Alberto to saddle Lucero immediately for a long ride. My mother called her, and they had a discussion. Tía Merce left in a fury, saying, "I don't care a fig what Dr. Kaplan says; he's too constipated, it clouds his thinking!"

Soon Tía Merce galloped through the entrance yard and disappeared down the road past the bridge. La Mamota dropped a pile of wool skirts she was carrying into a chamber girl's arms to cross herself. The chamber girl whispered, "The señora's out to the rauli mountains again. Been there several times, they say, like Señorita Madmosil Vicky used to."

"The Saintly Virgin have mercy on you, gossiping about your *patrona,*" la Mamota scolded her, taking the skirts back.

ONLY MADAME'S CLASSES made time move like the water that Eduardo let go through the irrigation ditches every morning. Under her nude portrait, Madame told us how poor and prodigiously talented musicians ended up playing for dukes and queens; how an inventive vaccine snatched from death entire flocks of sheep; how blood flowed from tiny streams to creeks and then rivers to the sea of our hearts; how faults inside our earth lost balance, tipped and caused earthquakes; how protons bounced inside atoms like Ping-Pong balls mimicking our planets; how a horrific ball of fire inside the earth grew lashing arms, creating volcanoes. You could have listened to Madame Chanel the whole day, if you could stop breathing that long, to avoid her awful breath.

Violin-and-accordion music and the creaking of wheels came from the road. Outside, chamber- and serving and kitchen maids rushed in great excitement, yelling, *"Gitanos! Gitanos!"* Madame released us. I ran to ask my mother permission to go see them. She went on wiping tiny brushes as if nothing were happening. "You may go"—she fanned a photograph to dry it—"but don't get too close in case they have lice." She didn't say, Your father's coming to get us right now, and we are leaving after you see the Gypsies. She mumbled, "This big mouth should look smaller."

The Gypsies had parked a colorful wagon at the entrance yard. While some men played music, women in dusty long skirts unfolded small decorated tables. Everybody from the houses, workshops and warehouses and the *almacén,* including Doña Gertrudis, came to watch. The *capataz* posted some foremen around. La Mamota insisted, "Don't you get out of my sight, my little ones; these heretics are not to be trusted. Once a year they come and clean everybody out; after a year goes by, they've all forgotten about it, but not me,

I don't forget a thing, nothing escapes me. *Mi* Señora Doña Mercedes ought to keep these pagans out of El Topaz instead of taking off to . . . Well, they bring bad luck."

If only Nanny Fresia were here to see all this. She could have told me so many strange things.

The Gypsy women swung their hips, rattling their discolored jewelry as if they owned everything in El Topaz. From behind their painted small tables, they called everybody as if they had known them all their lives. "Come here, handsome, come over here; let me tell you what's going to happen if you aren't careful! Come, lovely, let me tell you who loves you truly; come closer, my love, let me tell you who's been saying this about you. . . ."

Younger Gypsies did tricks in front of their wagon. A girl about Patricia's age bent her body as if it were an onion stalk. Gloria asked la Mamota how she could do that. "These heretics steal children and take out all their bones. When their wounds heal, they charge people to watch the poor things bend like that." Niceto hung on to Berta's apron.

Soon the Gypsy women were manipulating hands or cards or leaves inside cups, foretelling: "You're going to receive a present." "Your *patrón*'s going to see that your roof gets repaired." "Why do you think you'll never have children? You will, you will, your children are right on these lines, see?" "You're going to get assigned to a better working crew and get a pay increase; no, I don't know exactly how much." "You're going to close your *almacén* and open a big emporium in a coastal town." "You'll get your hair permed and be the most beautiful in all this land." "You will find a man that'll marry you legal and never hit you." "You'll find a woman who'll work hard and never open her mouth." "You'll go on a trip to Las Cabras and buy beautiful shoes with a heel that high." The listeners first looked at the palms of their hands with apprehension, then exposed their toothless gaps with pleasure.

The girls each gave a coin to a Gypsy woman and had their fortunes told. I was next in line. How could I get hold of a peso coin? Was Jaime Idarrázabal Ochagavía right about foil balls or would the Gypsy take part of mine? The Gypsy grabbed my hand and said, "Where's your coin, young one?" I shook my head. From under her skirt, she took out the coin Gloria, the last one, had given her. It was a five-peso coin. "Well, young one, I thought your friend had given me one peso—an honest mistake; I'm not trying to cheat you!" Maybe Nanny Fresia was right about a Guardian Angel hovering above you. "Let me see, young one; you'll be rich, but not for long; you'll take a long trip very soon; some day you'll cross the oceans and find love; your father will be sick many years from now; when you get to be that age, you'll be sick with the same thing; there's a divorce happening; this morning something horrible has befallen someone who's powerful. . . ."

A long trip very soon! I tried to act grand and serene like my mother. The Gypsy's hand holding mine disappeared; I was out on the motor bicycle waving good-by to the girls, smiling to the wind, gliding down the eucalyptus-lined road toward my own house, with Mami and Papi and my brother together, looking back at the dust between us and El Topaz, forever. I asked her, "This long trip, it's on a motor bicycle, right?" The Gypsy dropped my hand and went on to a nanny who was next in line.

When the girls compared the Gypsy's predictions, I didn't say a word about my trip; I couldn't wait to savor the whole thing when it happened. The Gypsy had also told the girls that this morning something horrible had befallen someone who was powerful. "I hope the old Madame tripped and a car went over her hat with the cherries," Gloria said. We all laughed thinking about the flattened cherries. Then I remembered about the divorce—it had to be the girls' Mumsy and Popsy.

WE PLAYED TAG inside the empty pool. The dogs, being country dogs, were afraid to descend the pool's steps and ran around the rim, yelping down. Madame and my mother strolled under the rose arbors in spite of the light drizzle. When they were near the pool, the breeze brought their words in between the dog's yelps. Madame said, "She's not familiar with Lady Chatterley, but she wants to find out what dancer Vicky found so fascinating about that big macho."

Their voices trailed off as my mother mentioned Dr. Kaplan.

Gloria scraped her shin on a step and yelled, "Ayyyy!" My mother and Madame came to the pool's edge and laughed when they saw us running down there. "The Gypsies told all of us that this morning something horrible happened to someone," we all said.

"It could be the old Madame," Gloria said hopefully.

My mother and Madame looked worried. Madame said, "Gypsies are very perceptive people. It could be they know something."

"These Gypsies have probably been all over El Topaz," my mother said. "They must have heard something."

My mother called Manuel. He said on his tippytoes, "I surely told Evaristo and Prudencio to go to the rauli mountains, Señora Pilar, as you asked. They do as I tell them."

Everybody waited for Evaristo and Prudencio to get back. They returned accompanied by the *capataz,* even more nervous than *peones* were normally in front of Tía Merce. The *capataz* asked if they could go to the *despacho.* La Mamota was summoned for the keys. We weren't allowed into the *despacho,* so we waited outside in the cart yard. After a while they let la Mamota in. We heard la Mamota scream for the Virgin and wail. They came out, all of them looking bad. La Mamota sobbed. "Something like this just couldn't happen in El Topaz, never, ever, ever, not in any ranch around here; not since the patriots drove the Spaniards out. I mean, sometimes they killed each other, but ay! Holy Virgin! What's everybody going to say?" Her face shone wet. She saw us. "Señora, I can't tell them. . . ."

A strange current went by; what was about to be revealed

was different, serious, frightening, and so it had a touch of thrill.

My mother took the girls to the gallery and told me and Niceto to wait outside. In a while we peeked through the door glass. My mother and Madame had their arms around Patricia. The twin nannies were holding the twins, who looked pale, very frightened, and bit their lips. My mother saw us and motioned for us to come in. "Listen, my children. You must be very mature about this. Mercedes . . . has died. I won't lie; you'll hear stories from the servants, and you should know the truth. She . . . she went to . . . to visit a man, a strange man who was very primitive. . . ."

"Ave María Purísima!" la Mamota cried, lunging to cover the girls with her big body. "Señora Pilar, there's no need . . ."

"I don't want the children getting distorted versions from the kitchen," my mother said firmly. Madame agreed with my mother.

"I don't get anything from the kitchen," Niceto said, offended, "not even from the pantry."

"What happened to Mercedes is that, well, her other friends had shunned her, and she looked for warmth from a man who was rather primitive, and bitter toward women from the houses, maybe felt ridiculed, or humiliated; he drank, and they had a fight—"

"Holy Mary, Martyr and Virgin," la Mamota interrupted. "Señora Madame, do something! That's not to tell the little ones; the only thing to tell them is about the politics; that's what it was, the ideas they put into the *peones'* heads, those agitators in Topotilla; always a rebel, el Gonzalo was, and Señor Don Juan Vicente, the Saintly Virgin forgive me, he encouraged . . ."

Madame patted her shoulder. My mother ignored her. My mother could be incredibly brave, or was it reckless? "This man drank too much." The rim of my mother's big black eyes shone red.

Patricia pushed la Mamota away. "Tía Pilar, how . . . how did it happen . . . ?" she said in a strange voice.

My mother thought for a minute. She was so pale, her hair looked even blacker. "It's better that you know now, Patricia. There's going to be a lot of talk. She didn't suffer, or know what happened; it was . . . with an ax. She didn't feel anything. . . . We'll send for your father right away."

Patricia stood silently with red eyes but no tears. There was a flicker of a mountain shack and a man's ax coming down and blood pouring out of someplace, but it was too horrible to consider, too horrible to make that head belong to Tía Merce, who was left whole, chuckling and sagging her chin and dropping sugar cubes in her tea with her long nails. One thing I was never ever going to do when I grew up was to go see primitive men.

On the veranda my mother told Manuel and Evaristo to go to the Undurragas' immediately and telephone Señor Miguel and the investigation officer in Topotilla, then fetch Padre Romualdo at Las Cabras. And to telephone the girls' uncles. Don't forget to call Señor Armando, she said loudly as they ran to the garages. Then she turned to a dazed chambermaid standing near. "Celia, come to my room, I need you to wash and iron some clothes for me, then bring me some *quillay* bark for my hair."

THERE WAS A LOT of discomforted confusion in the houses. Investigators from Topotilla came to ask questions because they had gone to the rauli mountains but had found no signs of el Gonzalo. Tío Popsy and his twin brother, who looked very much like him but had no pink, bald wart and a neat three-piece suit, sat in the gallery, drinking from big diamond glasses. Tío Armando gave orders and complained about all the craziness in the place. My mother wore her good blouse and first made her chignon carefully, then threw herself into Tío Armando's arms crying—I had never seen her cry like that—and her chignon fell apart. She thanked him over and over for being so strong and knowing what to do and how to take care of things so well. She told him he was the only person in the world who could do anything right, and now she had no one in the world and no place to go. This was strange, because my mother always seemed to know where to go and what to do.

We were dressed in black, from head to toe. The guanaco got a black ribbon on his neck, and the *capataz* distributed black armbands and veils to all the peasants. I was happy to see Nanny Fresia, who had an enormous belly. An assortment of friends, unknown relatives and odd people arrived with glum faces, and fought about where Tía Merce was going. My mother and Madame said she would want to stay in El Topaz. Tío Armando, Tío Toto and la Mamota said, preposterous! She was going to their family Carrara marble mausoleum. Tío Popsy drank from his glass.

Papi arrived on the motor bicycle. He demanded that Niceto and I remove the morbid and retrograde black clothes. Mami told him it took an earthquake or a murder to bring him to see us, and told me to ignore him. They locked themselves in her room. I waited on the veranda, outside her window, trying to decipher what they were saying. Thicker, moist air chilled my ankles and the back of my upper arms. In the gardens a veil of dew joined the nooks and crannies of tree bark, the spaces between bushes and the sky, like a friendship turned into a big gray conspiracy. My parents were still inside when Padre Romualdo came, and we all went to a mass for Tía Merce.

That afternoon a line of cars, headed by Tío Popsy's—with the girls' grandmother, the straw woman, Dr. Kaplan, Melons, and Lolita—followed a black carriage pulled by six black horses hatted with black feathers, carrying Tía Merce, with the guitar beside her. She would never come back to El Topaz. Suddenly, the roar of a motor bicycle and a cloud of dust unnerved the horses; Papi sped past the cortege. Mlle. Vicky stuck her head out of Tío Toto's car, yelling, "Wait for me, Julian! Wait for me! Well, all right! I'll see you in Galmeda!" The six black horses calmed down and continued their trot, removing Tía Merce from Paradise.

DOZENS OF CARS filled with relatives and friends left, but Tío Armando stayed to take care of things. My mother stopped crying and throwing herself onto him. Then they both seemed to feel much better and started taking horseback riding trips. Back from one of the trips, my mother's big dark eyes shone. Tío Armando stopped to talk to Niceto and me. "I'm now extending a formal invitation to you both for a guided tour of my rare tropical-bird collection. What do you say to that?"

My mother smiled at me as if I were the luckiest girl in the world to go see stuffed birds. What was a formal invitation? Was Tío Armando showing up at my bedroom door dressed as a king or something? I wanted to tell him, if we were going to Galmeda, I would just as soon be dropped at San Bernardo Street, if he didn't mind. However, he and my mother were keen for me to see his stuffed birds. He could drop me at San Bernardo Street afterward. If not, we could stop at Las Cabras.

Tío Armando turned to Niceto. "I own seven tropical stuffed birds; not ordinary birds like around here, more valuable than the ones in the aviary. They're just like in the movies. Do you want to see my tropical stuffed birds?"

"If you give me a Coca-Cola," my brother said.

It was so embarrassing the way Niceto extorted from everybody. They laughed. Tío Armando went to the *despacho* with the *capataz,* and Niceto and I followed my mother to her room to ask about Papi.

She put away photographs. "I will never, ever be forced into this humiliating, numbing endeavor again," she said, and sat to write at the windowsill. How strange that my mother was "forced" into something; wasn't she always in command? She gave us a happy smile and hugged us with both arms. "My children, everything has worked out as planned. It took months and months, but coming here was the correct action. We are leaving in the next few days."

The next few days! The next few days would be the happiest days of my life! The times when my father had said we were leaving, we didn't, but when my mother said it, that was it. Good thing Tía Merce was dead . . . well, that wasn't nice . . . that Tía Merce wasn't around to convince her to stay. "What time? What time?" I wiggled my legs and toes furiously. "Are we going on the motor bicycle?" Yellow flowers on the landscaped hill shone like tiny suns.

"Solita, you mustn't jerk like that; you make me dizzy. I must explain some things to you, but first I have to finish this letter." I looked at her writing. "This is not easy for me to do, Julian . . ." My mother pressed my cowlick. "Solita, you aren't reading other people's mail, are you? I must finish this to send it with Evaristo to mail at Las Cabras."

She was writing to Papi, finally. "When is Papi coming?"

My mother put her pen down. "I've been trying to tell you, Solita, but you're always running around somewhere. Your father won't be coming for us. Your father and I are separated. We're lucky that there's no need of a divorce, because marriages performed by the Republican militia during the Spanish Civil War aren't recognized either in Spain or abroad. But don't worry; children from those situations are considered legitimate. So your father and I . . . simply . . . we won't continue to live together. You're a big girl now; you have to understand that these things happen."

This, of course, was impossible, because Papi was renting the whole pensione for us, and *separated* just couldn't happen. Niceto pulled her sleeve. "So how will we get home?"

My mother kissed his head. "With a chauffeur; we are being driven." My mother's voice came from far away.

That horror that I had feared was lurching closer, but there was still time to stop it. "You and Papi can't get"—I couldn't say that word—"you're married. Paradise is where couples get joined, not . . . the other way. And Papi said . . ."

"My daughter, you must be understanding. Your father and I cannot live together, we couldn't go on. . . . You need to live in proper neighborhoods, go to good schools; your and your brother's health—you have to eat properly, get good medical care. And Julian . . ." Her voice was impatient. "I explained it to you."

Everything was ripped apart: the stairs in the pensione, soon to be our stairs; running after my father toward San Toribio Street; sweet grapes in the pensione's front yard; the alcohol-smelling Sunday paper; songs my parents sang when we went for walks; eating the egg in my soup because my mother said my father would be proud of me; my father saying, "My, you girls look gorgeous!"; the paved walk from the garden gate to the pensione's front door; my father telling what had happened when he went looking for work; the joyful light bulb hanging from the ceiling; the street-lamp putting shadows that moved with the slightest breeze on walls and ceilings . . . You can't. We're going to live in San Bernardo Street with Papi, I wanted to say. . . .

"Now, I must finish this letter and do a million other things. You understand, Solita. Take Niceto for a walk."

I couldn't cry. Walking through the garden paths, Niceto and I threw sticks for Coca-Cola. The gravel gave way over ground that had turned spongier. Bare branches in the trees twisted in anguish. A few dropped water on us that splashed into many tears. I sobbed. Niceto looked at me, scared.

MY MOTHER SAID Evaristo would drive the girls, Madame and la Mamota to Miguel's house in Galmeda, until arrangements could be made to send them to boarding school in France. She said she and Armando were getting married, no wedding, just what the law and the church required, in consideration of Mercedes' death, then we would go to Galmeda to live in Armando's mansion. My mother and Tío Armando went to Las Cabras with Tío Juan Vicente.

Patricia and Grace were ecstatic about going to boarding

school in France, but unhappy about their uncle and my mother. Gloria said, "So what if Solita will have a beach house in Tilipulli and a yacht? That's fine with me."

Her sisters left, saying, "Well, Solita isn't going to a French boarding school."

Gloria said her sisters were horrified at the idea of my mother having more things than their Mumsy, because Patricia always wanted to boss everybody and be superior. She asked me to invite her to the beach, because her Mumsy hated it and never wanted to take them. Maybe I could run away with Gloria. She didn't think it was a good idea. Then she told me that the big secret her sisters had kept her from telling me was that they had heard their *tío* say at dinner at their house in Galmeda that if he ever married a woman with children he would send them to boarding schools, because he had seen too many stepparents' lives made miserable by stepchildren, and later they had heard him tell my mother that I should definitely be sent abroad to escape my father's bad political influence. Gloria said her sisters would have died for me to go to a French boarding school when they were not going. She said that my mother didn't want me to go to a boarding school and that her *tío* had finally agreed I should stay here because I had made good friends with the visiting children, who came from the best families.

So that's why my mother had pushed me to be nice to Tío Armando and to get along with those children. Many times you didn't understand things. The girls and I had been working together for the same goal, but for opposite reasons. Sometimes enemies could work together. But no matter what, it was a bad idea to pretend that things that *were* happening weren't.

My mother and Tío Armando returned and said they were married. After we went to bed, champagne popped in the salon.

The next morning I watched my mother pack. She put my side-glancing doll in the suitcase. I clutched my foil ball. She didn't want me to take it, but I begged her. Jali and the dogs milled outside our room, knowing something was up. I wished we could take them. I was going to miss them terribly. And Madame a lot. And Gloria. More than a bit. We went outside.

Tío Armando's chauffeur opened the car door for us. Everything that had been coming apart burst; I ran back to the room. I fell on the bed and off it. While I tossed on the floor, endless craters with lava, as deep as the canyons where the Basilisco slid his repulsive reptile body, fought to pass through my eyes. Niceto stood at the door opening his huge eyes. My mother was a furious mass of silent motherhood coming toward me. Maybe I could stop the lava. "I'll go . . . live . . . with Papi." My voice came out in sobbing spurts.

"That's enough. Let's not be absurd. Your father's incapable of taking care of anybody. You'd starve to death; your teeth'd fall out. A girl belongs with her mother; we must stick together. What would people say if they find out you are so wicked you won't live with your own mother? You'll never find a suitable husband; no man in his right mind will marry you."

"I'll take care of myself! Then you'll want to come too. Papi said he was coming soon—" Sobs cut my voice.

"He did, did he? See how often he's been here. You have to understand, Solita, Julian's only interested in being celebrated, being honored like a lord, because his family was humble and resentful. All he cares about are his contacts to become *the* labor law expert in the New World. We mean nothing to him. And also, he's . . . well, you're too young to understand these things; you must do what I tell you."

My mother's words crept through my moist ears like fuzzy letters in a telegram. The letters got bigger and bigger, and I couldn't read the message. My mother was wrong. My father was coming. "I'm staying here. Papi's coming to get us."

"Now, I've taken enough nonsense from you," she whispered. "What a scene; you'd better not let Armando hear you." She closed the door. "You might as well know, your father has quite an interest in some . . . young thing who can be very good for his career, enough to give her gifts that should be coming to you. Not that he hasn't been chasing women all along; you'd have found out sooner or later, anyway. He has room only for whoever spoon-feeds his ego; he'll never have room for you in his life. Never."

I put my head between my knees; the sobs from my stomach bounced on my tights over and over; if I melted, I'd stop hurting.

"I'm deeply embarrassed at you. I can't believe you can be so selfish, so ungrateful, so lacking in consideration for your brother, for me, for your future . . . after all I've done for you, all the sacrifices . . ." The bottomless canyon was flowing down a mountain, and only a small part of it streamed out my eyes.

"You're going to live in a mansion, with everything a child could dream of, and I've done it all for you, so you stop that!"

Stop a sliding mountain?

"Will the mansion have an icebox," Niceto asked. "So I can suck on ice cubes?" He deserved to be thrown against the wall.

"Of course; not an icebox, a deluxe refrigerator, and telephones. You'll go to the best schools, play with children from the well-situated families in Galmeda."

"Oh, goody, I can get ice cubes," Niceto said. He deserved to get his head kicked.

"Now, my children, when we meet Armando's staff, you must be dignified and nice; first impressions are very important."

"Will other people move in with us too, like here in El Topaz? Refugees too?" Niceto asked.

"Of course not, my treasure. Armando doesn't like them; and I don't want to hear that word again—it would upset him."

So Padre Romualdo and Nanny Fresia's way to ask the Up Above didn't work. The lava inside me stopped. "If we can't go back to Spain and be in my own country, if we can't go back to France and be with my grandmother, if we can't live with Papi, I'm going to stay here, in El Topaz. I'll go live with Nanny Fresia."

"You want to stay here, do you? What if El Cid had said that? You and I would now be wearing veils." She made me stand up, handed me a handkerchief and whipped my dress into shape.

We left our room. I couldn't see much, except polite hugs, big eyes, tears, dogs running around excitedly. Someone told Manuel to put on the record that Señora Merce liked to have on for departing guests, called Brahms. My mother climbed into the car. The chauffeur sat Niceto inside, our suitcase in the trunk. A *puri* bird said, "*Chiiiirri-puri-puri-pui.*" The feathery leaves of the *aromo* nodded mysteriously. I could go to the public road and follow the train tracks all the way to Las Cabras and Padre Romualdo. No, I couldn't. I couldn't fly my magic carpet to San Bernardo Street, or to Las Cabras; it had been swallowed by the earthquake and was going to stay forever in El Topaz. Magic carpets existed only in fairy tales. When you wanted to go somewhere, you had to take yourself there, but you could choose your own road only if you were grown up. When it came time to look at stuffed parrots, I was going to pretend they were flying happily through the air. I wasn't going to play with anybody who didn't want me on their team. I wasn't going to follow anybody else around, no matter how colossally rich or elevated or anything. I wasn't ever going to accept anybody's spit. And when I grew up, I was never going to go to Paradise, nor do what the Romans did. I was going to do what the Gypsy said: cross the oceans and find love. I climbed into the car.

The dogs ran after us to the end of the front gardens. Under the bridge the willow branches pretended to follow the stream. My mother, Tío Armando, Niceto and I glided noiselessly through the road as the eucalyptus waved their long reddish leaves.

We stopped at the public road to let a bus go by. I said loudly, "What incredible colors the buses have in the New World," and threw my foil ball out the window. It rolled and stopped next to the iron post that supported the sign EL TOPAZ.

About the Author

ELENA CASTEDO was born in Barcelona, Spain, raised in Chile, and has lived on four continents. She received an M.A. from the University of California, Los Angeles, and a Ph.D. from Harvard University. The former editor of the *Inter-American Review of Bibliography* and the author of a critical study of Chilean theater, she lives in McLean, Virginia.